SUMMER AT SEA SHELL HARBOR

SUMMER

AT

SEA SHELL

HARBOR

RICHARD W. DUNNE

DONEGAL PUBLISHING COMPANY
LOS ANGELES

DONEGAL PUBLISHING COMPANY, LLC
Post Office Box 1018
Hermosa Beach, California 90254-1018
E-MAIL: editor@donegalpublishing.com
www.donegalpublishing.com
www.summeratseashellharbor.com
TEL: 310.379.5554
Donegal books are available from your favorite bookstore and amazon.com.

Library of Congress Control Number: 2004115759
Publisher's Catalog—in—Publication Data
Summer At Sea Shell Harbor/Richard W. Dunne
ISBN 978-0-9788128-0-5
ISBN 0-9788128-0-8 (Previously ISBN 1-932762-30-2)
Second Printing
Long Island—Fiction.
Coming of Age—Fiction.
Romance—Fiction.
New York—Fiction.
Fifties Fiction—Fiction.
I. Title
This book was written, printed and bound in the United States of America.

Dedication

To Eileen (my wife,) whose patience, understanding and unlimited support was immensely helpful and enabled me to write this book.

To Maxine (Shore) - This book is a direct result of your interest and encouragement of me as a writer. I would not have written it without you.

To Mom - You always said all I needed to do was apply myself. Thank you for giving me the drive to accomplish this.

One

"Mom, someone's at the door."

"Well, answer it, will you dear? I'm busy."

"Okay." Richie walked across the cabin's living room toward the front door. He was a slender young man with blond hair and blue eyes and had just turned seventeen a few weeks earlier.

Dressed in tan chinos, white tee shirt and a pair of topsiders, he whistled absentmindedly as he reached down to open the screen door. Outside, another boy about his age was standing there holding a box of groceries.

"This the Donnelly place?" the boy asked with an air of authority.

"Sure, c'mon in." Richie brushed a strand of hair away from his eyes as he sized the boy up. "That box looks kind of heavy. My mom probably wants it in the kitchen. This way."

"Nah, it's a cinch," the boy said. "I do this all day long." He followed Richie through the living room and into the kitchen at the rear of the cabin.

Although shorter than Richie, he was stockier, with dark wavy hair and muscular arms. His eyes were a dark brown, almost black, and matched the tee shirt he was wearing. A pair of worn jeans and dirty white sneakers completed his outfit.

"Mom, the groceries are here," Richie said as they reached the kitchen.

Mrs. Donnelly was busy cleaning and putting away the dishes she had packed and brought from the city. Blond and slender like her son, she looked up and smiled at the two boys.

"Oh, hello," she said. "You must be the boy from Treadway's Market."

"Yes, ma'am," he replied. "Name's Mickey. I make most of the deliveries here in the village. 'Cept on weekends. We don't deliver on weekends. Just Monday through Friday."

"Nice to meet you, Mickey. I'm Mrs. Donnelly and this is my son, Richard. We just drove out from the city. Oh, set the box down on the table for now, will you, Mickey? I'm trying to organize the kitchen and find out where everything goes. I still have the bedrooms to do yet."

Mickey did as she asked. "Most of the cabins are pretty much the same," he said. He walked over and opened a cupboard next to the refrigerator. "This is the food pantry and the dishes go over there next to the sink."

He pointed to a set of shelves but then dropped his arm abruptly. "That is..., I mean, most of the summer folks I know do it this way. You might have your own system that you use. I didn't mean to be..."

"Oh, that's all right, Mickey," Mrs. Donnelly said good naturedly. "I can use all the help I can get." She paused for a moment, then said, "It's pretty hot out today, would you like a cold drink?"

"Gee, thanks, Mrs. Donnelly," Mickey answered. He took a handkerchief from his back pocket and wiped his forehead. "It is pretty hot, considering it's only the end of June. Probably means the whole summer'll be hot."

"I hope so," Richie said. "I want to do lots of swimming this summer."

"Well, you came to the right place," Mickey said agreeably. "There's plenty of places to go swimming out here."

"Sit at the table," Mrs. Donnelly said. Mickey sat and took the bottle she offered him.

"Root beer. Nice and cold. We brought them with us from the city." She turned to her son. "Richard, would you like one?"

"Sure, mom". Richie sat at the table across from Mickey and watched him drink from the bottle. Mickey took three quick gulps and then wiped his mouth with the back of his hand. He saw Richie watching him and he smiled.

"Guess I was thirsty. I always swig it down like that when I'm thirsty." He put the bottle on the table. "So, you folks just came out from the city, huh? How long will you be here?"

"Till Labor Day," Richie answered, taking a sip from his drink. "You live around here, Mickey?"

"I live over in Bridgehampton," he replied. "It's a couple of miles from here." He took another swig from the bottle. "The whole summer, huh? That's great. You rent this place from old man Haddock? He handles most of the cabins in Sea Shell Harbor."

"Yes, I believe we did," Mrs. Donnelly said as she placed dishes in the cupboard.

"Figures. Old man Haddock's been around here for as long as anyone remembers. Born here. Everyone calls him Old Man Haddock."

"That's interesting," Mrs. Donnelly said.

"He's a nice old guy," Mickey continued," but if you ain't a year-round resident of the village, he'll barely talk to ya."

"Is that so?" commented Mrs. Donnelly.

"Yeah. He's afraid the summer folks'll like this place so much they'll want to move out here permanently." Mickey started talking in a funny, high-pitched voice, imitating Old Man Haddock.

"There ain't a nicer place to live in the whole gangdurled world but the winters sure get mighty cold and bleak and a person'd like to starve to death if'n he weren't smart enough to store up enough grub, 'cause you sure as heck can't make any money in this gosh-forsaken place in the winter!"

Richie and his mother both laughed. "Well, I don't think we'll be moving out here permanently any time soon," Mrs. Donnelly said.

Mickey finished the last of his root beer. "Well, if you do, don't tell Old Man Haddock." He stood up and carried the bottle over to the sink. "Do you want to keep the empty bottles here?" he asked, pointing to the storage area under it.

"Yes, that's a good place for them," Mrs. Donnelly agreed.

"That's where the Burketts kept theirs," Mickey said. "They own this cabin. I've been here many times. Their son, Eddie is a friend of mine." He opened the door and put the bottle away. "I can show you pretty much where everything goes, if you're not sure."

"Well, thank you, Mickey, but I think I can manage," Mrs. Donnelly said pleasantly.

"Where do the Burketts live if they rent their cabin out to other people for the summer?" Richie asked.

"Oh, they don't live here," Mickey answered. "They have a big house over in Sag Harbor. They're very rich, you know. They own quite a few of the cabins around here."

"Is that so?" Mrs. Donnelly started to unpack the groceries as she spoke.

"Yes, ma'am. Mr. Burkett is a lawyer in New York City but they spend the summers out here. Least they have for as long as I can remember."

"I think rich people are snobs," Richie declared.

Mickey looked at him and smiled. "Yeah, me too," he agreed. "Eddie's different, though. He don't act like a rich kid. He's a nice guy." He looked thoughtful. "I'll introduce you to him if you want."

"Well, I don't know," Richie said. "We'll see."

"Have you lived out here long, Mickey?" Mrs. Donnelly asked as she put the groceries away.

"Pretty much. I was born in Brooklyn but I moved out here when I was nine." He put his thumbs in the waistband of his jeans and lifted himself up on his toes. "I'm almost eighteen now," he said proudly.

Richie helped his mother unload the box. "We're from Brooklyn, too," he said with enthusiasm. "Flatbush. You know where that is?"

"I'm not sure, Richard."

"Richie. Call me Richie."

"Richie. I'm not sure," Mickey said. "Is it near "Williamsburg?

That's where I was born."

"It's not too far from it," Mrs. Donnelly answered. She turned to the boys. "Where do you go to school, Mickey?"

"Well, I used to go to Sag Harbor High but I..., uh, quit last year." Mickey's eyebrows knitted together and he frowned. "School's a waste of time," he said. "I'm planning on working all summer and when I get enough money, I'm gonna buy a clam boat. There's lots of money to be made clammin'."

Richie picked up a can of tuna and placed it in the pantry. "You quit school to go clamming? That sounds like a lot of fun in the summer but what about winter? You can't dig for clams in the winter, can you?"

"Sure you can," Mickey replied. "It's cold, but what the heck, I'm strong, I can take it."

Richie gave an involuntary shudder. "I wouldn't want to go out on a clam boat in the winter. I'd freeze to death."

"You just gotta dress warm, that's all," Mickey said with a laugh. "I guess I just have a thick skin. Really, though, you can make a lot of money clammin'. Twice as much in the winter as you can in the summer. You get used to the cold."

"Maybe it's not so bad then," Richie agreed. "I'm planning on finishing high school and then I'm going to college."

"Yeah? Where do you go to school?" Mickey asked.

"Midwood High. It's in Brooklyn. I'll be a senior there in September."

"That's cool," Mickey said. "I thought I wanted to finish high school and then go to college, but...," he hesitated for a moment, "ah, what the heck, I already quit so there's no use thinking about it."

"Richard, would you put these things away in the bathroom for me?" Mrs. Donnelly asked, interrupting them. She handed him several packages of soap and a box of toothpaste.

"Sure, mom." Richie took the items from her and left the room. Mrs. Donnelly waited until he was gone and then sat down at the table. "Mickey, sit down for a moment, will you?" she asked, pointing to the other chair.

"Sure, Mrs. Donnelly." Mickey sat across from her.

Mrs. Donnelly looked at him for a moment, then spoke. "Mickey, I don't mean to pry but you might want to consider returning to school. Even the best bayman could do with an education. There's no substitute for that, you know."

"Sure, I know that, Mrs. Donnelly," he said. "The thing is, I was never much good in school. Once I get the boat I can start making money and then..."

"Listen to me for a minute, will you?" Mrs. Donnelly folded her arms on the table and leaned forward slightly. "Mickey, I grew up on Long Island and I know a lot about working on the bay."

"You do?"

"Yes. Both my father and younger brother were baymen," she answered. "They spent years on the water harvesting clams. I can tell you, it's brutal work in winter. I could never understand how anyone would want to work out on that bay during the winter months."

She absentmindedly fiddled with her wedding band. "You know, the temperature often drops well below zero out on the water."

"Sure, I know that," Mickey said.

"And there's no protection from the icy wind when it blows in from the northeast," she continued. "Absolutely none. It chills everything in its path. My father was a physical wreck by the time he was fifty."

"Is he still clammin'?" Mickey asked.

"No, he passed away a few years ago."

"Oh." Mickey looked down at the table for a few seconds, then back up at Mrs. Donnelly. "What about your brother? Did he give it up?"

Mrs. Donnelly's eyes moistened and she was silent for a moment. "Ben was killed in a car accident when he was eighteen years old," she said. "It happened a long time ago when I was away at college."

"Gee, Mrs. Donnelly, I'm sorry to hear that." Mickey started to rise up from the table. "Maybe we shouldn't talk about it if it makes you sad."

"No, it's all right," she said, raising a hand to stop him. "I'm okay. I didn't mean to make you uncomfortable." She smiled at him.

"It's just that you remind me of him, that's all."

"I do?"

"Yes. You look a lot like Ben. Same build and you have dark, wavy hair and brown eyes like he had, although I think you're taller than he was."

"I'm five-foot eight," Mickey said.

"Five-foot eight," she repeated. "Yes, well, anyway, think about finishing school, will you Mickey? That's the only reason I brought it up. My brother never got to graduate before he died and it would be nice if you had that opportunity."

Mickey chewed on his lower lip. "I'll definitely give it a lot of thought," he said.

"Good." Mrs. Donnelly got up from the table and busied herself at the sink. "Do you have any brothers or sisters, Mickey?"

"I have a kid sister named Diane," he answered. "She's fifteen. It's just me and her and my mother."

"Again, I don't mean to pry, but what about your father?" Mrs. Donnelly asked.

"Oh, he lives in Queens. Him and my mother were divorced a long time ago. That's when we moved out here."

"What kind of work does he do?"

"He's in the construction business. I don't get to see him too often."

"Doesn't he ever visit you?"

Mickey shook his head slowly. "He never comes out here. Him and my mother don't get along. They hate each other. We used to take the train in to the city once in a while and see him there. Me and Diane. He'd take us to Ebbets Field to see the Dodgers play and then we'd go out to eat, but he stopped doing that a couple of years ago. Anyway, now that the Dodgers moved out to California, we can't even see them play anymore, either."

"Well, how does he feel about you leaving school?" she asked.

"Oh, he don't care what I do. Besides, I never asked him for permission. I make my own decisions about what I do." Mickey's body stiffened and his voice faltered slightly. "I don't let nobody tell me nothing."

"I'm sorry, Mickey," Mrs. Donnelly said. "I didn't mean to be nosy."

"It's okay, Mrs. Donnelly, it don't bother me none." He got up from the table. "I suppose I'd better get back to the store. Mr. Treadway don't like me to take too long. There's a lot of families arriving today and I got a ton of deliveries to make. It was real nice talking to you."

Richie returned to the kitchen just then and Mickey offered him his hand. "Hey, nice meeting you, Richie," he said.

Richie shook the offered hand. Mickey's grip was strong. "Nice to meet you, too."

"Hey, what are you doing later on?" Mickey asked.

Richie put his hands in his pockets and shrugged his shoulders. "I'm not sure. I thought I'd take a walk down to the beach and look around. I don't know anyone out here yet."

Mickey thought for a moment. "Why don't you meet me later and I'll show you around? I get off work at five. I know everyone around here. I'll introduce you."

"Hey, that sounds cool." Richie turned to his mother. "Is it okay, mom?"

"I guess so, dear," his mother answered. "As long as you promise to unpack your things and straighten up your room, first."

The two boys grinned widely and shook hands again. "C'mon," Richie said. "I'll walk you outside."

"So long, Mrs. Donnelly," Mickey called over his shoulder.

"Goodbye, Mickey," she answered.

Outside, Mickey straddled the bicycle he used to make deliveries and leaned forward over the handlebars. "Your mother's a nice lady, Rich," he said. "I wish mine was as nice as yours, but she's crazy."

"Crazy?" Richie asked, puzzled.

"As a loon," Mickey answered. "But, that's all right. She lets my sister and me do whatever we want, so it's not too bad."

"What do you mean, crazy?" Richie prodded.

"You know, nuts. She don't make any sense. She's always talking about stuff that happened years ago like it was only yesterday. Me and Diane call her The Mad Hatter." Mickey wiped his nose with the back of his hand. "It's not her fault, though," he continued. "Her family drove her nuts. My grandmother and my Aunt Edna. I hate them both. They're the ones who broke my parents up," he said bitterly.

"What do you mean?"

"They never liked my old man. To them, he was just a working stiff with no education. They thought they were better than him and they didn't want him to marry my mother." Mickey spun one of the bicycle's pedals with his foot. "He told me the whole story."

"Gosh, what happened, Mickey?" Richie asked, intrigued by the story. "How did they break your parents up?"

"Nothing really happened that you could pinpoint," Mickey said. "They just kept working on my mother, telling her my father was no good, that he was a bum and a bunch of other stuff. Finally, she couldn't take it anymore, so she got rid of him."

"Your father told you this?"

"Yeah, he..., ah, it's a long story, Rich. I'll tell you all about it some other time. Gotta go now. I'll tell you what, come down to the market around five. It's right around the corner, on Noyac Road. We'll go over to the Sugar Shack and see if anyone's around."

"What's the Sugar Shack?" Richie asked.

"That's where all the kids hang out. It's over by the beach. You never heard of it? They sell hot dogs and stuff."

"No, this is the first time we've ever vacationed here," Richie said.

"Well, I think you're gonna like it. Don't worry, I'll show you everything. There ain't nothing in Sea Shell Harbor that I don't know about." Mickey started to pedal away, then stopped. "Hey, you like girls?"

"Sure, I like girls," Richie said, laughing.

"Well, I know most of the girls around here, too. There's some really cute ones who come out here for the summer. I'll introduce you to some of 'em." Mickey's eyes seemed to sparkle as he said, "Hey, you know what, Richie? We're gonna have a great time this summer, what d'ya say?"

"I say, cool, Mickey. Sounds good to me."

Mickey patted Richie on the back. "All right, then, I'll see you later."

"Okay." Richie watched Mickey pedal the bicycle up the street, waiting until he turned the corner. There was plenty of time to kill until five o'clock, so he thought he'd go back inside and help his mother unpack and then straighten up his room like she'd asked.

He was glad he'd met Mickey today. Since he didn't know anyone yet, it was especially nice to meet one of the locals. Mickey could show him around and introduce him to some of the other kids. Best of all, he had mentioned knowing a lot of girls. Girls! That was a subject that occupied a good part of Richie's thoughts these days.

Ever since he'd turned seventeen, it seemed like he spent less time doing the things he used to do, like playing sports and collecting baseball cards. Now, he and his friends from his neighborhood in Brooklyn had started hanging around the local ice cream parlor and going to as many dances and parties as they could.

Any place where they might have an opportunity to meet girls, that's where they went. Girls! Their new social activity.

Oh, yes, it was going to be a great summer, Richie decided. Yes, sir, it truly was.

Two

At a few minutes before five, Richie was waiting outside Tread-way's Market. Treadway's, a small grocery store that sold groceries and locally grown fresh fruits and vegetables, had been operating in Sea Shell Harbor since the late nineteen-twenties.

Catering to the locals and tourists alike, it was a kind of informal gathering place, where, in addition to their needs, people could pick up some of the local gossip and other news of the village. Situated as it was right in the heart of the village, it was a busy place, with people coming and going most of the day.

The store was run by Aloyisus Treadway, a crusty old east-ender and his wife of fifty years, Anna. He was a mean spirited and sour-faced individual, unlike his wife, who was as pleasant and friendly to the customers as her husband was dour.

Most of the customers preferred to deal with Mrs. Treadway, who was the direct opposite of her husband and truly liked people. She was the one who usually waited on them while her husband busied himself in other parts of the store.

Mickey came out of the market a few minutes later and stopped to light a cigarette. He looked up and saw Richie standing there. "Hi, Richie, I see you found the place okay. You ready to go?"

"Ready as I'll ever be," Richie replied.

They started walking east on Noyac Road, past the gas station and hardware store. Mickey held up the pack of cigarettes. "Want one?"

Richie shook his head. "No, thanks, I don't smoke." He looked across the street at the Sea Shell Harbor Pharmacy, which occupied the ground floor of an older, two-storied building. It sat adjacent to the Haddock Realty Company, a newer brick building that had been built the previous summer.

Richie smiled as he remembered Mickey's earlier imitation of Old Man Haddock lamenting on the difficulty of making a decent living in Sea Shell Harbor. Old Man Haddock seems to be doing all right for himself, he thought.

Next to Haddock's was a deli with a sign in the window advertising hot coffee and sandwiches and next to the deli was Grace's Dress Shop.

The village reminded him of some of the smaller New England towns he had visited during previous vacations with his parents. The mostly wooden buildings were painted white and had large, screened-in porches, perfect for sitting outside on a warm, summer evening. Some of the houses featured a stained glass window or two.

Though only ninety miles to the east of New York City, this part of Long Island had a rural charm of its own, with its Colonial-era houses and manicured, freshly-mowed lawns. More so than the towns and villages closer to the city, with their brick and mortar dwellings and tract-housing developments.

Richie's father had told him there were still a couple of Indian reservations nearby, namely the Shinnecock and Montauk tribes. It kind of made him feel like he had somehow traveled back in time to another era. For some reason, he felt comforted by that feeling.

"How big is Sea Shell Harbor?" Richie asked as they continued walking.

"We just passed through the whole town," Mickey answered, as they reached the intersection with another road and turned left. "Well, almost through it, anyways. This is Beach Road. The Sugar Shack is down there on the left, do you see it?"

They were on a slight rise which offered an unobstructed view of the road and the waters of Noyac Bay in the distance. Mickey was pointing to a red speck about a half mile down on the left.

By squinting his eyes. Richie could make out a large, wooden structure painted a dull magenta, with white trim around the windows. It was set back from the roadway, on the beach side.

Closer to them but on the opposite side of the road, there was another wooden building with large plate glass windows. This one was painted gray and looked like a ship.

"What's that down there on the right?" Richie asked.

"That's a restaurant called The Salty Pirate. The older people go there, mostly. You gotta be eighteen to get in 'cause they sell liquor. We call it Grog out here. I'll be able to go there next year."

Mickey pointed again. "There's some more stores further up on the right, where Harbor Road crosses this one but you can't see them from here. There's another gas station and a florist on Beach and around the corner on Harbor you have Saint Matthews Church and the Sea Shell Harbor Community Theater."

"A movie theater?" Richie asked.

"No, that's over in Sag Harbor, about five miles away. You have to go there if you want to see a movie." Mickey put a hand on his forehead above his eyes and squinted. "This theater is where they put on plays and other stuff. Some real actors from TV and Hollywood come here to put on shows. They call it summer stock, I think."

"That's cool," Richie commented

As they walked by the Salty Pirate, Richie saw that the front of it looked like the bow of a fishing boat. Under the bow, there were huge wooden doors with polished brass fittings and round windows shaped like portholes were cut into them.

Large wood pilings stained dark with creosote and wound with heavy rope supported a slatted wooden walkway. It led from the edge of the parking area up to the front doors and was very nautical looking.

"No candy stores in the village?" Richie asked.

"Not here. There's a couple of 'em in Sag Harbor. We go over there a lot," Mickey said. "Sag is a lot bigger than this place and there's lots more to do over there, 'cept there's no place to go swimming. It's mostly yachts and big charter boats and stuff like that. I'll get Eddie to take us over there one of these days. He has a car."

Mickey lit another cigarette. "They sell candy and ice cream at the Sugar Shack, though." He dragged deeply and inhaled, then let the smoke out slowly. "You'll like the Sugar Shack, Rich. They got a soda fountain right in front as you walk in and in the back is a big dining room with lots of tables and booths along the side and they even have a juke box. You like music?"

"Sure. Rock and roll is my favorite."

"Yeah, me too. Hey, you sure you don't want a cigarette?" Mickey held the pack out towards him.

"Nah. I tried it once and they made me sick. Got dizzy and threw up. I decided I could live without them after that."

"Yeah, I know what you mean. I threw up my first time, too." Mickey laughed. "I was only twelve years old. I'm still smoking, though." He took another drag. "Anyway, the shack is packed just about every night in the summer."

"It sounds like a neat place," Richie said.

"Yeah," Mickey agreed. "The kids hang out mostly in the dining room and out on the deck. Friday nights are the best, 'cause they have a dance. The owner rigs the juke box so you don't have to put in any nickels."

"Really?" Richie liked that idea and he just remembered today was Friday.

"Yeah." Mickey nodded. "Ends at midnight. Friday nights are the coolest at the Sugar Shack." He finished his cigarette and flipped it ahead of them where it hit the ground, then stepped on it when they caught up to it.

Richie studied him out of the corner of his eye. Mickey's cool, he thought. He was glad they had met. Being a local, as year-round residents were called, Mickey was definitely qualified to show him around Sea Shell Harbor and introduce him to some of the other kids. He seemed nice enough and Richie felt comfortable being in his company.

Mickey also looked tough enough to handle himself in a fight if he had to, Richie thought. Definitely a rock, no doubt about it. He wore the uniform of a rock. Long hair piled on top of his head in a pompadour, with the sides combed straight back and culminating in a duck tail at the back of his head. With a garrison belt to hold up his dungarees and a tee shirt he wore with the sleeves rolled up, the look was completed.

Although it was the summer and Mickey wasn't wearing a leather jacket or engineer boots, Richie guessed that he probably owned both. Mickey would never be considered a collegiate, that's for sure, he thought.

Richie, on the other hand, would never be considered a rock. He looked like and considered himself a collegiate. He wore chinos and button-down shirts or V-neck sweaters and either white bucs or topsiders. Although he did wear his hair long like Mickey and he liked rock and roll music, that was where the similarities ended.

It took them about fifteen minutes to walk from Treadway's to the Sugar Shack. Richie laid out the route in his mind. Noyac Road to Beach Road, turn left and down the hill about a quarter of a mile. Once you see the Salty Pirate on the right, you're practically there. Pretty simple, he thought. He'd have no trouble finding it again.

When they reached the Sugar Shack, there were a couple of younger children playing in the sand alongside the parking lot. Richie glanced further up the road. Across on the other side, he saw the gas station Mickey had mentioned earlier.

"That's Harbor Road over there next to the gas station?"

"Right," Mickey said.

"And there's a church and theater around the corner on Harbor Road?" Richie wanted to be sure he knew where everything was.

"Yeah. Saint Matthews Church and the Sea Shell Harbor Community Theater. They're both on that road. Harbor Road only goes for a little ways before it dead-ends at the water, though. At Sag Harbor Cove. You could take a boat from there to Sag Harbor."

"Oh, I see." Richie added this latest bit of information to his memory.

Mickey turned and started to walk towards the rear of the parking lot next to the Sugar Shack. "The main entrance is actually at the back," Mickey said. He glanced up at the deck which ran along the outside of the building. "Nobody's here yet." He sounded disappointed. "They're probably all home having dinner."

He looked at Richie. "Don't worry, by tonight the place will be packed. Everybody in town hangs out here. C'mon," he said, gesturing to Richie, "let's go in and cool off. I'll show you the inside."

Richie followed him inside. The cool, dry air- conditioned atmosphere provided a welcome respite from the heat and humidity of outdoors. They sat down at the counter and ordered two cokes. As the drinks were placed in front of them, another boy about their age walked through the door. He was overweight and sweating profusely.

As he sat down a couple of stools away, the boy mopped his forehead with a sweat-stained handkerchief. He ordered a chocolate ice cream cone and when it was delivered to him, he attacked it with obvious delight.

"Hey, how're you doing, Frankie?" Mickey called to him, leaning forward so the boy could see him.

"Oh, hiya, Mickey," Frankie answered. He adjusted his glasses. "Didn't see you there. Whatcha doin'?" Frankie moved to the stool next to them.

"Not much." Mickey lit a cigarette, inhaled and then blew a smoke ring. "We just got here a minute ago. By the way, this is Richie, a friend of mine from Brooklyn. Richie, Frank Wittey."

"Nice to meet you, Frankie," Richie said, offering his hand.

"Same here." Frankie shook Richie's hand and smiled.

"Frankie's the local brain around here," Mickey teased. "He's very WIT-TEY!"

"C'mon, Mickey," Frankie protested. "Don't start that again."

"Just kidding you, Frankie." Mickey turned to Richie. "Frankie got the highest mark in science class last year, so I call him The Brain. Plus, his name is WIT-TEY, get it?" He nudged Richie gently in the side with his elbow. Richie gave Frankie a sympathetic look. "Yeah, I get it. It's a pun."

Mickey looked pleased with himself. Turning back to Frankie, he said, "Where is everybody, Frankie? I figured some of the gang would be here. You seen Eddie?"

"Burkett?" Frankie thought a moment. "He's over at Trout Pond with some of the other guys. Least he was a while ago." He used his tongue to swipe at a trickle of chocolate that was running down the side of the cone.

"They hanging out at Trout Pond today?" Mickey asked. "I figured they'd all be at the beach." He squashed the end of his cigarette into the ashtray on the counter.

Frankie mopped his brow again. "Nah, it was too hot at the beach, so everybody went over to the pond. It's much cooler over there. You just get off work, Mick?"

"Yeah. Five o'clock. What's happening at the pond? You think Eddie's still there? I gotta talk to him."

"Probably. Hey, you shudda seen what happened." Frankie started to laugh. "Kenny Simms was gonna jump off the forty-footer but he chickened out. He started crying when the guys wouldn't let him climb back down."

"You're kidding!" Mickey pounded the counter. "Kenny? Crying?"

"Yeah, like a baby." Frankie's head bobbed up and down as he laughed. "Eddie finally climbed up and made him jump from the thirty-foot marker. You shudda seen it. Kenny landed right on his fat ass. I couldn't stop laughing." Frankie was giggling insanely as he told the story.

"He get hurt?" Mickey inquired, leaning closer to Frankie.

"Nah, he's okay. Got a sore ass, that's all. That'll teach him not to go around bragging about how cool he is. Forty-footer my foot!" Frankie said derisively.

"Not too many guys have jumped from the forty-footer," Mickey said.

"Nope," Frankie agreed. "Not many. You, Eddie and Tommy Ryan are the only ones that I know of."

"And Billy Riley. Don't forget about him. He jumped last summer."

"Oh, yeah, that's right. I almost forgot about him. Add Billy Riley to the list." Frankie took another bite of his cone. "Hey, I haven't seen Billy yet. He coming back this summer?"

"As far as I know. I hope he shows up before the Fourth of July beach party," Mickey said. "I gotta see him about getting some fireworks."

"Yeah, I hope he does, too. He always has the best." Frankie finished the cone and licked his fingers. "Well, I better get going. Don't want to miss dinner. See you later, Mick."

"Okay, Frankie," Mickey said. "Say hello to your mother for me."

"Will do," Frankie said. "Nice meeting you, Richie." He got up from the counter and sauntered over to the door. Before walking through it, he turned to them and said in a voice like a radio announcer's, "Kenny Simms jumps from the forty-footer and breaks his ass! Ha ha!"

They could hear Frankie laughing all the way out in the parking lot. Richie turned to Mickey. "He's a funny guy, that Frankie."

"Yeah, Frankie's a cool guy," Mickey agreed. "Lives out here all year round, also. We used to go to school together, before I dropped out. His mom's all right, too. She lets us hang out at their house all winter when there ain't much happening out here. Feeds us all day long. Anything we want. Man, she's always cooking, that Mrs. Witty. I guess that's why Frankie is so fat."

"He is slightly overweight," Richie agreed.

Mickey looked at himself in the mirror behind the counter and ran his fingers through his hair, then stood up. "Let's go in the back and check out the juke box." He turned and headed towards the rear of the Sugar Shack with Richie following close behind.

They carried their drinks to the other room and found a table next to the juke box. Richie sat while Mickey stood in front of it, reading song titles. "You like Danny and the Juniors, Rich?"

"Sure." Mickey deposited a quarter and made several selections, then joined Richie at the table as the opening bars of At The Hop blasted out from the speakers. Their mood was instantly elevated as they sat and listened, keeping time to the music with their hands and feet.

"Yeah, Richie, this summer's gonna be great, I can feel it." Mickey was moving his whole body up and down as the song continued to play.

"It sure feels like it so far." Richie took a sip from his drink. "So, tell me about this place you and Frankie were talking about."

Mickey took another cigarette from his pack and lit it. "You mean Trout Pond?"

"Yeah. And what's the forty-footer?"

Mickey blew some smoke rings. "Trout Pond is a neat swimming hole about a mile from here, over in Noyac. Most of the kids hang out there when they're not at the beach. It's real nice. Out in the woods. There's these tall trees all around the water and we use 'em to jump from."

"That sounds like fun," Richie said.

"Oh, yeah, it's great. There's one really tall tree there we call Mighty Mo. Some of the kids made some platforms out of wood and stuck 'em in the tree. There's three of 'em. One at twenty feet, one at thirty feet and the highest one is at least forty feet up."

"And you jumped from the top?"

"Yeah, the first time when I was eleven," Mickey said proudly. "I was scared stiff, believe me, but I had to. I couldn't chicken out in front of my friends."

"You must be some kind of dare-devil," Richie said with admiration. "Forty feet is pretty high."

"Yeah, maybe I am," Mickey agreed. "Anyone can jump from the lower platforms, though. That's where all the little kids jump from. I was the youngest kid to ever jump from the top."

"What made you decide to try it?"

"My friends dared me, so I had to do it," Mickey said matter-of-factly. "The first time is the killer, then it's easy." After a pause, he said, "you want to try it, Rich?"

"Not me," Richie said quickly.

"Aw, come on, Rich. It's fun." Mickey was eyeing him closely.

"Well, I don't know, maybe," Richie said. "I'd have to see it first. We used to jump off the Plum Beach bridge in Brooklyn a couple of years ago. I don't know if it was forty feet or not but it was pretty high."

"You could probably do it with no sweat," Mickey said. "Heck, I did it when I was eleven. That's when it was scary. Now, it's a breeze."

"We'll see what happens, Mick," Richie said nonchalantly. "I can't guarantee anything."

"Well, if you jump off the forty-footer, the girls will treat you like a hero. They love it when we jump. Maybe I'll take you there tomorrow and you can check it out."

"Tomorrow?"

"Sure. I don't have to work, so we can pack a lunch and spend the whole day. You'll love it," Mickey said. "It's a beautiful place. Great for swimming."

"Well, I guess so," Richie said without enthusiasm. "That sounds good." He looked at his watch. "It's six-fifteen. I'd better head back home. My parents have this quirk about me being late for dinner."

"Yeah? I ain't got that problem. My old lady don't even cook for us half the time. She's usually half-bagged by then." Mickey took out a comb and ran it through his hair. His eyebrows knitted together, turning his face into a frown. "If it wasn't for Diane, we'd all starve to death. She usually makes supper for me."

"Where did you say you lived, Mickey?"

"Over in Bridgehampton. It's about three miles from here. I might as well go home for a while too and see what's shaking."

"How're you going to get there? Walk?"

"Nah, I'll hitch," Mickey replied. "Getting a ride out here is no problem at all. I hitch hike all the time. Most of the people around here know me."

They left the table and walked outside through a rear door. It opened onto a deck on which more tables and chairs were set up for outdoor dining. Mickey lit another cigarette. "You coming back tonight, Rich? It's Friday night. The place will be hopping."

I guess I will," Richie answered. "What time?"

"Around eight, eight-thirty. We can meet right here on the deck." Mickey made a sweeping gesture with his head. "C'mon, I'll walk with you back to Noyac Road."

They left the Sugar Shack and started walking back up Beach Road, the same way they had come. Mickey pointed to the water on their right, beyond the parking lot. "You can also get back to your house by walking along the water's edge but it takes a little longer. This way's faster."

Richie made a mental note of that. They continued walking and a few minutes later reached Noyac Road.

"So, I'll see you later, Rich," Mickey said. He crossed to the other side and stood there, waiting for a ride. Richie waved and started walking back toward Treadway's. Several cars passed him as he made his way along the road and when he glanced back to the spot where he had left Mickey standing, he was already gone.

SUMMER AT SEA SHELL HARBOR

Three

As Richie walked through the front door, he heard his mother call from the kitchen, "you're just in time for dinner, Richard! Better wash up!"

Richie washed his face and hands in the bathroom, then joined his parents in the small dining area adjacent to the living room. His father had arrived from the city a short time earlier on the Long Island Railroad and now that the unpacking and settling in were completed, the Donnellys sat down to enjoy their first meal together in Sea Shell Harbor.

Mr. Donnelly looked out from behind his wire-framed glasses. "I stopped by that market on Noyac Road on my way home to pick up a few things but the prices seemed a bit on the high side."

"You mean Treadway's?" his wife asked. "That's where I bought our groceries. Had them delivered earlier."

A portly man with grey, thinning hair and sparkling blue eyes, Mr. Donnelly had a self-deprecating sense of humor that others found endearing. "Don't think we can afford that place," he said. "I may look like I was born yesterday but I know when merchandise is marked up too high."

Though a pleasant and easygoing man, Mr. Donnelly was an astute shopper, the result of his training as an accountant. "Figure we'll do most of our shopping at the supermarket over in East Hampton," he said.

"Mickey says Mr. Treadway is a grouch and he raises his prices in the summer because he doesn't like tourists," Richie commented. "He said Mr. Treadway told him that when you see the customer start to cry, you know you charged him the right price."

"He did, eh? Well, who is this Mickey person?" his father asked.

"He's the boy who delivered the groceries," Mrs. Donnelly said. "He seemed like a nice boy. Friendly."

"Well, that's good," Mr. Donnelly said. "That also confirms what I suspected. Treadway's prices are much too high. How much did you spend on the groceries, dear?"

"It was ten dollars and some change," his wife answered. "I also tipped the boy a quarter."

"Ten dollars! And that's just for tonights dinner and tomorrow's breakfast. Why at this rate, we'll be broke in a week!" Mr. Donnelly took off his glasses and wiped them with his handkerchief. "It'll be worth the extra gas money to shop at the supermarket in East Hampton."

"Yes, dear," Mrs. Donnelly agreed. "The smaller markets usually charge more than the supermarket. We should probably use them only for the basics, like bread and milk."

Richie studied his parents as they talked about the prices at Treadway's. He admired them. As far as parents went, they were fairly lenient when it came time for his social activities and they gave him a generous allowance.

In return, he rarely ever caused them any problems. He studied hard in school and received good grades as a result. His teachers liked him and his parents were proud of him.

Although his father wanted him to be an accountant like himself, Richie wasn't sure what he wanted to do after college, or even what subjects to study. His own ideas tended to be more exotic. He thought he might want to become an airline pilot or maybe try for a career in law enforcement. He wasn't sure yet.

In his daydreams, he would sometimes be an FBI agent or perhaps even the captain of a big ship.

"Aye, aye, sir," his men would say as they saluted him and then turned away to carry out his orders. He'd be standing tall on the bridge, crisp and handsome in his captain's uniform, making sure the ship stayed on course as it sailed away to far-off lands.

He never imagined himself working as an accountant. He just couldn't put that scene in his mind. Oh, he could picture an accountant sitting at his desk with his sleeves rolled up, pencil in hand and jotting down numbers all day. Perhaps even wearing one of those green visors he had seen one of them wear in the movies.

Sure, he could picture it, all right. Only the face in the picture wasn't his. Not at all. He just didn't know yet what he wanted to do with his life but he figured he still had plenty of time to decide. He'd choose a career by the time he went off to college. In the meantime, just being seventeen was enough for him to worry about.

"Mr. Haddock at the realty company told me to try the Shopwell Supermarket over in East Hampton," Mr. Donnelly continued. "All the local people shop there."

"I just hope their produce can compare with Treadway's," Mrs. Donnelly said, as she speared a slice of tomato with her fork. "Even though the prices are high, the quality is excellent."

"I agree," said Mr. Donnelly. "Treadway's produce is locally grown. Can't complain about that. Just their prices."

"Great dinner, mom," Richie said as he wolfed down the fried chicken, baked beans and potato salad she had served. He was famished. More than that, he was in a hurry. He wanted to take a shower before he went out again.

Mickey had said there were plenty of pretty girls in Sea Shell Harbor and Richie wanted to make sure he looked his absolute best. Just in case he met any of them.

After cleaning his plate he excused himself from the table and went to his room where he picked up some clean clothes and then headed for the shower.

Finishing that, he toweled himself dry and put on a fresh tee shirt and a pair of faded jeans.

Even though he didn't have to shave regularly, he did so now and then splashed after-shave lotion on his face. He liked the smell of it and decided to add a little more, just to be on the safe side.

Next, he turned his attention to the most important part of his grooming - his hair.

Richie's hair was a light blond and he wore it a little longer than his parents preferred but they let him wear it the way he wanted. Some of his friends in Brooklyn still wore their hair in a crew cut but he felt he had outgrown that style, now that he was seventeen.

He decided to copy the way Mickey wore his. He combed his hair back away from his forehead and piled it high on top of his head in a pompadour. Next, he swept the sides straight back to form a duck's tail at the back of his head. After working at it for several minutes, he finally got it the way he wanted.

Examining himself in the mirror, he was pleased with the results. Not bad, he thought. After pulling the pompadour forward a little bit with his fingers, he decided he was ready. "Now, bring on the girls," he said aloud.

It was shortly past eight when Richie arrived at the Sugar Shack. He walked through the parking lot to the rear of the building and went up the stairs to the deck. It was filled with teenagers. Sitting, standing or leaning against the railing in small groups, they all seemed to be talking at the same time.

He looked around but didn't recognize anyone. The boys were neatly dressed in tee shirts and jeans or Bermuda shorts and wore sandals or sneakers without socks on their feet.

Some of the girls wore pastel-colored shorts and tank tops and some had on bathing suits under white, terry cloth robes that came down past their waists. The kids were all tanned and healthy looking, with freshly scrubbed faces and hair bleached lighter by the sun.

Richie stood at the top step and leaned against the wooden railing, surveying the situation. A couple of girls looked his way and smiled and he smiled back. He wanted to say something to them but felt a little shy because he didn't know any of them.

The kids on the deck all seemed to know each other, though. They acted like typical teenagers; laughing, talking loudly and pushing and shoving one another with equal abandon. Some of the guys and girls were sitting together at tables, snuggled up close

RICHARD W. DUNNE

and holding hands.

Feeling slightly self-conscious, he left the deck and went inside the Sugar Shack. It was crowded. All the stools at the counter were occupied and people were standing behind them, waiting to shout their orders to the harried countermen.

To the left of the door, the tables along the wall were also filled and several waitresses hurried back and forth, carrying trays of food to the hungry and impatient customers.

A pair of stereo speakers were mounted on the wall above the tables and loud music spilled out from them, almost managing to drown out the din of the crowd. Richie slowly made his way toward the dining room in the back, where he and Mickey had been earlier.

Sitting at one of the stools halfway down the counter, was Frank Wittey, munching on a hot dog. Glad to see a familiar face, Richie worked his way through the crowd until he was standing behind him. He watched as Frank held the hot dog up to his face and gave it a serious, almost loving look before he took a bite.

Richie tapped him on the shoulder. "Hi, Frank, have you seen Mickey?"

Frank swiveled around on his stool to see who it was. His eyes appeared huge from behind his glasses. "Oh, hiya, Richie. Mickey? Yeah, I think he's in the back." He pointed in the direction of the dining room. "He's in there with Eddie and some of the guys."

"Thanks," Richie said, patting him on the shoulder. "I'll see you later."

He turned and headed for the dining room. It took him a few minutes to weave his way through the crowd. I've never seen so many people all in one place, he thought. He remembered what Mickey had told him earlier that afternoon, the entire town usually showed up on Friday night.

There was a little more space in the dining room but it was still very crowded. The walk from the front of the Sugar Shack to the dining room reminded Richie what it felt like to be on the subway in Brooklyn. Wall to wall people.

Scanning the room, he saw Mickey sitting with two other boys at a table in the corner. They were laughing and smoking cigarettes. As he approached their table, Mickey looked up and waved. "Hey, look who's here. Richie, come on over and sit down." To the others, Mickey said, "this is the guy I was telling you about. Richie Donnelly, from Brooklyn. Richie, these are a couple of friends of mine, Eddie Burkett and Danny Shaw."

"How're you doing, Richie?" Eddie inquired, offering his hand. "Mickey's been telling us about you. From Brooklyn, huh?"

"Yeah. Nice meeting you." Richie shook hands with the two boys and gave them the once-over. Eddie was taller than the others and had short brown hair and blue eyes. He wore a white, button-down shirt, tan chinos and a pair of dockers, with no socks. He was quite good-looking.

Danny, on the other hand, was short, with dark features and a large nose. His hair was matted in places and looked like it hadn't been combed in a while. Parts of it stuck straight up from the top of his head.

"Hey, do you know my cousin, Pete Shaw?" Danny asked. He wiped his mouth with the back of his hand. "He's from Brooklyn, too. Bensonhurst." He had a high-pitched voice and seemed to whine when he talked.

"No, I don't think so," Richie answered. "I'm from Flatbush."

"Oh," Danny said. He sounded disappointed.

"He doesn't know everyone who lives in Brooklyn, you schmuck," Eddie chided him. "You have any idea how many people live in Brooklyn?" He playfully punched Danny in the arm.

"Well, I was only asking. Thought maybe he knew him that's all," Danny countered. "Can't a guy ask?"

"No, sorry, Danny. Don't know him," Richie said, soothingly.

"Don't mind him, Rich," Eddie said, smiling. "He's our court jester. We only keep him around for laughs."

"Oh, yeah, sure," Danny said. "And you're the class clown. Just 'cause you're older, doesn't mean..."

"That's right," Eddie said, interrupting him. He wagged his finger at Danny, as if scolding him. "Older and wiser and don't you forget it."

"The only thing I won't forget is how good your mother was last night. She was walking around the village with a mattress on her back, yelling, curb service!" Danny made a funny face and stuck his tongue out at Eddie.

Upon hearing that, Eddie picked up his bottle of soda and with his thumb covering the top of it, shook the bottle rapidly. When the liquid came rushing out, he squirted Danny with it. "All right, get your curb service over here," he said, laughing.

"Hey!" Danny jumped up from the table, trying to get away from Eddie and his weapon of fizzling soda.

Richie watched the friendly horseplay with amusement. He decided he liked these guys. They were funny and seemed to enjoy ribbing each other without hurting the other one's feelings.

Mickey, though, wasn't saying much, he noticed. He was quiet and he sat back in his chair, letting the others do all the talking. He seemed to have withdrawn and Richie sensed a change in his mood. He was not as animated as he had been earlier.

Eddie turned to Richie. "We were thinking about going over to Trout Pond tomorrow for a swim, Rich. You're welcome to come with us, if you'd like."

"Yes, I'd like that," Richie replied.

Mickey said you might want to try out Mighty Mo," he continued, raising his eyebrows quizzically.

"I don't know about that," Richie said, looking at Mickey. "Forty feet seems pretty high to me."

Mickey took a sip from his drink, looked at Eddie and then said in a quiet voice, "I didn't say he wanted to jump. All I said was, I told Richie about Mighty Mo and," he shifted his gaze to Richie, "that you would probably do it." He placed his glass on the table and looked back at Eddie. "That's what I said."

Eddie smiled at Mickey then turned to Richie. "You don't have to jump if you don't want to, Rich," he said.

"He can jump off off the lower platform," Danny interjected. "He don't have to jump off the top. We all did it but he don't have to." He looked at Richie and added, "you don't have to."

Richie looked at the three of them. "It almost sounds like I have to, now."

"We all did it," Danny repeated.

"Really?" Richie said, looking again at each of them. "You all jumped from the top? From forty feet?"

Eddie, still smiling, looked at him again. "Yup, from forty feet! It's sort of like an initiation out here, old sport." He gestured to Mickey and Danny. "All of us have done it at one time or another."

Richie had the impression they were testing him. Sort of feeling him out, to see what kind of a person he was. He didn't know for sure if they had jumped from the top of a forty-foot tree or if it was just friendly teasing.

Either way, he wasn't ready to commit himself to a jump like that and he wasn't the type to boast about his own adventurous undertakings, like jumping off the Plum Beach bridge.

Thinking about it now, it seemed like the bridge had only been about twenty feet or so, and that had been scary enough. Forty feet meant that the Trout Pond tree was twice as high. He didn't see how anyone could jump from that height without hurting themselves.

"Relax, Richie," Eddie said, patting his arm. "Don't take it so seriously."

"Hey, Mickey, there's Pat!" Danny said suddenly, pointing toward the dance floor.

"Where?" Mickey asked, looking to see where Danny was pointing.

"Over there. She's talking to Sally and some other girl." He glanced at Mickey. "No, on the other side of the dance floor. Do you see her?"

They all looked across the room to the spot where Danny had indicated. There were three girls standing across the room, talking to one another.

"Oh, yeah, now I see her," Mickey said. He turned to Richie. "Pat's the cute one with the dark hair. I noticed her at the end of last summer but I never got a chance to make my move. I was hoping she'd be back this year."

Richie picked Pat out from the three girls and nodded. "She is cute," he agreed.

"Who's that other girl with her and Sally?" Danny asked. "She's real pretty, too."

"Her name is Nancy," Eddie offered. "Forget about her, Danny. She's too classy for you."

"Says who?" Danny said indignantly. He nudged Mickey's arm. "C'mon, Mickey, let's go over there and talk to them."

Mickey didn't move but just sat there, looking over at the three girls, a bored expression on his face. "I don't know, Danny," he said. "We don't even know them."

"So what? We'll just go over there and meet them," Danny began to smooth out the hair on the top of his head with his fingers.

"I don't know if that's such a good idea." Mickey picked up his drink and took a sip. "You can't just barge in and start talking to people you don't know," he said. "It's uncool."

"Well, I know Sally. Let's get over there before some other guys move in on them," Danny persisted.

"Nah, you go, Danny. I'll wait here." Mickey took another sip of his drink. "This ain't the right time."

"Aw, you chicken!" Danny turned to Eddie. "C'mon, Eddie, let's go over there. You with me?"

"Easy, young Daniel," Eddie teased. "The night is young." He seemed amused by Danny's growing agitation.

"You guys make me sick! You're such babies!" Danny was starting to whine. He looked at Richie. "How about you,

"Richie? You got the nerve?"

"Sure, I have the nerve," Richie began, "but..."

"We'll just go over there and ask them to dance," Danny interrupted. "Please, Rich," he pleaded, "let's hurry, before..., darn! You see? Somebody else just beat us to it!"

Danny pounded the table with his hand. "Now look at them! They're out there dancing, right now! I told you we should've gone right over there! Now it's too late!" He slumped back in his chair, looking disgusted.

"We'll ask them later," Mickey said gently, as if to sooth Danny's feelings. "I just don't feel like dancing right now." He took the pack of cigarettes he had rolled up in his sleeve, tapped one out and lit it, then laid the pack on the table. "Like Eddie says, the night is young."

Four

Eddie looked across the table at Mickey. "What's the matter, Mick? You look down in the dumps tonight."

Mickey squinted back at Eddie, the cigarette dangling from his lips as he answered, "Oh, not much." He took the cigarette out of his mouth and laid it in the ashtray, then cleared his throat. "It's just my old lady, that's all."

"She giving you a hard time?" Eddie shifted in his chair, then put his arms on the table and leaned closer to Mickey.

"Nah. She just makes me mad, that's all." Mickey picked up his cigarette and took another drag. He inhaled the smoke and then blew a smoke ring as he exhaled. "She must've been drinking most of the day 'cause she was half-bagged when I got home. She and Diane were screaming at each other."

"Screaming?"

"Yeah." Mickey looked down at his glass for a second, then back at Eddie. "I hate it when she drinks."

"What were they screaming about?" Eddie folded his hands together as he sat and waited for Mickey's answer.

As he sat there observing him, Richie realized that Eddie had a natural charm that made him appear confident and self-assured. Sitting there like that, he reminded Richie of Mr. Cullen, his high school counselor.

"She was on Diane's back about wearing too much makeup,"

Mickey said. "Told her she was gonna attract the wrong kind of guy and a bunch of other stuff. Before I knew it, they were screaming and yelling at each other."

He stamped out his cigarette in the ashtray, then picked up the bottle and poured more soda into his glass. He took another sip. "I couldn't stand listening to them any longer, so I left."

"I'm sorry to hear that Mick," Eddie soothed.

"It's okay," Mickey said, then continued. "I just can't stand her when she drinks, that's all. She always seems to start hassling Diane as soon as she's had a few."

"That's what booze'll do for you," Danny offered.

Richie sat there, not saying anything. Since they had just met that afternoon, he didn't want to interject his opinions into Mickey's personal life. He didn't feel it would be proper. Since the others knew Mickey well, he guessed it was all right for them to do it.

As the music ended and people started to leave the dance floor, Danny looked up just in time to see Pat, Sally and Nancy walk through the rear exit which led to the deck. Following close behind were the three boys with whom they had been dancing.

"Hey, look!" he said, "those guys are moving in on the girls!" He struggled to get out of his chair. We gotta get out there, right now!"

"Will you just relax, Danny? Jeez!" Mickey said, sounding annoyed.

"I thought you liked Pat, Mickey," Danny argued. "You just gonna sit there and let somebody else move in on her?" He had managed to rise halfway up out of his chair and was gesturing wildly.

Mickey looked up at him and shook his head. "I told you, I don't even know her, you jerk! I can't go barging over there and cause a scene! She'll think I'm nuts! We gotta wait for the right moment..., you know, get properly introduced. Then we'll talk to them."

Danny stood up completely and moved his chair back out of his way. "Well, let's go and talk to Sally, then. I know her. I'll get her to introduce you."

Mickey looked up at him and raised an eyebrow. "You know Sally?"

"Sure, I...," Danny was stammering now. "Well, I don't exactly know her, but I see her around all the time."

"Sit down, you maniac," Mickey said, laughing.

Danny remained standing. "Come on, you guys, we're wasting valuable time! You gonna sit there all night? Let's go outside and talk to them! Maybe they'll have a couple of friends for you two." He gestured to Eddie and Richie and laughed. Richie smiled back at him.

"I know Sally," Eddie said. He gave Danny a big grin.

"You know Sally?" Danny's eyes widened.

"Yup. I know Pat, too. I dated both of them last year," Eddie said, matter-of-factly.

"Well, come on then, Eddie," Danny said. "Introduce us! Mickey, let's go!"

"You dated Pat?" Mickey asked Eddie.

"Well, it wasn't really a date," Eddie explained. "I took them for a ride on my boat, last summer. I thought they were a little too young for me at the time. Sally was only fourteen."

"They don't look too young to me," Danny said with a leer.

"They look a lot older now," Eddie agreed. He laughed. "What a difference a year makes. They sure filled out quite a bit, I'll tell you that. You want to go outside and talk to them, Mickey?"

Mickey thought about it for a minute. "Well..., okay, let's go! He who hesitates is lost."

The four boys left the table and walked outside. The deck was still crowded with teenagers and although they carefully scanned the crowd, they did not see the girls.

"Nuts! They're not here," Danny said. "Let's walk around to the other side and see if we can find them."

They headed along the deck to the other side of the building, looking at the faces in the crowd as they walked. There was no sign of them.

"Maybe they went back inside through the other door," Richie offered.

"Yeah, could be," Eddie agreed.

The four of them went back inside through the other entrance and made their way back through the crowd to the table where they had been sitting. No girls.

"We lost them," Danny said. He sounded disgusted.

"They gotta be around here somewhere," Mickey said.

Eddie snapped his fingers. "They probably walked down to the beach! Let's go there."

"Good idea," Mickey said.

The others followed Eddie as he retraced their route back outside, along the deck and down the stairs leading to the parking lot. They walked through the lot and climbed over the wooden fence which separated it from the sandy area on the other side.

Beyond the fence, there was a walkway made of wooden planks which had been laid down in the sand and led to the water, about a hundred yards away. This was the official Village of Sea Shell Harbor Beach, where everyone congregated in the summer.

As they started down the walkway, coming in the opposite direction was Mickey's sister, Diane. Almost as tall as her brother and bearing the family resemblance, she had long, blond hair which she had combed down over her shoulders and tied in the back with a red ribbon.

She was wearing white short shorts and a light blue, sleeveless blouse which matched the color of her eyes. A small mermaid was stitched across the left side of it, just above her ample bosom. Her shapely legs were already well tanned and she wore white sandals on her feet.

Standing there in the semi-darkness, with only the lights of the Sugar Shack illuminating her face, she looked quite stunning. "Hi, Mickey. Hi Eddie," she said, ignoring Danny completely. She gave Richie an appraising look. "Who's your friend?"

"Hi, Diane," Mickey said. This is a friend of ours, Richie, from Brooklyn. Where you been?"

"Down at the beach. Some of the kids got a bonfire going," she answered. "Where are you guys headed?"

"Thought we'd check out the beach ourselves," Mickey replied.

"Hey, you seen Pat and Sally in your travels?" Danny asked.

"Don't think I know them," she answered coolly. "I just passed a bunch of kids headed for the beach, though. Maybe they're in that group. Anyway, I'm on my way to the Sugar Shack to meet some of my friends. I'll see you later."

Before she could leave, Eddie stepped forward and blocked her path. "What happened to you last night, Diane? I thought you said you'd meet me at the shack?"

"Oh, I never got there," she answered easily. "My mother was being a pain in the neck, so I stayed home. Hope you didn't wait too long."

"Oh, not too long," Eddie said, glancing quickly at Mickey. "Left around nine-thirty. Took a ride to Southampton. Had a good time."

"That's nice," Diane said.

"I wanted to play some miniature golf," Eddie continued, "but it's no fun by yourself."

"Well, why don't you come back to the shack with me, buy me a soda and we can go golfing later?" she suggested. She looked at Richie. Her lips were a bright red. "Maybe Richie would like to play a game with us, too?" she asked.

"That's an idea," Eddie said, sounding less than enthusiastic. "You want to play some miniature golf with us, Richie?"

"Well..., not unless we all go," Richie answered. "I mean, I thought we were all hanging out together. We were just on our way to the beach, weren't we?" He was slightly puzzled by the sudden change in plans.

"You guys go," Eddie said. "Mickey, I'm gonna hang out with your sister and her friends for a while. You mind?"

"No, I don't mind," Mickey answered. "I guess we'll see you tomorrow."

"Okay. I'll pick you up at your house, say, one o'clock." Eddie looked at the others. "What about you guys? Danny? You coming to the pond tomorrow?"

"Can't," Danny said. "My old man wants me to help him around the house. I'll meet you tomorrow night at the shack, instead."

"Okay. What about you, Rich?"

"Sure, I'd like to go," Richie replied. "How do I get there?"

"Don't worry, we'll pick you up," Eddie said. "About one-fifteen, okay?"

"You know where I live, Eddie?" Richie asked. "Down on Chestnut."

"Yeah, I know where it is," he answered. He gave a chuckle. "My folks own the place. See you tomorrow."

"Good night, Richie," Diane said in a sultry voice. "It was nice meeting you." She gave him a dazzling smile.

"Same here," Richie said, smiling back at her. "Good night."

They parted company at that point. Mickey, Danny and Richie continued on toward the beach, while Eddie and Diane headed back to the Sugar Shack.

"Boy, your sister sure filled out, Mickey," Danny said as they continued walking. "Last year she was just a skinny kid, but now, gosh o'mighty, she's..."

"Hey, watch it, Danny, that's my sister you're talking about," Mickey said with a serious tone to his voice.

"You don't have to worry about me. I'm just making an observation, that's all," Danny whined. "I think Eddie likes her, though."

"Eddie? Are you kidding?" Mickey turned and gave Danny a scowl. "He's known Diane since she was eight years old. They're more like cousins to each other."

"Yeah, kissing cousins, if you ask me," Danny teased.

"Nobody asked you," Mickey said, sounding annoyed. "Look, man," he continued, "whatever they do with each other is their business. I don't interfere." He took a step closer to Danny. "But, I'm telling you, Eddie and Diane are just friends. She only likes to hang around with him because he has a car."

"Yeah, yeah, tell me another story," Danny said, keeping up the teasing.

"I'm telling you the truth, you dimwit. Besides," he turned and looked at Richie. "I think she likes you, Richie."

"Me?" Richie asked, giving Mickey a quizzical look.

"Well, she sure was giving you the eye," Mickey said.

"No offense, Mickey, but I think your sister's a little too young

44

for me," Richie stated flatly.

"With a body like that? You gotta be kidding, Richie," Danny said.

"Hey, you pervert!" Mickey lunged and made a grab for Danny.

Danny evaded his grasp and took off running toward the beach. Laughing now, Mickey started running after him. Richie hesitated for a moment, then joined in the chase.

They ran in the darkness, with Danny leading the way, followed closely behind by Mickey and Richie taking up the rear. They were laughing so hard, they were gasping for breath and almost fell in the slippery sand, finding themselves caught up in the gaiety and exuberance of their youth.

It was summer and they didn't have a care in the world.

Five

The next day, Saturday, was hot and sunny. A good day for swimming. Richie woke up late, had breakfast and then spent the rest of the morning straightening up his room.

At a few minutes past one, he was waiting outside the cabin for his new friends to pick him up. His parents had already left to spend the day with friends in Sag Harbor.

He sat on the top rail of the fence which surrounded the cabin's front yard and tossed pebbles into the street. The grass had been freshly mowed and a beautiful array of flowers had been planted along the fence line. The sweet aroma of roses and daffodils filled his nostrils and made him feel happy to be there.

Several of the other summer residents waved and said hello as they passed by on their way to Noyac Beach, which could be accessed by walking to the end of Chestnut Street. It was much closer than the Sea Shell Harbor town beach across the bay near the Sugar Shack and lots of people preferred Noyac Beach because it was less crowded.

As he sat there, Richie thought about the previous evening and events that had taken place. Of all the people he had met so far, he liked Mickey the best. Mickey was easy going and had a keen sense of humor, although Richie realized he could be moody at times.

Mickey had been quiet and withdrawn in the earlier part of the evening but had loosened up later on at the beach. They never found the three girls they'd been searching for but had managed to have a good time anyway. In spite of Danny's constant reminders about how they had let the girls slip through their fingers, the night had been a blast.

They'd sat around the bonfire with some of Mickey's other friends, listening to stories about some of the other people they knew in the harbor. It had been fun.

Richie guessed Mickey's home life was probably the reason for his moodiness. Of course, having parents who were divorced and hated each other, as Mickey claimed they did, could be rough on a person, he supposed. That was probably the reason Mickey's mother drank, he thought.

He tried to place himself in Mickey's shoes. What would his own life be like if his parents were divorced? Would that change everything? How would he deal with it? He just couldn't imagine anything like that and he hoped for Mickey's sake, that things would get better for him at home.

At one-fifteen, Mickey and Eddie pulled up in front of the cabin in Eddie's car, a brand new convertible. It was a real beauty, black with red leather upholstery and white sidewall tires. Eddie had the top down and the radio on, blasting out loud rock and roll music. The two of them looked spiffy in the convertible.

"Nice car," Richie stated as they stopped in front of him.

"Hi, Richie," Mickey greeted from the front passenger seat. "You ready to go?"

"Sure. You guys are right on time."

"Hiya, Richie. Hop in the back, will you, sport?" Eddie was peering out at him from behind a pair of aviator's sunglasses. "Mickey's riding shotgun today."

Mickey opened the door and leaned forward, pulling the back of the seat with him so Richie could climb in. "How're ya doing, pal?" he asked. "Hot enough for ya?"

"Just right," Richie answered. "I like it like this." He settled into the back seat. "How far is it to the pond?"

"About ten minutes from here." Mickey turned around in his seat to look at him. "You have a good time last night?"

"Oh, yeah, it was lots of fun. That Danny is some character, boy. And your sister's real nice, too." Richie looked at Eddie and asked, "how was the golf game?"

"What? Oh, we didn't go." Eddie whipped the car around in a u-turn as he spoke. "We just went back to the shack for a soda, then we went for a drive to Shelter Island. Quiet night." They drove up Chestnut in the opposite direction, stopped at the corner and then made a right turn on Noyac Road and headed west. Eddie picked up speed and after a mile or so, he suddenly turned left onto a smaller, barely visible, dirt road.

Richie was forced against the right side of the car as Eddie made the turn, nearly missing it. Anyone who was driving by and didn't know the road was there would probably never even see it, he thought.

"Nice move, Eddie," Mickey said. Eddie grunted.

They continued along the dirt road for another quarter of a mile until they came to a clearing in the trees. Eddie pulled the car off to the right and parked.

"This is it," he said. "We'll have to walk the rest of the way."

They left the car and started walking across the clearing, past several other cars that were parked there haphazardly, until they reached a dirt trail which led into the woods.

"Follow me," Eddie said to the others.

They started down the trail and, after about five minutes of hiking, Richie heard water splashing and voices laughing. A little further down the trail, they came upon another clearing, smaller than the first one where they had left the car, and surrounded by woods on all sides. Straight ahead, through the branches of the trees, Richie could see the pond.

On the banks along the waters edge, people had spread blankets on the ground and were lying on top of them. Some were sunbathing and others were swimming and splashing around in the water. The bank of the pond extended for several yards in either direction.

Richie looked around. On his right, the bank rose several feet above the pond and some of the younger children were diving into the water from a large rock. To his left, the bank disappeared into thick brush which grew right down to the waterline. Everyone looked like they were having a good time.

He followed Eddie and Mickey to a spot in the clearing near the water. Eddie spread a blanket down on the grass and started to take off his sneakers. "Let's hurry up and get into the water, you guys, I'm sweating like a pig."

They all stripped down to their bathing suits which they wore under their clothing. Mickey and Eddie finished first and raced each other to the edge of the pond, then dove into the water.

"Hurry up!" they called to Richie, who was still struggling to remove his jeans. "What're you waiting for?"

Richie finally managed to work his way free of his clothing and sprinted over to the water's edge. "Is the water warm, Mickey?" he asked.

"It's great, Rich. C'mon in."

Richie dove in and felt the cool water hit his body. It was clean and clear and felt wonderfully refreshing. He swam out to where Mickey and Eddie were floating on their backs, a few yards from the edge of the bank.

"So, how do you like Trout Pond so far, Rich?" Mickey asked.

"I love it," he replied. "I've never seen anything like it. This is paradise."

"Let's swim out to the raft," Eddie suggested.

Out in the middle of the pond where the water was deeper, there was a wooden platform, large enough to hold several people. The three of them swam out to it and hoisted themselves up.

Resting on top of four huge inner tubes, which had been previously inflated and secured to the platform beneath the water line to give it buoyancy, everything was held in place by wires attached to a large chain and heavy anchor from an old fishing boat lying on the bottom of the pond.

"This is our diving platform," Eddie said, "or, you can just lay out here and sunbathe."

"How deep is the water?" Richie asked.

"Nobody knows," Mickey said. "It's bottomless."

"Really?" Richie leaned over and looked down at the water.

"The pond is fed by an underground spring," Eddie said. "It's not really bottomless, but it's pretty deep. Thirty feet or so, at least."

"You guys ever try to touch bottom?"

"No, not me." Eddie shook his head. "Some kid drowned trying to do that, about…, when was that, Mick, about four years ago?"

"Yeah, I think so," Mickey answered. He came over to where Richie was standing and peered down into the water. "Don't try to swim too far down, Rich," he said. "Around twenty feet down, the land slopes in toward the middle of the pond. There's all kinds of tree roots and underbrush down there. The kid who drowned got tangled up in it and they didn't find his body until three days later."

"Did you know him?" Richie asked.

"Not really. I had seen him a couple of times before he drowned, though. He seemed like a nice kid." Mickey was silent for a moment. "Poor guy."

"They had to send divers down there to retrieve the body," Eddie said, picking up the conversation. "Don't worry, Rich, it's pretty safe. Just don't try to swim to China, that's all."

"You can bet on that," Richie said, stepping back from the edge. "Are there any fish in the pond?"

"Just some little ones. Not too many," Eddie answered. "Nobody really goes fishing over here. We go out in the bay to fish."

"There's some turtles and frogs, but not too many fish," Mickey said.

"Watch out for the big snapping turtles, though," Eddie teased. "They'll try to bite off your big toe."

As Eddie spoke, Mickey bent down behind Richie and reached over and pinched his big toe. Richie let out a scream and jumped up about a foot off the raft. The other two boys doubled over in laughter. "Got ya!" they both yelled simultaneously.

"You rats!" Richie grabbed Mickey's arm and pulled him to the edge of the platform where Mickey lost his balance and tumbled into the water. Next, he turned to Eddie, intent on grabbing him, too.

"Look out! Mad dog!" Eddie yelled. He avoided Richie's grasp and dove into the water, managing to safely elude him.

Richie assumed a Tarzan stance, throwing his head back and

beating on his chest with his fists. "Yahoo!" he yelled. "I'm king of the hill!"

Mickey and Eddie swam back to the raft and hoisted themselves up. They sat there trying to catch their breath from laughing so hard. Richie sat down next to them and laughed along with them.

Just then, a piercing cry filled the air from across the pond. "Geronomo!"

They looked up just in time to see a boy about fourteen hit the water. He made a large splash. Mickey pointed to a tree at the edge of the bank. "That's Mighty Mo," he said. "Some kids are jumping off of it."

Richie looked to see where Mickey was pointing. A huge syca-more tree, much taller than the others, jutted up and out over the water on the far bank. At that moment, another boy jumped from a point high up in the branches, about half-way up.

He seemed to hang suspended in the air for a moment, then, with arms flailing, fell rapidly toward the water. The boy hit the water as if he had been shot from a cannon, creating a large splash and making a noise that sounded like, ka-boom!

"Wow!" Richie exclaimed, looking up at the spot from where the boy had jumped. "That's high!"

Eddie and Mickey looked at each other and laughed. "That's only the twenty-foot marker," Eddie said. He then pointed to a spot in the tree, closer to the top. "That's where we jump from."

Richie craned his neck and looked to where Eddie was point-ing. "You gotta be kidding," he said. "Nobody could jump from there."

"We do it all the time" Eddie said seriously.

"Yup," Mickey agreed.

Richie sat there, shaking his head. "I don't believe it. It's not possible."

"If you don't believe us, we'll show you in a little while," Mickey said.

Eddie nudged Mickey in the arm. "You want to jump later?" he asked.

"Sure," Mickey said, sounding confident. "I could use the

practice."

"Come on," Eddie said. "Let's get back in the water. I'm starting to dry off." He dove into the water and Mickey and Richie dove in after him.

They swam around for a while and then headed back to the spot where they had entered the pond. They dried themselves off and laid down on the blanket to do a little sunbathing.

Richie lay on his back and closed his eyes, feeling a bit drowsy after the swim. He was thinking about the tree and had almost nodded off when he heard a velvety voice coming from somewhere above him.

"Hi, Eddie."

Richie opened his eyes and looked up, having to squint against the sun. Standing around the blanket and looking down at them were the three girls from the night before. The ones from the Sugar Shack that had caused Danny to get so worked up. What were their names? He thought for a second. Pat, Sally and..., oh, yeah, Nancy.

They were wearing bathing suits and carrying beach bags which they had slung across their shoulders. They seemed to be focused on Eddie and were smiling down at him. Eddie sat up and raised his sunglasses above his eyebrows. He smiled back at them.

"Oh, hello, ladies," he said. "Let's see...," he began, looking at each one of them. "Pat, right? Sally, and...,"

"Nancy," the other one said.

"Nancy," Eddie repeated. "It's nice to make your acquaintance." He gestured to the other two boys. "I'd like you to meet my friends. This is Mickey," he said, pointing to him, "and, that's Richie over there."

Mickey raised himself up on one arm and nonchalantly said, "Hi."

"Hi," Richie echoed, carefully looking each of them over and deciding they were all beautiful. Pat was the taller of the three and had dark brown hair, almost black, cut in a short pageboy style. Along with green eyes and a slightly up-turned nose, she was very attractive.

Sally was shorter than the other two, with medium brown hair and hazel eyes. A smattering of freckles splayed across the bridge of her nose and dotted her cheeks. Her teeth were crooked in the front but that somehow seemed to complement her appearance. She was cute in a perky sort of way and her alluring figure was her best feature.

To Richie, Nancy was the prettiest of the three girls. She had medium blond hair and the deepest and loveliest blue eyes he had ever seen.

Her fetching smile was caused by full red lips and dazzling white teeth that tantalized him to a degree he had never felt before. She was a dream. She was sexy. She was tempting. She was desirable. He was in love!

Pat was the first one to speak. "Where've you been hiding lately, Eddie?" she purred. "We haven't seen you since last summer. When are you going to take us out on your boat again? We've all decided we want to learn how to water ski this year."

Eddie stood up, stepped between Pat and Sally and put his arms around each of their waists. "Well, ladies," he said smoothly, "you've come to the right place. It just so happens that we're planning a little boat trip over to Robbins Island tomorrow, my lovelies. It's a great place to learn to ski. Why, we'd be honored if the three of you would join us."

"Oh," Sally said, sounding slightly disappointed. "We thought maybe you'd like to go skiing later on today."

"Can't today, I'm afraid," Eddie said. He turned and looked at her. The boat's in dry dock at the moment. I'm having the hull scraped. It won't be back in the water until tomorrow morning."

"Oh," Sally said in a small voice.

"Besides, my good friend, Richie, here," Eddie turned and gestured to Richie, "is making his debut jump from the top of Mighty Mo, today."

"Hey, Eddie," Richie began, getting to his feet, "I...,"

"You are?" Nancy asked, moving closer to him. She gave him another one of her fetching smiles.

As he straightened up, Richie found himself standing next to her and looking into her lovely blue eyes. He was further smitten.

She looked to be about sixteen, he estimated. Her skin was fair, not yet tanned by the summer sun. A few drops of moisture glistened on her skin, above her lips.

She looked at him and smiled, revealing her white, even teeth. She had a few randomly sprinkled freckles of her own, which only added to her beauty. With the sun radiating behind her as she stood there, she looked and felt like a vision, able to transmit her mesmerizing loveliness across to his awareness. He felt a sudden urge to kiss her.

Instead, he threw back his shoulders and assumed a military stance. "That's what they tell me," he said.

Pat moved over and stood next to Nancy. "Aren't you afraid?" she asked. "Hardly anyone has ever jumped from the top before."

"Well...," Richie began.

Mickey stood up and moved next to Richie. He looked directly at Pat and said, "I'm his trainer. I'm going to show him how it's done."

Pat looked back at him with an amused smile on her face but said nothing. Mickey continued talking.

"This is Richie's first vacation here, otherwise he'd have done it already," he said, switching his attention back and forth between Pat and Nancy. "And you're right, hardly anyone has ever jumped from the top before, because it's just too dangerous."

"Then why do you want to do it, if it's so dangerous?" Nancy asked.

"Because we like to live dangerously," Mickey said, boastfully. "Isn't that what life's all about? Adventure, excitement, danger...?"

"You're crazy if you jump from the top of that tree," Pat said, folding her arms in front of her. "Don't you know you could be seriously hurt? Why...,"

"I'll do it for you, my love," Mickey said gallantly. He bowed to her and tipped an imaginary hat.

"Don't do me any favors," Pat said, sounding slightly aloof. "Nobody has to commit suicide on my behalf."

"Oh, I want to see them jump," Sally said, excitedly. Her hair was tied in a pony tail and it moved up and down as she spoke. She wore a two-piece bathing suit, which complimented her generous figure.

Eddie, looking amused by the exchange between the others, moved in closer to Sally. "Tell you what, ladies. Let's all sit down and have some lunch and then perhaps a little later, we can attend to the suicide at hand."

He turned to Richie and said jokingly, "Richie, me lad, do you have any last requests before you die?"

Richie looked directly at Nancy. "A date with you, if I live through it," he said.

"That can be arranged," Pat said, answering for Nancy.

Nancy looked at her, then back to Richie. "If you live through it," she said with a smile, "I'll go out with you."

Mickey moved forward and looked at Pat. "And if I jump, will you go out with me?"

"I don't know about that," she said coyly. "Maybe. I thought you already had jumped."

"I did, but that was a long time ago. I haven't jumped yet this year. Come on, Pat," Mickey pleaded, "what do you say?"

"We'll see," she said. "If you live through it." Mickey smiled at her and she smiled back.

Eddie turned to Sally and bowed. "Shall we make it a three-some, my pet?"

Giggling, Sally answered, "Sure, why not?"

Six

The girls went to pick up their things and returned a moment later to join the boys for lunch. They sat on Eddie's blanket, eating sandwiches and getting further acquainted.

Nancy sat next to Richie and he was glad for the opportunity to talk with her. He moved closer. She sounded very friendly, conversing easily as they ate their lunch but he sensed that she was normally very quiet and reserved, perhaps even a little shy.

He was fascinated by her. He watched her out of the corner of his eye as she sat there, eating her sandwich with slow, deliberate movements. She was fawnlike, taking small bites and wiping her mouth with her napkin after each one.

Eddie was making Sally laugh by telling her funny stories. Every time he told a joke, she leaned forward and slapped his leg. The two of them acted like old friends and they seemed comfortable with one another.

Mickey's focus was on Pat, who was very animated and talked with exaggerated hand movements. She seemed to be interested in him, as well. She looked at him when she talked and directed most of her questions to him.

Nancy wasn't saying much. She just sat there, listening to the others talk. Richie liked that. He preferred girls who didn't try to dominate a conversation with meaningless chatter. Nancy had a quiet, studious look about her, but he sensed that she could hold her own in any conversation about any subject.

As they sat on the blanket, eating and talking, Richie learned that Nancy and Pat were also from Brooklyn and went to the same high school. They lived in the Marine Park section, which was only a few miles from his neighborhood in Flatbush and both were sixteen.

Sally came from Queens and went to a different school. She was fifteen and had met Pat and Nancy in Sea Shell Harbor the previous summer. The three of them were now good friends.

"I was born in Brooklyn, too," Mickey said, "but I moved out here when I was nine."

"Oh, that's nice," Nancy said. "You're both from Brooklyn. Where do you go to school, Richie?"

"Midwood High," he answered. "It's on Bedford Avenue."

"Pat and I both go to Saint Brendan's and Sally goes to Jefferson, in Queens," Nancy said.

"What school do you go to, Mickey?" Pat asked.

Before he could answer, Eddie and Sally got up from the blanket and announced they were going for a walk. "See you in a bit," Eddie said with a grin. Sally giggled as Eddie took her hand. They headed down a narrow path which led into the woods.

"Hurry back, you two!" Pat called after them, then turned to Mickey. "What school do you go to?" she repeated.

"Sag Harbor High School," Mickey answered. "I graduated last year." He glanced at Richie for a second, then turned back to Pat. "Next year I'm going to Southampton College."

Richie said nothing. It's his story, he thought. If that's what he wants to tell her, that's his business. Pat interrupted his thoughts.

"Are you two really going to jump from that tree?" she asked.

"Sure," Mickey said flippantly. "Why not?"

"It's very high," Nancy interjected. "I don't want to see you hurt." She looked at Richie as she spoke.

"We won't get hurt," Mickey reassured her. "Besides, Richie has to jump, now. You said you'd go out with him if he lived through it, remember?"

Richie smiled at Nancy. "That's right," he told her. "If I live through it, you'll go out with me." He leaned closer to her and looked into her eyes. "I'd jump from the Empire State Building if it meant a date with you."

Nancy placed her hand on his. "You don't have to jump. I'll go out with you, anyway."

"You will?" Richie asked, surprised.

"Yes, I will," she said. "So, you don't have to jump if you don't want to."

"That's good to know," he said. "Hey, Mickey, maybe I'll just take a rain check on the jump, after all. What do you think?"

"That's up to you, Rich," Mickey replied. He turned to Pat. "And what about me? Do I still have to jump or will you let me off the hook and go out with me, anyway?"

"I never said I'd go out with you," Pat said coyly. "I said, maybe, if you lived through it."

"Oh, so I guess that means I'm jumping," Mickey said.

"Well, how else will we know whether or not you live through it, unless you jump?" she asked teasingly. "Besides, I don't think you ever jumped from that tree, it's too high."

"Okay," Mickey said, standing up. "That settles it. I'm jumping." He started to take a step but Pat grabbed his arm.

"Come back, silly. I was only teasing." She stood up and moved next to him, then reached up and brushed a strand of hair away from his eyes. "You don't have to jump if you don't want to," she said softly. "I'll go out with you, either way."

"I'm glad to hear that," Mickey said, grinning widely. He took her hand and they sat back down on the blanket.

Eddie and Sally returned from their walk just then. As they sat down, Richie noticed traces of Sally's lipstick on his mouth. Eddie saw him looking and smiled. A moment later, he stood up and stretched.

"Well, lads," he said dramatically, "the appointed hour has arrived." He looked at Richie. "Who wants to go first?"

Nancy stood up quickly. "No! They've decided not to jump!"

"What?" Eddie stood with legs apart and hands on hips. "What is this? We've already decided that we're jumping."

Pat stood next to Nancy. "They don't have to jump on our account, Eddie. We told them...,"

Eddie interrupted her. "We're not doing this on your account, Pat. We're doing it on our account. Now, come on, you guys. Let's do it!"

"It's okay, Eddie," Mickey said. "It's no big deal. We can jump another time."

"What's with you guys?" Eddie asked sarcastically. "I leave for five minutes and when I come back, you don't want to jump anymore. What happened, you turn chicken?"

"Aw, Eddie," Mickey began, "it ain't that. We just...,"

"You guys are chicken!" Eddie stood there with a bored look on his face. He waited a moment and when no one else spoke, said, "okay, if you're not chicken, then let's go. Now, who's first?"

"I want to see them jump!" Sally hopped up and down and clapped her hands. "Come on, you guys!"

Mickey stood up. "All right, I'll jump. You go first, Eddie, then me, then Richie. Okay with you?"

"Yeah," Eddie said with a smile. "Now you're talking."

"Don't jump, Mickey," Pat said. "It's too high and you'll hurt yourself."

Mickey put his hands on her shoulders. "Don't worry, we won't get hurt. I gotta do it, now. Nobody calls me chicken!"

"Ready, Richie?" Eddie patted him on the shoulder. "You don't have to jump if you don't want to."

Richie looked at Nancy and shrugged his shoulders. "Yeah, I'm ready." I must be crazy, he thought.

As they started walking towards Mighty Mo, a younger boy of twelve, whom Mickey knew, stopped by to say hello. His name was Anthony. Mickey told him they were on their way to jump from the top of the tree.

Upon hearing this, Anthony started to jump up and down. "Wow, Mickey, the forty-footer?" he asked excitedly. "I gotta go and tell the rest of the guys!" He ran off in the same direction he had come from.

Just what I need, an audience, Richie thought. As they continued walking down the path which snaked through the woods and eventually led to the tree, his legs started to shake and he felt a tightness in his chest.

I can't do this, he thought. He felt a nervous spasm in his stomach and he took several deep breaths in an attempt to calm himself. It seemed to help for a little while.

Finally, after what seemed an eternity, they reached the base of the tree. Anthony and several of his friends were already there, waiting. Richie looked up.

It was the tallest tree he had ever seen. It had to be at least a hundred feet high and its trunk was as thick around as the columns of some of the buildings he had seen in the city.

Someone had nailed blocks of wood to the tree trunk to function as the steps of a ladder. These would serve to carry them up the tree to the top of the clouds. Or to oblivion.

Richie remembered the story of Jack and the Beanstalk. In that story, the prize was a goose that laid golden eggs. The prize here, if he lived through it, would be a date with Nancy. He guessed she was worth it.

Nancy stood next to him and watched him closely. "Are you sure you want to do this?" she asked.

"I'm sure," he said weakly. He couldn't back out now. He looked up again at the tree. It didn't seem as high to him now, and he relaxed a bit.

Eddie stepped up in front of him and gave him a friendly pat on the back. "I'll go first and Mickey, you follow me," he said with authority. "Richie, you take up the rear. Make sure you wait until I get to the first platform before you start climbing, okay?" Yeah, and the girls can pick up the pieces after I fall, Richie thought. "Okay, Eddie," he said.

Mickey nodded and Eddie placed his foot on the first wooden rung in the tree. As he started to climb, Mickey moved closer to the tree and waited as instructed. Eddie reached the platform and pulled himself up, then looked over the edge and called down to them. "All right, Mickey, start climbing."

Mickey turned to Richie. "Wait until I get up on the platform before you start climbing. You ready?"

Richie nodded. "I'm right behind you." He watched as Mickey began his climb.

Sally giggled nervously and covered her eyes. "Oh, I can't watch this. They're gonna get flattened."

Pat turned to her and put her finger to her lips. "Shh. You're the one who wanted to see them do it," she admonished.

"I know," Sally said. "But now I'm scared."

"Well, just relax and don't say anything," Pat chided.

Nancy moved closer to Richie and touched his arm. "Remember, you don't have to do this. I'll still go out with you."

"I know. I want to do it, though," he said bravely. "It looks like fun." He looked up and saw that Mickey had reached the platform. "Well, here goes. Wish me luck."

Nancy reached up and caressed his cheek. "Here." She kissed him gently on the lips. "For luck." As her lips touched his, Richie felt a sudden flow of energy course through him. It gave him a burst of confidence and, before he knew what he was doing, found himself climbing the tree. Seconds later, he had reached the platform where Mickey was waiting.

Mickey extended his hand and helped him onto the platform and Richie sat there for a moment, catching his breath. Eddie had continued climbing and was now almost to the second platform, thirty feet up.

Richie peered over the side and looked down at the water. This isn't so high, he thought. I can easily jump from here. As his confidence started to build, his nervousness began to fade.

"Okay, Richie, phase two," Mickey said. "You ready?"

"Yeah, let's do it," Richie answered.

They were squatting on the platform and Mickey leaned toward him. "Now, listen, Rich. The next step is a little harder, but not too hard. There's three wooden steps in the tree. You climb those. When you get to the last one, there's a branch on your left. Grab hold of it real tight, then reach up and over the platform with you right hand. There's a space in the wood, near the middle. Use that for a handhold. Just reach over and grab it, okay?

Richie nodded.

"Now, listen carefully. This is very important. Whatever you do, don't let go of the branch before you have a grip on the platform or you'll fall, understand?"

Richie nodded again.

"Okay. I'll be waiting for you up there. Once you have a grip on the platform, pull yourself up onto it. I'll help you. You follow everything I said?"

"Yeah, I understand," Richie said.

"Good." Mickey wiped his brow with the back of his hand. "Now, I won't be able to help you at the top, 'cause there's only room for one person, so I'll have already jumped by the time you get there. But you do exactly the same moves as this next one, okay? Three steps, grab the branch, then pull yourself up onto the platform. Easy, right?"

"Sure," Richie said.

"All right, here we go. Watch what I do. Start with your right foot, okay?" Mickey had his foot on the next rung and began to climb.

"Okay," Richie said.

Richie watched Mickey climb higher. Starting with his right foot, he navigated the three wooden steps. When he reached the last one, he grabbed a thick branch off to his left. Holding it tightly, he hoisted himself up until he could rest both feet on the top step.

Next, he reached up and found the handhold in the platform. Once he had a good grip, he was able to pull himself up and onto the platform. A second later, he was looking down at Richie from over the edge. "Now, you try it, Rich. Be careful."

Richie duplicated Mickey's movements, step by step. He took his time and moved slowly. It went smoothly. When he reached the point where he had a handhold on the platform, Mickey grabbed his arm and helped him up.

Once he was on the platform, Richie crawled slowly to the far edge and peered down at the water. He almost fell over when he saw how high up he was. It was much higher than he'd expected. He slowly crawled backwards to the center of the platform.

"I don't think I can jump from here, Mickey," he said, his voice almost cracking from fear. "It's too high." Then, realizing they weren't even at the highest point, he looked up and saw Eddie watching them from the top platform, another ten feet higher.

"How're you guys doing?" Eddie called down to them.

"We're okay, Eddie," Mickey answered. "We'll wait here until after you jump."

"Okay," Eddie replied.

Richie was starting to panic. "Mickey, I can't make it, it's too high." His legs started to shake again and he felt the familiar tightening in his chest.

"You'll be fine," Mickey offered.

"No. This is insane." Richie's palms were beginning to sweat. "You guys are used to this, I'm not..., ah, I just can't." He took a deep breath and continued. "I'm not used to jumping from trees, I..., I'm a city boy..., please, I can't do it." He felt himself losing control. He took another gulp of air, in a major effort to calm himself.

"Richie, calm down!" Mickey had him by the shoulders and was gently shaking him. "Take a deep breath. That's it. Now, listen to me. It ain't as high as it looks. It...,"

"You can call me a chicken, I don't care," Richie said between breaths.

"It only looks high," Mickey repeated. He spoke rapidly while continuing to hold on to Richie's shoulders. "Let me tell you something. Are you listening? You're doing exactly what everyone else who's ever jumped from this tree has done."

"What do you mean?" Richie felt numb.

"It's normal," Mickey continued. "Trust me. I was scared silly the first time I ever climbed up here, but I overcame it. Now listen, you won't get hurt, I promise you. It just seems higher than it really is. I'm telling you, Richie, it ain't that bad."

"I don't know, Mickey, I don't think I can," Richie said meekly. "I feel like I'm going to faint." He put his hand up to his forehead. It felt cold and clammy.

"Eddie!" Mickey called up to Eddie who was still watching them from the higher platform and trying to suppress a grin. "Eddie, tell him how scared we were the first time we jumped."

"Well, I don't know about you, but I was petrified," Eddie said. "It's normal, believe me." He wiped a bit of sweat away from his eyes. "Look, if you really don't want to jump, you can climb back down. We won't hold it against you. I'm ready to go, though. It's hot up here. What do you say? You guys coming or what?"

He moved away from the edge of the platform, but reappeared a second later. "The girls will probably think you're a wimp, though," he said, laughing. He stood up and, with a loud yell, jumped from the platform.

He went by them in a blur on his way down. They both leaned over the edge in time to see him hit the water cleanly, barely creating a splash. He popped up to the surface a moment later and swam to the edge of the pond. Standing at the water's edge, he yelled up to them, "come on in, the water's fine!"

Mickey turned to Richie. "See, Rich, there's nothing to it. You can do it too, I know you can. Just follow me and don't even think about it." He moved over to the wooden steps leading to the highest platform, then turned back to Richie. "Decide right here and now that you're going to do it, then climb up to the top and jump. Don't stop and don't look down. As soon as you get up there, do it!"

Richie took another deep breath. "You really think I can do it?" he asked.

"Sure," Mickey replied. "It's like jumping off the high board at a swimming pool. It's just a little higher, that's all."

The way Mickey was talking was reassuring. His voice had a hypnotic quality and, for the first time since he had reached the second platform, he felt as if he could do it.

"Don't worry about it," Mickey continued. "You can do it, I know you can. C'mon, you ready?" he asked. He offered his hand to Richie.

Richie took one more breath before he answered. "Yeah, okay. I'm ready." He shook Mickey's hand. "Let's do it!"

"Attaboy, Richie," Mickey said with enthusiasm. "I'll go first. As soon as you see me jump, count to ten and then climb up and jump. Don't stop and don't think about it. Just count to ten and go. Okay?"

"Just count to ten and go," Richie repeated.

"That's it," Mickey said. "All right, here I go. I'll meet you down there." He gave Richie a final pat on the arm and started climbing up to the top. A moment later, Richie saw him go flying past as he hurtled down to the water below.

Richie started counting. "One, two, three, four, five..., oh, please, God, don't make me do this..., six, seven, eight, nine, ten!" He stood up and without hesitating, climbed the rest of the way to the top.

Once there, he peered over the edge and looked down. The distance to the water was overwhelming and he almost turned around to go back. Instead, he rose shakily to his feet as his mind went blank. He leaned forward slightly and felt himself step off the platform.

For a second or two, it felt like he was suspended in mid-air, and then like his stomach was in his throat as he rapidly gained speed and fell to the water below. As he fell, his initial fear and queasiness left him and he let out a loud yell, just before he hit the water.

His momentum carried him under a good eight feet before he was able to pump his legs and rise to the surface. After breaking through to the top and taking in a large breath of air, a feeling of elation overtook him. He was laughing like a lunatic as he swam to the edge of the pond, where Mickey and Eddie were waiting for him.

As he left the water, Eddie pounded him on the back. "Hey, you're all right, Richie, you know that?" Mickey took his hand and pumped it vigorously. Richie looked at both of them and, grinning from ear to ear, said, "I did it! I did it!"

"You sure did," Mickey said. "We're proud of you!"

Seven

The girls were waiting for them when they returned to the blanket. As soon as they got there, Nancy reached over and took Richie's hand.

"Oh, thank goodness you're all right," she said breathlessly. "I don't know how you ever did it."

"It was easy," Richie said triumphantly. "Nothing to it."

"Richie's a real daredevil," Mickey said proudly, as the three boys dried themselves off and changed back into their clothes.

"And a real sport," Eddie added.

"Want to go for a walk?" Nancy asked as soon as Richie had his clothes on.

"Sure," Richie replied. "See you guys later," he said to the others. Mickey and Eddie both gave him a big smile.

They left the blanket and started walking along the path that led into the woods. Holding hands as they walked, they talked quietly and looked at each other often, beginning to feel comfortable with one another.

Richie was still excited by his daring leap from Mighty Mo, and now, finding himself alone in the woods with Nancy, who seemed to really like him too, he couldn't believe his luck.

Meeting her was, at this moment, the very best thing that had ever happened to him and he was especially thankful that his parents had decided to come here this year, instead of to the New Jersey shore as they had originally planned.

Even though he had enjoyed himself there in past years, nothing could compare to this place. Here it was, only his second day and things were going as smoothly as could be. He already had new friends and, best of all, he had met Nancy. Nothing could be better. It was a glorious day!

As they walked farther along the trail, the scent of lilacs permeated the air. They stopped for a moment and listened to the cicadas singing their songs from the tops of the trees, while a chorus of birds joined them in symphony.

They continued walking and came upon a fresh-water brook, which babbled and meandered on its way alongside the trail, adding a low murmur to the rustic peacefulness. Several frogs and crickets suddenly joined in, adding their own voices to create a cacophony of sound.

They found a fallen log in a small clearing and used it to rest for a moment. Richie turned to her and looked into her eyes. "I'm glad I met you, Nancy," he said seriously. "So am I, Richie," she replied, meeting his gaze.

He leaned closer to her and they kissed, tenderly at first, and then with more of an urgency. She traced a light pattern on his cheek with her fingers and sighed softly. They held each other tightly and kissed for a long time. "You're sweet, Richie," she said in a voice tinged with emotion after breaking off the kiss.

"So are you, Nancy," he replied, tenderly.

They kissed again several times. He was delirious with desire for her. Her essence overwhelmed him and delighted him with its intensity. He finally broke off the kiss and stood up. "I guess we'd better go back."

"I guess so," she agreed, getting to her feet.

They started walking back the way they came, each of them enchanted by the closeness of the other. Holding hands as before, they were each silent. No words were necessary.

They joined the others back at the blanket a few minutes later. When Eddie saw them he started laughing. "Hey, look at the lovebirds," he said. "We thought you two were lost in the woods. We were almost ready to send out a search party."

Nancy smiled shyly. "Oh, were we gone long?" she asked innocently.

"Not really, I was only kidding," Eddie said.

"We were checking out the woods," Richie offered. "It's really nice in there."

"Yeah, I'll bet it is," Eddie teased. "Did you see any woodpeckers?"

"Woodpeckers?" Nancy asked.

"Yeah, you know, they...,"

"Oh, Eddie, stop teasing them," Sally said. She poked him in the ribs. "Let's figure out where and what time we should meet tomorrow, 'cause it's getting late and I have to be home by five."

"Whoops." Eddie reacted to the poke in the ribs. "Okay, my love," he said. "Gather 'round and let's figure this thing out."

As they all sat back down on the blanket, Eddie went over the plans for the next day's boat ride. "The boat will be ready by ten o'clock, so let's all meet on the fishing dock at Mill Creek, say..., eleven. Is that all right with everyone?" he inquired.

After agreeing, they all gathered up their things and started walking back to Eddie's car. They piled in, with Eddie and Sally in front and the other four in the back. Pat had to sit on Mickey's lap in order to make room for all of them.

They dropped the girls off in front of Treadway's Market and continued on to the Sugar Shack. The three of them decided to go inside for a soda and sat at one of the tables in the back.

"Boy, what a day!" Mickey said as he lit a cigarette. "The girls are something, ain't they?" Richie and Eddie both nodded. "We got dates with the prettiest girls in Sea Shell Harbor, you realize that?" Mickey continued, excitedly.

"Here it is, the beginning of summer and we got it knocked." He poked Richie in the ribs. "What'd I tell you, Rich? Didn't I tell you you'd meet a girl, huh, didn't I?"

"You sure did, Mickey." Richie raised his glass to Mickey's and tapped it gently, then did the same to Eddie's. It made a clinking sound. "Here's to both of you, my new friends."

"Hear, hear!" Eddie joined in. "And here's a toast to you, too," he continued. "For jumping off Mighty Mo with barely a whimper."

"Hey, I forgot about that." Mickey raised his glass again. "Here's to you, Rich. For a minute back there when we were up in the tree, I didn't think you were gonna make it."

"I didn't think I was either," Richie said, laughing. "I was so scared, I thought I was going to faint."

"I almost did, my first time," Eddie offered. "Luckily, I was with Bruno Napolitano at the time. He told me if I didn't jump he was going to pull me apart and use me for crab bait." He chuckled. "I was more afraid of him than I was of falling forty feet, so I jumped. I'll never forget that day."

"Yeah, I'll never forget my first time, either," Mickey said. "I was too stupid to be scared. All I remember is that my friends kept calling me chicken and I was so mad that I just climbed up and jumped." He took a sip from his soda. "It's a funny thing, though," he continued, "you jump once and you're never really scared again, you know what I mean?"

"Yeah," Eddie agreed. "After the first time, it's almost like second nature."

"I guess you're right," Richie said. "I think I could do it again with no trouble at all."

"You'll have plenty of chances before summer's over," Mickey told him. Finishing his soda, he looked at the others. "What do you guys want to do now?"

"I think I'll drop you guys off and head home," Eddie said. "I'll meet you tomorrow morning at the dock."

"Aren't you coming back here tonight?" Mickey asked. "It's Saturday night."

"No, I'm taking Diane out to the movies tonight. I mean, is it all right with you, Mick?" Eddie asked sheepishly. "I told her I would last night. There's this picture playing at the drive-in she wants to see, and I...,"

"Hey, I got no problem with that," Mickey interrupted. "You two want to go and see a movie, why should I care? I just thought we'd all hang out together tonight, that's all."

Kissing cousins, Richie thought, remembering what Danny Shaw had said about them the night before.

Mickey looked at Richie. "Why don't you meet me here tonight, around eight o'clock, Richie? We'll find something to do."

"Sure," Richie replied. "Sounds good."

"Darn, we should have asked Pat and Nancy to meet us here tonight, too," Mickey said. "Why didn't I think to ask them?"

"I did already," Richie said. "While we were in the car. They're spending the night with their families."

"Oh." Mickey sounded disappointed. "Well, I'll just meet you here at eight, then."

"Okay."

"Eddie, let me catch a ride with you to Sag Harbor," Mickey said. "I'll hitch home from there."

"No problem," Eddie said. "Do you want me to drop you off, Richie?"

"Nah, that's okay. I think I'll try walking home along the beach. Thanks anyway."

"See you tomorrow, then. Do you know where the Mill Creek dock is?" Eddie asked.

"I'm not sure, exactly."

"It's right around the corner from your cabin, one block over from Chestnut. Just walk down your street towards the water and then turn left. Go one block, then make another left and you'll find it halfway up on your right. You can't miss it," Eddie assured him.

Richie repeated the directions, then said, "Okay, Eddie, thanks. I'll see you there at eleven and I'll see you back here tonight at eight, Mickey."

Eddie held out his hand. "Once again, that was a great jump, Rich. Welcome to the club."

"Thanks, Eddie," Richie said, shaking hands.

They walked outside and Richie watched them pile into the car. Eddie fired it up and pulled out of the parking lot and onto Beach Road. He gunned the engine and they took off, driving north towards Sag Harbor.

When he could no longer see them, Richie turned and headed

towards the beach. He remembered what Mickey had told him that by following the water's edge around the curve of the bay, he would eventually reach Chestnut street.

As he walked, he noticed numerous sea shells lying in the sand. He stopped for a moment and picked some of them up. Admiring them, he put a few of them into his pocket and threw a couple into the water.

Some of the shells looked like the ones in the brochure his father had brought home, back in March or April. He remembered reading it. It had described Sea Shell Harbor's many attributes, among them its abundance of exotic shells that collectors from all over the world prized and coveted.

According to the brochure, the village had been named Sea Shell Harbor because of its profusion of these colorful mollusks. The skeletal remains of scallops, cockle shells, arc shells and limpets were some of them, he recalled.

Children delighted in finding and gathering these treasures of the sea, and many a sea shell collection had been started right from these shores.

Adults, as well, collected these appealing crustaceans and they could be found for miles along its sandy beaches. They were pretty, he decided and put the rest of them in his pocket.

He decided to take off his sneakers. As he sat in the sand, he looked out at the water. The sun was reflecting off the surface and he had to put his hand over his eyes to block its glare. He squinted and looked out again.

There were pleasure boats anchored just off shore where the land curved around to meet its watery mate. A large boat, a yacht maybe, sat a little farther out on the water, rocking gently in the breeze. It truly is beautiful here, he thought. So peaceful and quiet.

A speedboat raced by a hundred yards out from where he sat, pulling a young woman on skis. The wind blew her hair straight out behind her where it met a cascading spray of water thrown up by the forward movement of the boat.

That looks like fun, he thought. He'd have to try that while he was here. Then he remembered he'd probably get the chance tomorrow, on Eddie's boat. He wondered if he'd be able to water ski. Heck, yes, he decided. He'd jumped off Mighty Mo, hadn't he? He could do anything, now.

He took off his other sneaker and got up, feeling the coolness of the sand on his bare feet. He walked for a while whistling a random tune, then broke into a trot and ran along the beach until he came to his street. As he turned onto Chestnut, he slowed down and walked the rest of the way home.

"Have fun today, dear?" Mrs. Donnelly asked at dinner.

"We had a great time, mom," Richie answered, attacking his corn-on-the-cob. "I went swimming with Mickey and his friend, Eddie, at a place called Trout Pond. Met some of the other kids, too. Eddie's the one whose parents own this cabin."

"Oh, he's the boy Mickey told us about yesterday, isn't he?" Mrs. Donnelly inquired.

"Yeah, the rich kid," Richie said, laughing. "He's okay, though. Not a snob like I thought he'd be."

"Well, that's nice," his mother said.

Mr. Donnelly looked up from his plate. "It sounds like you're off to a good start, Richard," he said.

"Yes, sir, I certainly am," Richie answered respectfully. Then, "Say, pop, how did you and mom ever find this place? It's much better than the Jersey shore."

"Friend of mine at the office told me about it," his father said. "It sounded interesting, so your mother and I took a ride out here one day in March to look it over."

"Remember that character we ran into in the real estate office?" Mrs. Donnelly asked.

"You mean that old goat who gave us a history lesson about the area? Sure, I remember," Mr. Donnelly replied.

"Yes, he's the one. You should have seen him, Richard." His mother looked amused. "Your father happened to ask the old gentlemen how long he'd lived here and he went into this long recitation about how his forefathers had come to settle in this area, remember, dear?"

Mr. Donnelly picked up his fork and made a stab in the air. "A safe haven in a stormy sea," he said, imitating the old gentleman's voice. "T'was God, himself, who led these kindred souls here in search of a place free from religious persecution, as was their lot before they came."

Mr. and Mrs. Donnelly both laughed as they remembered the incident.

"Well, they couldn't have found a nicer place," I told him. "And, do you know what he said to me?" Mr. Donnelly looked at his son, expectantly. Richie shook his head.

"He said, 'Aye, and we hope to keep it that way, the Lord be willing,' Can you imagine that, Richard? That pontificating, old...,"

"Dear!" Mrs. Donnelly interrupted.

"Codger," Mr. Donnelly said, finishing his description of the old gentleman. "You know the type, I'm sure. You can never win with those people. They always have to have the last word, regardless of the topic being discussed."

"I don't know, dear, most of the locals seem friendly enough," Mrs. Donnelly said.

"Oh, they're friendly enough. I just don't think they like us city folks." He turned his attention back to his dinner.

"The people I've met were all friendly to me," Richie said.

Mr. Donnelly stopped eating for a moment. He removed his glasses and rubbed his eyes before he spoke. "You're probably right about that, Richard," he said. "Don't mind me. That old fellow back in March just gave me a bad impression, that's all. I'm sure that doesn't mean everyone out here is like him." He replaced his glasses and resumed eating his dinner.

Richie thought about what his father had just said. It must be the older people out here he's talking about, he guessed. The kids my age are certainly nice enough. He put that thought out of his mind and continued eating. The image of Nancy came to him and he smiled as he cleared his plate of food.

Later that evening, he waited at the Sugar Shack until nine-thirty, but Mickey never showed. I wonder what happened to him? he thought, as he walked along Beach Road on his way home. "Probably couldn't get a ride," he said aloud. He guessed he would have to wait until the next day before he found out the answer.

That night, he dreamed of performing swan dives and back-flips from the top of Mighty Mo, while Nancy sat at the edge of the pond, clapping and cheering him on. In his dream, Eddie, Pat and Sally were also there, but no one knew where Mickey was.

They kept asking each other, "Where's Mickey? Where's Mickey?"

None of them could find him.

Eight

Everyone except Mickey showed up at the Mill Creek dock at eleven the next morning. He was late. He arrived fifteen minutes later, looking like he had slept in his clothes.

"It's about time, Mick." Eddie untied the mooring lines and threw them into the boat. "We thought you weren't going to make it."

"Sorry I'm late, you guys. Couldn't get a ride." Mickey looked at Richie and started to speak, then caught himself and said nothing.

"Climb aboard, everybody," Eddie said pleasantly.

The boat was an eighteen-foot Sun Cruiser made of fiberglass, white with red trim. It had an eighty-horsepower Mercury outboard motor mounted at the rear, and next to that was a swimming platform, equipped with a ladder for easy access to the water.

"Nice boat, Eddie," Richie said admirably.

"You like it?" Eddie gave him a big grin and showed him and Nancy around the boat. The others had all been in it the previous summer. "It's got a lot of extra gadgets for a boat this size," he boasted. "Power trim, depth finder, electric start. I even have a VHF navigational radio on board. We'll never get lost in this thing."

"How long have you had the boat?" Nancy asked.

"A couple of years, now. My dad bought it for me on my sixteenth birthday," Eddie said. "Mickey and I have been all over eastern Long

Island in this thing, huh, Mick?"

"Just about," Mickey replied.

Eddie instructed them to stow their things forward, under the bow. There were two bunks attached to the port and starboard bulkheads and under each one there was ample storage space.

Eddie moved over to the console on the starboard side. "All right, now listen up, everybody," he said. "This is how it works." He caught Mickey's eye and winked, then turned back to the others.

"Since I own the boat, I'm the captain and you have to do exactly as I say. Mickey is the first mate and the rest of you are the crew. That means, you follow all orders given by the captain or his first mate. Understood so far?"

"Yes, sir!" they answered in unison.

"Okay, Richie and the girls, find your seats and sit yourselves down." Eddie reached under his seat and pulled up a yachting cap which he placed on his head. It had gold braid on the visor, giving him the appearance of authority.

"First mate, Mickey, hand out the life preservers and make sure all lines are secure!" Eddie ordered.

"Aye, aye, Captain!" Mickey reached under the other seat on the port side and passed out life preservers to Richie and the girls, then climbed over the windshield and began to coil the bow line into a neat circle.

"Lines secured, Captain!" he called back to Eddie.

"Standby to launch!" Eddie primed the fuel line with the throttle and sat down behind the wheel. "First mate to act as lookout!"

"Aye, aye, sir!"

"Ready to start engine!" Eddie bellowed. He turned the ignition key to the right, engaging the starter, and the engine caught instantly. "Prepare to cast off!" he yelled to Mickey, then moved his hand over to the shift lever next to the throttle and moved it to the forward position.

"Aye, aye, sir!" Mickey used his feet to push the boat away from one of the wooden pilings on the dock as Eddie slowly eased the boat out into the channel. He stood lookout on the bow as Eddie advanced the throttle and the boat began to pick up speed. Eddie obeyed the five miles per hour speed limit until they cleared the Mill Creek inlet before he added more throttle. As soon as the boat cleared the last buoy, he added full throttle and turned to the others. "Hold on!" he yelled. The girls squealed with delight as the boat suddenly lurched forward. Its movement caused the bow to first rise up in the air, then slap back down against the water's surface in a steady tattoo.

Standing behind Pat and Sally, who were sitting in the port side seat, the wind and spray hit Richie and Nancy in the face and blew their hair straight back behind them. He looked at her and smiled. She was covering her face with her hands, so he put his arm around her and drew her closer. She snuggled up to him and buried her face in his shirt to escape the spray.

The boat's momentum had forced them backward so suddenly that they almost lost their balance. Richie had to grab on to the back of the seat to keep from falling, all the while holding on to Nancy with his other hand.

He looked forward and noticed Mickey sitting nonchalantly on the bow, legs crossed and holding on to a metal cleat attached to the hull. Mickey was faced into the wind and looked like he was enjoying himself.

Richie was having a great time and he guessed that Nancy was, too. He held on to her tightly, both laughing every time they were hit with a barrage of salt water and spray. He realized that not only was Nancy beautiful, she was fun to be with.

He was impressed with the boat's power. It moved along at a good clip and he had to raise his voice to make himself heard above the wind and the roar of the engine. "This is great!" he shouted to no one in particular.

When they reached the very end of the Jessup Neck peninsula which was off to their left, Eddie eased back on the throttle and the boat settled down into the water. They were moving along now at about twenty knots, the craft's normal cruising speed.

"We should be there in about ten minutes!" Eddie yelled. He made a ninety degree turn to the left and they were now traveling in a southwesterly direction. Robbins Island lay directly off the starboard bow.

Eddie glanced over at Richie. "Want to take the wheel for a while, Richie?" he yelled.

"Sure!" Richie let go of Nancy. "Hold onto the back of the seat," he told her. "This could get rough." He made his way over to the starboard side and stood next to Eddie. "What do I have to do?" he asked.

"Just sit here and hold her steady." Eddie moved out of his way so Richie could sit down. "Aim the bow at the center of the island," Eddie instructed him. "Keep one eye on the compass and try to maintain two-six-zero degrees."

"Okay..., I mean, aye, aye, sir!" Richie said, remembering that Eddie was the captain. He took hold of the wheel and the boat immediately started to veer left. He turned the wheel to the right and corrected his heading. Eddie climbed over the back of the seat and moved aft, then bent down to check on the steering cables and some other equipment.

"Don't sink us, Richie!" Pat called to him. "I promised Mickey a date, remember?"

Mickey, who hadn't said much so far, looked back at her and smiled. "That's right!" he yelled. "I haven't forgotten, either!"

The day was sunny and bright, except for a few scattered clouds in the distance and the engine seemed to purr smoothly as it moved the boat along the water at a steady rate of speed.

"Let's get rid of these clothes!" Sally called to the others. She started to remove her shorts and tank top, revealing a two piece bathing suit underneath. Pat and Nancy followed her lead.

Richie glanced over at them and was pleased when he caught a glimpse of Nancy's figure in her bathing suit. She's a real beauty, he thought. The boat started to drift to the left, again.

"Hold her steady, Rich!" Eddie yelled from the rear. "What's your heading?"

Richie squinted and checked the compass. It kept spinning back and forth until he was able to steady the boat enough to get a reading. "Two-fifty-five, Eddie!"

"Two-five-five!" Eddie corrected. "That's good enough. Now,

ease the throttle back about a third!" he commanded.

"Okay!" Richie moved the red lever back as instructed and the boat slowed down to about twelve knots."

"Now, turn left ten degrees!" Eddie finished his inspection of the cables and moved forward, next to Richie. "Try to aim for the southern point of the island, Rich. See it?"

Richie adjusted the wheel until he had it aimed the way he thought Eddie wanted. "How's this?" he asked.

"Perfect," Eddie replied. "Now, just keep it right there." He moved over to the port side and opened a long box which contained a pair of water skis and a tow line. After removing these and laying them on the floor of the boat, he returned to Richie's side.

"All right, I'll take it now, Richie. You did good." Eddie took the wheel and Richie moved out of his way by climbing over the rear of the seat. Eddie moved the throttle forward and the boat picked up speed. After a few minutes he throttled back again, slowing the boat down.

"We'll head around the south end of the island and beach her on the other side," Eddie said. "The water's pretty shallow over there, about eight feet. Perfect for skiing."

As he inched the boat around the island at a crawl, Eddie kept his eyes on the shoreline. "I'm looking for a good spot to land her," he said. Then, "I'm thirsty, anybody want a soda?"

"I do," Sally answered. "Me, too," Nancy said.

"Me, three," Pat said.

"I'll have one," Richie said.

"Sally, reach in the cooler behind your seat. They're in there. Get me one, too, will ya?"

"Mickey, do you want a soda?" Pat called to Mickey, who was still up on the bow.

"No, thanks, I'll wait until later," he replied.

Richie was aware that Mickey was acting very quietly as he sat on the bow. He just sat there and hardly talked at all. He wondered if the others had noticed it, too. "How're you doing, Mickey?" he yelled to him.

Mickey turned around and smiled. "I'm okay. I'm just a little tired, that's all. Didn't get much sleep last night."

Sally retrieved the drinks and passed them out to the others. She picked out a bottle of orange soda for herself and moved to the seat next to Eddie. "Oh, what a beautiful day," she said to him. "I just love being on your boat."

Eddie turned to look at her and clinked his bottle to hers in a toast. "A beautiful day for a beautiful girl," he said.

"I don't think I've ever been on a boat as nice as this one," she said, between sips of her drink. "Why, come to think of it, the only boat I was ever on was a rowboat. I was much younger, then. That was when we were up at the lake one year, and we...,"

"And the boat enjoys having you on it," Eddie cut in.

"Oh, I guess I'm talking too much, aren't I," she said good naturedly.

"Not at all," Eddie was quick to say. "Let's hear it for nice boats and nice girls like you."

"Why, thank you, kind sir," Sally said, looking pleased with his compliment. "And it really is a nice boat."

Nancy turned to Richie. "Have you ever been water skiing before, Richie?"

"No, I haven't." He turned to her. "I'll bet it's lots of fun, though," he said.

"I tried it last summer but I kept falling down." She adjusted the strap to her bathing suit. "I sure hope I do better this year."

"You will," he reassured her.

They had cruised around the end of the island and Eddie steered the boat to a small cove on the other side. It had a sandy little beach nestled between reeds of tall grass and some large rocks and he headed directly for it. As soon as he felt the bow make contact with the sandy bottom, he killed the engine.

Mickey jumped off the bow and waded ashore with one of the lines in his hand and secured it to a large rock lying in the sand. Richie stripped down to his bathing suit and joined the girls as they climbed out and helped push the boat onto shore until it was safely beached.

"We'll take a break here for a few minutes, then we'll get started.

Who wants to go first?" Eddie asked. Nobody answered.

"Come on, don't be shy, it's easy." Eddie looked at each of the others but no one volunteered. "Tell you what," he continued, "Mickey will go first to show you how it's done and then we can decide who goes next. That okay with you, Mick?"

"No sweat," Mickey answered.

They left the boat and settled down on the beach, relaxing and talking until they had all finished their drinks. After a few minutes, Mickey stood up and removed his shorts and tee shirt. "I'm ready," he said as he tossed his clothes into the boat.

"Let's do it!" Eddie got up and untied the line from the rock, throwing the end to Mickey, who coiled it up and secured it to the cleat on the bow. Mickey then helped Richie and Eddie push the boat back into the water, turning it around until it was facing the other way.

After helping the girls climb up the boat's rear ladder, Eddie and Richie joined them on board. Mickey remained on shore. Eddie threw the skis to Mickey and he sat down on the sand and put them on one at a time.

Next, Eddie threw him the end of the tow rope. Mickey grabbed it and waded into the water with the skis on his feet. "I'm ready whenever you are, Eddie."

Eddie started the engine, and as the boat began to drift away, Mickey crouched down in the waist-high water and pulled the tow rope toward him to keep it clear of the propeller.

"Richie, will you go back and stand on the platform to act as lookout?" Eddie asked, as he eased the throttle forward slightly. "Let me know right away if Mickey falls."

"Okay." Richie moved aft and took up a position on the platform. He smiled down at Mickey and Mickey smiled back at him.

"Ready, Mickey?" Eddie called out.

"Yeah!" Mickey yelled. "Let 'er rip!"

Eddie asked for the other's attention. "Now, for those of you who have never skied before, here's what you have to do," he began.

"You lean back in the water and raise the tips of the skis until they're sticking up about a foot. "As soon as the boat starts to pull you up, lean back a little farther. If you do it correctly, you should get up with no trouble."

"What happens if you fall at that point?" Sally asked.

Eddie looked at her and smiled, a twinkle in his eye. "If you fall at that point, we'll just start again," he said easily. "Now, once you're up, the boat will pick up speed. You'll have to keep leaning back, but not too far. If you lean back too far, you'll lose your balance. Basically, that's all there is to it." He looked at the others to see if they understood. "What happens if you get up, but then you fall after a little while?" Sally asked.

"Then we leave you there until you stop asking so many questions," Pat said. The others laughed.

"If you fall, just let go of the tow line," Eddie said. "The skis are designed to come off if you fall. All you have to do is tread water until we can turn around and pick you up. You'll be wearing your life preserver, so you won't sink."

He turned around in his seat and shouted back to Mickey. "Okay, Mickey, get ready, 'cause here we go!"

Nine

Mickey took a firm grip on the tow handle, leaned back into the water and raised the skis up slightly. The boat moved ahead slowly and the rope started to uncoil on the water's surface.

"Richie, let me know when the rope is almost played out!" Eddie yelled.

Richie gave him a thumbs up and kept his eyes on the rope. As soon as it was almost completely taut, he signaled to Eddie. "Now!" he yelled.

Eddie opened the throttle and the boat moved forward, pulling Mickey along with it. Richie watched him closely so he could see how he did it. Mickey leaned all the way back until he was up on the skis, then he straightened up slightly.

Richie noticed that there was a point in the maneuver where it looked like Mickey was about to pitch forward, but Mickey just gritted his teeth and leaned back as far as he could to counteract the forward pull of the boat.

"He's up!" Richie shouted to Eddie. So, that's how you do it, he thought. If you don't lean back far enough, you'll fall. If you lean back too far, you'll fall. Richie made mental notes to himself as the girls gathered around him on the platform to watch Mickey ski.

The boat moved through the water at a good rate of speed and Mickey skimmed along on the water's surface. He zig-zagged across the boat's wake several times, jumping over the trough of waves it made in the water.

"Oh, that looks like so much fun," Pat said. "I can't wait to try it."

"I hope I can do it," Nancy said. "Mickey makes it look so easy."

"I don't know if I'm ready for this or not," Sally said. It looks hard to me."

"Maybe we'd better let Richie try it before we go," Pat said mischievously. "If he gets hurt, then we'll know enough not to try it ourselves."

"Oh, thanks, Pat," Richie said good naturedly. "Make me the guinea pig, huh?"

"Do you think you can do it, Richie?" Nancy asked, concern in her voice.

"I think I can," he answered. "I'd like to give it a try, at least." Out of the corner of his eye he saw Mickey lose his balance when he tried to jump a wave. Mickey pitched forward into the water, letting go of the tow rope as he fell.

"Eddie!" Richie called out, "Mickey fell!"

Eddie immediately throttled back and put the boat into a wide turn to the left. He stood up and looked over his shoulder, eyes focused on the tow rope. "Always turn left so the line won't get caught in the prop," he said.

Richie and the girls could see Mickey bobbing up and down in the water a short distance behind them. He was laughing when they reached him and they helped him back into the boat. The skis floated nearby and Eddie steered the boat over to them.

"Grab 'em, you guys!" he shouted, over the noise of the motor.

Richie managed to snag one of the skis and Sally reached for the other one, but missed it by a few inches. She leaned over farther to make a grab for it and fell overboard into the water. She popped back up to the surface after a few seconds.

"Who pushed me over the side?" she asked between wild fits of laughter. She brushed her hair away from her eyes and dog-paddled over to the ladder.

"Eddie, you should have jumped over the side and saved me!" she cried, as she climbed up the ladder. The others could tell she was only being playful.

"I was going to, love, but I had to maneuver the boat away from you," Eddie said with mock seriousness. "Actually, that's a job for one of the crew members. Pat, why didn't you jump overboard and save her?"

Pat chuckled and pointed to Sally's chest. "Sally doesn't need any help from me," she said affably. "Not with those Mae West's she's sporting."

Sally looked down at her own chest and nodded in agreement. "She's right about that," she said good naturedly. "I'll never sink the way I'm put together."

"Amen," Eddie said.

Now it was Richie's turn. He put on a life jacket and jumped from the ladder. As he treaded water, Mickey handed him the skis one at a time and he managed to put them on his feet.

"Remember to keep your skis close together as the boat pulls you up, Rich," Mickey instructed him. "Stay loose. You ready?"

Richie nodded. "Ready!" I think, he thought.

"Okay, Eddie!" Mickey shouted. "Our first victim..., I mean, Richie, is ready!"

"Be careful, Richie!" Nancy called to him. She stood next to Mickey on the platform, appearing a bit apprehensive. Richie smiled up at her. "I will, don't worry." He blew her a kiss and moved his legs up and down in the water, trying to get a feel for the skis.

Pat and Sally sat on the starboard side across from Mickey and Nancy, facing towards the rear of the boat.

"This ought to be very interesting," Pat said impassively.

"You don't think he'll get hurt, do you?" Sally asked.

"No, I don't think so," Pat answered. "If he didn't break his neck jumping out of that tree yesterday, I don't think he'll have any problem with this."

Eddie reached for the throttle and moved it forward slowly. As the tow line stretched all the way out, Mickey signaled him and Eddie added full power. The boat instantly picked up speed and

Richie was pulled up on top of the water.

He wobbled slightly and began to lean back, almost making the transition to skiing, but a splash of water hit him in the face and he lost his balance. He pitched forward into the water head first and the skis flew off his feet .

As he skimmed along the water's surface on his belly, he remembered to let go of the rope. As soon as he did, his forward momentum stopped and he settled down into the water easily.

He saw where the skis were floating and paddled over to them, as Eddie turned the boat around in a slow, lazy arc. The boat pulled up next to him just as he reached the skis.

"You okay, Richie?" Eddie called down to him from the driver's seat.

"Yeah, just a little water in my eyes, that's all."

"Put the skis back on and grab the line when it comes back past you," Eddie said. "We'll give it another try. It's actually easier here in the deeper water."

"Okay." Richie put the skis back on and stabilized himself in the water. "I think I've got the hang of it now, Eddie. I'll do it this time."

Eddie smiled and waved, then slowly moved the throttle forward. "Good luck!"

Once again, Richie grabbed the tow line and treaded water, waiting for the slack to be taken up. He heard the engine whine as Eddie added full power and he prepared himself for the pull of the line. Remember to lean back, he reminded himself.

As the boat lurched forward, Richie leaned back to counteract the forward pull of the boat and was up on the skis a moment later. Sensing that he was about to lose his balance and fall forward, he leaned back as far as he could, and the next instant was skimming along on top of the water's surface.

He held the tow line tightly and stayed directly behind the boat, trying to get the feel of being on the skis. It was exhilarating! Feeling slightly more confident, he crossed from side to side behind the boat, just as he had seen Mickey do, and jumped over the waves in the boat's wake.

The wind was whipping into his face and making his eyes tear and the spray from the water was threatening to blind him again, so he squinted his eyes to protect them from the elements.

He looked up and saw Mickey and the girls waving wildly to him from the boat, and he let go of the tow handle with one hand and waved back. That almost caused him to lose his balance, so he quickly grabbed the handle again and held on with both hands.

Eddie put the boat into a shallow turn and Richie jumped over the waves in its wake. As they drew alongside Robbins Island, Eddie started pointing towards the shoreline.

Richie looked to his left and saw the beach where they had left their things. He nodded his head to show that he understood. He guessed that Eddie wanted him to let go of the rope and ski to the beach when they made another pass.

Eddie made another turn and steered the boat closer in to shore. The water here was about five feet deep, giving him ample room to maneuver. Just before they were parallel to the beach, Eddie added full power and made a ninety- degree turn to the left.

Richie cut across the boat's wake from left to right, picking up speed as he did in a whip effect. After jumping the waves on the right side of the wake, he let go of the rope and the momentum propelled him in towards shore. He almost made it all the way to the water's edge before he lost speed and settled into the water a few yards out.

"Outstanding!" he shouted to the empty beach. He sat down in the shallow water and removed the skis, then brought them ashore and laid them on the sand.

He turned around when he heard the boat's engine. The boat was only a few yards offshore and Mickey was standing on the bow with a line in his hand, just as he had earlier.

As the boat got closer, he jumped off the bow and waded in to join Richie on the beach. "You did great, Rich," he said in greeting. "You looked like a pro out there."

Richie beamed at the compliment. "That was fantastic, Mickey!" I never had so much fun in my life! Water skiing is the best!"

"Nothing like it," Mickey agreed. "It's almost as much fun as jumping off Mighty Mo, huh?"

"Better," Richie said. "It's not as scary."

Eddie killed the engine and he and the girls jumped into the water and pushed the boat up onto the beach. Nancy ran over to Richie and gave him a big hug. "You were wonderful," she said happily. "You made it look so easy."

Mickey tied the line to the same rock as before, then joined the others back at the blanket. "He only fell once," he said, patting Richie on the back. "Not too bad at all."

"Real good, Richie," Eddie said. "How did you like it?"

"I loved it," Richie answered. "I couldn't believe I got up so quickly." He picked up a towel from the blanket and used it to dry himself off.

Nancy moved next to him and took his hand in hers. "Richie's the one I want to take lessons from," she said sweetly. "He's a natural."

"Let's not get carried away, now," Richie said modestly. "I think I was just lucky."

"Let's take a break and have something to eat and then the girls can try it," Eddie said.

"Oh, goody, I'm starving," Sally said, patting her bare tummy.

"Me, too. Boating makes me hungry," Pat said. She took Mickey's arm and said, "C'mon, I'll help you get the food."

They brought the cooler, a picnic basket and another blanket from the boat and laid everything out on it. Eddie had thought to pack a portable radio and he placed that on the blanket and turned it on. While the girls busied themselves setting out the food and drinks, the boys played a game of tag in the sand.

"Everything's ready, you guys!" Pat called to them. "Let's eat!"

They all sat down on the blanket and the girls passed out the sandwiches and sodas. They sat there contentedly, eating and drinking and enjoying each other's company.

"I'm so hungry," Sally said as she wolfed down her sandwich. "Peanut butter and jelly is my favorite." She kept talking as she ate and a glob of jelly trickled down the side of her mouth. Pat looked over and made a face.

"Oh, Sally, you're such a slob," she admonished. "Wipe your mouth off before I get sick!"

Sally looked back at her and stuck her tongue out, which made Pat grimace even more. "Well, excuse me, Miss Perfect," she said. "I forgot to mind my manners." She looked at Eddie and smiled. "Eddie doesn't mind, do you, Eddie-kins?" She batted her eyelashes at him in an exaggerated movement. Eddie smiled back.

"No, I don't mind. I like your mouth, jelly or not." He reached over with a napkin and wiped a spot of jelly off her face, then kissed her.

Mickey, who was sitting on the other side of Pat next to Richie, touched his arm. "Sorry I didn't show up at the Sugar Shack last night, Rich," he said contritely. "I fell asleep on the sofa and when I woke up, it was already past ten."

"That's okay, Mickey," Richie answered. "I figured it was something like that. I hung around until nine-thirty, then I went home."

Nancy turned to him. "You really looked good on those skis, Richie," she said. "I can't believe you never skied before. Is it very difficult?"

"Not once you get the hang of it," he answered. "After lunch, it'll be your turn. Think you can do it?"

"I don't know. I'm such a klutz. I'm willing to try it, though."

Eddie finished his sandwich and drained the last of his soda from the bottle. "So, who's going to try to ski next?" he said, looking around at each of the girls. "Sally?"

"Oh, no, not me," she said. "I'm not ready. Pat, you go first and I'll go after you. Or," she turned to Nancy, "Nancy, why don't you try it? I don't want to be first."

Pat stood up and brushed sand from her bathing suit. "I'll go first," she said. "It looks easy enough."

Eddie and Mickey turned to each other and laughed. "It's easy enough, right, Mick?" Eddie said, mimicking Pat's voice. "Piece of cake!"

"Oh, definitely," Mickey agreed. "Nothing to it. Wouldn't you agree, Rich? You mastered the technique easily enough." He turned to Richie and winked.

Richie knew that it was harder than he had made it look. He'd just been lucky, that was all. Pat would probably be in for a surprise when she attempted it. "Absolutely nothing to it," he said.

That afternoon, they spent several more hours on the boat and at their little hide-a-way beach, swimming and water skiing. Pat and Nancy had both managed to master the art of skiing, but Sally hadn't been able to get the hang of it.

"I'm just too top-heavy," she'd said, to the others' amusement.

"And maybe a little bottom-heavy, too, don't you think?" Pat had kidded her.

At four o'clock, Eddie was guiding the boat back through the channel to Mill Creek and the dock. After tying up, he washed the boat down with fresh water from a nearby hose. The others helped clean up the sand and trash and afterward, they sat around on the dock, talking and making plans for later that evening.

They agreed they would go to a movie over in Sag Harbor and then to the Sugar Shack after that. When it was time to go, Richie and Nancy felt like walking, so they said goodbye to the others, who left in Eddie's car.

Nancy's parents had rented a summer house on the other side of Noyac Road, just up the hill from Treadway's Market. It wasn't too far from Richie's cabin. They held hands as they walked and Richie hadn't felt as comfortable with any other person as he now felt with her. It was as if he had known her all his life.

"See you later, Richie," she said breathlessly, when they reached her house. She kissed him and then turned and ran into the house.

"I'll pick you up at seven-thirty!" he called after her, then turned and started walking down the street.

Just as he got to Noyac Road, Eddie's car came to a screeching halt next to him, near the corner. It startled him for a moment until he saw who it was, then he relaxed and walked over to the driver's side. Eddie was sitting behind the wheel with a disturbed look on his face.

As Richie approached, Eddie turned off the motor and got out of the car, slamming the door behind him. "The cops just picked Mickey up!" he said excitedly.

"What?" Richie looked at him with disbelief.

"The cops! They just picked Mickey up outside the Sugar Shack! I don't know what's going on!" Eddie leaned against the car door and shook his head slowly from side to side.

Richie just stood there, mouth wide open, looking at him. He was utterly speechless. The day, which had started out so splendidly, had suddenly taken an ominous turn.

Ten

Richie met Nancy in front of her house at seven-thirty and they walked to the Sugar Shack from there. Pat and Sally were already seated at a table in the back.

As soon as she saw them, Pat blurted out, "Did you hear what happened to Mickey? The police picked him up."

"We heard," Richie replied. He and Nancy had been talking about it on the way over. He had repeated everything Eddie had said and then told her that he had no further information on the subject. After joining Pat and Sally at the table, he ordered two soft drinks from the waitress.

"Has anybody seen Eddie?" Richie adjusted Nancy's chair for her and sat down beside her.

"He's supposed to meet us here in a little while." Pat brushed her dark hair away from her eyes. "Gosh, I can't believe it! We had just pulled into the parking lot when a police car drove up next to us. They asked Mickey to come over to their car and the next thing we knew, he was in the back seat and then they drove away." She shrugged her shoulders. "I don't know what it's all about."

"When did this happen?" Nancy asked.

"Right after you left. We drove straight over here from the dock." Pat leaned forward in her chair and rested her head in her hands for a moment, then looked up at the others. "I really like Mickey, you know. I hope everything's all right with him."

"Didn't the police say anything to you?" Richie tapped his fingers nervously on the table. "Anything at all?"

"No, the one who was driving just called over and said, 'Hey, Mickey, come over here! We want to talk to you.' I guess they knew him, 'cause they called him by name." Pat took a tissue from the pocket of her shorts and dabbed at her eyes.

"Yeah," Sally agreed. "He walked over to talk to them but all they did was put him in the back seat and drove away." She screwed up her nose and frowned. "Can they do that? I told Eddie to go after them, but..." She let out a sigh and began to sip her drink.

"Did Mickey say anything to you, Richie?" Pat asked.

"About what?"

"About anything. Is everything all right with him at home?"

Richie hesitated a moment before answering. He didn't want to tell her what Mickey had told him about his mother's drinking, that was Mickey's place to tell her if he wanted her to know. "As far as I know, everything's all right," he said, a little uneasily.

"This is really puzzling," Nancy suggested. She paused as the waitress returned with their drinks and set them on the table, then went on after the waitress had left. "But there must be a logical explanation." She tapped her chin absentmindedly. "I'm sure everything will turn out all right," she said, then added, "hopefully, that is."

"Are we still going to the movies?" Sally asked.

Pat looked at her and frowned, green eyes blazing with anger. "With who, silly, ourselves? Mickey's not here and neither is Eddie! How do you expect us to get there? Walk?" She snatched up her drink and took a sip through the straw, making a loud, gurgling sound.

"Well, I'm sorry, Pat." Sally took a sip from her own drink. "You don't have to bite my head off. I just wanted to know what we're doing tonight, that's all." She turned away from Pat and stared at the wall, saying nothing further.

"We're waiting here until we find out what happened to Mickey!" Pat rummaged through her purse and pulled out her lipstick, which she applied to her lips with short, abrupt strokes.

"And, anyone who doesn't like it can leave anytime they want to!" She threw the lipstick back in her purse and took another sip from her drink, making another loud, gurgling sound.

Nancy leaned over and spoke in a low voice to Richie. "Let's go over and see what's on the juke box. Want to?"

"Sure." He stood up. "We'll be right back."

As they walked over to the juke box, Richie glanced over at the door just as Mickey and Eddie walked in from outside. "Look!" he said. He and Nancy turned around and returned to the table.

"Hello, everybody," Eddie said cheerfully. "Look who's here!"

"Mickey!" Pat stood up and gave him a big hug. "We were so worried about you! What happened?"

"Nothing, really." Mickey kissed her quickly. "Let's sit down." He grabbed two chairs from an empty table and he and Eddie sat down with the others.

"What happened?" Pat repeated impatiently.

"It was no big deal," Mickey began. "The cops found my wallet over in Southampton and they wanted me to come to the police station to fill out a form, that's all."

"Mickey called me at home when they were done and I went over and picked him up," Eddie said. He leaned over and gave Sally a kiss. "Do we still have time to make the show? It starts at eight forty-five."

Sally looked at her watch. "Plenty of time. It's only eight-ten."

"What was your wallet doing over in Southampton?" Pat asked.

"I must have lost it there the other day." Mickey leaned back in his chair and lit a cigarette, then laid the pack on the table. "I was over there running some errands for Mr. Treadway. Guess I lost it then. I didn't even realize it was missing until the cops told me they found it."

"So that's what all the fuss was about." Pat pointed to the pack of cigarettes. "Let me have one, Mickey." She held the cigarette to her lips as Mickey lighted it, then took a drag and blew a puff of smoke into the air. "I was so worried about you. I thought maybe you had been arrested or something."

"Me, too," Eddie said.

"Me, three," Sally said.

"Nah, that's all there was to it." Mickey dropped his cigarette to the floor and stamped it out with his sneaker. "We'd better get going if we're going to the movies."

On their way out, the girls decided to visit the ladies room. Eddie went outside to bring the car around and Richie was elected to take care of the check. He fished a dollar bill from his jeans and walked to the front of the building.

As he waited by the cash register, Mickey walked over and stood beside him. "Richie, do you think your parents would mind if I stayed at your place tonight? My old lady's been drinking again and I don't feel like being around her. "I'll understand if they say no."

"Hey, that sounds like fun! They probably won't mind. Let me call home real quick and ask them." Richie gave Mickey the money and the check. "Here, take care of this. I'll be right back."

He walked over to the pay telephone in the corner to make his call and came back a few minutes later. "They said it was all right with them, if you don't mind the pull-out."

Mickey gave him a lop-sided grin. "Not at all," he said. "Beggars can't be choosers."

In the ladies room, Pat put her arm around Sally and gave her a squeeze. "I'm sorry I was so rude to you before, Sally. Will you forgive me?"

"Oh, that's okay, Pat." Sally picked at her hair with her fingers, trying to rearrange her brown curls without a comb. "You were just upset, that's all. I understand." She looked at Pat and smiled.

"Yes, but that was no reason to take it out on you," Pat said contritely.

"Forget it. I have already." Sally gave her a quick hug. "Let's hurry, the boys are waiting."

They all met back outside where Eddie was waiting in the car. They piled in, this time with Nancy on Richie's lap to make room. Eddie put the car in gear and took off down Beach Road, heading toward the Harbor Bridge.

Sag Harbor was a ten minute drive from the Sugar Shack and the theater was located right in the heart of town, on Main Street. They found a parking spot nearby, left the car and went into the theater.

The film was a mediocre western which they barely watched. They sat in the last row of the balcony and necked, paying more attention to each other than to the picture.

After one particularly long and tender kiss, Nancy told Richie that she loved him.

"I love you, too, Nancy," he said.

She kissed him again. "Oh, Richie, I'm so happy."

After the movie, Eddie dropped Pat and Nancy off at their houses, then continued on to Richie's. Richie and Mickey got out of the car.

"See you tomorrow," Eddie said, as he and Sally drove away.

The two boys went inside. Mr. Donnelly was already sleeping but Mrs. Donnelly was waiting up for them. She asked them how the movie was and began making up the pull-out for Mickey.

"Good night, dear. Good night, Mickey," she said when she was finished. "I'm going to bed. Try not to stay up too late, now, all right?"

"Good night, mom."

"G'night, Mrs. Donnelly."

They waited until she had left the room before speaking.

Richie thought Mickey was a little nervous and ill-at-ease. "Let's go out to the porch," he said. "It's nice and cool out there."

"Thanks for letting me stay here tonight, Richie," Mickey said, after they were seated on the porch. "I really appreciate it."

"No problem, Mick."

"You have a good time tonight?"

"Great. How about you?"

"Oh, yeah, it was swell. I really like Pat. She's a lot of fun. Kisses nice, too."

"She likes you too, from what I could see. In fact, she told us she liked you tonight at the Sugar Shack before you got there."

"Yeah?"

"Yeah."

"That's good." Mickey scratched his nose. "Hey, you and Nancy sure hit it off. Right from the beginning, too."

"I know. I really like her a lot." Richie sat back in the chair and stretched his legs. They were beginning to feel sore from water ski-ing. "I'm glad you and Eddie took me to Trout Pond yesterday," he said. "I might not have met her, otherwise."

"Oh, you'd have met her sooner or later, Rich."

"You think so?"

"Sure. It's fate. You can't stop fate." Mickey was quiet for a mo-ment, not saying anything. He just sat there, staring off into space. After a few seconds, he said, "If not at Trout Pond, then somewhere else. Maybe the Sugar Shack or maybe the beach. Somewhere." He started fidgeting in his seat.

"You all right, Mickey?"

"Yeah, sure, I'm fine. Say..., Richie?"

"Yeah?"

"Listen, I got something to tell you. It's very important but I don't know where to begin...,"

"What's wrong, Mickey?" Richie straightened up in his seat, alert now.

"I think I'm in trouble."

"What do you mean?"

"The cops. I..., they think I broke into a house over in South-ampton."

"What?"

"Yeah. I didn't want to mention it in front of the others, especially Pat. I haven't even told Eddie. I guess I was just too embarrassed to say anything."

"They think you broke into a house?" Richie rubbed his face with his hands, then brushed his hair back over his forehead. "I thought they just wanted to return your wallet. Didn't they?"

"They did. At least they said they did, but when I got to the police station, they brought me upstairs to one of the rooms there and these two detectives from Southampton started questioning me."

"About what? What did they say?" Richie could barely see Mickey's face in the darkness.

"They had my wallet and they said they found it outside this house that had been burglarized, and...,"

"When? When was the house burglarized?"

"Last night."

"But didn't you tell them you lost it a couple of days ago?"

"Yeah, I did, but I don't think they believed me. I told them I thought I lost it somewhere on Montauk Highway when I was picking up that stuff for old man Treadway.

"Yeah, so...?"

"So they wanted to know how it got way over on South Lane where they found it."

"South Lane? Where's that?"

"It's about ten blocks over from where I said I lost it. It's a residential street. There's some expensive homes there, and..., God, Richie! I don't know how it got way over there! Some kid must have found it and dropped it there, or something. I..., I don't know how it got there!" He looked as if he was going to cry.

"Take it easy, Mickey," Richie soothed. "Maybe we can go over to the police station and talk to them. Maybe they...,"

"And tell them what? What could we say?" Mickey leaned forward and let his hands hang limply from his legs. "I don't think..."

"We'll just tell them the truth!" Richie said, interrupting him. "That you lost you wallet over there and that's all there is to it!"

"I don't know, Richie. I'm scared. They think I did it!" Mickey rose from his chair and started to pace back and forth in the porch.

"But they let you go, didn't they?" Richie raised his hands in a conciliatory gesture, like a preacher from a pulpit. "They wouldn't have let you go if they didn't believe you."

Mickey returned to his chair and sat down. "They said I could go while they checked out my story. They're gonna talk to old man Treadway first, to see if he really sent me over there, and...,"

"So, he'll tell them he did and then you're home free, right?"

"That part of it, yeah, but they're gonna wanna know where I was last night, who I was with..., I just don't know what I'm gonna do, Rich. They'll come back and arrest me if I don't have an alibi."

Richie's face took on a puzzled expression. "An alibi? What are you talking about? You have an alibi! You said you stayed home last night and fell asleep, right?"

Mickey stood up and started pacing the floor again. "Yeah, but I can't tell them that. They're never gonna believe I was there."

"Why not?"

"Who's gonna believe I was home sleeping? You think they will? Oh, God, Richie! I need help! Please!"

"What about your mother? She must have seen you."

"She was drunk. Passed out in her room. She don't know if I was there or not. Diane wasn't home, so nobody saw me there!" Mickey sat down again and buried his face in his hands. "Please, Richie, please! You gotta help me!"

"What can I do?"

Mickey was silent for a moment and then he looked up. "Tell them I was with you," he said softly.

"What?"

"Yeah. You and Diane. I was with both of you at the Sugar Shack last night. We hung out for a while and then we took a walk to the beach. Will you do it?"

Richie looked at him with disbelief as the significance of what he was saying began to register. Now it was Richie's turn to leave his seat and start pacing the floor. "Mickey, I can't tell them that!"

"Why can't you?" Mickey stood up and put his hands on Richie's shoulders. "Please, Richie, you gotta help me! They'll believe you. Please!"

"Mickey, I can't! It's just not right! I can't do it!"

"Why can't you do it? I thought you were my friend! "Why won't you help me?"

Richie moved away from Mickey's grip. "I don't know. It's just not right. I can't lie to the police. I..., I'll get in trouble!"

"Oh, so you'd rather I got in trouble for something I didn't do?" Mickey sat down heavily. "Thanks a lot, Richie," he said softly. "I thought I could depend on you." He was silent for a few seconds, then said again more loudly, "I thought you were my friend!"

"Shh, please, Mickey, don't wake my parents." Richie looked in the direction of his parents' bedroom, then sat back down across from him. "Look, can't you just tell them the truth? You were home last night. You fell asleep, that's all."

"I told you they won't believe me!" Mickey stood up and walked toward the front door, then wheeled around suddenly. "Diane is willing to say that the three of us were together, so why can't you? All you have to do is say you were with us last night! Why can't you do that, huh? Why can't you just do me a simple favor like that?" Mickey was angry now. His hands were on his hips and he was glaring down at Richie.

"A simple favor?" Richie got up and walked over to where Mickey was standing. "You want me to lie to the police for you, and that's a simple favor?" He shook his head. "I can't do it, Mickey!"

"Well, thanks a lot, then, friend!" Mickey pushed open the screen door and stormed out of the house. "You'd rather see me go to jail for something I didn't do!" he yelled, then ran up the street.

"Mickey!" Richie ran out the door after him.

Mickey was halfway up Chestnut now, heading towards Noyac Road. He was faster than Richie and with the head start he'd had, Richie doubted he would be able to catch up with him.

Richie ran faster. "Mickey!"

Mickey had already reached the corner and was about to turn left. Once he turned the corner, he'd be gone.

"Mickey, wait up!" Richie ran as fast as he could, trying to close the gap between them, but Mickey turned the corner and disappeared out of sight.

"Okay, I'll do it!" Richie yelled into the darkness. He stopped running and had to lean on someone's fence to catch his breath. He looked around but couldn't see more than three feet in front of him. The night was pitch black and there were no street lights out here in the country.

After catching his breath, Richie started walking back toward his house. The whole episode had confused him and he now felt depressed and completely drained of energy. His only thought was to reach his room and fall exhausted into bed.

"You promise?" It was Mickey. He had come up behind Richie in the darkness and now put his arm over Richie's shoulder. "You really mean it, Rich? You'll help me?"

"Yeah, I'll do it, Mickey," Richie said with resignation. "Just tell me what you want me to do and I'll do it."

"That's great, Richie. Come on, let's walk down to the beach and we'll go over everything. We have to get our stories straight." Mickey playfully punched him in the arm. "Don't worry, Rich, you won't get into trouble. The cops out here are just a bunch of hicks. They ain't like the cops in the city. We just stick to our story and we're home free. Trust me."

Trust me. The words reverberated in Richie's head. I trust you, I guess, he thought. I just don't know now whether or not I trust me.

They walked to the end of Chestnut Street and climbed over the barrier where it dead-ended at the beach. They continued walking in the sand until they found a spot near the water and sat down.

Mickey seemed to be in a much better frame of mind now than he had been a few minutes ago, but Richie felt terrible. He had a headache and was very tired. He only wanted this night to be over with, and the sooner the better.

Mickey laid out the plan of action. "Okay, here's what we'll do," he said.

Eleven

Richie slept until nine o'clock the next morning after a fitful night of sleep. He and Mickey had stayed down at the beach until well past midnight, going over the plan for Mickey's alibi.

He went into the kitchen and poured himself a glass of orange juice and a bowl of cold cereal. Mickey had already left for work at Treadway's and Richie remembered that his parents had told him they had to drive to the city today, so he was alone in the house.

He sat at the kitchen table and went over everything in his mind. The story they had concocted was that Mickey, Richie and Diane had met at the Sugar Shack at eight o'clock Saturday evening. They had stayed there for about an hour and then gone down to the beach. They were at the beach until after eleven o'clock.

"Make sure you tell them we were there until after eleven," Mickey had said. "That should cover us for the whole evening."

"What's so special about eleven o'clock?" Richie asked. "Why not ten or ten-thirty?"

Mickey became agitated. "Look, Rich, could you just stick to the time I tell you? We have to get it down exactly so our stories match! I already told Diane to say we left at eleven, so that's what she's going to tell the cops! Eleven, Rich. Eleven!"

"All right, Mickey, eleven." Richie replied. "We left the beach at eleven o'clock." What was Mickey getting so excited about? he thought. I'm trying to help him, aren't I? "Then what?" he asked.

"After that, me and Diane walked you to your house and then we hitched a ride home from there. That should cover it," Mickey said.

So that's where they stood. Mickey had gone over the story several times to make sure that Richie understood the plan. Only after Mickey was satisfied had they walked back to Richie's house and gone to bed.

Richie drained the last of his juice and went over the story again for his own benefit. It seemed okay. He'd been at the Sugar Shack on Saturday night all right, but he'd been there alone. Neither Mickey nor Diane had been there with him. That's where the story changed.

Had anyone else seen him there? He thought for a minute. He hadn't seen anyone else he knew except..., Frank Wittey! Frank had been sitting at the counter when he'd first walked in, he remembered.

Richie had said hello to him and recalled asking him if he had seen Mickey. That's right. He had told Frank he was meeting Mickey there. That was good. It could only help make their account of the evening more credible, just in case the cops wanted to talk to any other witnesses.

Frank would remember seeing him there, he guessed. At least he hoped so. But I was there, he reminded himself. Stayed until nine-thirty. It was Mickey and Diane who hadn't been there that night.

"God, why am I doing this?" he asked out loud. He didn't want to lie to the police. Not really. He was scared. If the police ever found out he was lying, it'd be all over. He'd be in trouble for sure.

What would they do to him? Could they charge him with a crime? Possibly. What kind of a crime? Obstruction of justice? Maybe. Giving false witness? That sounded too religious. Giving a false statement? Probably. Something like that.

Would they send him to jail? Reform school? Maybe to a place like Attica. Or Sing Sing. He'd heard of those places. They were upstate. Up the river. Yeah, that's where they'd send him. Up the river. He'd be a convict. A hardened criminal, sent up the river. The Hudson River.

His body shuddered involuntarily, reminding him of his situation. This was a real dilemma. He needed to get a grip on things. He had to somehow convince himself that Mickey and Diane had been with him the other night. But he wasn't a very good liar and he hated not telling the truth.

No matter what mistakes he had made or what kind of trouble he'd ever found himself in, he had never lied about it. It went against his nature. He had always told the truth. That was something his parents had instilled in him at an early age.

"Honesty is always the best policy, son," he remembered his father saying to him many times. "No matter what, always tell the truth. Lying about something will only make things worse."

Richie believed that. Honesty was always the best policy. Then, why was he now going against that belief? Why was he going to lie for Mickey? It didn't make any sense to him. And lying to the police, no less. He just didn't understand it.

He stood up from the table and decided to take a shower. He was supposed to meet Nancy and some of the other kids at the town beach at noon. After toweling off and combing his hair, he went back to his room and put on a clean tee shirt and a pair of khaki shorts over his bathing suit.

Since it was only a little after ten, he decided to read for awhile. But as he lay on the bed, his mind kept wandering and he had difficulty focusing on the pages of his book. He kept going over the story in his mind, again and again, trying to lock it in. He closed his eyes.

He was entering the Sugar Shack. There was Frank Wittey, sitting at the counter. He was eating a hamburger. No, a hot dog. Frank was eating a hot dog.

"Hi, Frank, seen Mickey?"

"Hi, Richie. No, I haven't."

"I'm supposed to meet him here. See you later."

"See you."

Now, walk to the back room and sit at a table. Look around. Nobody here that I know. A couple of vaguely familiar faces. Where's Mickey? Not here yet. Look at the time. Eight-twenty. Where's

Mickey?

Order a malt from the waitress. Chocolate. She brings it to the table. Take a sip of the malt. It's good. Chocolate's my favorite. Check the time. Eight-thirty. Still no Mickey.

Walk over to the juke box. Put a dime in, play two songs. Earth Angel and Story Untold. The Penguins and The Nutmegs. My two favorites. Walk back to the table. Sit down again. Think about Nancy. Wish she was here. Can't wait to see her tomorrow. She is my Earth Angel.

Songs end. Check the time. Eight forty-five. What happened to Mickey? Maybe he's having trouble hitching a ride. Getting fidgety. Finish the malt. Waitress walks by. Pay for the malt. Waitress brings back my change.

Get up from the table. Take a walk outside. Sit at a table on the deck. Crowded out here. Lots of kids. They all seem to be having fun. Look around for a familiar face. I don't know anyone here, either.

This is no good, where's Mickey? He should've been here by now. Check the time. Nine o'clock. "I'll wait another ten minutes, then I'll...," Now I'm talking to myself out loud. I'll wait another ten minutes. If he doesn't show by then, I'll walk down to the beach. He might be there.

Did I misunderstand him? Don't think so. He said eight o'clock, didn't he? Definitely no Mickey here. Wait! Something's wrong! Back up. Go back inside. Sit at table. Malt. Juke box. Nancy. Wish she was here.

What time is it? Eight-thirty. Keep going back. Further. Back. Back. What time, now? Eight-twenty. Look around the room. Where's Mickey? I don't think he's going to show.

Wait! There he is! He just walked in. Who's that with him? Diane? It's Mickey's sister, Diane. What's she doing here? Mickey and Diane. They're coming over to the table.

"Hi, Richie!"

"Hi, Mickey. Hi, Diane."

"Sorry we're late. Couldn't get a ride. We were supposed to meet you at eight."

"Both of you? I thought just Mickey. Oh, that's right, I'm meeting both of you. Mickey and Diane. Together. I'm meeting both of you here tonight. How are you? Nice to see you both. Want a drink? I just had a malt. Chocolate. It's my favorite. Nothing for you, you say? Okay. The juke box? Sure. Here's a dime. Diane will go.

"Oh, I see you have good taste. You played two of my favorites. Earth Angel and This Is My Story..., I mean, Story Untold. That's right, Story Untold. I almost forgot. What time is it? Nine o'clock? Do I want to go to the beach? Sure."

We're at the beach now. Diane and me and Mickey.

"Where's your date, Mickey? Why am I with Diane? I'm supposed to be with Nancy. She's my girl, you know. What? Diane likes me? Can't be. She's too young for me. No, Diane, you can't kiss me. I'm Nancy's girl. I mean, Nancy's my girl. Why are you kissing me, Diane?

"Yes, I like it. Yes, you're a good kisser. I thought you were Danny's girl. I mean, Eddie's girl. What? You're nobody's girl? I see. Yes, I told you I like it. With a body like yours, who can resist?

"Kiss me again, Diane. Yes. Oh, sorry, Mickey. I didn't mean to..., I mean, she's your sister and all."

"Diane likes you, man. Don't you see the way she looks at you? You, Richie. Only you. Want to kiss her again? Go ahead."

"Mickey, how could you? Your own sister and all? Oh, I see. She's older than she looks. What? Look at her body? "Yes, I see it. Yes, Diane has a beautiful body. Kiss me again, Diane. Kiss me again. Mickey says it's okay. Yes, I like you. I do."

Richie woke up with a start. He rubbed his eyes. Must have dozed off, he thought. God, what a dream! He yawned and looked at his watch. It was eleven forty-five. I'll have to hurry if I'm going to meet Diane and the others..., I mean, Nancy and the others at noon.

Feeling slightly groggy, he went into the bathroom and splashed cold water on his face, then brushed his teeth again. For a brief moment he thought he could smell perfume. He sniffed at the air a few times. Nothing.

Richie met his friends at the beach at a few minutes past twelve. Nancy, Pat, Sally and Eddie were sitting together on a blanket close to the water. The day was hot and sunny but there was a breeze blowing in from the water and it cooled the air down to a pleasurable level.

Adjacent to them on another blanket was Danny Shaw, Frank Wittey and some other kids Richie didn't know. Eddie introduced them.

"This is Richie Donnelly, everybody. Richie, meet Judy, Eileen, Kenny and Gail. You already know Danny and Frank."

"Nice to meet you." Richie waved to them.

"Hey, Richie, welcome to the club," Danny said. "I hear you made the mighty leap from Mighty Mo. This guy is no sissy," Danny said to the others. "His first time at Trout Pond and off he goes, right from the top."

"Yeah, and he didn't land on his ass like you did, Kenny," Frank said, clapping Kenny Simms playfully on the back.

"Don't remind me," Kenny said good naturedly. "It still hurts when I sit down."

"Then don't sit down," Eileen said with a straight face.

After a few more pleasantries, Eddie organized a game of beach volleyball, guys against the girls. The girls won the game and then they all went for a swim. The water was a nice respite from the hot sun and it made Richie feel better than he had all morning.

Afterwards, he and Nancy walked over to the Sugar Shack for a hot dog and soda. They sat at a table outside on the deck and talked about the up-coming Fourth of July celebration which was being held in the village the following weekend.

"I just love July 4th, Richie, don't you?" Nancy gave him a big smile. "It's one of my favorite holidays."

"Mine, too," Richie agreed, looking at her with admiration. She looked very attractive in her white bathing suit. Her hair was matted and curled up at the ends from the time spent in the water and she had a bit of dried sand stuck to the side of her neck.

"I heard there's going to be a big parade down Noyac Road in the morning," he commented.

"Yes, that's right. They have it every year," she said. "People come from all over Long Island to see it." She wiped a strand of hair away from her eyes. "After the parade, they have a picnic and barbecue over on Harbor Road and when it gets dark, they put on a big fireworks display down at the beach."

"That sounds like fun," Richie said.

"Oh, it is," Nancy said cheerfully. "And the kids are having a beach party right before the fireworks start. Would you like to be my date, kind sir? I'm in need of an escort."

"Why I'd be happy to, fair maiden. What time shall I come and call for you?"

The waitress brought their food and went back inside. As she opened the door, they could hear music coming from the juke box. The song playing was Story Untold, which, when Richie realized what it was, reminded him of his dream earlier that morning. He frowned.

"Is anything wrong?" Nancy asked. She was watching him closely.

"What? Oh, no. No, everything is fine."

"Oh, you had the strangest look on your face just then, that's all."

"Sorry." He looked at her and smiled. "So, tell me more about the Fourth of July festivities," he said, changing the subject.

They talked some more about the parade and other activities the village fathers had planned for the following weekend. Since it was the largest annual event in the area and heavily advertised, it usually drew hundreds of people from the surrounding communities and elsewhere.

After a while, Nancy looked up at Richie. Her blue eyes sparkled. "Eddie said he'd take us over to Southampton tonight to play some miniature golf. Want to go?"

"Sure. Anything you want to do is okay with me."

She blew him a kiss. "Sally told me he already asked her to go steady. He's going to give her his high school ring as soon as she can get a chain for it."

Richie raised his eyebrows. "Really? Boy, that was fast! They only met the other day."

"Well, when two people really like each other...," She gave him a sideways glance.

He had thought about asking Nancy to go steady but didn't want to rush things. Now he sensed that she wanted him to. What would he do about a ring, though? He wouldn't receive his own high school ring until the fall, when he would be a senior.

She wiped a bit of mustard from her mouth. "I think it's so romantic, don't you, Richie?"

"What? Oh, yes. Very romantic." He suddenly decided he would ask her to go steady, too. Not right at this moment, though. Tonight. It would be more romantic then.

"Of course," she went on, "I'd have to know a boy longer than a few days before I'd consider anything as serious as going steady." She looked at him seductively.

"Of course," he agreed. He took a sip from his drink. "Uh, just how long?"

"Oh, maybe a week."

They both burst out laughing.

"How long have we known each other?" he asked.

"Two days."

"Seems longer."

"Yes, it does."

"Seems more like a week to me."

"It does?"

"Well, almost a week. By tonight it'll feel more like a week, don't you think?"

"Oh, Richie, you're so sweet!" She got up from her chair and walked around to his side of the table, then sat on his lap. She put her arms around his neck and kissed him. "I love you," she murmured.

He held her tightly and returned her kiss. Tonight, he thought. I'll ask her tonight.

After a while, they left the Sugar Shack and returned to the beach. The kids were in the middle of another game of volleyball, so they sat on the blanket and waited for them to finish. When it was over, they all decided to go for another swim.

"Let's have a game of topple," Eddie suggested.

"What's that?" Richie asked.

Eddie explained how the game was played. "Everyone splits up into teams, with a guy and a girl on each team. The girls climb on the guys' shoulders and then each girl tries to topple the other one by pulling them off the guys' shoulders into the water. Sort of like a free for all. The team left standing up at the end wins."

Everyone thought it was a good idea and they divided up into teams. Eddie and Sally, Nancy and Richie, Frank and Eileen, Danny and Gail and Kenny and Judy. As they waded into the water, a wave caught Frank off guard and he and Eileen immediately toppled into the water.

"Hey, that's not fair! Interference!" Frank protested loudly, after coming up for air. "We got hit with a wave!"

"Sorry, Frank, waves count," Eddie said, as Sally caught Gail around the neck from behind and toppled her from Danny's shoulders. "No interference."

Richie noticed Eddie and Sally moving towards them so he backed away and was about to warn Nancy to be on her guard when Kenny slipped behind them and Judy pulled Nancy off his shoulders. They both fell into the water, laughing hysterically.

Now it was down to just two teams, Judy and Kenny against Sally and Eddie. They circled each other slowly several times, each team eying the other warily.

Kenny moved forward to close the distance between them as Judy leaned over and tried to grab Sally by the arm. Sally managed to push Judy off to the side, which almost caused Judy and Kenny to lose their balance. Kenny immediately pulled back, trying desperately to maintain his balance.

Eddie and Sally used the distraction to move behind them and Sally successfully pulled Judy from Kenny's shoulders. "We win!" Sally yelled triumphantly. They played several more games and Eddie and Sally won every time.

After the others congratulated them for being the undefeated champions, Sally boasted that it was because she had a lot of upper body strength. They all agreed.

After the last game, everyone returned to the blankets to rest and sunbath. After about ten minutes, Richie heard someone call his name. He looked up and saw Diane standing over him.

"Richie, I've got to talk to you."

Twelve

As Richie stood up, Diane took his arm and led him away from the blanket. "Let's take a walk," she said.

Nancy gave him a puzzled look but said nothing. Richie looked back at her and shrugged his shoulders. "Be back in a minute, Nancy."

He and Diane walked along the beach in the direction of Noyac Road, away from the others. Diane held on tightly to his arm. "Mickey asked me to talk to you, to make sure we have our stories straight, okay, Richie?"

She smiled sweetly at him, revealing tiny dimples on her cheeks. She was wearing pink shorts, a white tee shirt with a plunging v-neck collar and a pair of sandals.

Her toenails were painted a bright red and her blond hair, already starting to turn lighter from the sun, was combed back into a pony tail and secured with a pink ribbon.

Richie nodded. "We went over the story pretty thoroughly last night," he said. He noticed that her face was flushed, as if she had just left a sauna and she seemed to be slightly out of breath.

"I know. He wanted me to reassure you and tell you not to worry." She let go of his arm and turned to face him, taking one of his hands and holding it with both of hers. "As long as we all agree on where we were and what time we were there, there's no reason to be concerned about the cops, Richie."

"Ah, Diane, I think I'd better tell you something." He worked his hand free and stood there fidgeting nervously. "I've been thinking about this all morning, and...,"

"Let's sit down over there." Diane pointed to a spot in the sand on top of a little bluff which overlooked the water. From it, they had a good view of Noyac Bay, which curved around to the west and formed a small, crescent-shaped patch of beach where the water met the land.

Richie had almost decided that he couldn't go through with it. He had gone over it again and again and there was just no way he was going to lie to the police. The thought terrified him and he had planned on telling Mickey when he saw him later that day.

"I'm glad you're going to help us," she continued. "Mickey really needs all the help he can get. You're a good friend to do this," she said warmly.

"That's just it, Diane," he began. "I don't know if I'd actually be helping him or not by lying to the police. I really don't think it's necessary. If he just tells them the truth...,"

She gave him a hard look. "It's too late for that, Richie," she said softly.

"What do you mean?"

She leaned back against the sand and extended her legs out in front of her, then picked up a handful of sand and slowly let it drop through her fingers. She looked away from him as she said, "I already spoke to the police and I told them what we agreed upon." She turned back to face him. "So you can't back out now."

"You already talked to them?" Richie brought his legs up and leaned forward, resting his chin on his knees. "When did you see them?" he asked.

"They came by my house this morning, around ten o'clock." She leaned closer to him and gently touched his arm. "Richie, it's going to be all right." She was tracing small patterns on his arm with her fingers. "I'm sure they believed me."

Her touch caused goose bumps to appear on his arm and he felt tingly all over. He found himself staring at her breasts, then caught himself and looked away. Diane saw him looking and smiled.

"Mickey really likes you, Richie. He thinks you're a cool guy. She squeezed his arm. "I like you, too." She wore no make-up except for a dab of lipstick and some eye shadow. She was very pretty. He shifted uncomfortably and mumbled his thanks. There was something about her that was familiar but he couldn't put his finger on it. It came to him suddenly, a strong feeling of deja vu. Her perfume!

He remembered his dream, when he had fallen asleep in his room that morning. The scent of her perfume was the same as in his dream! It had been so strong and vivid that he could still smell it even after he woke up! In the dream, she had kissed him.

This was crazy. He liked Nancy and even though he planned on asking her to go steady with him, here he was, sitting alone with Diane and remembering a dream in which she had kissed him. The whole thing was strange and didn't seem right.

She leaned closer to him. "Will you do it, Richie?"

He turned and looked deeply into her eyes. They were blue, like Nancy's. Lighter, though. A lighter blue. Her lips were fuller, too. He focused on her mouth. Her lips were parted slightly, just ever so slightly.

He was attracted to her, he realized. She was very pretty. No, she was beautiful. And God, so sexy, so very sexy. He turned away from her.

"I just don't like the idea of lying to the police, Diane, that's all, and I wish Mickey had told them the truth. I mean, he was home asleep, what's wrong with that?"

"He was afraid they wouldn't have believed him."

"I don't see why not," he said. "It's not so far-fetched. Heck, I fell asleep in my room this morning after breakfast." He found a small pebble in the sand and threw it towards the water. "It happens sometimes."

"You don't know Mickey. He's..., well, the cops are always giving him a hard time. They treat him like a juvenile delinquent just because he got..., just because he dropped out of school."

Richie was surprised to hear this. "Really?"

"Yes." She made a face like she had just eaten a slice of lemon. "Anything that happens in this town, the first person they come looking for is Mickey. They're always bugging him."

"I didn't know that."

"Well, it's true. He doesn't deserve it, either, Richie. He's my brother and I'd do anything for him." Diane crossed her legs at the ankles. 'Mickey looks out for me, too. Whenever I have a problem, he's always there for me."

"Couldn't you have said Mickey was with you and Eddie that night? You were with Eddie, weren't you? What if they question Eddy?"

"They won't. And no, we can't say Mickey was with me and Eddie. Eddie wouldn't go for it. He's..., well, let's just say that Eddie takes care of Eddie."

"Yeah, but...,"

"Mickey doesn't want Eddie involved in this. Eddie's parents are very rich and...," Diane uncrossed her legs and drew them up in a lotus position She sat upright and turned to face him. "Let's just stick to the plan, okay, Richie?" She squinted at him. "You're not backing out, are you?"

He avoided her eyes. He wanted to say, yes, I'm backing out. Instead, he heard himself saying, "No, I'm not backing out. I'll tell them we were all together Saturday night."

Diane gave him a big smile. "That's great! The police probably won't ask you anything, anyway. Mickey just wants you to be ready in case they do." She took his hand again. "I really appreciate what you're doing, Richie. If there's anything I can ever do for you...," Her voice got lower and softer and she leaned forward suddenly and kissed him on the lips. "Just let me know, all right?"

The kiss took him by surprise. "Oh, uh, sure." He absentmindedly wiped his mouth. The smell of her perfume was all around him now, permeating his senses. He could feel a wave of excitement ripple through his body, threatening to overtake him. An odd feeling, something he wasn't used to.

Nancy popped into his mind. He'd left her sitting on the blanket and she was still there, waiting for him.

"We'd better go back," he said, not wanting Nancy to wonder what happened to him, why he was taking so long.

They stood up and Diane came into his arms. She hugged him tightly and Richie could feel her body pressing against his. She kissed him again. "Thanks, Richie. You're really a great guy." She slowly relaxed her embrace and took a step backward. "Remember, if there's anything I can do, anything at all, call me, okay?"

"I will, Diane."

They walked back the way they came. As they approached the blanket, Diane reached over and gave his arm a squeeze. "Gotta go, doll," she said. "I'll see you around." She veered off and started walking in the direction of the Sugar Shack.

Richie returned to the blanket, feeling a bit apprehensive. Nancy was sitting there alone, a puzzled look on her face. She put a hand over her eyes and squinted up at him. He smiled weakly and sat down beside her.

"Who was that girl, Richie?" His body cast a shadow over her face and she lowered her hand. She looked at him curiously while her fingers worried the strap of her bathing suit. On her finger was a silver ring with a small pearl set in the center. He hadn't noticed it before.

"Oh," he replied. "I thought you knew her. That was Mickey's sister." He tried to act nonchalant. "Diane," he added, almost as an afterthought.

"Mickey's sister? Oh," she said, as if it made all the sense in the world. Then, "what did she want with you?"

"Just wanted to give me a message from Mickey, that's all. Nothing important." He shifted his eyes away from her and watched some little kids playing with their pails and shovels in the sand. He felt uneasy now and thought that his voice sounded a bit shrill, like it was about to crack.

"I see. She's very pretty, isn't she?" Nancy was tracing a pattern in the sand with her fingers and not looking at him. "Is she going out with anyone?"

Richie looked towards the water. Eddie and Sally were playing another game of volleyball with some of the others. "She, uh..., I don't know. She probably has a boyfriend, I'm sure." He added, "she's only fifteen."

"Oh." Nancy looked at him and smiled. She appeared to relax a bit and moved closer to him. "What do you want to do now? Want to go for a swim?"

"Sure." He stood up and extended his hand to her. She took it and he helped her to her feet. She continued to hold it tightly as they walked down to the water and dove in, releasing it only then. He felt more relaxed now.

Mickey showed up about an hour later and they all sat on the blanket and made plans for the Fourth of July beach party later that week.

"Hey, Mickey, we'd better line up some fireworks for Friday," Eddie said. "It's already Monday and we don't want to wait 'till the last minute, do we?" He stood above the blanket looking down at the others, flexing his muscles like Charles Atlas.

"You're right," Mickey replied. "I guess Billy Riley isn't coming this year. Haven't seen him, yet. Maybe it's time to make a run into the city. Want to go tomorrow?"

"Too soon," Eddie said. "How about Wednesday?"

"Okay. I'll call in sick and we'll leave early." Mickey turned to Richie. "Want to take a ride to the city with us on Wednesday, Rich?"

Richie thought a moment. "Maybe. What time do you think we'll be back?"

"What time do you think we'll be back, Eddie?" Mickey asked.

"Well, we may not have to go all the way in to the city," Eddie said. "I have a friend in Hempstead who says he can get us anything we want. So, figure we'll be back by dinnertime."

"Okay, count me in," Richie said.

It was after five o'clock now and the beach was starting to thin out as people left to return home for dinner. The sun ducked briefly behind a cloud in the distance and Richie felt a momentary chill in the air. He stood there for a second, staring off into space and losing himself in his thoughts. He felt uneasy again but he wasn't quite sure why. Then he remembered.

A seagull flew by and called to him, snapping him out of his reverie. He looked up. The girls had already dressed and were gathering up the rest of their things, preparing for the walk back to the parking lot. He quickly put on his shirt and shorts and then helped them fold up the blanket.

They all started walking up the path towards the Sugar Shack. Eddie's car was parked next to it, in the lot. He and Mickey strolled ahead of Richie and the girls and were talking animatedly about the price of fireworks, what kind and how many they should try to purchase on Wednesday. Frankie, Danny and the other kids Richie had met earlier had already gone home. He and Nancy walked together, with Pat and Sally directly behind them.

In the parking lot, they made plans to meet later that evening for a ride to Hampton Bays. Mickey and Eddie knew of a place there where they could ride go-karts, an activity, they assured Richie, that was more fun than anything. Since he had never been on a go-kart in his life, he readily agreed.

After walking Nancy to her house, Richie turned and headed back the other way. He reached the corner and turned left on Noyac Road. Again, he lost himself in thought. It seemed as if his life had suddenly turned complicated. At least it appeared that way.

He went over a few things in his mind. Meeting Nancy had been wonderful; that, he was sure of. Mickey's problem, on the other hand, had suddenly become his problem and that was where the complication in his life seemed to begin. But what could he do about it?

His face felt sunburned and he thought he'd better use suntan oil the next time he went to the beach. He touched it gingerly. He hoped his nose didn't start to peel. He wanted to make sure he looked his best for Nancy and having a red, skin-peeling nose was no way to accomplish that.

On the other hand, he knew it wouldn't bother him if Nancy's face was sunburned and her nose peeling. Not in the least. Nothing could mar the beauty of her features. God, she was beautiful, he thought. He touched his face again. It probably wouldn't bother her either.

Back to Mickey. Lying to the police for Mickey was an idea

that had frightened him at first but after talking with Diane, it had become less of a problem. It certainly didn't seem to bother her or Mickey. They didn't have difficulty with it. Maybe he needed to toughen up and not be such a sissy about it.

He began to feel reassured. After all, they were all in it together, weren't they? Mickey, Diane and now, himself. Diane had told him not to worry, so he wouldn't. The police probably wouldn't even ask him anything, she had said. Hopefully, that was true.

Even though he wished he hadn't told Mickey he'd lie for him, he realized he had promised him and he wasn't going back on his word now. And that was that. He'd had the opportunity to back out during his walk with Diane, but somehow she had convinced him not to. So he wouldn't. Heck, what were friends for, anyway? The memory of Diane's perfume and the way she had felt in his arms came flooding back to him. He remembered the way her lips had felt on his, moist and exciting. There was definitely something about her that attracted him, he admitted to himself.

As he walked along Noyac Road, he daydreamed. He and Diane were dancing at the Sugar Shack. They were alone on the dance floor and the song playing on the juke box was Earth Angel. Diane was holding him tightly and kissing him, while her fingers twirled their way through his hair.

Nancy walked in and saw them. "You'll have to choose between us," she said.

Richie came out of his fantasy and saw that he was almost at the cabin. This is crazy, he thought. I love Nancy and I choose her, no question about it. Diane is only a kid. She's fifteen years old! Not only that, she's Mickey's sister. "I'm not getting involved with her," he said aloud.

A dark green sedan was parked across the street from the cabin. Sitting in it were two men. As Richie glanced briefly over at the car, a trickle of sweat started to work its way down under his armpit, causing a tickling feeling on his skin underneath his shirt.

As he was about to turn up the walkway to his front door, a voice called out, "Richard Donnelly?"

Thirteen

Richie stopped and looked over at the sedan. The two men in it got out and approached him. As they crossed the street, he knew instinctively that they were police officers.

The taller of the two had his identification folder in his hand and Richie could clearly see the gold badge it contained. "Are you Richard Donnelly?"

"Uh, yes, I am." Richie immediately felt weak in the knees.

"I'm Detective Shaunessy and this is my partner, Detective Robbins." He put his identification in the inside pocket of his jacket and buttoned it. Richie caught a glimpse of his gun which was stuffed into a holster and clipped to the belt on his right hip.

"We're with the Southampton Police Department," Shaunessy said. "Mind if we talk to you?"

Before Richie could answer, the burly one, Robbins, who was shorter than Shaunessy by several inches, stepped forward. He had dark, curly hair, bushy eyebrows and a scowl on his face. He spoke brusquely. "Your parents at home?"

Richie, suddenly ill-at-ease, took a step backward before answering. "No, my parents went to the city today. I was just on my way home from the beach."

He glanced up at the two detectives. The one calling himself Shaunessy had red hair and freckles. His face seemed kinder and he spoke more softly than Robbins.

"Richard, we'd like to talk to you about a burglary that occurred last week in Southampton. What do you know about it?"

"Why, I, uh..., I don't know anything about it," Richie stammered. His face began to twitch at a spot just below his right eye and he moved his hand up to cover it.

"Didn't your friend tell you all about it?" Robbins asked accusingly.

"Who? What do you mean? I don't understand." Richie was frightened now and he had a sinking feeling in the pit of his stomach. He reached out and held on to the fence railing to steady himself.

"Bernie, take it easy on the lad, will you?" Shaunessy stepped forward. "Richard, can we talk inside your house?" He placed his hand on Richie's shoulder and gently turned him around to face the cabin. "This is a serious matter and we'd like you to cooperate with us, all right? Let's just go inside and see if we can straighten it out. It won't take long."

Richie nodded. "Sure." He led them up the walkway to the front door. After unlocking it, they all went inside and sat down on the porch. He looked up anxiously at the two detectives.

Shaunessy spoke first. "Richard, do you know a boy named Mickey McKee?"

"Yes, I, uh..., sure. He's a friend of mine." Richie licked his lips nervously.

"And how long have you known him?" Shaunessy leaned forward with his hands resting on his knees. He eyed Richie closely.

"I just met him last week, the day we arrived here. He delivered groceries to the cabin."

"So you haven't known him long?" Robbins asked.

"No. I, uh..., we got here last Friday and I met him then." Richie folded his hands together and placed them on his lap.

Robbins stood up suddenly. "He tell you what he did with the stuff?" he asked loudly. He bent over and stuck his face a few inches from Richie's, one bushy eyebrow raised.

Richie instinctively drew back in his chair. He looked away from Robbins and turned to Shaunessy. "What stuff?" he asked. His eyes were wide with fear and he avoided Robbins' stare.

"Bernie, please, if you don't mind," Shaunessy cut in. He began speaking slowly and deliberately in a softer voice. "Richard, we have reason to believe your friend was involved in a house burglary over in Southampton last week and we need your help. We'd like to clear it up as soon as possible, so anything you can tell us will be greatly appreciated."

"But I don't know anything about it! Mickey was with me Saturday night," Richie blurted.

Robbins pointed his finger at Richie. "Who the hell said anything about Saturday night, sonny? We never mentioned anything about Saturday night! We said it happened last week!" Robbins turned away from him and then suddenly whirled back around.

"You'd better come clean with us, kid! Tell us what that punk friend of yours did with the loot, you understand me?"

Richie started trembling and moved farther back in his chair, trying to get away from Robbins and his tirade. He was almost frozen now by fear and anxiety.

"What loot? I don't know what you're talking about!" Richie's eyes filled with tears and he almost started to cry. He rubbed at them anxiously with his fingers, trying desperately to compose himself.

"All right, Bernie, that's enough," Shaunessy said firmly. "Let me handle this." He stood up and took Robbins by the arm, steering him toward the screened door. "Go "outside and have a cigarette. Let me continue with this, okay? There's no need to raise our voices."

Robbins gave him a scowl and then looked past him at Richie. "Jack, just give me a minute alone with this kid and I'll get the truth out of him!" He moved a step closer to Richie and made a motion as if to grab him. Richie almost wet his pants.

Shaunessy held him back. "That won't be necessary, Bernie," he said soothingly. He tightened his grip on Robbins' arm. "Take a break, will ya? You've had a rough day. Let me handle this, okay?" He eased him closer to the door.

"All right, you handle it!" Robbins pushed open the door with his shoulder and stepped outside. He stood on the top step for a moment, then turned around and glared in through the screen at Richie.

He slowly took out a pack of cigarettes and put one in his mouth. It dangled from his lips and bounced up and down as he spoke. "But he better not lie about it, that's all I have to say!"

"Don't worry, he won't." Shaunessy waited by the door until the other detective walked across the street to the car, then turned back to Richie.

"Richard, I have to apologize for my partner's behavior. He's been under a lot of pressure lately but that's no excuse for him to be rude. We just want to get at the truth, here. You can understand that, can't you?"

Shaunessy sat back down. He reached into the side pocket of his jacket and pulled out a pack of chewing gum, took a piece for himself and offered the pack to Richie. "Gum?"

Richie shook his head. "No, thanks."

The detective continued. "Richard, I just want to ask you a few questions and I hope you answer them truthfully. He unwrapped the gum and stuffed it into his mouth. His words were slightly muffled as he chewed. "Just a few questions and then we'll be on our way, okay?"

Richie nodded.

"Now, where were you on Saturday evening around eight o'clock?"

Richie's heart pounded and he was barely able to speak. "I was at the Sugar Shack," he said nervously.

"The Sugar Shack?"

"Yeah. It's a place over on Beach Road where all the kids hang out. They sell hot dogs and soda and stuff."

"I see. Was anybody with you?"

"Well, I saw Frank Wittey when I got there. He was eating a hamburger - no, a hot dog, at the counter when I walked in. I think it was around eight o'clock." Richie quickly glanced at the detective, then looked down at his sneakers. "Yeah, a hot dog," he added.

Detective Shaunessy removed a small notebook from his breast pocket and started jotting down the information. "Did you talk to him?"

"I asked him if he had seen Mickey because I was supposed to meet him there."

"And Mickey wasn't there?" Shaunessy eyed him closely.

"Well, not right away. He...," Richie stopped to think. He was worried now. The other detective, Robbins, had frightened him so much that all he wanted to do now was tell the truth. He didn't want to get in trouble over this. He could picture Robbins' face. The detective was snarling at him and pointing his finger at him accusingly.

Robbins. The name rang a bell. Where had he heard it? Oh, yeah, Robbins was the name of the island Eddie had taken them to on his boat yesterday. He wondered if the island had been named for the detective or if it was somebody else's family name. He'd have to ask Mickey about it.

He didn't like Detective Robbins. He had no right to yell at me, he thought. Plus, he called Mickey a punk. Mickey's no punk. He's a good guy and he's my friend.

"Richard?" Shaunessy was tapping the eraser end his pencil on his front teeth. "Was Mickey there or not?"

"What? Oh." Richie made his decision. He would protect Mickey from Robbins. "He came in later, around eight-fifteen, eight-twenty." He brushed his hair away from his eyes and looked up confidently at the soft-spoken detective. There. He'd said it. It was done. He had lied for his friend. The heck with Robbins, he thought. He's a creep! He shouldn't have yelled at me like that! I'm not a little kid! I have to protect Mickey! He suddenly felt better.

"Was anyone else with him?" Shaunessy asked.

"Um, let's see..., yeah, he was with his sister, Diane."

Richie told Detective Shaunessy the story they had concocted about being at the Sugar Shack for a while and then ending up at the beach at eleven o'clock. As he told it, it seemed real to him, just as it had been in his dream.

We were there, he repeated to himself several times, reinforcing the lie in his mind. The three of us. Me, Mickey and Diane. I danced with Diane at the Sugar Shack and she kissed me at the beach. No, wait. That happened today. She kissed me today at the beach. He could still smell her perfume.

"Okay, Richard." Shaunessy's voice snapped Richie back to the present. "Your story checks out with what we already know. We'll talk to Frank Wittey and if he remembers seeing you there we won't have to bother you again."

The detective rose from the chair. "One more thing, which my partner has already brought up. How did you know the burglary took place on Saturday night?"

Richie stroked his chin nervously. "Mickey told me he lost his wallet over in Southampton last week and that you questioned him about a burglary that happened on Saturday night, that's all."

"Oh, I see." Shaunessy looked at him for a moment and then extended his hand. "Well, sorry to have bothered you, Richard. If we need to talk to you again, we know where to reach you."

Richie shook the detective's hand which dwarfed his own. "How come you thought Mickey did it?" he asked with a puzzled expression on his face. "Just because he lost his wallet over there?"

"He's been in trouble before, son," Shaunessy said tightly. "I just hope you realize what kind of person you're associating with, because you seem like a nice, clean-cut kid to me."

"Hey, Mickey's a good guy," Richie protested. "I know I just met him a couple of days ago and everything, but I'm sure Mickey wouldn't do anything like that. What..., ah, what kind of trouble was he in?"

Shaunessy hesitated before answering. "That information is normally confidential but I think I'll make an exception in this case. Like I said, you seem like a nice kid, Richard. I wouldn't want to see you get into any trouble because of the company you're keeping.

"McKee was expelled from Sag Harbor High School last year for stealing money from the principal's office. He spent six months at Lincoln Hall. That's a reform school, upstate." Richie had heard of it. Shaunessy stretched his six-foot frame, then relaxed. "Just be aware of the kind of people you associate with, Richard," he reiterated. "I want to help you. That's the only reason I'm telling you this."

Richie was stunned and didn't reply. He accompanied the detective outside and they stood in front of the cabin. He glanced across the street at the car but couldn't see inside.

Shaunessy saw where he was looking and said, "Once again, I apologize for my partner. He gets a little excited sometimes."

A little? Richie thought. "Oh, that's okay," he said.

He stayed there and watched the detective walk across the street to the car. Shaunessy opened the door and entered the vehicle. Richie went back inside and peeked out through the window.

He could see the two detectives sitting in the front seat, talking. Cigarette smoke wafted out through the window on the passenger side and after several minutes, Shaunessy started the car and pulled away from the side of the road. Richie watched until it was no longer in sight.

He went into the kitchen and poured himself a glass of water. His mouth was dry and his hands were shaking as he brought the glass to his lips. He had trouble swallowing it at first, but finally managed to get the water down. "Oh, God!" he said aloud.

He wandered aimlessly around the cabin for a while, opening closet doors and noticing where everything was kept. He was actually seeing the cabin for the first time. He hadn't spent much time there except to eat and sleep. Most of his time in Sea Shell Harbor had been spent outdoors with his new friends.

He went outside through the rear kitchen door. There was a small yard surrounded by five-foot tall forsythia bushes and off to one side, a small cement patio with a picnic table in the center. He saw that the grass needed cutting and he decided he'd mow the lawn tomorrow and surprise his parents.

His parents! They'd be home any minute! The thought of them coming home suddenly made him uneasy and he went back inside the cabin to his room and laid down on the bed. He fell asleep a few minutes later.

Fourteen

"**I** was scared out of my wits!" Richie said, looking across the table at Mickey. "I thought one of cops was going to beat me up!"

They were sitting in the rear of the Sugar Shack next to the juke box, sipping cokes. Richie was telling Mickey about the detectives' earlier visit. He had called Mickey at home after his impromptu nap and they had made plans to meet right after dinner.

The nap had managed to put a bit of distance between the questioning by the detectives and his parents' arrival home, so that he'd been relaxed enough to act normally by the time they'd returned from the city. Dinner had been a pleasant and uneventful affair and the detectives' visit had seemed like just another dream.

Richie felt a lot happier now than he had earlier. He went to the juke box, popped a nickel in and made a selection. The music to 'Why Do Fools Fall In Love' came up just as he returned to the table and sat down.

"One of the cops was okay," Richie continued, "but the other one was a real creep. The nice one made the other cop wait outside while he questioned me. I told him exactly what you told me to say." Richie looked across the table at Mickey for approval.

Mickey took a sip from his glass. "Mutt and Jeff act."

"What?"

"Mutt and Jeff act," Mickey repeated. "They pulled a Mutt and Jeff act on you, Rich."

"What do you mean?"

Mickey reached for the pack of cigarettes lying on the table, took one out and lit it. He took a deep drag and let the smoke out, blowing smoke rings into the air. "You know, good cop, bad cop. It's a routine they do." He laughed.

"I don't follow you," Richie said.

"It's simple. One cop plays the good cop and the other one the bad cop. The first one pretends to be angry and makes you think he's going to hit you, then the other cop pulls him away and tells him to go in the other room. Or, in this case, outside." Mickey took another drag from his cigarette and blew more smoke rings.

"And then, the one who's playing the good cop questions you and you start to feel like the good guy is your long lost buddy." He gave Richie a sour look. "You end up spilling your guts," he said sarcastically. "They do it all the time."

"Well, I'll be darned," Richie slammed his glass against the table. "You mean that's what they did to me?" He had finished his coke and now he fished out a piece of ice from the bottom of his glass and started to chew on it. "Well it didn't work. All it did was make me angry enough to lie to them with no trouble." Richie laughed now. "I think the joke is on them, instead."

"You mean you never heard of that ruse?" Mickey snuffed out his cigarette in the ashtray. He looked amused. "Boy, Richie, for a city kid you sure got a lot to learn. All cops are flim flam artists."

"Guess so," Richie agreed.

"So what else did they say?" Mickey leaned back in his chair and clasped his hands behind his head.

Richie pondered whether or not to tell Mickey what Shaunessy had said about him getting into trouble and being sent to reform school. He decided against it. Somehow, he felt that telling him would betray a confidence between himself and Shaunessy.

Instead he said, "The red-headed one said they're gonna talk to Frank Wittey and see if he remembers seeing me here on Saturday night. Said they probably won't have to bother me again."

"Was Frank here Saturday night?"

"Yeah, I saw him when I first got here but I think he left right after that. I don't remember seeing him later on." Richie finished chewing the ice and fished out another piece from his glass.

"Then we're home free, Rich," Mickey said. His face lit up and he gave Richie a big smile. "Frank won't know that I wasn't here at all if he left early. He saw you, though?"

"Yeah."

"Perfect. He'll tell the cops he saw you, so that means you were here like you said. Maybe he'll even tell them he saw me, too. I mean, he sees me here practically every night anyway, and Frank isn't exactly the smartest guy in the world, you know?"

"I thought he was very witty," Richie said jokingly.

"Yeah, right, witty but not too bright," Mickey said, tapping the side of his head. "And you and Diane both told them you were with me, so that means I was here, too! We have it covered, Rich." He chuckled.

"I guess we do," Richie said, pleased by the way things were shaping up. With Mickey's assurances, he was feeling much more confident now and it felt good.

Mickey unclasped his hands and placed them on the table, then leaned forward. "Look, Richie, I really appreciate what you did for me today. I won't forget it, either. You're a good friend and friends have to stick together."

Richie nodded.

"I didn't want to get you involved but I knew the cops would never believe I was home sleeping that night, even though I was." He lit another cigarette. "It's better this way. All you had to do was tell them a little white lie and now everything's cool. I'm in the clear."

"You think so, Mick?" Richie asked hopefully.

"I know so. Don't worry about it, Rich, it's guaranteed." Mickey played a drum roll on the formica table top with his fingers. "Hey, what time is Eddie picking us up?"

"He said around eight." Richie looked at his watch. "It's almost eight, now. He's picking Sally up first, then meeting us here, then we'll go and pick up Pat and Nancy at Pat's house."

"Good. Let's go outside and wait for them."

They left the Sugar Shack and walked outside to the parking

lot. Mickey put a muscular arm around Richie's shoulder as they walked.

"You know, Rich, Diane really likes you. She was talking about you tonight all during dinner. You ought to take her out one of these nights. I think the two of you would really hit it off. What do you say?"

Richie stopped walking. "Gee, Mickey, I'm kind of going out with Nancy right now. In fact, I was planning on asking her to go steady with me tonight."

They hoisted themselves up and sat on the top rung of the fence which separated the parking lot from the beach access and Richie looked out over the expanse of sand towards the water.

The evening air was cool and mild with little humidity, and the sky had just turned a mixture of blue and indigo, pulsing and shimmering with the approaching darkness. A narrow band of gold and red, with intermittent streaks of purple, stretched across the lower part of the horizon, just above the distant water.

The deck outside the Sugar Shack was starting to come alive with teenagers, as if the salty night air and changing sky had suddenly caused them to become animated. Bursts of laugher and joyful dialogue, mixed with rock and roll music from the juke box inside, drifted across the lot and blended in with the nautical sounds from the bay. All of it eventually found a path to his senses.

He scanned the evening sky. An Eastern Airlines constellation was cruising silently overhead, heading in from the south and the Atlantic Ocean. It made a left turn above him, probably on its way to Idlewild Airport, he guessed. He looked up and saw the Eastern logo, a contemporary bird on the outermost of its triple tail configuration. As it cruised away, the sound of its four engines reached down and lulled him into a feeling of peace and security. He felt at ease with himself and the world.

"Are you sure you want to get serious so soon?" Mickey asked. "Play the field, man. You'll have lots more fun that way." Mickey took a comb from the back pocket of his jeans and ran it through his dark hair. "Diane don't care if you date other girls. She just wants you to take her out once in a while, that's all."

"I don't know, Mickey. We'll see."

"Think about it, Rich." Mickey put the comb back in his pocket.

"I will."

Eddie and Sally drove up a few minutes later. Mickey and Richie climbed into the back seat and Eddie drove off in the direction of Noyac Road.

Pat lived only a few blocks from Nancy. The girls were waiting outside as Eddie pulled up and he got out of the car like a gentleman and opened the door for them.

When everyone was safely seated in the car, Eddie peeled out with a squeal of the tires and headed south on Scuttlebutt Road. When they reached Sunrise Highway, he turned right and headed west to Hampton Bays, about a twenty minute drive.

They spent the rest of the evening there, racing each other around the go-kart track and then stopping at a local diner for ice cream.

At eleven o'clock, Richie and Nancy were sitting in front of her house, kissing passionately.

"Will you go steady with me, Nancy?" Richie asked between kisses.

"Only if you promise you'll kiss me like this every night," she answered sweetly.

From his pocket, he produced an inexpensive gold-plated ring he had picked up at a drugstore in Hampton Bays earlier that evening. He placed it on the third finger of her left hand. "As soon as I get my senior class ring, I'll give it to you," he told her.

"Oh, Richie, it's beautiful." She kissed him tenderly, then more urgently. "I love you, Richie," she said.

"I love you, too, Nancy," he replied. "I really do."

Fifteen

It rained all day Tuesday. The beach was deserted and most people seemed to be staying indoors. The wind blew a steady torrent of rain in from the water as Richie made his way along Beach Road to the Sugar Shack. He was supposed to meet the others there at eleven o'clock and it was almost that time now.

He shifted the umbrella that he had found in one of the closets in the cabin to his left, trying desperately to shield himself from the sideways downpour caused by the wind, but he was still getting soaked.

A black convertible, tires whistling on the wet pavement and traveling just a bit too fast for the road conditions, came hurtling towards him from the opposite direction. Richie could make out two figures sitting in the front seat.

Eddie's car, top up to protect it from the weather, slowed down and, skidding slightly, turned into the parking lot directly in front of him. Eddie parked in one of the spots at the rear, then he and Mickey exited and began to run towards the building in an effort to escape from the rain. Mickey saw him and waved. "Hurry up, Richie!"

Richie caught up to them just as they reached the door of the Sugar Shack. Eddie gave him a friendly grin and held the door open for him. "Some beautiful weather we're having, huh, Richie?"

Richie's hair was drenched and hanging down over his eyes. He folded the umbrella and walked in ahead of Eddie. "Unbelievable," Richie said, brushing himself off.

Eddie pointed to the umbrella. "You sure that thing is working, Rich? You're soaking wet, my friend."

"Not too well, I guess," Richie agreed. Eddie's hair he noticed, was still perfectly in place.

The three boys walked in and headed for the back room. Richie took a detour to the men's room to dry his hair and recomb it before joining the others. Mickey came in behind him.

Richie used half a package of towels to dry his hair before he was satisfied, then stood in front of the mirror combing it and trying to get it just right while Mickey busied himself in one of the stalls behind him.

"So did you ask her, Rich?" Mickey called out from inside the stall.

Richie looked at his reflection in the mirror and smiled. "Yup," he answered. He gently pulled at the front of his hair with his fingers and when it was just the way he wanted it, smiled again. "Last night, in front of her house."

Mickey walked over and stood at the mirror next to him. He rinsed his hands and then started on his own hair. "I don't know, Richie," he said with mock seriousness. "Now you're gonna be tied up with one girl for the rest of the summer. You sure that's what you wanna do?"

Richie turned and faced Mickey. "Oh, yeah, Mick. I'm sure." He put his comb back in his pocket and smoothed out the collar of his shirt. "I never met anyone like Nancy," he said cheerfully. "I may even want to marry her some day."

"Marry her? Oh, no, Richie's hooked!" Mickey looked at his own reflection in the mirror, a horrified expression on his face. "Did y'all hear that, Mickey?" he said with an exaggerated southern drawl. "Richie's done gone went and fell in love!"

He moved over and put his arm around Richie's shoulder. "I'm just joking, Rich," he said in his normal voice. "Nancy's a nice girl and you're a lucky guy."

"Thanks, Mickey," Richie said appreciatively.

They finished up in the bathroom and headed for the back room to join the others.

"Maybe I should ask Pat to go steady with me," Mickey said just before they reached the table.

"Now, that's not such a bad idea," Richie agreed. "If Eddie asks Sally to go steady, too, then we can all hang out together all summer. It'll be fun."

"Maybe." Mickey said.

Nancy, Pat, Sally and Eddie were already sitting at a table in the back. Mickey and Richie joined them and they ordered cheeseburgers, french fries and cokes for lunch. Richie and Nancy left the table and walked over to the juke box. They stood in front of it holding hands while they picked out several selections. When the food came, they went back to the table and listened to music while they ate their lunch.

For a rainy day, it was going as well as any other, Richie thought, as he sat there eating his cheeseburger. Of course, he was with his steady girl and his new friends and right at this moment, he didn't care if the sun ever shined again.

It was summer, school was out, and he was on vacation in one of the nicest places in all of New York, Sea Shell Harbor. No matter what happened after today, he knew he would always remember this one, magical moment. He sat there and savored it.

After about an hour, Eddie drove them over to the Noyac Teen Center, down the road from Treadway's and past the firehouse. They spent the afternoon there playing ping pong and knock hockey.

Some of the other kids Richie had met at the beach were also there, including Danny Shaw and Frank Wittey. Danny, as it turned out, was a whiz at ping pong and he beat everyone he played. After winning each and every game he played, he would snicker across the table at his opponent and say, "Yuk, yuk, yuk."

At one point during the afternoon, Richie noticed Mickey and Frank Wittey sitting alone in a corner. Mickey was talking animatedly and using his hands to gesture while Frank nodded his head up and down as Mickey talked. He wondered what it was they were discussing but decided it was none of his business. He wouldn't pry.

At four o'clock, they decided to leave and go home.

Eddie gave them all a ride to their front doors since the storm seemed to have gotten worse. The wind had picked up and the rain came beating down. It hit the ground in wide, watery sheets and reduced the visibility through the car's windshield until it was almost nonexistent.

Richie thought of asking Nancy if she wanted to come over to his house that evening, but the girls had already made plans for a slumber party at Pat's house. They wouldn't be seeing the boys until the next evening when they returned from their fireworks acquisition expedition. It seemed like a good idea, since the weather was terrible anyway.

They dropped the girls off first, then Eddie backtracked and drove Richie home.

"We'll pick you up at ten o'clock on the corner, Rich," Mickey said as Richie got out of the car. "Don't be late."

"I won't." Richie made a dash for his door to avoid the rain, now coming down in buckets.

After dinner, Richie and his parents spent the rest of the evening playing cards, then he decided to go to bed. He first secured permission from them for the ride to the city with Mickey and Eddie the next day but had carefully avoided any mention of buying fireworks.

At ten the next morning, Richie was standing at the corner of Noyac Road and Chestnut Street, waiting for his ride. It had rained again earlier and the sky was still overcast with a slight drizzle in the air.

He looked at his watch. It was almost ten-fifteen. They were late. A few minutes later, a beat-up, green Chevy coupe pulled over to the side of the road. Mickey was sitting in the front passenger seat.

"Hop in, Rich," he said, leaning out the window.

Next to him, sitting behind the wheel in the driver's seat, was a young man Richie had never seen before. Richie gave Mickey a puzzled look as he climbed into the back seat. He was even more surprised when he looked and saw Diane sitting there.

"Hi, handsome," she said.

"Oh, hello, Diane," he said awkwardly. "How are you?"

The man in the driver's seat appeared to be in his early twenties. His brown hair was closely cropped in a crew cut and he had a long, pointy nose. He needed a shave. Richie wondered who he was.

"Where's Eddie, Mickey?" Richie asked. "I thought he was driving us."

Mickey turned around in his seat and looked back at Richie and Diane. A toothpick was sticking out of the corner of his mouth.

"He couldn't make it this morning. Something came up at the last minute." He removed the toothpick and held it in his fingers. "Charlie said he'd take us instead. Oh, I almost forgot," Mickey said, "this is Charlie McGee. Charlie, Richie Donnelly."

Charlie turned and extended his hand. He smiled, revealing a set of yellow, crooked teeth. "How ya doin', Richie?" He had a high-pitched voice. "Glad to meecha."

Richie shook his hand. "Me, too." Their names rhyme, he thought. Mickey McKee and Charlie McGee. I wonder where Mickey met this guy? He gave Charlie a weak smile in return. "You from Sea Shell Harbor?"

"Nah. Bridgehampton. I used to go to school with Mickey." Charlie reached between his legs and brought up a can of beer. He took a sip. "I was a couple of years ahead of him, though. He was only a freshman and I was already a junior."

Richie noticed that all three had cans of beer and there were already several empties on the floor of the car. Diane reached into a bag at her feet and brought out another. She offered it to Richie.

"Want a beer, Richie?"

Richie held up his hand and shook his head. "Oh, not right now, Diane, thanks. I just had breakfast."

"Okay, doll." She smiled sweetly at him. "Be a party pooper. I'm having my breakfast right now." She took a big slug of her beer and put the other unopened can back in the bag.

"Oh, no, it's not that," Richie said defensively. "I'll have one a little later, maybe."

"I'll hold you to that, Richie," she said.

Charlie eased the car out onto Noyac Road. "Gimme another

one, Diane," he said over his shoulder. He belched loudly and tossed the empty can into the back without looking. "S'cuse me."

Richie caught the can with his left hand and put it on the floor. He gave Charlie a rueful look but said nothing. Diane handed Richie a can from the bag and he passed it up to Charlie.

"Charlie just happened to come by my house this morning, Rich," Mickey said, turning to look at him. "So when Eddie called and said he couldn't make it, Charlie agreed to drive us."

"That's cool," Richie said.

"We won't have to go all the way into the city, either," Mickey continued. "He's got friends in Hempstead who he says can fix us up with some good fireworks, right, Charlie?"

"Yeah, man, anything you want. Rockets, Roman candles, cherry bombs, stuff like that. Good prices, too." Charlie grinned at Richie through the rear view mirror. "How much you guys wanna spend? Twenty? Thirty?"

"Gee, I don't know," Richie said. "I've only got about five dollars with me."

"Five bucks? Ha!" Charlie snickered. He made a razzing sound with his lips. "Whaddaya think you'll get for five bucks? Couple of lady fingers, maybe. Maybe even a box of sparklers, if you're lucky." He laughed. "Hey, Mickey, your friend's a real big spender, ain't he?"

Richie felt his face flush and he had a sudden urge to tell Charlie to stop the car and let him out. He didn't need any aggravation from someone he'd just met, not when he'd rather be spending the day with Nancy, anyway. He decided he didn't like Charlie very much and he certainly didn't like being made fun of in front of Mickey and Diane. Why is Mickey with this loser? he wondered.

"Shut up, Charlie!" Mickey said easily. "Don't mind him, Rich," he said to Richie. "He's just kidding around with you." Mickey gave Charlie a little more than a playful punch in the arm. "Right, Charlie?"

"Yeah, yeah," Charlie said. "Just foolin' around. Don't mind me. Actually, five bucks'll get ya a pretty good assortment of stuff, Richie."

They reached Sunrise Highway and Charlie made a right turn. He pulled into the first gas station he came to. "Gotta get gas," he said. "You got money, Mickey? Put a couple of bucks in, will ya? That'll cover it. Got to hit the bathroom."

The three boys left the car and Diane remained inside. While Charlie sauntered over to the restroom located around the other side of the station, Mickey and Richie leaned against the car and waited for the attendant to finish up with another customer.

Mickey pointed to the gas prices posted on a large sign at the edge of the station, near the road. "Twenty five cents a gallon?" he complained to Richie. "That's what they mean by highway robbery. Boy, I'm telling you...,"

"I wish Eddie had come with us instead of this guy, Mickey," Richie said, interrupting him. He folded his arms in front of him and watched the cars going by on the road. "Where did you say you know him from? High school?"

Mickey took out a pack of cigarettes and put one to his lips, then realizing where he was, refrained from lighting it. "Yeah, Sag Harbor High. Charlie's all right, Rich, he's...,"

"You sure he's cool, Mickey?" Richie said, interrupting him again. "How old is he, anyway? Don't you think...,"

Mickey started to laugh and turned to face him. "Don't worry, Rich, he's okay. Charlie just takes a little getting used to, that's all. Yeah, he's older than me. He's twenty or twenty-one but he acts younger."

"He acts like a little kid, if you ask me," Richie said indignantly.

"Relax and have a beer, will you, Rich? We'll have a good time today. Make the best of it."

The attendant came over and Mickey handed him two dollars. "Two bucks, please," he told him. "Besides," he continued, "if he hadn't come over this morning, we wouldn't've had any way to pick up the fireworks. We would've been screwed for the fourth."

"I guess you're right," Richie reluctantly agreed. "He just better lay off me, that's all."

"Don't worry, he will. If he don't," Mickey held up a fist, "I'll pop him one."

He grinned at Richie, then leaned in the car window. "Diane, give Richie a beer, will you?" He took the beer from her and handed it to Richie. "C'mon, Richie, drink this and relax a little, will you? Let's have some fun today!"

Richie took the beer and climbed back into the car with it. Diane handed him a can opener. What the heck, he thought, as he punched two holes in the top of the can. "No sense in being a party pooper, right, Diane?" He looked at her and smiled.

"Way to go, Richie." She held her can of beer next to his. "A toast. Here's to good times and silent mimes," she said with a giggle.

"Cheers." He took a sip. The beer was ice cold and had a bitter taste. He pretended to like it. "Good beer," he said.

The attendant finished pumping the gas just as Charlie returned from the rest room. He and Mickey got back in the car. "Let's hit the road," Charlie said as he cranked the engine. "Diane, pass up a couple more beers."

Mickey reached over and took the beers from her, then opened them with the can opener that was dangling from a string attached to the dashboard. He handed one to Charlie and took a sip from the other one.

Charlie drank greedily from the can, emptying half of it in three large gulps. He belched again loudly. "Ah, we're off." He put the car in gear and pulled out onto Sunrise Highway.

Richie relaxed in his seat and drank the beer. Glancing at Diane, he wished it was Nancy sitting next to him and not her. He realized that if he had known the day was going to start out like this, he never would have agreed to go, but, he figured, he might as well make the best of it. He took another sip.

The ride to Hempstead took just under two hours. Surprisingly, Charlie was a careful driver. He kept the car under the speed limit and didn't make any unnecessary lane changes. At the Hempstead exit, he left the Southern State Parkway and headed north on Uniondale Avenue.

Richie finished his second can of beer and Diane immediately handed him another one before he even had a chance to get rid of the empty can. He accepted it and popped two holes in the can. "Thanks, Diane," he said thickly.

His face felt a little fuzzy and there was a warm glow spreading out from his stomach to the rest of his body. He was starting to feel a little giddy and a lot more relaxed.

"How are you doing, Richie?" Diane asked sweetly.

"Pretty good, Dee Dee, pretty good." Richie laughed out loud, amused by his modification of her name. "Oops, I'm sorry, I meant to say Diane." He turned to her and grinned foolishly.

"That's all right, sweetie, you can call me Dee Dee." She moved closer to him and touched his arm. "I like Dee Dee."

He held up his can in a toast. "To Dee Dee," he said, then took a big slug from the can. "This is really good beer, you know, Diane? I mean, Dee Dee."

In Hempstead, Charlie pulled up in front of a Chinese laundry and backed into a parking space. They were on a side street just off Fulton Avenue, the main thoroughfare which ran the entire length of the village. It was not in the better section of town.

Charlie turned off the ignition and turned to Mickey. "Okay, you guys decided on what you want me to buy?"

Richie started to reach into his pocket for his money but Mickey held up his hand. "Don't worry about it, Rich. This one's on me." He handed Charlie a wad of bills. "Get whatever you can with this," he told him. "Make sure you get plenty of rockets and cherry bombs."

Charlie counted the money. "Wow! There's fifty bucks here! What the hell did you do, Mickey, rob a bank?" He whistled. "I'll get you the whole damned fireworks factory with this much!" He opened the car door and climbed out, then leaned in the window. "You guys wait here. I'll be back in a little while."

They watched him walk down to the end of the street and turn the corner. "Mickey, what are you doing?" Richie leaned forward and held on to the back of Mickey's seat. "I can't let you pay for everything. Take the five."

Mickey turned and smiled broadly. "Don't worry about it, Rich. I'm flush."

"Where'd you get the money, Mickey?" Diane asked.

"I've been saving it from my job," he answered. "This year, we're gonna have a great Fourth of July." He snapped his fingers. "Right?"

"Yeah, but fifty bucks is a lot of money," she continued. "You sure you want to spend that much?"

"Yeah, I'm sure," he said. "I'm tired of always worrying about money all the time. This year's gonna be different."

"You know you're supposed to give mom some money," she said.

Mickey raised his beer and took a sip. "I'm not giving her any more money, Diane." He sounded annoyed. "All she does is buy booze with it. No, this year, we're gonna celebrate in style."

He drained the last of his beer and crumpled up the can. "I got the money, so quit worrying about it, will ya?" He handed Diane the crumpled beer can. "Give me another one, Dee."

Diane reached into the bag and brought up a can. "This is the last one. We'll have to pick up some more before we head back."

"You feel like drinking some more beer, Rich?" Mickey asked.

Richie was halfway through his third beer and was beginning to feel tipsy. The others, who had consumed several more than he had, showed little if any, effects. "Sure," he said easily. He was beginning to loosen up and enjoy himself.

"Okay," Mickey said. "I'll walk back to that deli we passed and pick up some more. You two wait here in case Charlie comes back before I do."

"Roger," Diane said.

When Mickey was out of sight, Richie turned to Diane.

"You think they'll sell it to him?"

"Why not?" she replied. "He looks old enough. Mickey'll be eighteen next month, anyway, so it's no big deal." She reached into her handbag and took out her lipstick, uncapped it and lightly dabbed her lips. "That's one thing I like about living in New York. The drinking age is only eighteen. Most other places, it's twenty-one. Least it is in Jersey and Connecticut."

"Sure, but you're only fifteen," he teased.

"That's true, but most of the guys I go out with are eighteen or older, so getting beer isn't much of a problem for me." She looked at herself in the mirror and smacked her lips. Satisfied, she put the lipstick back in her bag, turned to him and smiled. "Got the picture now, Richie-poo?"

"I do." Richie finished the beer he had been nursing and reached past Diane to throw it into the bag with the rest of the empty cans. Diane brought her hand up to take the can from him and accidentally knocked it out of his hand. "Oops." she said.

They both laughed and simultaneously bent over to pick up the can from the floor of the car. Their hands touched. Her skin felt soft and warm. He managed to pick up the can and hand it to her.

"Thanks, handsome," she murmured.

She was wearing a short, cream-colored skirt which amply showed her attractive legs and the cut of her green cotton blouse was tight across her chest. He looked at her and felt silly for no reason that he could think of. He gave her a goofy smile.

She looked back at him, staring into his blue eyes with her own, lighter blue. "Do you think I'm pretty, Richie?" she asked, almost in a whisper.

"Yes, I do, Diane," he answered in a voice that sounded husky. "I think you're very pretty."

"So, why haven't you asked me out?" She moved her hand up and touched his face, brushing her fingers lightly across his cheek.

"I don't know, I, uh..., well, I'm kind of going steady with Nancy right now." He started to blush.

"Kind of going steady?" She smiled at him and continued to caress his cheek.

"No, not kind of. I mean, I am going steady." He could smell her perfume.

He let his eyes wander over her, taking in everything. She had an ample figure. Stacked was the term he'd heard older guys use to describe a well built woman. Diane was stacked. Not only that, she was beautiful.

She leaned closer and he felt her breast touch his arm. He felt himself becoming aroused by her closeness.

"I really like you, Richie," she said breathlessly. She put her arms around him and drew him closer. Nancy doesn't have to know anything. I won't tell her."

"Diane, I...,"

"Ssh. Kiss me, Richie." She embraced him and her lips closed over his. They felt warm and sweet and he felt his resistance slowly begin to melt away. He held her tightly and returned her kiss, gently at first, then with an increased sense of urgency.

She caressed his leg and his arousal increased. He kissed her harder and put all thoughts of Nancy out of his mind. Her kiss became more passionate. He could feel her tongue pressing against his teeth, gently probing.

Time and awareness drifted away. Nothing else mattered and nothing else existed for him at this moment except the feel of her lips and the smell of her perfume. He was hopelessly and completely captivated.

Sixteen

Richie lay sleeping with his head on Diane's lap. They were now on one of the back roads that crisscrossed the farmland north of Sunrise Highway and led up to Sea Shell Harbor.

Earlier, Charlie and Mickey had returned to the car with the beer and fireworks and they had left Hempstead for the return trip home. Mickey had gotten back before Charlie. After seeing Richie and Diane locked in a passionate embrace, he remarked, "I see you two are finally getting properly acquainted."

Diane laughed and Richie smiled sheepishly.

"You'd better keep what you just saw to yourself, big brother," Diane said. "Richie is going steady with another girl, you know."

"My lips are sealed," Mickey said as he handed her a bag containing two six-packs of beer. He kept a can for himself. "Except to drink this," he added.

Richie was embarrassed but said nothing. He knew he was slightly drunk from all the beer he had consumed but he also knew

it was no excuse for having taken up with Diane. He decided to put the situation out of his mind for now. He'd deal with it later, when he'd had a chance to think about it.

Charlie returned to the car right after that, carrying two large shopping bags. He placed these in the trunk, then climbed behind the wheel and started the motor. After pulling away from the curb, he looked over at Mickey. "I'm gonna take the L.I.E. back to Noyac," he commented. "It's faster." He took Hempstead Turnpike east to the Meadowbrook Parkway, then headed north to the Long Island Expressway.

"Okay by me," Mickey answered. He took out his pack of cigarettes and lit one. "How'd you make out with the fireworks?" he asked as he exhaled.

"I got enough 'works to start World War Three," Charlie answered proudly. "More than enough."

"It's going to be a bang of a fourth," Diane added from the back seat. She looked over at Richie and winked, then handed him a beer.

During the ride home they consumed several more beers and all four of them were feeling the effects of the alcohol. Richie felt sick at one point and Charlie had to pull the car off to the side of the road so he could throw up.

"Your friend's a real seasoned drinker, huh, Mickey?" Charlie taunted as Richie climbed miserably back into the car.

"Leave him alone, Charlie. He ain't used to drinking, that's all. You okay, Richie?" Mickey asked.

"Yeah, I'm all right. Just let me lay down for a while." He stretched out on the back seat with his head resting on Diane's lap and was asleep only a few seconds later.

Mickey turned to Charlie. "Let's stop somewhere and pick up some coffee. I think Richie could use some."

"Good idea," Charlie agreed. "I could use some myself." He left the expressway at the next exit and headed south on the William Floyd Parkway. "We can stop at the Southampton Diner," Charlie said. "They got good coffee there."

"Cool," Mickey said. "Then we can take one of the back roads up to Noyac. He pointed to the exit sign up ahead. "Here's Sunrise, now."

Charlie steered the car east on Sunrise Highway. After several miles, the sign for the Southampton Diner loomed up, indicating it was located just ahead on the right. He turned off the road, pulled the car into the lot behind the diner and parked.

"I'll go inside for the coffee," Mickey said. "You ditch the beer cans, Charlie." He left the car and walked to the front entrance, went inside and ordered four containers of coffee and four donuts to go.

It started to rain again just as Charlie was hauling the bags of empty beer cans to the trash bin behind the diner. Instead of continuing on, he decided he didn't want to get wet, so he threw the bags on the ground and ran back to the car.

He failed to notice the police car parked at the rear of the lot. When they heard the clatter of the empty cans hitting the pavement, the two officers, sitting in the car and drinking coffee, looked up just as Charlie began running.

Mickey returned to the car and Charlie drove out of the parking lot and away from the diner. He turned left on Scuttlebutt, one of the back roads leading up to Noyac. They had gone less than a mile when he happened to glance into the rear-view mirror and saw the police car behind him.

"Cops!" He poked Mickey in the ribs. "There's a cop car following us!"

"What?" Mickey turned around in his seat and looked out the rear window, just as the driver of the police car activated his lights and siren.

"We got to make a run for it!" Charlie yelled. "Hold on!" He floored the gas pedal and the Chevy lurched forward, instantly increasing the distance between the two cars.

"What the hell are you doing, Charlie?" Mickey screamed. "Pull the car over, you idiot! We didn't do anything!"

"Can't!"

"What're you talking about? Pull over, I said!" Mickey punched Charlie hard in the arm with his fist. "You crazy or what? Pull the damn car over!"

"The car's not mine!" Charlie's eyes widened as he glanced in the mirror. The police car was closing the distance behind them as the rain came down more heavily.

"What're you saying? Whose car is it?" Mickey braced himself as the car picked up speed.

"Stolen!"

"What?"

"It's stolen! I stole the car!"

"You what?" Mickey's mouth was wide open as he looked at Charlie with disbelief.

The commotion in the front seat wakened Richie and he sat up, then was thrown against Diane as Charlie whipped the car around a curve at high speed. "What's going on, Mickey?" he asked groggily.

Charlie's knuckles were white as he gripped the wheel tightly and answered for Mickey. "I stole the God-damned car!"

Richie felt his stomach grumble and he felt sick again. "Oh, no! You idiot!" he yelled at him.

Diane moved closer to Richie and held on to his arm. "Richie!" she screamed.

"Yell at me later!" Charlie bellowed. "Right now, we gotta lose these cops!"

The distance between the two cars increased momentarily as Charlie skidded around several curves in the road. Richie and Diane held on to each other tightly as they were thrown back and forth in the rear seat. She started to cry softly and Richie did his best to comfort her. The sound of the police siren was deafening and the rain came down in buckets, barely allowing them to see the road ahead.

"Head for the country club, Charlie!" Mickey yelled as he kept his eyes on the rear window. "You're losing them!" He took the bag of donuts and coffee they hadn't had a chance to drink and threw it out his window. It sailed high in the air and splattered against the windshield of the pursuing police cruiser, momentarily blinding its driver.

The police car swerved and skidded on the wet pavement until the driver finally lost control. It fishtailed wildly, then skidded across the pavement and landed in a drainage ditch which ran along the side of the road. The sound of the siren immediately died down and the car sat off the road at a crazy angle, hopelessly stuck in the ditch.

"Yeah!" Mickey yelled wildly. He pounded on the dashboard as hard as he could. "We did it, Charlie! We lost them!"

"Thank God!" Charlie kept the accelerator pressed all the way to the floor and the roar of the car's engine seemed to get louder as they sped along the rain-slicked road. There was a sudden popping noise from under the hood and smoke started billowing up from underneath the car.

"I think she blew a rod!" Mickey yelled. "Turn in there!"

There was a dirt path about fifty yards ahead which led off to the right. "Hold on!" Charlie cut the wheel sharply and the car spun around completely before crashing into a tree with a loud rupturing of metal and shattering glass.

The force of the impact slammed Richie and Diane into the side of the car's interior and Richie's head cracked into hers. Charlie gripped the steering wheel tightly and Mickey managed to hold on to the door handle long enough to slow his momentum before centrifugal force caused him to collide into Charlie's body. The movement caused Charlie to hit his head against the driver's side door, almost knocking him unconscious.

The entire left side of the car was demolished, rendering the door on that side inoperable. Mickey recovered quickly. He spun around and looked back at Diane and Richie, who were tangled up together in the back seat. They looked almost comical. "You guys all right? C'mon, we gotta get out of here!"

They managed to pull themselves together and scampered out of the car through the passenger side door. Charlie shook his head from side to side and blinked his eyes rapidly.

"You all right, Charlie?" Mickey asked as he grabbed him by the shoulders and looked in his eyes. The loud wail of another police siren could be heard in the distance.

"I'm okay, I guess," he answered meekly.

"C'mon, we've got to leave right now," Mickey said urgently. "The cops are coming!"

They ran through the woods as fast as they could, with Mickey leading the way, Charlie right behind him and Richie and Diane taking up the rear. Richie grabbed Diane's hand and pulled her along.

Mickey knew exactly where they were. It was a hiking trail which ran parallel to the road they had been on and would eventually lead them up to Noyac Road and the country club. It was surrounded by thick woods and the deeper into the woods they ran, the more chances they had for eluding the police. After running for several minutes, they reached Noyac Road and cautiously ran across it. On the other side, was the South Hills Country Club. They quickly ran into the thick brush surrounding the club's perimeter and disappeared.

Running through the brush for several hundred yards, they came upon the golf course's seventeenth hole. Mickey held up his hand and placed it to his lips. He cautiously peered out across the neatly trimmed grass of the fairway and then motioned them forward. They hurriedly ran across the fairway and into the woods on the other side.

As they moved in a low crouch across the grass, Richie turned to look behind him for the first time since they left the car. He was relieved to see nobody was chasing them.

Mickey turned to the others and said in a low voice, "Follow me." They followed him single file through another several hundred yards of woods until they reached the far eastern edge of the golf course.

"Noyac Bay's up that way," he said, pointing to the north. "There's plenty of places to hide." He turned left and signaled to the rest of them. "This way."

They ran for several minutes, until Mickey suddenly stopped. He peered around through the trees, then signaled for them to follow him again. He turned right and ran down a barely discernible path which led them out of the woods and onto a narrow, dirt road which ran from south to north, adjacent to the woods and the golf course. Mickey turned left and ran along the side of the road next to the trees. They slowed to a trot but kept moving. Following close behind Charlie, Richie looked past him and saw that the road dead-ended up ahead at the water. He wondered what Mickey had in mind for getting them past this next obstacle.

He turned around to check on Diane. The side of her face was swollen and the area just below her right eye was beginning to turn black and blue. She squeezed his hand and gave him a weak smile. He smiled back at her.

Mickey turned around and spoke softly to the others. "C'mon, it's just a little bit farther."

"Where we goin', Mick?" Charlie asked, almost out of breath.

"I just remembered, I got a friend who lives over here," Mickey answered. "We can lay low at his house." The rain had stopped and a hint of sunlight peeked out from the clouds.

They moved carefully along the side of the road, ready to sprint into the woods at the first sign of a car, until they finally reached the other end. Directly ahead were the marshy waters of the bay. Mickey held up a hand. "This is it!"

Across to the right and set back from the road, was a small wood-framed house, barely visible behind the large hedges that surrounded it. A gravel driveway ran from the road, up between the hedges and continued past the side of the house to the rear. The house had faded white paint and peeling yellow trim around the windows and the grass in the front needed mowing. It didn't look like anyone was home.

"Isn't this Speedy Downey's house?" Diane asked.

"Yeah," Mickey answered. "Let's go and see if he's home. Be real quiet and follow me."

He walked slowly up the driveway with the others following close behind. At the rear of the house, the driveway curved around to the left. Several yards beyond the house and next to a large, dilapidated old barn was a wooden dock. Tied to the dock and resting quietly in the water, was a small runabout, equipped with a thirty-five horsepower outboard motor. Eighteen-year-old Speedy Downey, slim with red hair and freckles covering his face and arms, was sitting at the edge of the dock, his feet dangling over the side. He was busily working on a set of crab nets and didn't hear them enter the yard.

Mickey stopped. "Speedy?" he called cautiously.

Speedy looked up from his task and saw his friend Mickey peering down at him. He gave him a toothy grin. "Mickey!"

Seventeen

The four of them, exhausted from their ordeal, walked over to the dock and sat down next to Speedy. Richie started to feel pain on the left side of his face. He touched it gingerly and winced when he felt a stinging sensation.

"What happened to you guys?" Speedy asked, looking at each one of them.

"Car wreck," Mickey answered tersely. "We just outran a Southampton cop car that was chasing us." He pointed to Charlie. "Charlie wrapped his car around a tree in Harper's Woods."

"You mean the car he stole," Diane added angrily.

Speedy dropped the crab net he was working on and stood up quickly. "My God, you guys all right?" His face showed concern as he bent over and looked at each of them closely. "You all look terrible! I'm gonna go into the house for some water and towels so you can clean yourselves up."

"Speedy, can we lay low here for a while?" Mickey asked. "We need time to pull ourselves together." His shirt was ripped and hanging out of his jeans and there was caked, dried blood covering part of his left arm.

"Sure, Mickey. There's nobody home but me. I'll be right back!" He ran across the yard to the back door of the house and went inside. The others remained sitting and continued to take stock of their injuries.

The right side of Diane's face was swollen and the area just below her eye and above her cheek bone was bruised and discolored. Part of her jaw was also swollen due to the impact with Richie's head. She rubbed it slowly and checked her mouth to see if any of her teeth were loose.

Richie's left eye had started to close and the entire left side of his face was swollen and bruised and had started to turn black and blue. He was having trouble seeing out of the injured eye, so he just sat quietly on the dock and held a bloody handkerchief to his face.

Charlie had a golf ball-sized lump on the side of his head where Mickey's elbow had smashed into it and he complained of a headache and nausea. Other than minor cuts and scratches on his face and arms, sustained from the car's impact with the tree and from running through the woods and brush, he was in fairly good shape.

Mickey had survived the wreck with nothing more than a gash on his arm, a couple of sore ribs on his left side and a painful elbow. "I think I scraped my arm when I was running through the woods," he said to no one in particular. While they waited for Speedy to return with the towels, they vented their anger at Charlie. Richie was the first to speak.

"You damn idiot!" he yelled. "You could have gotten us all killed! Where do you come off, picking us up in a stolen car and not even telling us it's stolen? What kind of...!"

Diane cut him off. "Yeah, Charlie, that was a pretty dumb move you made! First you steal the car and then you try to outrun the cops! That was real bright of you! Just what the heck is going around in that pinhead of a brain of yours, huh? Look at us! We're all beat up!"

She stood up and pointed her finger at Richie. "Look what you did to Richie! Oh, my God, Richie! Your eye is completely closed!" She took a step closer to Charlie. "I'm gonna give you a black eye, you creep!"

Mickey stood and stepped in front of her. "Keep your voices down! You want the cops to find us?" He motioned for Diane to sit down. "Relax, sis, I'll handle this."

Diane moved away and sat down next to Richie. As she fussed

over him, Mickey reached down to where Charlie was sitting and grabbed the front of his shirt.

"Get up, Charlie," he said in a low, menacing voice. "You got some explaining to do." He made a fist with his other hand and stuck it in front of Charlie's face. "Start talking right now or you're gonna get a fat lip!"

"Okay, okay!" Charlie protested. "Lemme go, Mickey! I'm sorry about what happened! Just let me explain, please?"

Mickey let go of his shirt and Charlie started to fall backwards. Mickey reached out to steady him. "Start talking, Charlie," he said.

"I was gonna tell you," Charlie began, wiping his shirt with his hands to smooth it out, "but then we started drinking and it slipped my mind. I was gonna tell you later, I swear! I forgot, that's all! I would've told you, honest!"

"Where'd you get the car, Charlie?" Mickey stood in front of him with his hands on his hips, talking in an angry voice. "C'mon, let's hear it!"

"From a guy who lives near me, old man Archer!" Charlie held his arm up in front of his face as if to ward off any possible blows Mickey might throw. "He's just an old wino who lives down the street from me. He's drunk most of the time. Probably don't even know I took the car!"

Charlie lowered his arm and looked at Mickey fearfully. "Look, Mick, I didn't really steal the car. I just, uh, borrowed it without asking him. He left the keys in it. I was just gonna take it for a ride and, uh..., well, then I saw you hitching and..., I just got carried away, that's all!"

"You stole the car, Charlie!" Diane yelled at him. "You stole the lousy car and you almost got us killed!" She started to stand.

Mickey placed a hand on her shoulder to hold her down. "Calm down, Diane, let me handle this!" She reluctantly settled back on the dock.

"Look, Charlie," Mickey continued, "if the cops had caught us, we'd all be in trouble for car stealing, not just you. I don't think they'd agree that you just borrowed the car, do you?" Mickey folded his arms on his chest and stood there looking at him.

"I guess not," Charlie said with resignation. He gently fingered the lump on his head. "Okay, you're right, I stole the car. I'm sorry I got you involved, I really am. But, I was gonna tell ya, I swear!"

Mickey unfolded his arms and his expression softened. "All right, now we're getting somewhere. No sense in everyone getting bent out of shape over this. It was a stupid thing to do, we all agree on that." He looked at Diane and Richie. "Right?" They nodded.

"But it's over and done with." He started to pace back and forth on the dock. "Now we gotta figure out what to do next."

"But look at Richie's face!" Diane protested. "It's all black and blue and his eye is screwed up! How are we gonna explain that?"

"Be quiet a minute, will ya? I gotta think here!" Mickey looked down at Richie who was sitting on the dock, cradling his head in his hands. "You feeling all right, Richie?"

Richie raised his head slowly. "I think so. I can't see out of my eye, though."

Speedy returned with towels and a first aid kit. He placed the kit on the dock and passed the towels out to the others. He filled a plastic bowl with water from a faucet next to the dock. "Dip the towels in here," he said, "while I find some iodine."

Mickey sat down and followed his instructions, then passed the bowl around to the others. "Thanks, Speedy."

"So, tell me what happened, Mickey." Speedy found the iodine and a piece of gauze in the kit and handed it to him. "After you clean the cut with the water, put some of this on it."

As Mickey related what had happened, Speedy played the role of nurse, tending to each of their injuries like a concerned mother hen. His slender fingers worked rapidly, opening bandages and wetting them with iodine before he passed them around to those in need.

"Looks like you got the worst of it, Richie," he said. "You and Diane could pass for twins, 'cept her eye ain't closed like yours." He dabbed at Richie's face with another piece of bandage and gently applied iodine to some of the cuts on his arms.

As Speedy tended to his wounds, Richie said, "My parents are going to blow a fuse when they see me looking like this." He shook his head slowly. "I've never been in trouble with the police before but now all I've got is cops in my life."

Mickey moved over and squatted down next to him. "You're not in trouble with the cops, Rich," he soothed. "They don't know it was us in the car. All we gotta do is hide out here for a while until the coast is clear."

"I'll help you," Speedy said. "You can stay here as long as you want. My parents are visitin' my cousins in Connecticut and they won't be back until tomorrow." He looked at Richie and gave him a big smile, revealing a slight gap in his front teeth.

"What time is it, Speedy?" Mickey asked.

Speedy looked at his watch. "Three o'clock."

"What time do you have to be home, Rich?"

"No later than six. My folks like me to be home in time for dinner." Richie stood up shakily, then had to reach out to Mickey for support. "Wow, I feel a little dizzy!"

"You better sit back down, Rich." Mickey helped him lower himself on the dock. "We gotta figure out what we're gonna do. Anybody got any ideas?"

"We should stay off the main roads in case the cops are out there looking for us," Diane offered. "At least until it gets dark."

"That's too late. It doesn't get dark until after nine o'clock and Richie has to be home by six." Mickey took a wet towel, lifted his shirt and pressed it against his sore ribs. "Maybe we can call Eddie to come..., nah, forget that idea, he's not home."

"My parents are still going to wonder what happened to my face," Richie said.

"That's true," Mickey agreed. "Okay, everybody think! First, we got to get back to Sea Shell Harbor without being seen. Then, we got to think of something to tell Richie's parents about why his face is all messed up."

After several minutes of silence, Speedy spoke up. "I got an idea!" he said, green eyes sparkling. "We can take my boat from here, cruise around Clam Island and tie up at the Mill Creek dock! You can walk home from there!"

"Hey, that's a good idea," Mickey said, snapping his fingers.

"But, how did Richie get hurt?"

"We'll say he fell down in my boat and hit his head on my outboard motor." Speedy bounced up and down on the balls of his feet. "If you want, Richie," he continued, "I'll walk home with you and help convince your parents that's what happened. I'm sure they'll believe it."

Richie was thoughtful for a moment. "You know, it might work. I just hate to lie to my parents, that's all."

"Sometimes you gotta lie," Speedy said. "What d'ya say?"

"It's worth a try. I can't tell them what really happened." Richie looked up at him. "You'd be willing to do that, Speedy? Talk to my parents for me and all?"

"Sure, why not? You're a friend of Mickey's, ain't ya? Any friend of Mickey's is a friend of mine." He spat through the gap in his front teeth. "Don't worry, I'm a good talker. I'll convince your parents that's what really happened. They'll never know it ain't the truth."

"Well, I wish there was another way but I certainly can't tell them what really happened. My father would have a stroke.

"Can you see it? Hi, mom, hi, dad. I'm home."

Richie imitated his father's voice. "Hello, Richard, and how was your day? Well, let's see, dad. I took a ride in a stolen car with Mickey, Diane and Charlie. We drove over to Hempstead and picked up a ton of fireworks and then, on the way home, we..., wait, first we drank some beer and got pretty drunk! I got sick and threw up and then we were involved in a high speed chase with the cops and we ended up in a car wreck. We got away clean, though."

Richie was thoroughly into it now. He stood up uneasily and switched back to his father's voice. "Why, good show, son! At least you managed to elude the police! I'm proud of you!"

Diane started to laugh and the others joined in, even Charlie. Richie's monologue had broken the tension and he was beginning to feel better. After thinking it over some more, he agreed that Speedy's plan was the best course of action.

"Okay, we'll do it your way, Speedy," he said.

They went over the plan several times. Since Eddie had been unable to drive that morning anyway, they decided to eliminate any mention of Hempstead. Instead, they would say that they had spent most of the day at Speedy's house and had gone fishing in Speedy's boat after it stopped raining.

Speedy planned to bring along some fish he had caught that morning to embellish the story. They'd say they had gone fishing on the boat and at one point, Speedy had added too much throttle, causing Richie to fall and hit his head. Speedy and Mickey would accompany Richie home to lend moral support.

Since Diane had visible injuries, she would remain behind at Speedy's house until Speedy and Mickey returned and then she and her brother would spend the night there. Charlie would make his own way home from the Mill Creek dock. After agreeing to all the details, they swore an oath of secrecy.

Everyone but Diane piled into Speedy's boat and he lowered the motor into the water and fired it up. The trip around Clam Island took less than twenty minutes and before they knew it, they were tied up at the Mill Creek dock. They bid Charlie goodbye and walked around the corner to Richie's.

As the three of them paraded up to his front door, Richie took a deep breath to ready himself for the ordeal ahead. The smell of fish that Speedy had slung over his shoulder was beginning to make him sick but he took several more breaths and the feeling passed.

It went surprisingly easy. After their initial shock at seeing him in his battered condition, his parents' only concern was for his comfort and well being. They listened politely as Speedy told his story and accepted his version of events without question.

Speedy was completely convincing as he apologized to Richie's parents for his carelessness. In fact, Speedy was so believable that Richie almost began to believe the story himself, going so far as to describe his fall and Speedy's expert administering of first aid. Mrs. Donnelly invited the boys to stay for dinner but they politely declined. "Have to get the boat back before dark," Speedy said. "We'd love to stay some other time, though, Mrs. Donnelly."

Richie walked them outside and they made plans to meet at the Sugar Shack the next day. Now that the worst was over, Mickey's only concern was where to purchase some more fireworks before

Friday's beach party.

"I don't think it would be a good idea to go back and pick up the ones we left in the trunk," he joked.

"We can pick up fireworks at Shelter Island tomorrow night," Speedy said. "My friends over there will probably have some."

"Yeah? Good, I'll ask Eddy to drive us," Mickey said. "You wanna come along for the ride, Rich?"

"Now where have I heard those words before?" Richie said, laughing. "No, count me out this time, Mick. I've had enough excitement to last me for a long time."

Mickey started laughing with him. "I guess you have. I hope you're not going soft on me though." He and Speedy turned to leave. "See you tomorrow, Rich."

"See you."

Mrs. Donnelly continued to make a fuss over Richie, despite his assurances that he was all right. He ate a light dinner and decided to turn in early. As he was saying good night to his parents, his father looked up from his newspaper. "That's some shiner you have there, Richard," he said with a chuckle.

Richie lay awake for a long time before finally dropping off to a fitful sleep. Although happy that they had avoided serious trouble, he was disturbed by some of the events that had taken place the past few days.

It was bad enough, he felt, that he had lied to the police for Mickey. Now they had almost gotten killed. This was not even taking into consideration the trouble they would have been in if the police had caught them in the stolen car.

That Charlie is a real loser, he thought. What kind of people does Mickey associate with, anyway? He made a promise to himself that he would never have anything to do with Charlie McGee again, ever.

As he dabbed at his eye with a damp cloth, he thought about his friendship with Mickey. He knew Mickey was a cool guy and he sincerely liked him. Even though they had only just met the week before, he felt as if he had known him a lot longer.

One thing in Mickey's favor was the fact that he hadn't known the car was stolen. He had gotten just as upset as Richie had when he found out. Richie had even thought Mickey was going to beat Charlie up that afternoon at Speedy's house.

Then he remembered what Detective Shaunessy had told him, about Mickey being sent to reform school for stealing. That information had disturbed him a lot. He felt like asking Mickey about it but wasn't sure it was a good idea. Anyway, it was Mickey's business and he wasn't going to pry. Mickey was entitled to mistakes just like anybody else, wasn't he? He'd made a serious one himself, today, hadn't he? Climbing into that stolen car?

They'd have sent him to reform school for sure if he had been caught in that car, so he couldn't hold something like that against Mickey.

Still, certain things nagged at him. Mickey just didn't seem like the kind of guy to be stealing money from the principal's office or anywhere else, for that matter. Sure, he was no sissy. He was downright tough when you thought about it. But just because Mickey drank beer and smoked cigarettes didn't make him a juvenile delinquent.

No, whatever the reason, it didn't concern him, Richie told himself. He trusted Mickey. Today had been just an error in judgment on all their parts. Besides, except for his black eye and assorted bruises, he had escaped relatively unscathed. For that, he was thankful.

Diane came to mind. That was another disturbing situation. What had happened between them today had surprised him and he couldn't help feeling angry with himself for allowing it to happen. He should have exercised more control, that was for sure.

Diane was a friend and nothing more. No matter how pretty or sexy she was, his heart still belonged to Nancy. He loved her! He wasn't about to let Diane or anyone else sidetrack him again. He drifted off to sleep and started to dream. In his dream, he was standing in front of Nancy's house, calling her name. The door opened and Diane came out. She waved to him. "Come on in, Richie, there's nobody here. We can be alone." She blew him a kiss.

She was dressed in the same tight blouse and shorts she had been wearing today. They served to enhance her lovely curves. She beckoned to him. "Come here, Richie, I want to kiss you."

He turned and ran up the street, towards Noyac Road. What is she doing there? he thought. It's Nancy's house. Where is Nancy? He started to run faster. "Nancy!" he called out as he ran. "Nancy!"

Eighteen

Richie arrived at the Sugar Shack the next day at noon. His mother had wanted him to stay home and rest, but she reluctantly agreed to let him go after he promised to be careful.

The sky was overcast and there was a slight chill in the air. He wore a blue windbreaker over his tee shirt and a pair of jeans and sneakers. Even though the sun was hiding behind the clouds he wore dark sunglasses to hide his black eye.

They were all at a table in the back room when he arrived. Pat and Mickey, sitting close together and next to them, Eddie and Sally. Nancy was by herself off to one side, and Speedy was standing in front of the juke box. When she saw Richie, Nancy ran over to him.

"Richie! Oh, I'm so glad to see you! Are you all right?" She cupped his face with her hands and kissed him gently. "I was so worried about you!" Her blue eyes sparkled with a mixture of happiness and fear.

"Hi, Nancy," he said affably. "I'm okay, don't worry."

She took his hand and held it tightly as they walked to the table. "Let me see your eye," she said with some anxiety. "Mickey and Speedy already told me what happened."

"It's not so bad," he said as he removed his glasses. "I just can't see very well, that's all."

Nancy stared at him for a second and winced. "It looks pretty bad to me," she said. "Does it hurt?"

"A little."

As they sat down across from the others, Mickey got up from his chair and came around to their side of the table. He stood behind Richie and squeezed his shoulders.

"Here he is, you guys! The summer's first casualty of Speedy's Boating Service!"

Speedy looked over from the juke box and made a funny face, then stuck out his tongue. He strolled over to the table and joined the others. "Don't worry, I'm heavily insured," he said as he sat down. "How're ya feelin', Richie?"

"Better than I felt yesterday," Richie replied. He removed his jacket and hung it on the back of the chair. "My eye is still puffed up but it doesn't hurt as much. I'll be fine in a couple of days."

"I hope so, my handsome sailor," Nancy cooed. "We can't have you going around with a black eye for the rest of the summer."

"Richie, can I talk to you?" Mickey gestured with his head towards the door. "Let's take a walk outside for a minute." He took Richie's arm and helped him to his feet, then steered him towards the back door.

"Be right back, Nancy," Richie said.

They stood leaning against the deck railing. Mickey was silent for a moment before he spoke and he seemed a little ill-at-ease.

"I just want to apologize to you for all the trouble I caused in the past few days, Rich. I never should have brought Charlie around yesterday. I'm sorry I did."

Richie adjusted his sunglasses. "You didn't know what was going to happen, Mick," he said. "It wasn't your fault."

"I know, but Charlie's too much of a wild man. I never know what he's gonna do next." Mickey took a handkerchief from his pocket and blew his nose. "Anyway, I'm real sorry."

"It's okay, Mick. It's over and done with. You didn't know Charlie was going to steal a car."

"No, I guess not. Hey, let's see your eye." Mickey took a cigarette from his pack and lit it while he waited for Richie to remove his glasses. "Wow, that's some shiner you got there."

"Yeah, it's a real beauty, isn't it?" Richie put his glasses back on. "How're your ribs?"

"Not as sore as they were yesterday."

"I guess we're all lucky it wasn't much worse," Richie said, nodding his head. He gave Mickey a serious look. "We could have been seriously hurt in that car, Mick."

Mickey massaged his left side where the ribs were bruised. "You're not kidding. I been thinking about that a lot since yesterday." He stared off into space for a second, then looked back at Richie. "Lucky thing it didn't happen on Dead Man's Curve. We'd all be history."

"What's Dead Man's Curve?"

Mickey squinted against the cigarette smoke. "A hairpin curve on Noyac Road, a little ways between here and Sunrise Highway. A lot of people died there in car wrecks."

He took a final drag then flipped the cigarette out towards the road. It landed in a small puddle and fizzed out. "You must've drove past it on your way out from Brooklyn."

"I don't remember it."

"It's treacherous, let me tell ya. If you take the curve too fast, you could lose control of your car." Mickey turned around and rested his elbows on the railing, staring out towards Beach Road. He looked thoughtful. "I knew some people who died there," he said.

"You did? I'm sorry to hear that." Richie tried to picture the curve in his mind. He couldn't remember it.

"Frank Wittey's old man got killed there. It happened a long time ago," Mickey took a cigarette out of his pack and it dropped down into the sand on the other side of the railing. He didn't seem to notice. "Me and Frank were little kids, around eight or nine at the time. Frank never talks about it."

"Poor Frank," Richie said somberly.

"Yeah." Mickey fished another cigarette out of his pack and lit it. "I don't know what got into Charlie, stealing a car like that. I know he's done a lot of crazy things but never anything this serious. This one really takes the cake."

"I would never hang around with a guy like him, Mickey," Richie said. "Sooner or later he'll get you into serious trouble."

"I suppose you're right. I mean, I know what a screw-up he is, but I always wind up feeling sorry for him." Mickey took a deep drag from his cigarette. "He don't have any friends because nobody will hang around with him. Except me," he added.

"Well, I can see why." Richie remembered Nancy was still waiting for him inside. "Hey, we'd better go back in."

"Okay. Oh, by the way, the girls have been pumping us about yesterday. Me and Speedy told them what we agreed on, that we were at his house first, then we went out on the boat and that's how you got hurt."

"That's good," Richie said agreeably. "It's better if they don't know what really happened, just in case the cops come around asking questions."

"Yeah. Oh, and one more thing. I sort of told Eddie what really happened yesterday."

"Oh, no! You told him the truth?"

"Yeah, but don't worry, Rich, Eddie's cool. He won't tell anyone else." Mickey dropped his cigarette on the deck and stepped on it. "Ready to go back in?" "Sure. Say, Mick, are you sure Eddie won't tell anyone else? You didn't mention anything about me and Diane, did you?" Richie asked.

"Nah."

They walked back inside and joined the others. Nancy cuddled up next to Richie and held on to his arm. "Where have you been, sugar plum? I missed you."

"Hey, Richie, want to go for a boat ride?" Eddie teased.

Richie smiled self-consciously. "No, thanks, Eddie. I had enough boating for a while. Maybe next week."

"You didn't have half as much trouble jumping off Mighty Mo. Now look at you." Eddie slapped him playfully on the back.

"Guess I'm better with trees than I am with boats," Richie said.

"Quit teasing him, Eddie," Sally said, her expression slightly pouting. "It could've happened to anybody, even you."

"If I'd been driving the car we wouldn't have..., I mean, the boat..., oh, never mind."

Alarmed, Richie looked over at Eddie. Eddie avoided his gaze and instead, turned to Speedy. "Hey, Speedy, I'll take you out on my boat and give you a few lessons in seamanship, what do you say?"

"Sure, Eddie," Speedy said good-naturedly. "Anytime."

The waitress came over to the table and they all ordered cokes. Eddie gave Sally a quarter and she and Pat walked over to the juke box. "Hey, Mickey, where's your sister today?" Eddie asked.

"Haven't seen her since we left Speedy's house. She's probably home by now." Mickey looked at Eddie and made a face. "What time are we meeting tonight?" he said, changing the subject.

"Around seven-thirty," Eddie answered.

Nancy didn't seem to hear what Mickey and Eddie were saying. She turned to Richie. "Why didn't you call me yesterday if you didn't go to Hempstead? I was home all day with nothing to do."

"I'm sorry, honey," Richie said. "I should have. I was going to call you but then we went out on Speedy's boat and I never got the chance."

"You could have called me last night."

"I know, but I went to bed early. I wasn't feeling well."

"Oh, my poor baby," she soothed. "It's all right, I forgive you."

Pat and Sally returned to the table and sat down and Pat turned to Nancy. "Nan, we're going to Shelter Island tonight with Eddie and Mickey," she said. "Are you two coming?"

Nancy looked at Richie. "I don't know. Are we, Richie?"

"I'd rather skip it," he said, sounding a bit tired and weary. "Why don't we just hang around here, tonight? I don't really feel up for the ride."

"All right, my wounded sailor." Nancy leaned over and kissed his cheek. "I'd rather be alone with you, anyway."

Eddie looked across the table at Speedy. "Are you sure we can get fireworks on the island?"

"Sure, no problem. I have a friend over there who sells 'em. Carl Boucher. You know him?"

Eddie thought for a minute. "Big guy with red hair?"

"Yeah, that's him."

"I know of him. Doesn't he hang around with some of the guys from Greenport?"

"He might. He works on the ferry. He's got the Shelter Island to Greenport run, so it's possible."

"That's the guy," Eddie said. "Carl Boucher. They call him, 'Red'. Boucher's okay but he hangs around with a bunch of punks. Most of them I can't stand."

"How come?" Speedy asked.

"We had a run-in with some of them last year, remember, Mickey? Skippy Leonard and a couple of other creeps. They used to hang around next to the ferry landing in Greenport. Gave us a hard time last year when we pulled in there for gas."

"Yeah, I remember," Mickey said. "We had a fight with Skippy and his friend - some skinny guy - can't remember his name." Mickey smiled. "They thought they were tough, but me and Eddie straightened them out."

"Couple of hard rocks, huh? What happened?" Speedy asked.

The others leaned forward and listened intently as Mickey began to tell the story. "Me and Eddie pulled into the bait and tackle shop to get gas for the boat one day last summer. There was this girl we knew from school who had moved there and we were talking to her.

"Two of the Greenport locals, Skippy Leonard and one of his skinny friends, come over and Skippy starts to mouth off so I had to punch his lights out. Nothing major." Mickey leaned back in his seat and grinned proudly.

Eddie picked up the story. "You should have seen it. Mickey really clocked the guy, embarrassed him in front of his girl friend. Next thing we know, the skinny guy runs into the candy store and tells some of their other friends and they come running out to punch our lights out."

"There were at least six of them," Mickey said.

"Anyway," Eddie continued, "Red Boucher sees what's going on and he steps in. Didn't like the idea of six against two. He stopped them and we got the heck out of there."

"The skinny guy is screaming that he's going to take care of us the next time he sees us but we never heard from him again," Mickey said. "They're all just a bunch of punks."

"Those guys from Greenport are nobody to mess around with," Speedy warned.

"Well, I wouldn't want to tangle with your friend, Boucher, that's for sure," Eddie said. "The others I could handle in a fair fight. One on one."

"Boucher's pretty big," Speedy agreed.

"He don't scare me," Mickey said. "I'd fight him."

Eddie turned to Pat. "Mickey's not afraid of anyone," he said admiringly.

Speedy looked at the others. "We don't want any gang wars on the island tonight, you guys. Let's just go there, pick up the stuff and leave. If anyone else from Greenport is there, we'll just ignore them."

"Sure, no problem," Eddie said. "So, we're leaving at seven-thirty, right?"

"That okay with you, Mick?" Speedy asked.

"Sure. Let's all meet here and leave right after that."

They finished their cokes and decided to spend the rest of the afternoon at the teen center. Most of the kids went there when the weather was bad. Since they all couldn't fit in Eddie's car, they decided to walk.

"I hope the weather clears up by tomorrow," Richie said as they walked up Beach Road on their way to the teen center.

"It will. It never rains on the Fourth of July," Mickey said.

"Usually rains on the day after, though," Eddie offered. "All those firecrackers and rockets bring on the rain. Old Indian legend."

"Gee, the Indians must have been real smart, to be able to predict the weather like that," Sally said, to everyone's amusement.

Pat linked her arm through Mickey's as they walked. "I missed you, yesterday, you know. Thought you'd at least be at the Sugar Shack last night." "We spent the night at Speedy's house," he answered.

"Who? You and Richie?"

"No. Me and Diane. We took Richie home after he got hurt and then went back to Speedy's house."

Nancy, who was walking beside Richie directly behind Pat and Mickey, heard their conversation. "I didn't know Diane was with you yesterday, Richie," she said. "I thought it was just you, Mickey and Speedy."

"She, uh, came along for the ride," he answered uncomfortably.

"What ride? I thought you said you went out on Speedy's boat?"

"That's what I meant. The uh, boat ride."

"Oh. Who else was there?"

"Just me, Mickey, Diane and Charlie. And Speedy."

"Charlie? Who's Charlie?"

"Charlie McGee, friend of Mickey's from Southampton. He was there, too."

"I see."

"I thought I mentioned him," Richie said uneasily.

"No, I never heard of him until just now," Nancy said. "It's all right. It's not important." She turned away and looked out towards the water.

"I should have called you and invited you along, but I didn't know we were going out on the boat. It was a last minute thing. We were supposed to go to Hempstead with Eddie to pick up the fireworks, but when he couldn't make it, we stayed at Speedy's house and ended up on his boat instead. Charlie drove us over there from my house."

"How did Diane happen to be there?"

"She, uh, was in the car with Charlie and Mickey." Richie felt uncomfortable now and decided to change the subject. "Hey, you guys, what's the plan for tomorrow's celebration?"

"First, there's a parade through the village at eleven o'clock," Eddie said. "After that, a fair and carnival in the vacant lot next to town hall. It usually lasts until six. Nothing after that until the beach party at nine."

"Everyone in the whole town'll be there," Mickey added. "The fireworks start as soon as it gets dark. That's the best part of the day, Rich, the beach party."

"Oh, I can't wait," Nancy said. "It sounds like fun."

"Last year we had the best time," Pat said over her shoulder to Nancy and Richie. "We went out on my friend's boat and watched the fireworks from the bay."

"What friend?" Mickey asked.

"Oh, nobody you know. Just a guy I knew last summer," Pat answered mischievously. She smiled. "You don't have to worry about him. He moved away."

"Sounds like a summer romance kind of person," Mickey teased.

"Oh, silly, it wasn't like that. He..., hey, wait a minute! Who were you with last year and what were you doing?"

Pat poked him playfully in the ribs.

Mickey winced but pretended not to feel the pain. "Well, let's see, I was..., don't ask," he said, laughing.

"I guess I'd better not. You probably romanced at least half of the girls here last summer, if I know you." Pat looked at Mickey, eyebrows raised.

"Not half, Pat. Mmm, maybe a third."

"Yeah, I'll bet!" She made a grab for him but he bolted out of her grasp and made a run for it, laughing out loud as he scooted away from her.

"Come back here, you!" she called, taking off after him.

"Whoa, there they go!" Eddie said. "C'mon, let's go after them!" He took off running with Sally and Speedy right behind him.

"I'll race you to the teen center, Richie!" Nancy broke into a run and followed the others.

"You're on!" Richie ran after her. "Hey, you're pretty fast!" He let her get a little ahead of him before he picked up speed and caught up with her.

"Not bad for a fella with only one eye," she said, running beside him.

They spent the rest of the afternoon at the teen center, playing ping pong and listening to records. At five o'clock when the center closed, they all walked back to the Sugar Shack.

Eddie offered to drive them home but Richie and Nancy elected to walk instead. The others piled into his car and drove away.

"See you guys later," they called after the car.

Richie was lost in thought as they walked to Nancy's house. There were several things bothering him. Why did Mickey seem to take things so lightly, he wondered? His attitude about the car chase, lying to the police and pretty much life in general seemed, to Richie, a little too nonchalant. Mickey just didn't seem to let anything bother him.

On the other hand, maybe Mickey had the right idea. His own attitude was starting to get the best of him. Maybe he worried too much about everything. What with the car chase, getting hurt and all the lies he was involved in, his life seemed to have become more complicated with each passing day. Maybe he just needed to lighten up and not worry so much.

There was also Diane to think about. He had to admit he was attracted to her. She'd aroused feelings in him he'd never had before. He knew he didn't love her, not like he loved Nancy, but there was definitely something going on. Whatever it was, it was a problem he'd have to work out before too long.

He had a sudden urge to take Nancy aside and tell her everything. That would ease his conscience. Just blurt it all out and tell her. About lying to the police for Mickey, getting drunk yesterday, and the real reason he'd gotten hurt.

She'd understand, wouldn't she? Maybe. Maybe it wouldn't bother her. She had to admire him for telling the truth. Just tell her everything, Richie. All of it. Except for one small detail. Diane. How would he ever be able to explain being in Charlie's car with her? Getting drunk with her and making out with her? There was no way. He couldn't tell Nancy about Diane. He'd lose her for sure.

No, Diane would have to remain their secret. His secret and Diane's secret. And Mickey's. And Charlie's. And, and, who else knew about them? Eddie? Did Eddie know? Oh, God! Life was just too complicated!

"Are you okay, Richie? You have the strangest look on your face." Nancy was watching him closely.

"Oh, sorry." He smiled at her. "I was just thinking about the beach party tomorrow night, that's all." Darn! Another lie! My life is just one big lie after another now, he thought bitterly.

They walked the rest of the way in silence, both of them lost in their own reflections. They kissed when they reached her house.

"See you after dinner, Nancy."

"I'll be waiting," she said breathlessly. Then, "Richie?"

"Yes?"

"I love you."

"I love you too, Nancy."

Nineteen

Richie arrived at Nancy's house at seven-fifteen and found her waiting for him outside. The weather had finally broken and the skies were cleared of the last of the rain clouds which had slowly moved off to the east. The evening air was warmer but there was no trace of humidity.

Nancy wore a white cotton blouse, jeans and sandals with no socks. Her blond hair fell loosely about her shoulders and curled up slightly at the ends. Her tanned face enhanced the color of her eyes and seemed to make them appear an even deeper blue than before.

"You look pretty tonight, Nancy." He moved closer and kissed her.

"Thanks. You look handsome tonight yourself, Richie." She returned his kiss then took his arm as they walked back towards Noyac Road.

"Are you sure you don't want to go with the others tonight, Richie?" she asked. "Shelter Island is real pretty. It might be fun."

"I'd kind of like to be alone with you tonight, sugar." He put his arm around her waist and drew her closer. "I still feel a little wobbly from yesterday. We can always go there another time." He studied her face, trying to gauge her feelings. "If you really want to go, I guess we could," he said.

She shook her head and turned, wrapping her arms around him

in a quick maneuver. "Being alone with you sounds like a much better idea." She tilted her head and looked up at him. "I'd much rather have you all to myself than share you with Mickey and Eddie."

They continued walking until they were almost at the Sugar Shack. Stopping on the side of the road, they kissed for a long time, oblivious to the occasional passing motorist. The toot of a car horn made them relax their embrace and they looked up in time to see Eddie make a left turn into the parking lot next to the Sugar Shack.

"There's Eddie now," Richie said. "I guess they haven't left yet. Let's go inside and say hello."

Mickey, Eddie, Pat, Sally and Speedy were sitting at a table in the corner of the dining room. Several teenagers were out on the floor, dancing to the music of Bill Haley & The Comets' Rock Around The Clock.

"Here's the lovebirds now," Eddie said as Richie and Nancy approached the table. The others greeted them and made room so they could sit down.

"You guys coming with us tonight?" Mickey asked.

"No, we'll take a rain check, Mick," Richie answered. "We're gonna take it easy and just hang around here tonight."

"Not a bad idea," Mickey agreed. "That way you'll be in good shape for tomorrow's festivities." He peered at Richie. "How's the eye?"

Richie was still wearing his sunglasses and everyone watched as he removed them. The swelling around his left eye had gone down considerably and he was able to open it a little. The surrounding area was still severely discolored, making it look worse than it really was.

"A little better than yesterday, I think." Richie gingerly rubbed the area around his eye. "It should be okay in a couple more days, I hope."

"I sure am sorry I made you fall, Richie," Speedy said with mock seriousness. "I was a little too heavy-handed with the throttle."

Richie winked at him with his good eye. "That's okay, Speedy, I'll recover."

Nancy stood up. "Be right back, you guys. Have to visit the

little girls room."

"I'll go with you," Sally said, rising from her chair. "We can chat."

As she started to leave the table with Nancy, Eddie suddenly stood up. "Oh, Sally, let me talk to you for a minute, will you?" He took her arm and led her away from the table.

"Sure, Eddie. I'll catch up to you in a minute, Nan!" she called over her shoulder. Nancy nodded and kept walking.

Eddie took Sally's arm and the two of them walked over to the door and stepped outside.

Pat looked across the table at Richie. "Speedy isn't the only one who's heavy-handed, isn't that right, Richie?"

Richie was puzzled by her remark. "What?" he said.

"There seems to be a lot of heavy-handedness going on around here, wouldn't you say?" Pat picked up her drink and took a sip, eying him over the glass.

Before Richie could reply, Mickey stood up and reached for Pat's hand. "Let's dance, Pat."

"I don't feel like dancing right now," she said petulantly.

"Sure you do. You promised to teach me how to do the Lindy, remember? C'mon, sweetheart," he coaxed.

Pat reluctantly got up from the table and took Mickey's hand. They walked out to the dance floor and joined several others moving in time to the music.

Richie looked over at Speedy. "What's with her?"

Speedy shrugged his shoulders. "Beats me," he said indifferently. "I just wish everyone would quit wasting time. We need to get to Shelter Island before my friend leaves, if we want to pick up any fireworks tonight." He looked around anxiously. "We were supposed to leave by seven-thirty and it's already ten to eight."

"How far is it from here?" Richie asked.

"Not too far. It's about five miles from here to the ferry, another ten minutes to cross the channel, then another couple of miles to where we have to go." Speedy looked at his watch. "If we leave right now, we can be there by eight-thirty."

"That's not bad," Richie said.

"Yeah, but the last ferry leaves the island at nine-thirty. That only gives us an hour there to take care of business." Speedy nervously shifted around in his chair. "That's if we leave right away."

Eddie and Sally returned to the table and Speedy stood up. "Come on, you guys!" He fidgeted impatiently. "We have to leave right now if we want to be out of there in time to catch the last ferry!"

"Okay, we're leaving right now." Eddie picked up his glass and drained the last of his soda, then called out to Pat and Mickey. "Hey, Arthur Murray! Speedy says we have to leave right now or we'll miss the ferry!" Eddie and Sally bid Richie good night and started walking towards the door. Pat and Mickey returned and gathered up their things. "Sure you don't want to come along, Richie?" Mickey asked.

"No, some other time. We'll just stay here tonight."

"Okay. Come on, Pat. You ready Speedy?"

"I was born ready, Mick," Speedy replied. He moved off towards the door.

Pat picked up her purse and handed Mickey his cigarettes. To Richie, she said coldly, "Tell Nancy I'll talk to her tomorrow." She turned and started walking towards the door.

"What's the matter with Pat?" Richie asked.

"Who knows? Women are hard to figure, Rich." Mickey put the pack of cigarettes in his pocket and turned to leave.

Richie put his hand on Mickey's arm. "She acts as if she's angry with me about something. What did she mean by that remark, about being heavy-handed? That was a little strange."

"Beats me. I think she's just in a bad mood, Rich. Don't pay any attention to her."

"Mickey!" Pat was calling to him from the door.

"I'd better get going," Mickey said. He patted Richie on the shoulder. "Meet you tomorrow morning at eleven, okay? Have fun tonight."

"Yeah, you too." Richie started to reach into his pocket. "Oh, by the way, Mick. Why don't I give you some money for the fireworks? I still have that five from yesterday."

Mickey held up a hand. "Nah, that's all right, Richie, keep it. This is my treat."

"But it already cost you fifty dollars and we won't even be able to use the stuff we left in Charlie's car. Where are you getting all this money, Mickey?"

"I'm independently wealthy, Rich," Mickey said with a grin. "Don't worry about it." He hurried outside to catch up to the others.

After a few minutes, Nancy returned from the ladies room. "Did everyone leave already?"

"Yeah, they had to hurry to catch the ferry," Richie answered. "Pat and Sally said they'd talk to you tomorrow."

"Oh, good, we're finally alone, then." She cuddled up close to him and took his hand. "Aren't you going to ask me to dance, my handsome young sailor?"

"I'd love to. You'll have to lead me, though, 'cause I can't see very well."

They danced to several songs before returning to the table. There, they spent the next hour talking and feeding each other french fries and potato chips. They had just decided to walk down to the beach and were gathering up their things when Frank Wittey walked in and noticed them sitting there. He came over to their table.

"How're ya doin', Richie?"

"Oh, hi, Frank," Richie said. "Do you know Nancy?"

"Haven't had the pleasure," Frank said.

"Nancy, this is Frank Wittey, a friend of Mickey's. Frank, Nancy."

"Hello, Frank."

"Pleased to meet ya." Frank reached down and picked up a french fry from the table and stuck it in his mouth. "Have you guys seen Mickey tonight?"

"He left about an hour ago with Eddie and their girl friends," Richie said. "Went over to Shelter Island. Speedy Downey was with them, too."

"Oh, I see." Frank pointed to Nancy's plate. "You want the rest of those fries?" She shook her head and Frank stuffed several of them into his mouth. Nancy suppressed a giggle.

"Richie, when you see him, tell him I talked to the cops and everything's cool. He don't have to worry about nothin'."

"Oh, okay, I'll tell him," Richie said uneasily. Not wanting Frank to say any more in front of Nancy, he quickly said, "I'll see him tomorrow."

"Thanks, Rich." Frank picked up the last french fry from Nancy's plate and popped it into his mouth. He smiled down at her as he turned to leave. "Nice meeting you," he said.

Nancy looked at Richie. "What was that all about?"

"I'm not sure," Richie answered, a bit uncomfortably. "Probably something about Mickey's wallet." *There I go again,* he thought, *lies, lies, lies.*

"Oh, that's right," Nancy said. "I forgot about that." She pushed her chair away from the table. "Come on, let's hurry. The submarine races are starting up any minute."

"Hey, I'm supposed to feed you that line," Richie said happily.

They paid the check and left the Sugar Shack. Outside, the sun was just beginning to set as they walked through the parking lot towards the beach.

"Oh, look, Richie! Look how beautiful the sky is. Let's hurry!" Nancy took his hand and pulled him along. "Come on, one eye, I'll lead the way." Richie dutifully followed.

They sat by the water and watched the sun disappear below the horizon. They could hear the gentle lapping of small waves at the water's edge and except for the occasional cry of a seagull off in the distance, there was no other sound except their own breathing.

The sky turned a brilliant red and was streaked with sinewy patterns of deep purple clouds which seemed to have moved in suddenly, filling the spot where the sun had been only moments before. The air was still and warm and a sliver of a moon appeared low on the horizon off to the southwest. The night enticed and beckoned.

"It's so peaceful here, Richie," Nancy said in a soft voice that was almost a whisper. "I wish I could live here all the time."

"Me, too," he agreed.

"Wouldn't that be great? Living here all year round?" She gave a small sigh. "The city feels so crowded sometimes. All that noise and traffic. I can hardly stand it anymore."

"Me neither."

Nancy stared out over the water and remained quiet for a time. "It's a shame that nothing seems to last very long," she said wistfully. "Everything changes so quickly."

"I know. Brooklyn is the same way. A lot of people we used to know have moved away. The old neighborhood just isn't the same as it used to be. I hardly know anybody there, anymore."

Nancy fiddled with her ring, twisting and turning it around on her finger. "My father is always talking about moving down to Florida as soon as he retires. Says he can't take the winters like he used to."

"What does he do?" Richie asked.

"He's a policeman."

"Oh." A wave of apprehension hit him in the stomach for a moment, then, realizing his foolishness, he smiled to himself. "Mine's an accountant," he said.

"That's nice." She let go of her ring and began to trace patterns in the sand with her fingers. "I don't know if he really would, though. I think he just likes to talk about it," she said.

"Well, I hope he doesn't," Richie said. "I'd hate to see you move away now, just when we're getting to know each other." He reached over and took her hand, squeezed it, then brought it up to his lips and kissed it gently.

"Would you miss me?" She squeezed back.

"Sure."

"Are you glad that you asked me to go steady, Richie?" She reached over with her other hand and touched him gently near his injured eye.

"Of course I am. Why do you ask?"

"I don't know. I just want you to be happy, that's all. I wouldn't want you to feel trapped."

"I would never feel that way with you."

"Some guys feel trapped when they go steady. They still want to date other girls. You don't want to date other girls, do you,

Richie?"

"Of course not, Nancy. You're the only girl for me. I don't want to date anyone else."

"Are you sure?"

"Sure I'm sure. Hey, what's all this about?"

"Oh, no reason. I guess I'm a little insecure. I just want to be sure that you love me."

"I do, Nancy. I do."

She removed her hand from his and went back to tracing patterns. "What about Mickey's sister?"

Richie stiffened and started to feel a little tense. "What about her?" he asked cautiously.

"I heard that she has her eye on you."

"Who told you that?"

"Oh, it's not important. Nobody told me, really."

"But someone must have told you."

"Well, I heard Mickey and Eddie talking at the Sugar Shack yesterday, before you got there. They were sitting out on the deck and didn't see me at first. I heard Mickey tell Eddie that Diane has the hots for you. That's how he put it." She cocked her head to one side and looked at him.

"Mickey said that?"

"Yes. They stopped talking as soon as they saw me, though. It didn't really bother me at first, but then I remembered the other day at the beach when she came by looking for you and you took a walk with her."

"That was nothing, Nancy, really. She just wanted to tell me something about Mickey, and..."

"I believe you, Richie. I'm just jealous, that's all. Don't mind me." She leaned over and kissed him, gently at first, then with more passion.

They held each other tightly, kissing and moving slowly backwards until they were lying side by side on the sand. Nancy broke off the kiss.

"She's very pretty, Richie. She might tempt you."

"Diane doesn't mean anything to me, Nancy." He stroked her

cheek and looked into her eyes. "You're the only girl I want. I love you." He drew her closer and kissed her again.

She kissed him back, adding short little pecks around his mouth. "Are you sure? I wouldn't blame you if you fell for Diane. She's much prettier than I am."

Richie brushed her hair away from her face. "Believe me, sugar, you're the only one for me. Diane doesn't stand a chance." He leaned closer to kiss her again but instead she turned her head away.

"Not only is she pretty, she's also very sexy. She has a very nice figure, Richie. Better than mine."

"She can't hold a candle to you." He kissed her again.

"She has the hots for you."

"Don't be silly, Nancy, she..."

"I have the hots for you, too." She wrapped her arms tightly around his neck and pulled him closer. He was lying almost on top of her. "I'd do just about anything for you, Richie, do you know that? Do you?"

Her words came out in short, rapid bursts. Breathless streams tinged with youthful passion. She kissed him again, more urgently now.

He felt himself getting aroused as she pulled him closer and he moved on top of her, forgetting everything else for the moment except his own passion. I love you, Nancy, he thought. I love you.

Their kisses became more intense as they lay there, lost together in a whirlwind of mutual desire. He felt a great intimacy with her. It was as if they were soaring through the air, then tumbling down slowly and gently in a free fall. Together.

She loves me, too, he thought. She loves me, too. He could smell her. The scent of her perfume was tantalizing. It was..., no! What am I doing? I can't do this with Nancy!

But he wanted her. Her perfume was driving him crazy! Wait a minute! What's going on here? That's not Nancy's perfume I'm smelling, it's..., Diane's!

It was Diane's perfume! She was the one he wanted, not Nancy! He could never think of Nancy that way. Not..., sexually. Nancy was too sweet and innocent and he had too much respect for her to think of her like that.

Diane was a different story. He didn't think of Diane as innocent. She was more..., womanly. Her kisses were more intense, more passionate. It was Diane who stirred up his sexual fantasies, not Nancy. He loved Nancy. He could never..., not unless they were married.

Richie relaxed his embrace and moved away from her, embarrassed now by his behavior. He sat up. "I'm sorry, Nancy," he stammered, "I..., I guess I got carried away."

Nancy sat up and straightened out her clothing. Her face was flushed. "It's all right, Richie. I wanted you, too." She moved back into his arms and he held her there, gently, tenderly. They sat like that for a long time, neither of them speaking.

"We'd better head back," he said finally.

"I love you, Richie."

"I love you, too, Nancy."

"Tell me I'm the only girl for you."

"You're the only girl for me."

"Tell me Diane doesn't stand a chance with you."

"Diane doesn't stand a chance with me."

"Oh, Richie, I'm so happy." She turned her face to his and kissed him. "You're the only boy I'll ever love."

They stood and turned away from the water, brushing sand away from their clothing. The crescent moon was off to their left, almost below the horizon now. Holding hands, they walked slowly back towards the Sugar Shack.

It hardly seemed like any time had gone by when they found themselves standing in front of Nancy's house. She came into his arms and they stood like that without speaking for several minutes. Then, after a final good night kiss, they parted company.

The night was quiet as he walked along Noyac Road, with only the occasional lights and sounds of a passing vehicle to intrude into the silence and gentle darkness. As he passed Treadway's Market, he caught sight of his reflection in the plate glass window. For a moment he thought it was someone else and he gave a slight start, then realizing his mistake, relaxed again.

He'd been thinking about it all the way home and he decided

now that he would tell Nancy the truth about the past week. No more lies, he told himself. He would tell her everything.

He would tell her about the visit from the detectives and the fact that he had lied for Mickey. He'd tell her about the car chase, the drinking, the wreck, how he really got hurt, all of it. He would even tell her about Diane.

Being alone with Diane in Charlie's car. There would be no more secrets from Nancy. He hoped she would understand why he had lied and forgive him. She had to. Honesty was the best policy. She'd understand.

The moment he decided to tell Nancy his dark secrets, it felt as if a giant weight had been lifted from his shoulders. He tried to whistle but was unable to because he couldn't stop grinning. He turned the corner at Chestnut and began to skip along the street, like a little kid. He felt a little foolish at first, then remembered it was dark and no one could see him.

He stopped and looked up at the sky. The moon was gone now but the stars were big and bright, some as large as golf balls. "Deep in the heart of Texas", he sang softly to himself.

The milky way was a shimmering cluster of twinkling, little white blobs and out of the corner of his eye, he caught the tail end of a shooting star. He started to skip again, then began to run.

"I can't wait until tomorrow!" he yelled out loud.

Twenty

Richie woke early the next morning with mixed feelings of excitement and apprehension. It was Friday, July Fourth. Independence Day. He sat up in bed and rubbed his eyes, thinking about what lay ahead and what he had decided to do.

He had dug himself a hole and it was rapidly becoming deeper, filling up with lies and deceit. Now it was time to climb out and face reality.

As he swung his legs over the side of the bed and stood on the floor, he couldn't help feeling angry with himself. He realized he was stuck in a series of lies and evasions, almost like a fly in a spider's web. He began to wonder. Why had he allowed it to happen?

He wished he could somehow be transported back to simpler, more innocent times. Times when he had nothing to be ashamed of and nothing to hide.

He looked out his bedroom window. The sun was shining and the thermometer attached to the side of the cabin indicated eighty degrees. Another beautiful day in Sea Shell Harbor. It was to be his day of reckoning. It could also be the day his own independence would end.

The more he thought about it, it seemed as if Mickey was leading him down a path that was now closing in on both of them. The more they traveled down it, the narrower it became.

He knew it wasn't all Mickey's fault. He had to share some of the blame, too. Things were getting out of hand, though. The way they were headed, it was only a matter of time before something really bad happened.

As he walked slowly into the bathroom, a plan started to take shape in his mind. He would spend the day with Nancy and the others, watching the parade and then attending the carnival and fair. He'd say nothing to her until that evening when they would all gather at the beach for the party and fireworks.

As soon as the right moment presented itself, he would ask Nancy to take a walk with him. Then he'd tell her the truth, from beginning to end. Starting with the night Mickey asked him to lie to the police for him and ending with his romantic encounter with Diane in the stolen car. He would leave nothing out.

Had it only been a week ago since he'd arrived in Sea Shell Harbor? So much had happened in one week. It felt more like a year. Funny how time seemed to be distorted when you looked back on something that had already happened.

He'd try to explain to Nancy how he'd refused to lie for Mickey at first, but changed his mind when Mickey became upset and ran off. He'd tell her how he'd been afraid of losing him as a friend and so had relented. He'd also tell her how frightened he'd been when the police came to his house and how he'd almost told them the truth right then and there.

If the one cop hadn't been such a creep, he would have, no doubt about it. He hadn't been aware of the Mutt and Jeff tactic then, but he was now. He hoped Nancy would understand. It was because of his friendship with Mickey that he'd allowed his own judgment to become clouded.

Richie ran water into the basin and splashed some on his face. Suppressing a yawn, he stared at himself in the mirror. He felt a sudden twinge of apprehension as he thought about the possible consequences of telling Nancy about Diane. What would she say? How would she take the news?

Nancy loves me, he thought, in an effort to reassure himself. She'll understand. I was drunk and Diane made the first move. I didn't plan on it happening. She enticed me with..., with her beautiful lips, and her fabulous figure.

And her perfume.

He shook his head to clear it and moved away from the mirror. It felt like he was sitting in a courtroom, pleading his case and protesting his innocence before a jury. He picked up his toothbrush and began to brush his teeth.

I am innocent, he thought warily. Well, maybe not totally innocent but not guilty either. He visualized himself sitting in the witness chair, nervously attempting to answer the questions being put to him by the attorney for the prosecution. The attorney was a woman with dark hair and she..., it looked like Pat! She stood in front of him with her hands on her hips and a stern look on her face. "Answer the question, Richie! Did you kiss Diane?"

He looked anxiously around the courtroom. Over in the witness section sat Mickey, Charlie and Speedy, waiting their turn to testify. A lone juror sat in the jury box. Nancy! She was eying him intently but he couldn't bring himself to look at her. Instead he looked up at the judge, who looked down on him with an amused smile. Eddie?

"I'm afraid you'll have to answer the question, Richie," Eddie, the judge stated without sympathy. "Did you or did you not kiss another girl?

"I'm innocent, your honor! I swear! Diane made me do it! She made me!" Richie snapped out of his reverie and rinsed his mouth with water. He looked in the mirror again and carefully studied his reflection. Was he guilty or innocent?

He removed his underwear and stepped into the shower, reached for the knobs and turned on the water. He adjusted them until he had the desired combination of hot and cold. The water soothed his body and he began to relax.

He hadn't planned to kiss Diane, he reminded himself. Even though he had kissed her it wasn't, what was the word, premeditated? Yeah, that was it. He hadn't premeditated the kiss, Diane had. Still, he had liked it and had kissed her back. He couldn't deny it. He tilted his head back and let the water run down over his face.

So what was he, guilty or innocent? Not guilty? Not innocent? A little of each? He wasn't exactly an innocent bystander to the whole thing, no. For whatever reason, he'd been a willing player. He had to admit that. But he hadn't planned any of it. It was confusing.

Nancy will understand, he told himself, more to bolster his confidence than anything else. She loves me, doesn't she? With that positive thought he turned off the water and breathed a sigh of relief.

His shower completed, Richie dressed and then went into the kitchen to see about breakfast. There was money and a note on the table. He picked up the note and read it. His parents were spending the day at a nearby cabin with friends and wouldn't be back until evening. There was a number where they could be reached in case of an emergency.

He made himself some bacon and eggs and poured a large glass of orange juice. Sitting at the table eating his food, he felt relieved that he wouldn't have to deal with his parents right then. He'd be able to talk to Nancy first before having to worry about them. One thing at a time.

After eating, he cleaned up the dishes and returned to the bathroom to rinse out his mouth and comb his hair. He splashed cologne on his face and checked himself in the mirror one last time. His left eye was still black and blue, although the swelling had gone down considerably. He looked presentable enough. Next, he walked into the living room and began searching for his sunglasses. He found them on a table in the porch, exactly where he'd left them the night before. He put them on and left the cabin.

He met Nancy in front of her house and together they walked over to the Sugar Shack. They were supposed to meet the others at eleven. A slight breeze mixed with salt spray was blowing in off the water as they walked up the steps to the outer deck. Small patches of swirling sand skittered around the edge of the parking lot, creating miniature versions of desert sand storms as they were carried along by the wind.

The two of them walked into the dining room through the rear door and looked around. Only Speedy was there, sitting by himself at a table in the corner.

"Hey, Speedy!" Richie called.

Speedy looked up and saw them. Talking rapidly and waving his arms, he rose from the table and walked across the floor, meeting them halfway. "You should've been there!" he said excitedly. "What a nightmare!" He started to bounce up and down on the balls of his feet. "I told them not to get involved in nothin' but Mickey wouldn't listen!"

Richie looked at Nancy. She raised her eyebrows questioningly and he turned back to Speedy. "What are you talking about, Speedy?" What happened?" "I told them, I told them, but Mickey wouldn't listen! We had the firecrackers and we were just gettin' ready to leave, but then Mickey had to go and start trouble!" Speedy's arms were flailing back and forth.

"Speedy, calm down a little, will you?" Richie said, with a bit of authority. "Tell us what happened."

The three of them walked outside and sat at a table. Nancy on one side of Speedy and Richie on the other.

Nancy said calmly, "Tell us what happened last night, Speedy. Start at the beginning."

Her voice seemed to have a soothing effect on him. Speedy relaxed, took a deep breath and then started to speak. "Okay. Let me start at the beginning. Let's see, we were..., everything went smooth as silk at first." He rubbed his nose nervously.

"After we left you, we headed up One-Fourteen to North Haven. We caught the ferry for Shelter Island right away and everybody was happy. It was a beautiful ride." He started to twitch in his seat but Nancy placed her hand on his arm.

"It was a beautiful ride," she said.

"Yeah. So we get to Shelter Island and Eddie heads up North Ferry Road to The Heights. We pull up in front of Maxie's and my friend Boucher's waitin' for me."

"The guy with the fireworks." Richie stated.

"Yeah. He's waitin' in front of the candy store, just like he said he'd be, so I get the money from Eddie and Mickey.

"Twenty from Eddie and thirty from Mickey."

"Thirty from Mickey?"

"Yeah, I give it to Boucher, he takes a walk, then comes back ten minutes later with the goods. He hands 'em to me, then he leaves again. No problem."

Speedy cracked his knuckles. "Man, he had all kinds of stuff," he said, looking back and forth at the two of them. "Rockets, candles, M-80's, you name it! Everything we could possibly want for tonight!"

"What happened next?" Richie asked.

"Eddie puts the bag of firecrackers in his trunk and just as we're about to leave, these three guys come out of the candy store."

Nancy tapped Speedy on the arm. "What three guys?"

"One of them is Vinnie Armadello, big guy from Greenport. One of them is Stevie Miller. He's the skinny guy Mickey was talkin' about the other night, remember?" The one he had trouble with last summer?" Speedy swiped at his nose. "The third one I didn't know."

"Yeah, so?" Richie prodded.

"So, Mickey yells over at the guy, 'Hey, Skinny, you lookin' for Charles Atlas?' Somethin' like that." Speedy took another swipe at his nose. "I tell Mickey to clam up, but it's already too late."

"What do you mean?" Richie leaned forward, impatient for Speedy to continue. "What happened?"

"They must've heard him because the three of them start to walk over to the car. Next thing I know, Mickey hops out of the back seat and leans on the car, arms folded across his chest, like a tough guy."

"Then what happened?" Nancy asked.

"Stevie comes up to Mickey and says, 'Wha'd you say?' So Mickey says, 'I heard Charles Atlas is looking for ya. He wants to use you as a ninety-seven pound weakling for his comic book ads.' The guy got all puffed up but Mickey just laughed."

"That wasn't very nice of him," Nancy said, sounding puzzled by Mickey's behavior.

"I know." Speedy glanced at her. "Next, Mickey says to the guy, 'Don't you remember me?' The guy says no and Mickey says, 'Yeah, last summer. My friend and me were gettin' gas over in Greenport and we were talkin' to a girl we knew from school. You got all bent out of shape over it.'

"Stevie says he don't know what Mickey is talkin' about and they turn and start to walk away but Mickey calls him a ninety-seven pound weakling again and tells him he shouldn't stick his nose where it don't belong or he's gonna knock it off his face."

"Oh, no," Nancy groaned. "Mickey said all that?"

"Yup, and they still didn't do nothin'. All Vinny and Stevie do is laugh at Mickey like he's a jerk or somethin'. Then they walk away and Mickey starts walking behind them, giving them the high sign."

"What's that?" Nancy asked.

"You know." Speedy made a fist, then stuck up his middle finger. "The high sign."

Nancy turned to Richie, covering her mouth to suppress a giggle. "Oh," she said.

"Meanwhile, I'm yellin' at Mickey to get back in the car and let's go." Speedy shook his head slowly. "I can't believe we're still there, horsin' around."

"What happened next, Speedy?" Richie asked.

"Mickey only goes a few feet before he comes back to the car, only the third guy starts following him back to the car. The guy sees Sally sittin' in the front seat and he leans over and says to her, 'Nice pair of jugs you got there, Sweets.' Sally got all red in the face."

Nancy opened her mouth wide, then brought her hand up to cover it.

"Next thing I know, Eddie leaps out of the driver's seat and punches the guy in the face. Vinnie and Stevie come running over and Mickey punches Stevie in the stomach and he goes down on the sidewalk. Then, Mickey and Vinnie start wrestling."

"Wow," Richie said. "A regular donnybrook." He glanced at Nancy. Her eyes were as wide as saucers and her hand still covered her mouth. "What happened next?" he asked.

"The girls are screamin' at the top of their lungs and I'm yellin' at everybody to get out of there before the cops show up. Meanwhile, Stevie gets up and jumps on Mickey's back and the other guy comes up behind Eddie and grabs his neck.

"Eddie and the one guy are wrestling on the ground and Vinnie and Stevie are both fighting Mickey, two against one. Eddie starts yellin' at me to help Mickey." Speedy raised his palms up to indicate helplessness.

"Now, Richie, I ain't no scrapper. I'm a hundred and fifty pounds, soaking wet. I can't fight my way out of a paper bag." He lowered his hands and looked down at the table dejectedly.

"Come on, Speedy," Nancy prompted, impatiently. "Finish the story!"

Speedy nodded and resumed talking. "I didn't know what to do at that point. Everybody's rollin' around on the ground and screamin' and yellin'. All of a sudden, I hear Mickey yell, he can't breathe!"

Speedy slapped the table top with the palm of his hand. "So, I pick up a coke bottle that was lyin' on the seat, climb out of the car and I hit Vinny over the head with it!" Speedy looked proudly at the two of them.

"You what?" Richie couldn't believe what he was hearing.

"Yeah. I didn't know what to do, Rich," Speedy protested meekly. I mean, two against one? That ain't fair. Anyway, Vinnie goes down like a dead weight and everybody stops fightin'. Eddie gets up and screams, 'Let's get out of here!' So, we all pile in the car, Eddie starts it up and we peel out!"

"Unbelievable!" Richie shook his head slowly as he digested the story.

"As we pull away I hear one of them yell how they're comin' down to Sea Shell Harbor to even the score."

"How badly was the boy hurt?" Nancy asked, her face showing concern.

"Not too bad," Speedy replied. "He wasn't bleedin' or nothin' 'cause I didn't hit him that hard. I just wanted to get him off Mickey."

"Then what happened?" Richie asked.

"We got out of there and headed straight for the ferry. Caught the last one just in time."

"What about Mickey and Eddie?" Nancy asked. "Are they all

right?"

Speedy looked at her and then turned to Richie and laughed. "Actually, Eddie has a black eye just like you, Rich."

"He does?" Richie couldn't suppress a smile.

"Yeah, he sure does. Mickey's okay, though. He bruised his knuckles a little bit, that's all. He's fine." Speedy was thoughtful for a moment. "But now there's gonna be a war for sure."

Nancy looked at Speedy and grimaced. "I never could understand why people have to use physical violence against one another."

"Mickey started it," Speedy protested weakly. "I tried to tell him to cool it but he wouldn't listen. For a minute there, it looked like everything was gonna be okay, but then the guy made that remark about Sally's, uh, I mean her..., um..."

"Sally's jugs," Nancy said, finishing the sentence for him. "Don't worry, Speedy, I know what they are."

Speedy gave her an embarrassed look. "Yeah, thanks. Well, then Eddie went crazy," he continued. "I never saw him like that before. He went wild. I think he would have really hurt the guy if he could've. Thank God we got out of there when we did."

"Where are they now?" Richie asked.

Speedy shrugged his shoulders. "I don't know. We were supposed to meet here at eleven to watch the parade but I haven't seen them since last night."

The staccato tattoo of snare drums beating out a marching rhythm could be heard in the distance, followed by the musical presentation of several brass and woodwind instruments playing 'The Stars and Stripes Forever'.

"The parade is starting!" Speedy exclaimed. Let's go out to the road so we can see it!" Without waiting for the others, he stood up from the table and vaulted over the deck's wooden railing, then began running towards Beach Road. "Come on, you guys!"

Richie and Nancy climbed over the railing and followed him, hurrying to catch up. "Wait up, will you, Speedy?" Richie called. Speedy was already at the side of the road, looking north in the direction of the approaching parade.

"It just started," Speedy said when they caught up to him. "Let's walk up to Village Drive and see if they're over there. That's where the parade will end." He led them up Beach Road toward the sound of the music.

The parade was turning left from Beach Road onto Village Drive just as they arrived and the three of them stood at the corner watching the marchers. Behind the band were groups representing various social and civic organizations; the boy and girl scouts, several veterans associations and the local police and fire departments.

With their uniforms gleaming and shining from hours of spit and polish, the participants marched proudly and happily in time to the music. Richie felt a pang of excitement. It reminded him of the times his parents had taken him into Manhattan to watch the annual Saint Patrick's Day Parade on Fifth Avenue.

They moved farther down Village Drive as the parade continued on for another quarter mile. At the village square, the marchers dispersed to both sides of the road, bringing the parade to its happy conclusion.

On either side of Village Drive, booths had been set up to display a wide assortment of goods. The vendors were doing a brisk business selling hot dogs and hamburgers, soft drinks, ice cream, cotton candy and other treats to the large holiday crowd. The mood was festive as children ran excitedly from one booth to the next, followed closely behind by their parents with money in hand.

In addition to food, there were booths selling arts and crafts, tee shirts, sandals, sunglasses, nautical items and souvenirs of Sea Shell Harbor. Across the street towards the end of the fairway, there was a large open field where a ferris wheel and other carnival rides had been set up.

To the delight of the children, there were strolling clowns handing out balloons, jugglers and magicians and a hurdy gurdy man with a little monkey who begged for coins. There was even an eight-foot tall clown on stilts.

Beyond the carnival rides, there was a livestock exhibit, petting zoo and still more booths offering various games of chance and skill. One of them featured a Gypsy fortune teller.

"Where the heck do you suppose they could be?" Speedy asked

as he busily scanned the faces of the crowd.

"Beats me," Richie answered.

"Maybe they're still at home," Nancy suggested. "After all that excitement last night, they were probably tired and slept later than usual."

"Could be, but I got a feeling they're around here someplace." Speedy continued to look around and noticed the fortune teller's booth. "Let's ask the Gypsy to look into her crystal ball," he added jokingly. "She'll be able to find them for us. Richie and Nancy laughed.

As they reached the end of the line of booths, Richie glanced across the street. Sitting at a picnic table on the other side of Village Drive were Mickey, Eddie, Pat and Sally. They were eating hot dogs and drinking from paper cups.

"There they are!" he yelled to the others.

Twenty-One

When Mickey looked up and saw Richie, he began waving excitedly. "Over here, Rich!" he yelled. Nancy and Speedy followed him as Richie quickly crossed the street.

Everyone started talking at the same time until Eddie put up his hand for silence. "Whoa!" He had to shout to be heard over the clamor of their voices and the parade noise. "Let's take a walk," he said.

They followed him past the fair booths and carnival rides to the edge of Village Drive. Here, the road dead-ended in a grove of tall marshy grass and reeds and there was a dirt path leading down to the waters of Sag Harbor Cove which lie beyond.

It was quiet and secluded here, with only the squawk of an occasional sea gull or the croaking of a bullfrog to break the silence.

"Let's go down to the cove," Eddie said.

They climbed over a wooden barrier designed to keep motorists from continuing into the marsh and walked along the path which snaked along through the tall grass down to the water's edge.

It was much hotter in the reeds and Richie could feel the sweat start to trickle down the back of his neck. Eddie found an old tree stump and sat down and Sally came up behind him and sat next to him.

Eddie picked out a blade of grass and snapped it off, then stuck it in his teeth. The others gathered around the log and squatted down next to him. Speedy was the first to speak.

"Where the heck you guys been? We been looking all over town for you!"

"Sorry about that, Speedy," Eddie replied. He was wearing his aviator's sun glasses which hid part of his face. "I know we were supposed to meet you at the Sugar Shack but my parents insisted that I have my eye looked at, so I had to see the doctor first. I was late picking the others up. Figured we'd meet up with you sooner or later."

"Well, okay," Speedy replied, sounding somewhat appeased by Eddie's explanation.

Eddie removed his sunglasses and turned to Richie. "Looks like we're twins now, Richie," he said with a laugh. "Same eye, too!"

"Well, I'll be darned." Richie was surprised to see Eddie's left eye had been blackened and bruised much like his own. "You've got a real beauty there."

Eddie punched him playfully on the arm and began to speak with a British accent. "Doesn't hurt too terribly, old man, but it certainly makes it difficult to see where I'm going. Had to let Mickey have a go at navigating the motor car this morning."

"Oh, Eddie, you're so funny!" Sally gripped his arm and lay her head on his shoulder.

"Guess what Eddie told his parents, about how he hurt his eye?" Mickey asked. The others shrugged and looked at him expectantly. "Said he fell on Speedy's boat." He chuckled loudly. "Can you believe that?"

"You did?" Speedy asked Eddie.

"Yeah. I told them we went night fishing on your boat and that you pulled into the dock just a bit too fast." Eddie spit the blade of grass out of his mouth. "The boat slammed into the dock and I went flying forward and hit my head on one of the tie-down cleats." He put his glasses back on and grinned at Speedy. "Good show, old man!"

"Boy, what a bum rap I'm getting," Speedy said good naturedly. "My reputation as a skipper is sure being bandied about."

"Sorry, Speedy, it was the only thing I could think of at the time," Eddie offered.

"It's okay, Eddie," Speedy said. "As long as it worked, that's all that matters."

Sally reached up and tousled Eddie's hair. "My poor babykins got himself a little boo boo," she said soothingly. She raised up and kissed him gently on the cheek. "Mommy's kisses will make it all better."

Eddie tilted his head to the side and smiled. "Doctor says it'll be okay in a couple of days but the more kisses from you, the better."

"I nominate Richie and Eddie for purple hearts," Speedy said. He stood up and walked behind Eddie. Placing his hand on Eddie's shoulder, he announced, "Ladies and gentlemen, I give you the second casualty of Speedy's Boating Service!"

They all laughed.

"You guys are lucky you decided not to come with us last night," Eddie said to Nancy and Richie. "Did Speedy tell you what happened?"

Richie stood and stepped on the edge of the log, then leaned forward and rested his arm on his leg. "He gave us a quick rundown," he said. "Who were those guys, anyway?"

Mickey answered for Eddie. "Just some Shelter Island riff raff," he said. "Remember that guy from Greenport I was telling you about? Well, it was him and two of his buddies. Speedy says his name is Stevie Miller."

"And the other guy was Vinnie Armadella," Speedy added. He wiped his nose on the sleeve of his tee shirt. "He's from Greenport, too. I never saw the third guy before, though." Speedy straightened up and stuck out his chest. "Vinnie's a big monster but he was no match for 'Lightnin' Speedy Downey'. He never even saw it comin'." He made a swiping motion with his arm to recreate the blow he'd made with the coke bottle the night before. "Look out, you big lout!" he said menacingly. "How did the fight start?" Nancy asked.

Sally spoke up. "One of them made a remark about my chest," she said, arching her back to emphasize her breasts. "So Eddie had to defend my honor." She raised up and kissed him again. "My hero." She settled back on the log and continued speaking. "Then, two of them jumped Mickey and started to beat him up!"

"You mean, tried to beat me up," Mickey said, correcting her.

"What were you doing, Eddie?" Nancy asked. "Why didn't you try to help him?"

"Eddie was fighting the other one at that time," Sally said quickly in his defense. "There were three of them, after all. Pat and I were screaming for help at the top of our lungs."

"Finally, Speedy picked up a coke bottle, jumped out of the car and hit the big one over the head with it," Pat added.

Nancy let out a gasp.

"He had to," Pat said defensively. "They were trying to hurt Mickey and that was the only way he could stop them."

"It worked, too!" Speedy said proudly.

"It was terrible," Pat added, "but they started it!"

Richie looked at Mickey. "Is that the way you remember it, Mick?"

"Pretty much," Mickey answered. "I was duking it out with Stevie, and Eddie was fighting the other guy. Next thing I know, Vinnie jumps me from behind. If Speedy hadn't conked him over the head when he did, it might have been a lot worse. You can see what they did to Eddie's eye."

"I wonder why the three of them would just walk over to the car and insult Sally like that?" Nancy asked. "I mean, if all of you were just minding your own business..."

"Actually," Mickey said, "I started the whole thing."

"You started it?" Nancy asked.

"What do you mean, Mickey?" Eddie interjected. "You didn't do anything. They insulted Sally!"

"Yeah, true, but I called Stevie a ninety-seven pound weakling first, don't you remember?" Mickey lit a cigarette. "I shouldn't've done that."

"So what!" Eddie said indignantly. "You were just kidding around, weren't you? They had no right to say that to Sally. That was uncool!" He put his arm around Sally's shoulder. "Nobody talks to my girl like that, I'll tell you!"

Sally looked up at him and batted her eyelashes.

"They probably wouldn't've said anything if I hadn't made fun of Stevie," Mickey continued. "I started it. Nobody likes to look like a jerk in front of their friends."

"You didn't mean anything by it, Mickey," Pat said.

"I know, but I should've kept my mouth shut. They weren't bothering us." Mickey dropped his cigarette and squashed it into the sand with his sneaker. "When I saw Stevie coming out of the candy store, I remembered the beef we had last summer. I just wanted to make him look stupid, that's all. It was dumb."

"Well, maybe so," Eddie admitted, "but his friend had no right to pick on Sally. She wasn't bothering anyone."

"No, I guess not," Mickey agreed. "Well, at least nobody got hurt too bad." He looked at Eddie's face. "Except for your eye, maybe."

"And Vinnie's head," Speedy said smugly. "Anyway, let's all just forget about it, okay? It's over."

"That's just the point, Speedy, it ain't over yet," Mickey warned.

"What do you mean, Mick?" Richie asked.

"Stevie and his friends ain't gonna just let it go like that," Mickey said. "They'll be coming over here one of these days to finish it." He made a fist and held it up menacingly in front of the others. "You can be sure of that."

"You think so?" Eddie asked.

"Yeah." Mickey turned to Speedy. "You heard them, Speedy. What'd they say?"

"They said they'll be coming over to Sea Shell Harbor to even the score!" Speedy looked grim. "That's what they said."

"Do you really think they will?" Sally asked, alarmed. She clutched at Eddie's arm. "Oh, Eddie, what are we gonna do?"

"Don't get excited," Pat said. "They're probably just bluffing. Don't you think so, Mickey?"

"Could be," Mickey answered. "Then again, maybe not. Vinnie Armadella ain't the kind of guy who takes a crack over the head lightly." He pointed to Speedy. "Especially from a "pipsqueak like you, Speedy," he said jokingly. Then, more seriously, "I think we should be ready, though, just in case."

"Ready for what?" Nancy asked.

"I don't know, exactly. Just ready, that's all." Mickey raised his arms over his head and stretched. "Listen, let's not worry about it right now, okay? We can't let them spoil our fun. I don't think they'll come over here on the Fourth of July, there's too many people in town. Let's just do what we planned and worry about it later."

"I second the motion," Eddie said.

"What do you say we get going?" Mickey started walking back towards the road and the others followed. "We'd better stay alert, though, just in case," he said.

When they reached the road, Eddie asked, "What do you guys want to do first?"

"Oh, I want to ride the ferris wheel," Sally said. "Come on, everybody, let's go for a ride on the ferris wheel!" She squealed with delight.

"Okay," Eddie said. "Everyone agreed?"

Richie turned to Nancy. "Want to?"

"Oh, that sounds like fun," she said agreeably. "Let's."

"After that, let's get something to eat," Speedy said. "I'm starving to death."

They started running towards the carnival area and stood on line for the ferris wheel. They spent most of the afternoon riding it and some of the other attractions. After a few hours, they found a picnic table and loaded up on barbecued chicken, baked beans, corn-on-the-cob and ice-cold watermelon. For desert, they stuffed themselves with cotton candy, soda, pretzels and ice cream until they couldn't eat another bite.

They threw balls at wooden milk jugs, tossed rings at empty coke bottles, threw darts at balloons filled with water and tested their strength by swinging a heavy sledgehammer at a wooden peg, trying to ring the bell. Mickey was the only one who succeeded.

They went on several rides and played more games of chance. Eddie won a large teddy bear for Sally when he managed to dunk a basketball into a basket three times in a row. Finally, they had their palms read by the gypsy fortune teller, who predicted long and prosperous lives for all of them.

At five o'clock, they decided to take a break. They would go home and freshen up before returning in time for the evening festivities. It had been a glorious day so far, but the best was yet to come - the beach party and fireworks.

They left the carnival and walked along Beach Road to the Sugar Shack where Eddie had parked his car earlier.

"You guys want me to drive you home?" Eddie asked Richie and Speedy. "Mickey and I are going to my house for a while but we can drop you off, first."

"I'll take you up on that," Speedy said.

"I think I'll walk Nancy home, but thanks anyway," Richie said. "Oh, Richie, I'm going with Sally to Pat's house, so you won't have to," Nancy said. "I'll meet you at the Sugar Shack later, instead."

"Oh, okay," Richie said. Then, "I'll just take the beach route home from here, Eddie. Walk off some of that food I ate. I'll see you all later."

"Meet us here around seven-thirty, Rich," Mickey said.

"Okay." Richie kissed Nancy and watched as she left with Pat and Sally. She turned around and blew him a kiss. "See you later, Richie," she called.

Eddie, Mickey and Speedy drove off in the car and Richie walked along the water's edge and around the curve of the bay to Chestnut Street. Remembering what his friends had told him earlier, that this would be the best Fourth of July celebration yet, he was gripped with a feeling of elation.

If today was any indication, he thought, it certainly will be. When Richie had mentioned what a good time he was having that afternoon at the carnival, Eddie had looked at him and said with a big grin, "Rich, it's just another summer day at Sea Shell Harbor."

Arriving home, he decided to skip dinner. He was still full from all the food he had eaten that afternoon. Since his parents weren't home anyway, he thought he'd just take a shower and relax until it was time to go out again.

He went out the back door into the yard and sat in a lawn chair. Leaning back and stretching his legs out in front of him, he put his hands together behind his head, lacing his fingers together.

As he sat there soaking up the atmosphere in the garden, he decided he felt good about himself. Today had been an exceptional day but tonight would be even better. Once his planned talk with Nancy at just the right moment was completed, his conscience would finally be clear.

He thought about Mickey and decided he felt better about him, also. Mickey had taken responsibility for starting the fight and he was glad for that. It reaffirmed his opinion about his friend. He knew that Mickey was a good person at heart. All he'd done was make a few mistakes, just like anyone else. You couldn't fault a guy for that.

At seven-thirty, freshly showered and smelling of fresh lilacs from the after-shave lotion he'd used, Richie was waiting for his friends in the parking lot outside the Sugar Shack. Tucked under his arm was a woolen blanket Eddie had asked him to bring. Eddie and Mickey were bringing beer and snacks.

As he stood there, he decided he wouldn't drink much beer that evening. He didn't really like the stuff. Just one to be sociable, he thought. Besides, he wanted his mind to be clear when he talked to Nancy.

Speedy showed up first, then a few minutes later, Eddie and Mickey drove up in Eddie's car.

"Where's the girls?" Richie asked after they had parked.

"Aren't they here yet? They're probably still at Pat's."

"Should be here soon." Eddie got out and opened the trunk. "You know how women are when they get together and start yakking, Rich. They forget all about the time." He handed a bag to Richie and one to Speedy.

"Got beer, ice, pretzels and potato chips. Grab the cooler, will ya, Mick?"

Mickey reached into the trunk and picked up the cooler which was sitting next to a large plastic bag. "What about the fireworks, Eddie?"

"They're in the bag," Eddie replied. "We'll come back for them later, right before it gets dark." He picked up another bag and a blanket and closed the trunk.

They walked to the beach carrying the supplies and found a

spot near the water. Eddie pointed north. "That's where they'll be setting off the fireworks display," he said. "We'll have a good view from here." He turned to the others and gave them a wide grin. "After that, we'll loosen the girls up with this beer and hopefully create our own fireworks."

"Hurry up darkness and don't be late," Mickey said.

"Amen," Speedy added.

Richie and Speedy spread the blankets out on the sand and Mickey placed the cooler on one of the corners. Eddie took the beer out of one of the paper bags and transferred it to the cooler, then emptied a bag of ice on top. He closed the lid.

"That'll keep things nice and cold," he said.

The beach was starting to fill up with people and just as Richie was starting to wonder what was keeping the girls, Pat and Sally came walking up to the blanket.

"Hi, everybody," Sally said, plopping down next to Eddie.

Pat sat next to Mickey, took the can of beer from his hand and took a sip. "Starting without me, I see," she said

"Hi, babe," Mickey said.

Richie was puzzled. "Where's Nancy?" he asked Pat.

"Oh, she went home to change," she answered nonchalantly. She avoided looking at him.

"Did she say what time she'd be here?" Richie asked.

Pat looked at him and shrugged her shoulders. "She didn't say."

"H'mm." Richie thought for a moment. "I wonder if she thinks I'm meeting her at her house?" He stood up. "Maybe I'll walk over there."

"I don't think that's a good idea," Pat said.

Richie looked over at Pat. "What do you mean?" he asked, slightly confused. He glanced at Mickey with a puzzled look on his face.

"What's going on, here, Pat?" Mickey asked. "Do you know something we don't?"

Pat looked away for a moment, saying nothing, then turned back to Mickey and took another sip from his beer. "What makes you think there's anything going on?" she asked coyly.

Richie shifted his attention to Sally. "Sally, can you tell me what's going on? Do you know where Nancy is?" Sally looked away sheepishly. "I'm not one to tell a sad tale," she said in a small voice.

Richie was growing angry now. "What are you talking about, Sally?" She didn't answer. He looked at Pat. "What's going on, Pat?" When she didn't answer he crossed to the other side of the blanket and kneeled down in front of her.

"Look, Pat," he said, trying to keep his voice under control, "you've been acting pretty strange lately and I'd like to know why. What have I done to deserve this? Now, tell me what's going on, will you? Where's Nancy?"

Pat turned away, still saying nothing. After a moment, Mickey took her by the arm. "Hey, Pat, what's the big idea? Richie asked you a question, so why don't you answer him? What's going on?"

Pat looked at Mickey and pouted. "I don't want to talk about it," she said petulantly. "Let Nancy tell him herself."

"Tell me what?" Richie demanded.

Sally stood up and brushed sand from her shorts. "Come on, Eddie, let's take a walk down by the water." She took Eddie's hand and pulled him to his feet.

"Um, we'll be back in a few minutes," Eddie said. He appeared bewildered as she led him away in the direction of the beach.

Speedy sat alone on the other blanket, drawing patterns in the sand with his fingers. When Eddie and Sally started to walk away, he stood up quickly. "Wait up, you guys, I'll go with you!" he called after them.

Pat finally looked at Richie. "Nancy's not coming tonight," she said. "She's mad at you."

"Mad at me? For what? What did I do?" Richie anxiously brushed a few strands of hair away from his eyes and waited for her to reply.

"Why don't you ask your girlfriend what you did?" Pat said coldly.

"My girlfriend? Who, Nancy?" Richie was completely confused now. He turned to Mickey. "Mickey, would you please ask Pat to stop playing games and tell me what's going on here?"

Mickey tapped Pat on the arm. "C'mon, Pat, stop playing games. What do you know that we don't?"

Pat sighed and looked at Richie. "Nancy isn't coming tonight, Richie. She told us to tell you to have fun without her. She also said to tell you that she wouldn't want to get in the way of you and your girlfriend."

"What girlfriend? What are you talking about?" Richie asked, exasperated.

"Nancy knows all about you and Diane, Richie!" Pat spat the words out as if she had a bad taste in her mouth. "She knows all about that little love scene in what's his name - Charlie's - car! She also knows that you lied to her about where you were and how you got hurt! She knows everything!"

Richie was speechless. Flabbergasted, he sat in front of Pat, his mouth wide open, unable to speak. Finally, he managed to gasp, "Oh, no!"

"She's not very happy with you at all, Richie," Pat continued. "In fact, she's very angry with you! And, for your information, so am I! You have some nerve, leading my friend on like that, you..., you..., two-timer!"

Richie stood up, incredulous. His ears were ringing and his head started to pound. He felt his face flush.

Pat continued her tirade. "And all along, you were sneaking around with Diane! What a guy!"

Richie felt tears well up in his eyes. Humiliated by Pat's remarks, he looked around wildly, unable to think clearly. "You told them!" he yelled, pointing his finger at Mickey. "Thanks a lot, Mickey!" He turned and ran off in the direction of the parking lot. He could hear Mickey calling after him.

"Wait, Rich! Hey, Richie, I didn't..., Richie, wait a minute, will ya?"

Twenty-Two

Richie ran all the way to Nancy's house. Racing up to the front door, he rang the bell and stood there, trying to catch his breath. He wiped the sweat from his face with his handkerchief and tucked his shirt back into the waistband of his jeans.

He wondered how Nancy had found out about Diane. Had Mickey told Pat and Sally what really happened that day and had they told Nancy? He'd thought that at first. Now he wasn't so sure. He didn't believe Mickey would betray a confidence. They had sworn an oath of secrecy!

Mickey told Eddy, though. Richie remembered talking to Mickey on the deck of the Sugar Shack, the day after the car wreck. Mickey informed him then that he had told Eddie. "Don't worry, Rich, Eddie's cool," Mickey said. Eddie wouldn't tell anybody else.

Did Mickey tell Eddie about Diane? Richie asked him if he'd said anything to Eddie and Mickey said he hadn't. Then, how in the world had Nancy found out? This was a real mystery and Richie was determined to learn the truth. Either Mickey told Eddie and then Eddie confided in Pat and Sally or, Mickey spilled the beans to Pat and Sally himself. Either way, Nancy knew about Diane.

He rang the bell again, but there was no answer. He wondered if Nancy was inside and just wasn't answering the door, then realized no one was home. The house was too quiet. She must have gone out. Maybe she had thought things over and decided to talk to him about it. She might be at the beach right now, waiting for him!

Richie considered leaving Nancy a note but discarded that idea. He had nothing to write with, anyway. Instead, he started walking back to the beach. He needed to talk to Nancy as soon as possible. There was no time to waste. If she'd only give him a chance, he knew he could explain it all to her. He hoped she would understand.

He felt terrible as he walked along Beach Road. Knowing he'd made the biggest mistake of his life didn't help matters much. He certainly didn't want to lose Nancy over it. I should have stayed home that day, he told himself over and over.

But he hadn't stayed home. He'd gone along with them, even after he'd had misgivings. He'd gotten in the back seat of Charlie's car and sat next to Diane. He'd taken the beer she offered and he had kissed her. That was the truth of the matter and he had nobody to blame but himself. "Oh, Nancy," he said aloud. "I don't want to lose you!"

When he reached the parking lot, he decided to look in the Sugar Shack first. Maybe Nancy was in there having a coke or something. He veered off and went up the stairs and through the main entrance, walking rapidly past the counter into the dining room. It was crowded and most of the tables were occupied. There were kids out on the floor, dancing.

He scanned the faces of the people at the tables but didn't see her. He checked the dance floor. No. Where could she be? She wasn't home and she wasn't here. Maybe she was at the beach.

He'd go there next. He threaded his way past the dancers and went out the rear door. On the deck, he quickly looked around. She was there! Sitting alone at a table against the railing in the far corner. His heart skipped a beat.

"Nancy!" He walked over to her table and sat down across from her. "I've been looking all over for you!" He was filled with apprehension. "I, uh, thought we were supposed to meet here at seven-thirty?"

Nancy turned away. "I have nothing to say to you, Richie."

"What do you mean, sweetheart?" He felt the sweat in his armpits and a chill ran up his back. "I don't understand."

"I'm sure you do." She turned to face him and looked at him coldly.

"Can't we talk about it?" He reached forward to take her hand but she snatched it away. Her eyes were red as if she had been crying which only made him feel worse. "Please let me explain, Nancy," he said meekly. "I think..."

"There's nothing to explain, Richie!" she interrupted. "Pat and Sally told me all about you and Diane," she said derisively. "How you spent all day Wednesday together, making out in the back seat of someone's car. There's no explanation required!"

"I'm sorry about that, Nancy, honest. There's no excuse for what I did. I was drunk and..."

"You were drunk?" Nancy's lips curled together as if she had a piece of lemon in her mouth and her face turned red with anger. "Well, that explains it all then, doesn't it! You were drunk! You told me you spent the day on Speedy's boat with Mickey and that you got hurt when you fell over and hit your head on the motor!

"Now I find out you weren't on Speedy's boat at all! You went to Hempstead with Diane and Mickey and some guy named Charlie and then you were involved in a car chase with the police! That's how you got hurt!"

"Yes, Nancy, but..."

"Now you're trying to explain it all away by telling me you were drunk?" She stood up and looked down at him. "Do you really think that would excuse you for what you did?" She placed her hands on her hips and glared at him, her eyes burning with fury. "Do you?"

"No, Nancy, I don't." Richie raised his palms up, in a helpless gesture. Trying his best to placate her, he said, "Please, sit down for a minute, will you? I want to tell you how sorry I am. I didn't mean..."

"What are you sorry about, Richie?" Nancy asked, still standing. "That you were with Diane or that I found out about it?"

"No, that's not what I'm trying to say. Diane doesn't mean anything to me. It wasn't the way you think. I..., we were..." Richie felt his face flush as he tried desperately to think of the right words.

"Spare me, Richie. I don't want to hear any more. You've already lied to me enough as it is." Nancy removed the ring he had given her and placed it on the table. "Here, this is yours," she said, sliding it across the table toward him.

"No, Nancy." He stood. "Please, keep the ring. I want you to have it. Can't we just talk things over?"

"No!" she said coldly. "There's nothing to talk about."

Richie felt his eyes start to water as he held the ring out to her. "Don't do this to me, Nancy," he pleaded. "I love you. Please, don't."

"If you'll excuse me, I'm busy now." She turned and started walking towards the door.

Richie put the ring in his pocket and followed her. Just as she reached the door, a boy Richie didn't know stepped through it. He was carrying two glasses of coke.

"Oh, there you are, Nancy," he said. He handed her one of the glasses. "I was just bringing these over to our table."

The boy was dressed in what the kids referred to as the collegiate style. Button-down shirt, tan chinos and white bucs. He was two or three inches taller than Richie and looked like an athlete. His hair was closely cropped in a crew cut.

Nancy accepted the glass and took his arm with her other hand. "John, do you think we could sit inside? The air is getting a bit thick out here."

"Sure thing." The boy she called John put his arm around her waist and led her inside. "There's still a few tables left."

Richie followed behind them. "Nancy!" he called. "Will you please wait a minute? Let me talk to you!"

Nancy and John stopped and turned to look at him. "I already told you, Richie," Nancy said, "there's nothing to talk about."

"Friend of yours, Nancy?" John eyed Richie curiously.

"Not really," Nancy replied. "Let's go."

As they turned to leave, Richie closed the distance between them. He reached over and touched Nancy's arm. "All I want is a minute of your time, Nancy. Can't you give me one minute?"

John, who was in front of Nancy, quickly moved around her and stood facing Richie. "Who are you and what do you want?"

He asked menacingly.

Richie sized him up. He appeared older than Richie and was extremely well built, like a football player. His arms were massive. Richie determined that if it came down to a physical altercation between them, he would probably be the loser. He didn't care.

"This doesn't concern you, fella," Richie said, trying to move around him.

"I think it does," John said. He shifted his weight from side to side, effectively blocking Nancy from Richie's view.

"Get out of the way!" Richie shouted, trying to see around him. "It's none of your business!"

"I'm making it my business." John turned to Nancy and handed her his glass, then turned back to Richie and pushed him. "She doesn't want to talk to you, so why don't you leave her alone?"

Richie eyed him coldly, angry at having been pushed. He grabbed the other boy's arm and tried to move him aside. He couldn't budge him.

John wheeled and and grabbed Richie by the front of his shirt. "You little punk! I'll blacken your other eye if you don't quit bothering her!"

Nancy screamed as John gave Richie a harder shove. The force sent Richie flying backwards into one of the tables. He knocked over several glasses and broke them as he fell to the floor. He lay there trying to catch his breath.

"Stop it, John!" Nancy shouted. "Leave him alone! You're twice his size!"

"Well, he'd better cool it, then!" John answered loudly.

Nancy set the glasses down on an empty table. "Come on, let's go!" she said, nudging him in the arm. With John following close behind, she quickly walked through the back door and disappeared.

Richie lay on the floor, moaning softly as he waited for his strength to return. Mr. Meyers, who owned the Sugar Shack, had heard the commotion and ran over to help Richie to his feet.

"Are you all right, son?" he asked as a crowd started to gather.

"Yeah, I'm okay," Richie answered meekly. "Just let me catch my breath." He got shakily to his feet and looked around the room.

Faces peered back at him but there was no one there he knew. "I'm sorry for all the trouble," he said, apologetically. "How much do I owe you for the broken glass?"

"It's all right, son," the owner said. "We'll take care of it. Maybe you'd better go on home, now."

"Okay." Richie brushed himself off and walked slowly to the door. He paused there for a second, then went outside. He leaned against the fence rail until he was breathing normally again, then walked down the stairs and headed for the parking lot.

He still felt a little shaky from the fight and had to stop for a second. What the heck had just happened? He leaned against a parked car and tried to think. Everything had been going so well, until now. All of a sudden, not only had he lost his girlfriend, he was completely in the depths of despair! He was more confused than ever, now. Exactly what had caused everything to change so quickly? Between this afternoon and evening his life had suddenly made a one-hundred-eighty degree turn for the worse. This afternoon, Nancy still loved him, now she wanted nothing more to do with him. She had shut him out of her life, probably for good.

Who was this new boy, John, and what was he doing with her? Richie instinctively knew he was a serious rival for Nancy's affections, but when had that started?

John had looked vaguely familiar but Richie couldn't quite place him. He seemed to know Nancy pretty well, though. I guess Nancy has a few secrets of her own, he thought wryly.

Richie suddenly remembered where he had seen him before. His first night in Sea Shell Harbor, the night he had met Eddie and Danny Shaw. At the Sugar Shack! Nancy had been there with Pat and Sally and Danny had wanted them to ask the girls to dance. Richie remembered Danny had gotten all bent out of shape when they took too much time and the girls ended up dancing with other boys.

John was the one Nancy had been dancing with. She had also left the Sugar Shack with him, he remembered. Richie felt a pang of jealousy. She's not wasting any time, he thought. She's already going out with someone else.

He reached into the pocket of his jeans. He took out the ring and stood there staring at it for several minutes. He felt like crying. Giving her his high school ring as soon as he received it had been his plan, but that didn't seem likely now.

He pictured her face. Nancy. Nancy, please don't do this.

John's face suddenly intruded into his thoughts. He was scowling at him and snarling, causing Nancy's image to fade. John pointed his finger at him and yelled, "Get out of here, you punk!" Next, he turned and swept Nancy into his massive arms. They danced away from him and John bent down and kissed her. She kissed him back. Nancy was kissing John. Nancy. His girl.

"Richie!" The sound of Mickey's voice snapped him out of his reverie. He looked up. Mickey was approaching from the direction of the beach.

"Where you been, Rich? I been looking all over for you!"

Richie gave him a blank look and said nothing. He felt very tired, like he just ran five miles without stopping to rest.

"Are you all right?" Mickey stood directly in front of him, arms folded. His face showed concern.

"Sure, I'm okay," Richie answered in a low voice. "Nancy's new boyfriend just threw me across the dance floor of the Sugar Shack, that's all."

"What? What are you talking about?"

Richie related his encounter with Nancy and John and how he had ended up on the floor. "The guy's as big as a house," he concluded.

"Let's go find them and I'll straighten him out," Mickey offered. He made a fist and held it up in front of him. Richie considered Mickey's offer. "No, that wouldn't do any good, Mick." It'd just make Nancy hate me even more."

"What are you talking about, Rich?" Mickey asked. "Nancy doesn't hate you."

"Well, she doesn't like me anymore, that's for sure."

"She'll get over it." Mickey moved over and leaned against the car next to Richie. He looked thoughtful. "Who is this guy, John, anyway? Where'd Nancy meet him?"

"I don't know where she met him, but she was with him last

Friday night at the Sugar Shack, remember? The night you introduced me to Eddie and Danny. My first night here. His name is John, that's all I know."

"Oh, yeah, I remember now. Pat and Sally were there, too."

"Right. They ended up leaving with those guys that night. Do you remember that?"

Mickey scratched his head. "That's right." He was silent for a moment. "But that don't mean anything, Rich. He's probably just a guy she knew before she met you. That doesn't mean he's her boyfriend or nothing."

Richie was skeptical. "Maybe not, but all I know is, this afternoon everything was cool. Nancy and I were going steady and now we're not. She hates my guts." He looked Mickey in the eye. "How did Nancy find out about Diane, anyway? Who told her?"

Mickey looked down at the ground, avoiding Richie's gaze.

"Come on, Mickey," Richie said, more forcefully. "Who told "her?"

"Pat and Sally told her," Mickey answered, in a small voice. "After we left them this afternoon, when they went to Pat's house. I just found out myself."

"I figured it was something like that," Richie said disgustedly. "But who told Pat and Sally? Did you?"

"No, I didn't, Richie. Honest." Mickey scratched his head again. "Eddie must have. He's the only other person who knew, besides Diane. And she didn't tell them."

Richie looked at Mickey with skepticism.

"I didn't say a word to them, Richie. I swear, I didn't. It must have been Eddie." Mickey fumbled around in his pockets for cigarettes. He found the pack and pulled one out.

"Give me one," Richie said.

"What?"

"A cigarette. Give me a cigarette."

"You sure?"

"Sure I'm sure." Richie took a cigarette from the pack and put it in his mouth. "What's the big deal? You think I've never smoked a cigarette before?"

"Okay." Mickey lit a match and cupped it in his hands. He leaned over and held it under Richie's cigarette. Richie puffed on it until it was lit.

"Thanks." Richie took a drag and coughed twice, then took a smaller one. He drew the smoke deep into his lungs and immediately felt dizzy. "Not bad," he said. "But I like Luckies better."

Mickey lit his own cigarette. "I used to smoke Luckies until I climbed onto a Camel. Now I smoke these."

Richie took another drag. "You shouldn't have told Eddie, Mick. Especially the part about Diane. It was supposed to be a secret."

"I know, Richie. I'm sorry. I didn't think he'd tell Sally. I told him not to tell anyone else. He promised me he wouldn't."

"Well, if you ask me, Eddie's got a big mouth. I know exactly what happened, now. Eddie told Sally and then Sally told Pat. I should have known something was wrong, the way Pat's been treating me lately. The two of them just couldn't wait to tell Nancy."

Richie dropped his cigarette on the ground and stepped on it. "I can't believe Nancy wouldn't even let me explain," he said, dejectedly.

"Pat told me Nancy was really bummed out about it when they told her, Mickey said. "Started crying and everything. She wanted to find Diane and tear her hair out." Mickey beamed. "That means she really likes you, Rich. She wouldn't get mad like that if she didn't care."

"You think so?" Richie asked hopefully. "She sure didn't act like it when I saw her tonight."

"Sure she does," Mickey said confidently. "You'll be back together in a couple of days. You'll see."

"That would be nice," Richie said.

"Yeah. Just give her a couple of days to stew about it, then she'll come around." Mickey took Richie by the arm. "C'mon, let's go back to the beach and join the party. It'll be dark soon and time to shoot off the fireworks."

"I don't know, Mick."

"C'mon, you've been through too much to miss the fireworks. Nancy will get over it. You can call her tomorrow."

Richie hesitated. "I don't know if I want to hang around with Pat and Sally tonight. I'm mad at them for spilling the beans to Nancy. Eddie, too, for that matter."

"So, don't talk to them," Mickey said. "Hang out with me. There's other kids there you know."

Richie wasn't sure he wanted to see anyone at the moment, but he didn't want to be alone, either. "I'm too depressed to have fun," he said.

"It's the Fourth of July, Rich," Mickey said soothingly. "Come to the party, you'll feel much better. Besides, Pat and Sally feel bad about it. They never thought Nancy would break up with you over it." Mickey patted his arm. "You know how girls are. None of 'em can keep a secret. Come on."

"Well, maybe for a little while." Richie allowed himself to be led along by Mickey. They stopped at Eddie's car and Mickey used Eddie's keys to open the trunk.

"Can't forget these," he said, reaching for the bag of fireworks. He pulled out the bag and closed the lid. "What a blast these'll make!"

"This was supposed to be the best Fourth of July ever," Richie said grimly. "Instead, it's the worst one of my life."

"Cheer up, Richie," Mickey said. "I'll have Pat talk to Nancy tomorrow. She'll get the two of you back together."

"I hope so," Richie said. "All I can think of is Nancy walking away with that guy. That's all I can picture in my mind."

"She doesn't like that geek." Mickey stuck out his tongue and made a face. "She's probably just trying to make you jealous, that's all."

"Well, she's sure doing a good job of it."

"Forget about it for a while, Rich." Mickey laid the bag of fireworks on the ground and massaged his sore ribs. "Like I said, it's the Fourth of July and we have a ton of fireworks, so let's have some fun."

"But I just broke up with my girlfriend."

Mickey picked up the bag of fireworks and swung it over his left shoulder. He put his right arm around Richie and said, "Then, it's time to get drunk, Rich!"

Twenty-Three

Richie sat alone on his blanket, drinking from a bottle of beer. The others were gathered on the blanket next to him but separated by several feet. He had decided not to say anything to Pat, Sally or Eddie, figuring that the silent treatment was the best course of action.

He was furious with the three of them, though. In his mind, they had betrayed him. By causing the news of his romantic encounter with Diane to reach Nancy, she had turned around and dumped him for another guy. He blamed them.

Pat and Sally had caused the most damage. They were the ones who told Nancy. But Eddie had to share some of the blame, too. Wasn't he was the one who had spilled the beans to Sally after Mickey asked him not to say a word to anyone? The way it seemed to Richie, everyone had ganged up on him and caused him irreparable pain.

By the time he'd finished his third bottle of beer, he was feeling a bit tipsy. He didn't care. What was there to care about? He signaled to Mickey that he wanted another. Mickey, who was trying to maintain diplomacy by spending time on both blankets, came over with another bottle.

"You're really knocking off the beers tonight, Richie. This is your fourth. I'm only on my second." He popped the cap off the top of the bottle for Richie and handed it over.

"So what?" Richie replied indifferently. "I intend to knock off a lot more before the night is over." He took a swig from the bottle and wiped his mouth with the back of his hand. "Let me have another cigarette, will you?"

"Don't you know that smoking will stunt your growth?" Mickey asked in a light attempt at humor. He held out the pack. Richie took a cigarette and Mickey lit a match for him. He took a deep drag and inhaled.

"Doesn't matter much now, does it?" The alcohol had put Richie in a melancholy mood. "When you break up with your girlfriend, nothing really matters anymore."

"Come on, Richie, stop feeling sorry for yourself," Mickey said, as he lit a cigarette for himself. "Didn't I tell you everything is gonna be all right? You and Nancy will get back together real soon."

Mickey squatted down next to him and spoke in a softer voice. "I talked to Pat. She feels really bad about the whole thing and she's going to have a chat with Nancy tomorrow."

"So now I'm feeling sorry for myself, am I?" Richie asked, ignoring the latter part of Mickey's statement. His feeling of anguish was starting to get the better of him and he wanted to lash out at someone, anyone. Mickey would do. He stood and looked down at his friend.

"Maybe if you had kept quiet about that day, none of this would've happened. I'd be here with my girl right now, instead of sitting alone like some jerk!" Richie was swaying from side to side as he lashed out at Mickey.

"Hey, Richie, I didn't mean..."

"But no," Richie continued, cutting him off, "you had to go and blab to Eddie!" He looked at Mickey, his expression one of disgust. "That guy couldn't keep a secret if his life depended on it!"

Richie was shouting now and the others on the adjacent blanket were beginning to take notice. When Richie saw Eddie looking at him, he directed his tirade at him.

"That's right, Mr. Eddie Big Mouth, I'm talking about you!" He pointed to Pat. "And you, Miss Pat Spill The Beans! And you," he pointed to Sally, "Miss Sally Nice Set of Jugs! You're all nothing but a big bunch of gossips!"

"Richie, please." Mickey stood and tried to console him but it was no use.

"You heard me!" Richie said to Eddie.

"Knock it off, Richie!" Eddie shouted. "You have no right to talk to us like that!"

Richie took several steps toward the other blanket. He was intoxicated from the beer and his words came out slurred. "Who's gonna make me, Eddie, you?" Eddie eyed him warily. "You're drunk, Richie," he said. "I'd suggest you lay down for a while and sleep it off."

Richie moved over to the other blanket and stood in front of Eddie. He was rocking back and forth on the balls of his feet. "Well, maybe you're right! Maybe I am drunk, but at least I know how to keep a secret!"

Eddie stood and faced him but kept his distance. "If you can't stand the heat, old man, you'd better leave the kitchen."

"Oh, really? What a clever remark! Did you think that one up all by yourself, Eddie?" Richie took a long pull from the bottle. "Or maybe you borrowed it from old Harry S. Truman."

"Nobody forced you in the car with Diane, Richie. You brought all this on by yourself." Eddie folded his arms in front of his chest.

Richie gave him a look of contempt. "From what I hear, you spend a little back seat time with Diane yourself from time to time. Isn't that true?" When Eddie didn't reply, Richie said, "Well, isn't it? Answer me, Eddie!"

"What is he talking about, Eddie?" Sally asked.

Eddie ignored her. "I'm not going to talk to you while you're in this condition, Richie. You're drunk and you're upset. Just try to calm down, will you? We can discuss it tomorrow."

"Come on, Richie." Mickey had come up behind him and was trying to coax him back to the other blanket. "This won't solve anything.

Speedy, give me a hand here, will you?" Speedy, who had been sitting quietly the whole time, got up and helped Mickey lead Richie away. "I think I'd like to say somethin'," he said. "Richie, I don't blame you for being ticked off. They done you wrong, man. They shouldn't've said anything to Nancy."

When they had Richie sitting down, Speedy spoke directly to Mickey. "You know, Mick, he's right. We swore an oath of secrecy, didn't we? Eddie had no right to tell the girls."

Speedy gave the others on the other blanket a derisive look, then turned back to Mickey. "You shouldn't've told Eddie," he said accusingly.

"I know," Mickey said. "I goofed."

It was dark now and the sky was being lit up by the fireworks display over the bay. Beautiful bursts of colorful skyrockets and cluster bombs illuminated the sky at thirty-second intervals and could be seen for miles.

"Oh, how pretty!" Sally squealed with delight from the other blanket. "Come on, everybody, let's go down by the water and watch from there." She got up and headed toward the water with Pat and Eddie following behind her.

"Coming, Mickey?" Pat called.

"Be there in a minute," Mickey replied.

Pat stopped and walked back to them. She took Mickey's arm. "Maybe if I talked to Richie, it might help. Should I?"

Mickey shrugged. "You can try."

Pat sat down directly in front of Richie. "I know you're mad at me, Richie, but can I talk to you?"

"About what?" Richie took another sip from the bottle. His eyes were glazed and he stared at her blankly.

"I never wanted you and Nancy to break up," she began. "I was angry when I heard about you and Diane and I admit, I wanted to hurt you. That's why I told her. I thought I was just looking out for my friend, that's all."

Richie took another sip of beer. His words were slurred as he spoke. "Wha's done is done. No use fretting 'bout it."

"What I didn't realize," Pat continued, "was how much Nancy would be hurt by my telling her. I never wanted that, you know."

"No, you wanted to hurt me, tha's all."

"I guess I did," Pat agreed. "I'm sorry."

"Well, what can you do?" Richie said in a sing-song voice. "Times are tough." He put the bottle to his lips.

Pat reached over and stopped him. "Don't you think you've had enough for one night, Richie? Getting drunk won't solve anything."

"P'haps not," Richie said, pulling the bottle away, "but at least'll make me feel better for a little bit while." He took another sip.

Pat stood up. "I know you think I'm a meddler, Richie, and maybe I am, but I don't think drinking is going to bring Nancy back. You'll just wake up tomorrow with a hangover."

"So, wha'f I do?" Richie said defiantly. "Who cares?"

"I care," Pat said. "And Nancy cares."

"Nancy doesn't care!" Richie cried. "She's already going out with someone else!"

"She does care, Richie!" Pat said forcefully. "I know she does. She really likes you, you know. It's just that she was really hurt when she found out about you and Diane, that's all. She'll get over it."

She gave him a sympathetic look. "If you want me to, I'll talk to her for you." She reached over and touched his arm. "Richie, I really think you're a nice guy and I want to see the two of you get back together again." She tried to take his hand in hers.

Richie moved his hand away. He wasn't having any of it. The alcohol had gotten to him, eliminating all chances of reasoning with him. He got to his feet unsteadily and spoke in a loud voice. "Don't do me any favors, Pat! You've done enough damage for one day!"

He moved closer to her, staggering slightly and pointing his finger at her. "Sure, I made out with Diane! I admit it! I made a mistake! I was drunk and I got carried away!" His stomach was churning and he felt sick. "But it was between me and Diane! It wasn't anyone else's business!" He was lurching back and forth now, gesturing wildly.

"Come on, Richie, take it easy," Mickey said.

"No, I won't, Mickey! You come on! You still have your girlfriend but I've got nothing!" Richie shouted. "The trouble is, you all have big mouths! Can't keep secrets!"

Richie went to take another forward step and fell flat on his face. His head began to spin and he thought he was going to be sick. He rolled over on his back and closed his eyes. "Big mouths," he muttered, more to himself than anyone else. He continued to lie there with his eyes closed.

"I think he passed out." Mickey bent over to take a closer look.

Richie opened his eyes and lifted his head. "Wrong again! You think I'm passed out?" He got to his knees and waited for the feeling of nausea to pass, then stood up shakily. "It'll take more than a couple of beers to make me pass out."

He staggered to the other blanket where the cooler was, lifted the lid and took out another beer. He paused for a second, then turned around and looked at Mickey. "You wan' a beer, Mick?"

Mickey shook his head. "No, I've had enough. Don't you think you've had enough, too, Richie? You still look a little tipsy."

"Had enough?" Richie laughed. "I'm just getting started, Mick! You're the one who said it was time to get drunk, remember?" He opened the bottle and took a sip. "It's the Fourth of July! Come on, you bunch of sissies!"

Richie was thoroughly intoxicated now and his feelings were out of control. He took another pull from the bottle while they stood on the blanket and watched him.

The image of Nancy in John's arms came back to haunt him. He took the bottle and threw it as hard as he could toward the water.

"Richie! You're out of control!" Mickey started to move towards him.

"I make one lousy mistake with Diane and my life gets ruined over it," he said angrily. He looked at the others accusingly.

Pat tried to speak. "Richie, we didn't mean..."

Richie pointed his finger at her. "You told Nancy!" he said loudly. He shifted his finger to Mickey. "And you told Eddie!"

"Richie, we've already been over this," Mickey said.

Richie walked to the edge of the blanket and looked sadly down at the sand. He felt dejected. "If everyone had just kept quiet about it nothing would have happened! Are you happy now? You broke us up!" He had tears in his eyes.

"You're drunk, Richie!" Mickey said. "You don't know what you're saying. Come with us. We'll just shoot off these fireworks and forget the rest for now, okay? We can straighten everything else out tomorrow, when you're feeling better. Pat will help, won't you, Pat?"

"I don't want her help! And I don't want to shoot off any fireworks, either!" Richie was in a rage now. He stepped closer to Mickey and tapped him on the chest. "Where did you get all the money for those fireworks, anyway, huh? Fifty the other day and thirty last night!"

"I already told you," Mickey said calmly. "I've been saving."

"Saving my foot!" Richie spat. "You robbed that house in Southampton, didn't you?"

"No!"

"And then you had me lie to the police for you, didn't you?"

Pat's eyes widened. "What is he talking about, Mickey?"

"Oh, you didn't know about that, did you, Pat?" Richie said mockingly. "You think I'm such a creep but maybe you ought to know what your boyfriend, Mickey's been up to! He made me lie to the police for him and then he tried to fix me up with his own sister! Remember, Mickey? 'Diane really likes you, man', remember?"

Richie turned to Pat. "Then he shows up that day with some loser named Charlie, they're in a stolen car and we almost get killed! But I'm the bad guy?"

"You think I robbed that house, Richie?" Mickey asked in a soft voice. "Do you?"

"What house?" Pat exclaimed. "What are you talking about, Richie?"

"Yes, I do," Richie said, ignoring her. "If you had nothing to hide, you wouldn't have lied to the police! You would have told them the truth!"

Pat's face showed utter disbelief. She shifted her gaze between the two of them. "Would somebody please talk to me?"

"I told you why I couldn't tell them," Mickey said.

"Sure, Mickey. You think I believe that now? You robbed that house and then you used me to cover it up! I lied to the police for you and I kept my mouth shut about it! But when I needed your help, what did you do? Huh? You couldn't even keep a secret about me and Diane! No, you had to go and tell Mr. Big Mouth, Eddie!"

"I can't believe you're doing this, Richie," Mickey said quietly. "I thought we were friends."

"We are friends! Do you think I'd lie to the police for you if we weren't friends?"

"Not any more we aren't." Mickey studied Richie for a second, then turned away.

"Oh, so now we're not friends anymore, is that what you're saying?" Richie said to Mickey's back. "Well, that's okay with me, Mick!" Richie turned to Pat. "I suppose we're not friends anymore, either, huh, Pat?"

"I want to be your friend, Richie," Pat answered softly.

"Yeah, sure you do. You and Sally couldn't wait to screw me up with Nancy, though, could you? Some friends! And Nancy? She's already out with another guy. She wouldn't even give me a chance to explain, first!"

Richie turned to leave, then stopped and looked back at Pat. "Well, you know what I say? I say the hell with all of you!" He stormed away from the blanket, leaving Pat, Mickey and Speedy standing there. No one called after him. The tears which had been trying to work their way out flowed easily now, blurring his vision. He wiped at his eyes furiously, unable to see where he was going. It's all over, he thought, miserably. Everything.

The level of his rage had taken him completely by surprise. It was totally out of character for him. He couldn't remember ever having such strong feelings of hostility before. He was having trouble trying to understand it. Was it because his emotions and frustrations had been building up inside of him the past week?

If such was the case, they had finally burst out of him, taking the form of an explosive tirade against his friends. Former friends, he thought, cynically. He felt remorse.

He was already sorry for the things he'd said to Mickey and couldn't believe he had done it with such vehemence. Even in his drunken state he knew that was wrong, but part of him still didn't care. He felt Mickey and the others had betrayed him and because of that, he had lost Nancy. So that's how it had come out. What was done was done.

Richie walked with his head down, kicking up sand as he went along. Some Fourth of July, he thought wryly. He'd already lost his girlfriend and now he was alone and friendless.

He realized he had no one to blame but himself. It was his own stupidity that had led him to where he was at this moment. He'd yielded to temptation and he'd gotten caught. Case closed. It was that simple.

He looked at his watch. It was only nine-thirty. Too early to go home. His parents were out and he didn't feel like being alone in the cabin. Not tonight, of all nights. Alone? He'd have to get used to that. He'd be alone for the rest of the summer, it looked like. He'd never be able to face any of the kids again.

The Sugar Shack stayed open until midnight on Fridays and Saturdays and he decided to go there for a cup of coffee. Time to sober up before he found himself in more hot water.

Richie trudged through the sand, hoping he wouldn't run into anyone else he knew. He wasn't in any mood to answer questions about the condition he was in, or why he wasn't with his friends.

No, all he wanted was a cup of coffee and then he would go home to bed. Summer was over as far as he was concerned. There was nothing left for him in Sea Shell Harbor. Nothing at all.

"Richie, where are you going?"

Richie looked up toward the source of the voice. It was Diane. She was coming his way from the direction of the Sugar Shack. A slight evening breeze lifted her long blond hair from her bare shoulders. She wore a pair of shorts, sandals and a halter top that barely covered her breasts. She gave him a dazzling smile. Diane. The cause of all his problems.

"Hello, Diane," He said, returning her smile with a weaker one of his own. "What are you doing here?"

"I was looking for you," she said.

Twenty-Four

Richie stopped and waited for Diane to reach him. "Well, you found me," he said listlessly.

"Where are you going?" Diane gave a little toss of her head to move her hair away from her face.

"No place special." Richie was swaying slightly. "Need a cup of coffee. Had too much to drink."

"Where's everybody else?" she asked.

"Down at the beach shooting off fireworks."

"Well, how come you're not at the beach?"

"Had enough fireworks for one night." Richie lurched sideways and Diane put out a hand to steady him.

"Are you okay?" She looked at him more closely. "What's wrong, Richie? You look like you just lost your best friend."

"Maybe I have," he replied.

"Want to talk about it?"

"I don't know, I..."

"Come on." Diane took his hand and led him over to the edge of the parking lot. They leaned against the fence and she focused all her attention on him. "Now, tell me what happened," she commanded.

Richie began to speak. Tentatively at first, then more freely and with great emotion. Once he started, the words came gushing out of him like a raging river flowing to the sea.

Telling her first about the argument he'd had with the others, he then backtracked and began to tell her everything that had happened since he'd seen her last.

Diane let him talk, murmuring only an occasional, "Oh," or "Gee". When he finished, she was thoughtful for a moment before speaking. "Richie, I'm sorry for what happened but I'm not going to apologize for my part in it. I've already told you how I feel about you and nothing will ever change that." She touched his arm lightly.

"You told me you liked another girl and I respected you for that, but Richie, did you ever think maybe she's not the right one for you? I mean, if she's already going out with another guy, she couldn't have liked you very much to begin with."

"Nancy said she loved me," he said in a low voice."

Diane moved closer to him and gently touched his cheek. "I don't really know and I guess I shouldn't say anything about her because that's between the two of you. I do know this, though. I'd never hurt you the way she did. She's already out with someone else, but I'm here with you. If she really loved you, she wouldn't do that to you."

Richie listened quietly to Diane's words, letting them all sink in. Nancy had hurt him tonight. Hurt him deeply. He agreed with Diane on that point. She hadn't even given him a chance to explain. "Maybe you're right," he said. "Maybe she didn't love me."

"I don't know, Richie, only she can tell you whether she did or didn't. I will tell you one thing. You're wrong about Mickey. He is your friend and he thinks the world of you."

"But, he..."

"Maybe he shouldn't have asked you to lie to the police for him," she interrupted. "Maybe that was a mistake. He didn't rob any houses, though. I know my brother and he wouldn't do anything like that. No, he was home that night like he said. He just didn't think the police would believe him, so he asked us to help him."

"But where did he get all the money for the fireworks?" Richie asked. "He spent over eighty dollars. That's a lot of money, Diane. He can't make that much delivering groceries, can he?"

Richie gently rubbed his bruised face with the tips of his fingers.

"And how could he ask me to lie to the police? I only met him a week ago. He had no right to ask me to do something like that."

"I don't know where he got the money, Richie, but he didn't steal it. I'm sure he didn't. As for the police, he asked me to lie to them because I'm his sister and I'd do anything for him, including that."

"But I'm not family."

"He asked you to lie because he thought of you as a good friend. Somehow, he knew he could trust you to help him. Who else besides me would have done it? You think Eddie would have lied for him?"

She answered her own question. "He wouldn't. As much as Mickey likes him, he would never ask Eddie to do anything like that because Eddie just isn't as good a friend as you are. Believe me, I know."

"But Mickey and I just met," Richie protested. "How could he think that? He's known Eddie a lot longer."

"That doesn't matter, Richie. Mickey has a special quality that enables him to judge people. It's like he can see inside them or something and know what that person is really like."

Diane leaned back against the fence and folded her arms. "Look, I've known Eddie for a long time, too. I've even dated him. But when you get right down to it, we're worlds apart." She smacked her lips and went on. "Eddie's a little rich boy from the other side of the tracks. He hangs around with us, but we really move in different social circles. He's going places and we're not. Why, he's never even invited me to his house!" She looked angry now.

"Believe me, Richie," she continued, "there's just no way Mickey would ever ask Eddie to lie like that for him. No, he'd only ask a real friend. A friend like you."

Richie stood beside her with his hands in his pockets, staring at the ground. He was silent for a moment, thinking about what Diane had just said. Finally, he said, "I wasn't a real friend tonight. I said some terrible things to him."

"He'll understand, Richie. He knows what kind of pressure you've been under lately. We do talk a lot, you know."

Richie smiled for the first time that evening. "You do?"

"Sure we do. Mickey and I are very close. There's a lot about us you don't know. We haven't had it too easy in this town ever since my parents split up." Diane glanced over at him. "You might even say we're the town misfits."

Richie raised his eyebrows but said nothing.

"That's right. She picked at a piece of paint chip on top of the fence. "Nobody would ever say anything to our faces but we know what people think. Our family reputation isn't entirely spotless." She gave a cynical laugh. "Some people can really be cruel."

Richie looked at her as if seeing her for the first time. He suddenly felt a closeness to her that hadn't been there before. He studied her face for a long time. There was an ever so slight sprinkling of freckles which ran from one cheek across her nose to the other one. She was very attractive, he realized. "You're a pretty smart kid for a fifteen-year-old," he said finally.

"Actually," she said, "I'm sixteen. Today's my birthday."

"What? You were born on the Fourth of July?"

"Yeah. Pretty neat, huh?"

"I'll say." Richie was starting to feel better. The effects of the alcohol were beginning to fade, along with his anger. He ran a hand through his hair. "I've got to talk to Mickey," he said. "I said a lot of things to him I shouldn't have. I don't want him to be mad at me."

"Don't worry, Richie. Mickey doesn't get mad very easily. Like I said, he'll understand. He knows how upset you were."

"You think so?"

Diane moved closer to him. "Mickey really thinks the world of you, Richie. He never wanted you to get caught up in his troubles." She turned and moved in front of him, facing him, then put her arms around his waist and hugged him. "Some things just happen, that's all."

He put his arms around her shoulders and drew her closer. "What kind of things?" he asked.

"Like the other day in the car." She looked up at him. "I wanted you to kiss me and I should have left you alone. I'm sorry."

She felt good in his arms, comforting. "I wanted to kiss you, too."

"But you were going steady with someone else and I should have respected that. Besides, you had been drinking and you weren't thinking clearly."

The scene with Nancy and John earlier in the Sugar Shack came to mind. He remembered John pushing him and knocking him down, then Nancy taking his arm and leaving with him. Feelings of anger and jealousy came rushing back to him but he managed to push them aside.

He looked down at Diane. "I was drinking tonight too, but I believe I'm finally starting to think clearly about you for the first time," he said.

"Thinking clearly about me?"

"About you and me."

"What do you mean?"

"I'm thinking about how I'd like to kiss you again."

"You are?" Diane's arms tightened around his waist. "Are you sure, Richie? I don't want you to do anything you're not sure of."

Richie pulled her closer to him and kissed her. "I'm sure," he said. He kissed her again, enjoying the feel of her lips against his. They were soft and tender. Her enticing perfume was enveloping him, making him giddy.

"What about Nancy?" she asked breathlessly.

"Nancy?" He pictured Nancy's face. She was kissing John. "She's out with someone else tonight." He kissed Diane again. "It's a funny thing, but I haven't thought about Nancy at all for a while now. All I'm thinking about right now is you, Diane."

It was true. It was as though his feelings for Nancy had suddenly disappeared. She had killed them tonight by her actions. Nancy had betrayed him and he forced himself not to care about her anymore. Maybe the spark that had existed between them had already died.

On the other hand, there was a spark between himself and Diane, now. It had existed the other day in the car and now, at this moment, it had suddenly ignited and burst into flame. Fueled by their mutual passion for each other, the fire was threatening to burn out of control.

"Let's go somewhere," Diane said between kisses.

"Where?"

"Somewhere we can be alone."

Richie thought for a moment. "Come on." He took her hand and they started walking out of the parking lot towards Beach Road. "I know a place where we can go."

"Where?" Diane asked.

"My house. There's nobody home."

They strolled up Beach Road, holding hands. When they passed the Salty Pirate, the aroma of barbecued steak and grilled onions drifted out from the restaurant's kitchen and greeted them.

Mixed with the sounds of music and merry conversation coming from the dining room and bar area, it helped to create a festive atmosphere. The place was packed with the Fourth of July holiday crowd.

"I'm getting hungry," Diane said.

"Me, too," Richie agreed. "It looks like those people are sure having fun," he said, gesturing toward one of the picture windows in the bar. "We can have fun just as well as anyone," Diane said seriously. "It's up to us." She gave his hand a gentle squeeze.

"I hope you're right."

"Are you sure your parents won't mind you bringing guests over when they're not home?"

"Nah, they won't mind," Richie said. "They told me to have a good time, tonight." He laughed. "Besides, they're celebrating the holiday with friends and they won't be back until very late."

"Neat," Diane said.

When they reached the cabin, Richie opened the door and led her inside. He walked over to the radio in the living room and turned it on, then fiddled with the dial until he found a rock and roll station. He pointed to the sofa. "Make yourself comfortable," he said. "I'll be right back."

He went into the bathroom and brushed his teeth to get rid of the taste of alcohol before returning to the living room. "I can make you a hot dog or something if you're still hungry."

"No, that's okay, I'm not really that hungry. Do you have anything to drink, though, like a coke?"

"Sure, let me check the fridge." He went into the kitchen and pulled out two bottles of coke from the refrigerator, then returned to the living room. Diane was still sitting on the sofa. She crossed her legs and patted the seat beside her.

"Take a load off," she said. He sat beside her and they sipped their cokes, not saying anything. Finally, she put her bottle on the coffee table and turned to face him. He looked at her expectantly.

"Richie," she began, "I want you to know that no matter what happens after tonight between you and Nancy, I really do care for you and I've decided that I'll take any time I can have with you."

"It doesn't look like there'll be anything happening between Nancy and me now, Diane. She dumped me." He took a sip from the bottle. The coke tasted much better than the beer he'd had earlier.

That may be true," she said, "but things can change. I just want you to know how I feel about you, that's all." She picked up her drink and took another sip. "How do you feel about me?"

He held his bottle in both hands, rolling it back and forth between his fingers. "I like you, too, Diane," he said. He stopped rolling the bottle and took a sip. "Probably more than I realized," he added.

"You're not just saying that to be nice, are you?"

"No. I liked you right from the start, believe me."

"How come you didn't ask me out then? Was it because I was Mickey's sister?"

"I don't know. That probably had something to do with it. And I guess I thought you were too young for me. Anyway, then I met Nancy and got distracted." "Do you think I'm too young for you now, Richie?"

"No, I don't." He looked at her admiringly. "Not at all."

They sat on the sofa listening to the radio for a while, neither of them speaking. She held her bottle to her lips and watched him as he fidgeted nervously.

"What a night," he said finally.

She smiled at his discomfort. "Life is hell and then we die," she said. She continued to watch him closely. "Of course...," she started to speak and then hesitated.

"Yes?"

"Life can also be heaven," she said, gazing into his eyes. "That is, if you want it."

"You really think so, Diane?"

"I know so." She finished the last of her coke and stood. "Finished?" she asked, pointing to his bottle.

"Yeah." He took a final sip, then handed her the empty bottle.

"I'll put these away for you." As she turned and started to walk to the kitchen, he got up and followed her. Diane was putting the empty bottles in the sink when he came up behind her and placed his hands on her waist.

She turned around and came into his arms, kissing him and wrapping her arms around him. He kissed her back, gently at first, then with more passion. Her body moved against his and she held him tightly. They kissed for a long time before breaking it off, still holding on to each other. Both of them were breathing heavily.

"Happy birthday, Diane," he whispered, enjoying the feel and smell of her.

"I have a present for you," she said breathlessly.

"But it's your birthday, not mine," he said.

"It doesn't matter, Richie. This is something I want you to have." She kissed him again, more passionately than before. "Where's your room?"

"Over there," he said, pointing in the general direction of his bedroom. "Why?"

"Come on." She took his hand and led him towards his room. When they were just outside the door, she turned and embraced him. "If you only knew how excited you make me feel, Richie. If you only knew." She kissed him again. "I go ape over you."

He was overwhelmed by her ardor. "What's the present?" he asked when she broke off the kiss.

Diane took his hand and pulled him into the bedroom, then closed the door behind them. "Me," she answered.

Twenty-Five

Richie woke up Saturday morning with a slight hangover and mixed feelings of sorrow and happiness. He felt sad when he thought about Nancy breaking up with him but he was thrilled with the way things had worked out with Diane. Diane excited him like no girl ever had before.

He knew he wasn't in love with her. No, it was a physical attraction that existed between them. He also realized that it had been there from the very beginning. Even though he had tried to push it aside, it was so strong it had blotted out everything else from his mind.

Richie sat up in bed and stretched, then walked over to the bathroom. He recalled the fight he'd had with his friends. That bothered him and he knew he would somehow have to try to make amends. Vaguely remembering some of the terrible things he'd said to Mickey the night before at the beach, he couldn't believe he'd been that resentful.

He knew a lot of his anger could be blamed on the beer he'd consumed but he'd also have to give serious thought to some of other reasons. Standing in front of the mirror and examining his reflection, he made a vow he would never touch a drop of alcohol again for as long as he lived.

He picked up his toothbrush and started brushing his teeth. He couldn't wait to see Diane again. She had thrilled him beyond his wildest imaginations, transforming him from an awkward, innocent teenager to a sophisticated man of the world.

Being with her last night had been like having a new toy to play with and he was looking forward to playing with it again. Diane had completely captivated him with her womanly charms and there was no turning back now.

His parents had returned home shortly after one o'clock in the morning. He and Diane had fallen asleep on his bed but were awakened by their voices in the kitchen. The sound of the refrigerator door opening and ice cubes tinkling in a glass indicated they were probably having a nightcap before retiring.

Richie and Diane had quietly and hurriedly put on their clothes and then she had left by climbing out his bedroom window. She assured him she would get home safely and not to worry. "See you later, lover," she had said. They made plans to meet that evening.

The day was hot and humid and Richie was already starting to sweat. He thought about going to the beach, but decided against it, figuring he'd probably run into someone he didn't want to see. He wasn't ready to face any of the gang yet, not until he figured out what he'd say to them. That is, if they even wanted to talk to him. Maybe he'd go over to Sag Harbor and catch an afternoon matinee. At least the theater would be air conditioned.

After showering, he dressed in a pair of shorts, tank top and sandals, then went into the kitchen to make himself some breakfast. His parents were nowhere in sight and he wondered if they were still sleeping.

As he poured himself a glass of juice, he saw the note taped to the refrigerator door. It was from his mother. It said his parents were spending the day on the boat of their new friends, the Kramers and wouldn't be home until dinner.

That was fine with him. He preferred being alone at the moment. It would give him a chance to think and he had a lot of that to do. Sorting out the events of the day before would take a lot of time. I'm a man, he thought, as he sipped the juice. It was time to start thinking like one.

He had planned on informing his parents about Mickey and

the police today, but it could wait until another occasion. Since he and Nancy were no longer going steady, the urgency was gone and he was in no rush to tell them.

It was funny, he thought. Whenever he thought of Nancy now, the emotion was gone and in its place was a strange calmness. Maybe Diane was right. Maybe Nancy hadn't really loved him in the first place but had only been mouthing the words. Maybe.

He knew he had loved her, though. He was sure of it.

That wasn't something he could fake. Nevertheless, where she was concerned, there was now merely a sort of void in his heart.

Had going all the way with Diane made him feel that way about her? No. It had started before that, when he'd seen Nancy leave the Sugar Shack with her new boyfriend, John. Something inside of him had clicked off. The feelings of jealousy and humiliation he'd experienced on the dance floor had been the catalyst, effectively killing his feelings for her.

It didn't seem to matter to him anymore. Being with Diane had taken over and finished the job. It was Diane who was foremost on his mind, now. He still cared for Nancy in some ways, he supposed, but since he had messed up so badly in her eyes, he figured she no longer felt the same way about him.

"Oh, well, water under the bridge," he said out loud. "I've got Diane." He picked up his glass and drained the last of his juice. Diane would be his girl from now on. Richie and Diane. It had a nice ring to it, didn't it? Yes. Richie and Nancy. Nope, that didn't sound right. Not anymore.

There was a knock on the door just as he was finishing the last of his toast. He got up from the table and went inside to answer it. It was Speedy. He was out of breath and all sweaty from the heat.

"Hi, Speedy," he greeted. "What brings you here?"

"I gotta talk to you, Rich!" Richie invited him in. Speedy looked excited as he mopped at his brow with a damp handkerchief. "What's up?" Richie led the way to the living room and offered him a seat.

"After you left last night, the fireworks really exploded," Speedy began excitedly. He stood in front of the sofa bouncing up and down on the balls of his feet, then began to pace back and forth.

"I know," Richie said. "I saw some of them before I left."

"No, that's not what I mean. I'm talkin' 'bout the human fire-works. Man, you should-a seen it!"

"Sit down, Speedy," Richie pointed to the sofa, "and tell me what happened."

Speedy sat in the same spot Diane had occupied the night before. He fidgeted nervously until Richie sat in the chair next to him. "You want something to drink?" he asked.

"No, I'm okay." Speedy closed his eyes, leaned back and rested his head on the rear of the sofa for a moment, then opened them again and leaned forward. "After you left," he began, "all hell broke loose."

"What are you talking about?" Richie asked, puzzled.

Speedy rubbed his nose vigorously the way he did whenever he was excited. "Well, the first thing that happened was Mickey had an argument with Pat, Sally and Eddie. Told them they all had big mouths, and that because of them, you and him weren't friends no more."

"He did?" Richie was surprised to hear this but also pleased that Mickey had stood up for him. "Yeah. They didn't wanna hear it and so they ended up havin' a big fight. Pat and Sally got mad and left with Eddie." Speedy laced his fingers together and cracked his knuckles. "Me and Mickey started drinkin' beer after that, then we remembered we still had the fireworks, so we lit some of 'em off.

"After a while, Mickey says we should go over to your house and get ya 'cause he promised you fireworks for the fourth and he didn't want you to be mad at him any more."

"Mickey said that?" Richie was amazed.

"Yeah. Said all the trouble was his fault and he wanted to make it up to you." Speedy leaned back and crossed his legs. "He told me about the cops and what you did for him, then he said he couldn't let this go on any longer. He wants to talk to you and try to straighten everything out."

"It wasn't all Mickey's fault," Richie said. "I have to share some of the blame, too. I was drunk last night."

"Maybe so, Rich, but they had no business squealin' on you to

Nancy like that," Speedy said seriously. "They really screwed you up! Anyway, we start packin' everything up so's we could come over here, and then they showed up."

"Who showed up?"

Speedy started counting on his fingers. "Stevie Miller, Vinnie Armadella, Carl Boucher and about five other guys."

"You're kidding!"

"No, I swear. I almost wet my friggin' pants. I was busy gettin' the rest of the fireworks together, when I look up and see Vinnie standin' over me." Speedy stood up from the sofa and started gesturing with his hands.

"Richie, this guy is a moose! Next thing I know, he's got me by the throat and he's yellin', 'This is the guy that hit me!'. I almost blacked out right then and there!"

"Oh, no!" Richie said.

"Then two of 'em grab Mickey and they start twistin' his arms behind him - he looked like a pretzel - and askin' him, 'Where's the other guy?'" Speedy bent his arms behind his back to show Richie what it looked like. "I'm tellin' you, Rich, I was never so scared in my life! I almost fainted on the spot!"

"God! What happened next?"

"Well, Vinnie lets go of my throat and I fall down in the sand. I'm figurin' he's probably got a bottle or somethin' and he's gettin' ready to hit me with it, but nothin' happens. I look up and there's my friend, Carl Boucher, the guy we bought the fireworks from."

"Yeah? Come on, Speedy, what happened next?" Richie urged.

"Yeah. So, Boucher steps in front of Vinnie and says to me, 'Speedy, I didn't know you were involved in this.' I says, yeah, Carl, looks like I am, and he says, 'Well, why did you hit Vinnie over the head with a coke bottle?' and I says, 'cause they had Mickey on the ground two on one and I had to do somethin'. It wasn't a fair fight."

Richie shook his head slowly from side to side. "I can't believe it."

"Believe it." Speedy gave Richie one of his goofy grins. "Then, all of a sudden, Mickey breaks loose from the two guys who're holdin' him and he runs over to Carl. Everyone's lookin' at Mickey to see what he's gonna do, then Mickey says, 'Look, Boucher, this is all my fault, so leave Speedy out of it!'

"Carl says, 'What do you mean?' and Mickey tells him how it's really between him and Stevie and if anyone's gonna fight, it should be them."

"What happened next?"

"Carl has Mickey tell him the whole story from beginning to end." Speedy paused a moment to catch his breath. "When Mickey's finished, Carl thinks it all over. He's like a mediator, you know? Anyway, Carl finally says the whole thing is bein' blown out of proportion and, since it wasn't a fair fight at Shelter Island, Stevie and Mickey should duke it out."

"Boucher said that?"

"Yeah, but Stevie says he ain't gonna fight Mickey alone. He wants them all to beat the hell out of us and then go find Eddie and take care of him, too. Carl says, 'No, it ain't gonna happen that way, it ain't a fair fight.' Then Vinnie says it ain't fair lettin' me get away with hittin' him over the head like I done, that I should be punished for it. He tells Carl to let him deal with me one on one and that's a fair fight." Speedy paused, looking at Richie with wide eyes, then continued.

"Before Carl can say yes or no, Mickey says, 'Tell you what, Boucher, I'll fight all of you one at a time but leave Speedy alone. He was just tryin' to help me out, that's all.' Can you believe it, Rich?" Speedy asked happily. "Mickey offered to fight all of 'em one at a time, to save me from a beatin'."

Richie nodded. "What did Boucher say when he heard that?"

"He says somethin' like, 'Hey, I admire a guy who would risk his own neck to save a friend.' Then, he looks at Stevie and says, 'There ain't gonna be no more fightin'. You and Mickey shake hands.' Next, he turns to Vinnie and says, 'You're twice as big as Speedy. I ain't gonna let you fight him neither. Everybody just shake hands and let's get out of here.' Then they left."

"Just like that?"

"Yup, just like that. It was unbelievable, Richie," Speedy said proudly. "I never seen nothin' like it. Mickey talks eight guys out of wantin' to make mince meat out of us. Pretty cool, huh?"

"I'll say." Richie got up from his chair. "Come on, Speedy, let's go out to the kitchen and I'll make us a cup of coffee." Richie had started drinking coffee only that morning, figuring he was a man now and that's what men drink.

"Sure." Speedy followed him into the other room.

They sat at the kitchen table drinking the coffee and Speedy went over the story again, embellishing it this time with vivid descriptions and sound effects. Richie pictured menacing faces on large, muscular bodies bent on pulverizing the two innocents, Mickey and Speedy.

He was impressed by Speedy's description of Mickey's behavior in the face of adversity. Mickey had come through in a crisis and Richie was proud of him. He decided he had to see him as soon as possible. First, he wanted to apologize for his own behavior, and second, he wanted to try and make amends for the night before.

"Mickey wants to see you, Rich," Speedy said. "He wants to tell you that he ain't mad at you no more and he's still your friend. He hopes you ain't mad at him no more, either. He had to work today because of the holiday but he'll be gettin' off around three. Can you meet him at the Sugar Shack around three-thirty?"

"Sure. Tell him I'll be there. I really didn't want to fight with him in the first place. I think all the beer I drank got the best of me."

"Boy, I'll say," Speedy agreed. He laughed. "You were really smashed last night. We could've used you when those guys from Shelter Island showed up. The way you were actin', you would've scared them all away." He finished his coffee and stood.

"Gotta go now. I'm goin' fishin' on the boat for a couple of hours. You wanna come along?"

"No, I don't think so. Thanks, anyway, Speedy. I think I'll just hang around here for the rest of the day. The heat is making me tired, so maybe I'll take a nap. I still have a "headache from last night." Richie picked up the empty cups and took them to the sink.

"Okay, then, I'll see ya later." Speedy got up from the table and they walked back through the cabin to the front door. After saying their goodbyes, Richie went to his room to lie down for a while.

He was in the middle of a dreamless sleep when loud banging snapped him back to consciousness. He woke with a start and sat upright on the bed, disoriented for a moment. When he realized the banging was someone knocking loudly on the door, he went inside to answer it.

He had fallen asleep with his clothes on and he smoothed out the wrinkles with both hands as he shook the cobwebs out of his head. He was whistling a nondescript tune as he walked through the cabin out to the porch to open the door. His heart leaped into his throat when he saw them standing there. It was the two detectives from the Southampton Police Department, Shaunessy and Robbins.

"Got a minute?" Robbins asked sarcastically. He had a smirk on his face. Shaunessy looked grave.

Richie stepped back inside and held the screen door open for them. He nervously eyed Shaunessy, whose face betrayed the seriousness of the situation, then Robbins, who looked extremely angry. His legs started to shake uncontrollably.

"We'd like a word with you," Shaunessy said without a trace of his previous kindness. Richie led them to the living room, offered them the sofa, then sat down in the chair across from them. He looked at them with absolute fear and trepidation.

"Kid," Robbins began seriously, "you utter one sentence that doesn't have a ring of truth to it and I'll slap the cuffs on you before you can say boo, understand?"

Richie swallowed hard and nodded.

"You know why we're here, Richard?" Shaunessy asked.

"I think so," Richie answered meekly.

Shaunessy looked at his partner as if to say, let me do the talking, then spoke. "Why did you lie to us, son?"

"I thought I was helping Mickey," Richie answered truthfully.

"You thought you were helping Mickey by lying to us about where the two of you were that night? What good did you think that would do?" Shaunessy's demeanor softened somewhat.

"Didn't you think we'd eventually find out the truth?". Robbins squinted his eyes at Richie and looked at him intently.

Richie raised his hands in a helpless gesture. "I don't know, I...,
Mickey told me you wouldn't believe he was home that night sleeping, so we made up that story."

"You're damned right we wouldn't!" Robbins said harshly. "We
know where your friend was that night, all right. Over in Southampton burglarizing a house!"

"Mickey wouldn't do that," Richie protested. "He..."

"Come off it, kid," Robbins spat. "What dream world you living in?"

Shaunessy touched Robbins lightly on the arm. "Richard, all
of the evidence points the finger at Mickey. He lied to us about his
whereabouts that night. He's been flashing money around..."

"Who told you that?" Richie interrupted.

"Never mind who told us. It's true, isn't it?" Robbins asked
caustically.

"Bernie, please." Shaunessy smiled sweetly at his partner and
continued speaking. "Richard, we're convinced that Mickey is the
one we're looking for. He's been in trouble before for stealing, I already told you that. Now he's gotten you in trouble by having you
lie for him. What kind of a friend would ask you to do something
like that?" Shaunessy slowly shook his head and his voice became
more sympathetic. "He's using you, son. You've got to stop trying
to protect him."

Tears started to well up in Richie's eyes. "Mickey wouldn't do
anything like that. I know him."

"Where's your parents?" Robbins asked suddenly.

"They're out on the water with friends," Richie replied uneasily.
"The Kramers. They'll be home later."

"We're going to have to talk to them about this," Shaunessy
stated. "What time will they be home?"

"Around six, I think," Richie answered unhappily.

"All right, now listen." Shaunessy reached into his shirt pocket
and took out a business card. He looked at it, then handed it to
Richie. "Have your father call us on Monday at this number. He's
going to have to come into the station with you next week. You're
going to give us another statement, Richard, and this time it had

better be the complete truth. Do you understand?"

Richie nodded. "Yes, sir. Am I..., uh, am I in trouble?" he asked timidly.

"I'm afraid so, son," Shaunessy answered gravely. "How much depends on you. If you come clean with us and tell us the truth, it might not be too bad. It's really not up to us, though. The district attorney will decide." Shaunessy stood up, followed quickly by Robbins. "Just tell us the truth, Richard. That's my advice."

"I will." Richie looked up at the two of them and spoke in a small voice. "What about Mickey? What kind of trouble is he in?"

"He's under arrest!" Robbins said loudly.

Shaunessy corrected him. "Mickey will be placed under arrest as soon as we pick him up. We have people out looking for him right now. If you know where he is, you'd better tell us. Make it easier for him. Do you know where he is?"

"Well, I...," Richie was about to tell them he thought Mickey might be at Treadways when Robbins cut him off.

"If you know, tell us right now, sonny!" he yelled. "Or you'll find yourself sleeping in the cell next to him! Now, where is he?" Robbins stood in front of him, looking down at him menacingly. "Don't you dare lie to me, either!"

"I don't know where he is!" Richie shouted. The hell with you, Mutt, he thought, remembering what Mickey had told him about the Mutt and Jeff act cops liked to stage.

Although he was the most frightened he'd ever been in his entire life, he found the strength to resist from the way Robbins was treating him. He wasn't going to tell Robbins anything, he decided. Let him find Mickey himself.

"All right, Richard, take it easy." Shaunessy motioned to his partner. "We'll be going now. Make sure your father calls us on Monday. If we don't hear from him then, we'll have no choice but to come back and place you under arrest as well, understood?"

"Yes."

After the detectives had gone, Richie remained sitting in the chair for a long time. His mind and emotions were racing up and down like a yo yo. He knew he was in serious trouble, now. What was he going to do? What would his parents say when they found out? Nothing like this had ever happened before. They'd disown him for sure.

He sat there dejectedly, head in hands and close to tears. They'll never understand, he told himself. Never in a million years. Not only that, his life would never be the same after this.

He'd lost it all. Nancy, his friends, his freedom. The summer was ruined and the crowd had broken up because of this. It was all gone, everything. Even Diane! He'd probably never see her again, either.

He got up from the chair and started to pace back and forth around the room. He went into the bathroom and looked at himself in the mirror. He looked haggard. Their were circles under his eyes and his skin was pale and pasty. He was a mess!

"What do I do now?" he asked his reflection. Everything was in chaos. "Oh, God, help me! Help me!" He ran out of the bathroom and into his bedroom, throwing himself on the bed as the tears finally came. He cried uncontrollably for several minutes until, finally, the tears subsided and he lay there sobbing quietly.

After a few more minutes, he straightened up and sat at the edge of the bed, feeling calmer now. Take it easy, Richie, he thought, don't lose control.

His inner voice was speaking to him, trying to reason with him. It's all right, man. Stay cool. The words were soothing, comforting. Everything was going to be all right. They were Mickey's words, he realized. Calm down, relax. Take it easy. Don't worry about a thing. Words Mickey had said to him many times.

He sat there quietly, letting his emotions settle and trying to compose himself. He was a man now and it was time to start acting like a man. Last night with Diane had changed him. He was all grown up, now. Experienced. He could handle the problem. There had to be a logical answer.

Just stay on top of it and meet the problem head on, the voice told him. It wasn't the end of the world. He just had to think things out very carefully, that's all. He could do that.

The card Shaunessy had given him was still in his hand. He looked at it and was instantly beset with doubt. Oh, God, his parents! What will they think? How will they react?

Easy now, the voice said. They'll understand. The truth. Just tell them the truth, that's all you can do. Tell them the truth, Richie. Be a man. You are a man. A man!

Another loud knock on the door. Richie almost jumped out of his skin. He wiped his face with his handkerchief as he slowly walked to the door to answer it, almost expecting to see Shaunessy and Robbins standing there, handcuffs in hand. It was Diane and she was crying.

"Oh, Richie!" She moved into his arms and held him tightly for several seconds, then eased her grip and looked up at him. "The police are after Mickey!"

"I know," he answered gently. "They were here."

"What are we going to do?"

"Come on inside, Diane. We have to think this thing through."

Twenty-Six

Diane was agitated. "We have to warn Mickey!" she said anxiously. "We can't let the cops get him!"

Richie led her inside to the kitchen. "Take it easy, Diane." He gripped her shoulders, trying his best to keep her calm. "Tell me what happened. Did the police talk to you?"

"No." Diane moved away from him and started speaking very rapidly. "They talked to my mother - at least she was sober for a change - I was in my room but they didn't know that. I listened through the door."

She paced the floor as Richie watched her. She looked good, dressed in white shorts and matching halter top. Memories of the night before flooded his senses, distracting him from the seriousness of the moment.

"What did they say?" He caught her hand with his and with the other pointed to one of the kitchen chairs. Diane stopped pacing and sat down. Her frightened blue eyes locked onto his as he sat down across from her.

"I'm scared, Richie," she declared. "The cops said Mickey was in a lot of trouble and that if my mother knew where he was, she'd better tell them."

Richie raised his eyebrows. "And?"

"My mother told them she didn't know. She hadn't seen him since yesterday." Diane looked nervously around the room, as if expecting the police to come barging in at any moment. "Said he might be with Eddie."

"No," Richie said. "He's not with Eddie."

"I know. The cops told my mother they had already talked to Eddie and Mickey wasn't with him. Eddie told them he hadn't seen Mickey since last night at the beach."

"Speedy told me Mickey was going to work today."

"He was? I wonder if the cops know that?" Diane fidgeted at the table and Richie reached over and took one of her hands in his. "Do you think they know where Mickey works?" she asked.

"Probably. They seem to know everything else about him. They told me Mickey had been spending a lot of money lately," Richie patted her hand.

"They did? They told my mother the same thing. Said Mickey had been flashing a lot of money around and wanted to know if she knew where he got it." Diane squeezed Richie's hand. "They knew he spent quite a bundle on fireworks. At least eighty bucks worth."

"They knew the exact amount?"

"Uh, huh. How could they know that, Richie? You didn't tell them, did you?"

"No. They told me they knew about the money but they didn't mention how much or how they found out about it. I wonder..."

"I bet Eddie told them," Diane said, her expression changing to a frown. She rubbed the side of her face. "Damn him! He just can't keep his mouth shut about anything, can he?" She was glowering as she spat out the words. "Ooh, he makes me so mad!"

"Why do you think it was Eddie?" Richie asked.

"It had to be him, Richie. He's the only other person the cops talked to who knew Mickey had money. I haven't talked to them and you didn't tell them, so it had to be Eddie."

"It is starting to look that way," Richie agreed.

"Mr. Smooth Talker, Eddie! Wait until I get my hands on that creep!" Diane made a fist and pounded on the table with it. "I'll teach him to squeal to the cops!" Her shoulders drooped slightly and she sat there for a moment, pouting. Richie said nothing, deciding to let her vent her anger.

"He's real slick when it comes to charming all the girls around here, but when it really counts, what does he do? Mr. Swanky Eddie Burkett spills the beans to the police!" She held up her fist. "I'd like to give him a fat lip! That's what I'd like!"

Richie was surprised by her scorn for Eddie. "Calm down, Diane," he said gently. "Getting mad at Eddie won't help Mickey. We've got to think about this and find a solution."

"I suppose you're right," she reluctantly agreed. "But what do you think we should do? We can't just sit here and not do anything."

"I don't know. What can we do? The cops will probably find Mickey before we do." Richie said.

"We could try to warn him. Tell him they're after him and then help him get away." She stood up and started to run towards the door. "Come on, Richie, we have to hurry."

Richie managed to stop her. "Wait, Diane. We have to think this over carefully, first." He envisioned Robbins coming at him with a pair of handcuffs while Shaunessy stood there wagging his finger. He blinked his eyes and shook his head to rid himself of the vision. "Mickey isn't the only one who's in trouble. I am, too. And probably you, as well."

Diane looked at him, concern showing in her eyes.

"We both lied to the police for him," Richie said, remember?"

"Sure, but they don't know we lied," she protested.

"Yes, they do. I don't know how they found out, but they did. They were here about an hour ago and they said they know I lied. That means they know you lied, too."

"Oh, Richie," Diane moaned.

"They also said I could be arrested for it, so we have to be very careful what we do from now on. I don't want to go to jail, do you?"

"No," she answered meekly.

"They want my father to call them on Monday." Richie took the card out of his pocket and showed it to her. "If he doesn't call, they said they're coming back here to arrest me. They're probably looking for you, too."

"I don't care if they are!" Diane said belligerently. There was a hint of arrogance in her voice. "We have to help Mickey!" Then more softly, "Let's at least see if we can find him and tell him the cops are after him. We can do that, can't we, Richie?" She reached up and gently caressed his cheek. "Couldn't we at least do that?"

"I suppose we could at least do that much," Richie agreed. He felt all tingly from her touch. "Speedy said that Mickey's supposed to be working until three. Let's walk up to Treadway's and try to find him."

"Okay," Diane said, "let's do that." She gave him one of her dazzling smiles.

Richie took her hand. "We have to be very careful, though, Diane. If the police ever find out we're interfering, we'll be in worse trouble than we are now."

"We'll be careful." She hugged him. "I love you, Richie, you know that? Being with you last night was wonderful." She relaxed her grip and backed up a step to look up at him. "How do you feel about me, Richie? Do you love me?"

Richie hesitated before answering. Diane's words both thrilled and comforted him. It was a heady experience, being told by the second beautiful girl in less than a week that she loved him. First Nancy, now Diane. He believed she meant it, too, unlike Nancy.

Nancy couldn't have truly loved him and then treated him like she'd done the night before. He asked himself the question, had he really loved her? He thought he had, but maybe not. Maybe it had been just infatuation, like the song. Maybe he was just too young to love anybody.

"Well, I..., I like you a lot, Diane," he said awkwardly. He bent down and kissed her. "An awful lot."

"But you don't love me." It was a statement.

"Well, I..."

"It's okay. You don't have to answer that question, Richie." She kissed him back. "It's not fair of me to put you on the spot." She smiled at him. "As long as you like me a lot, I guess that will have to do for now."

"I do, Diane," he said with sincerity. "I like you an awful lot." He kissed her again and they held each other tightly for a long time.

They left the cabin a few minutes later and nervously walked up to Treadway's Market, feeling like fugitives on the run. They went inside and asked for Mickey. Mr. Treadway told them Mickey hadn't reported in for work that day.

"Had to have my nephew make the deliveries," he said with his eastern Long Island nasal twang, "but he ain't as good as Mickey is. "Takes too durn long." They thanked him and promised to have Mickey get in touch with him as soon as possible. They left the market and started walking back to Richie's, trying to decide what their next move should be.

As they walked down Chestnut Street, they noticed Speedy heading toward them from the opposite direction. When he saw them, Speedy waved. "Hey, you guys!" He ran over to them. "The cops are after Mickey!" he said excitedly.

"We know, Speedy," Diane said. "We're looking for him, too, so we can warn him."

"Mickey already knows about it," Speedy said. "He's over at my house now, hidin' out. He sent me over here to get ya, Richie." Speedy jerked a thumb over his shoulder. "Come on, my boat's around the corner at the dock. We can use it to get back to my place."

As they headed to the dock where the boat was tied up, Speedy filled them in on what had transpired since he'd left Richie's house, earlier. "Mickey was on his way to work this mornin' when he saw a cop car parked outside Treadway's," Speedy began.

"He wasn't sure if they were lookin' for him or not, but he wasn't takin' no chances so he cut over to your house, Rich. Figured he'd first call old man Treadway from there, to see if anything was cookin'."

Walking along next to Diane and Richie, Speedy looked like a ten-year-old. "When he came around the corner and saw those other two cops walkin' across the street to your door, he split in a hurry." He took out a handkerchief from his back pocket and blew his nose loudly.

"He hitched a ride to my house," Speedy continued, "just as I was gettin' ready to leave in my boat. He told me what happened and then sent me over here to get ya." He blew a stream of spit out through the gap in his front teeth, then looked up at the two of them and smiled. "Man, ain't this excitin'?"

"What does Mickey want with me?" Richie asked curiously.

"I don't know. He just told me to get a-hold of ya."

"God, what a mess we're in," Richie said morosely. "When is it all going to end?"

Diane took his hand and gave it a squeeze. "Seems like it," she said, with equal gloom.

Speedy navigated the boat around Clam Island and tied up at the dock behind his house. It was slightly cooler around this side of the bay, and a gentle breeze was blowing in from the northwest. Mickey was sitting there, waiting for them. When he saw the boat approach, he broke out in a big grin.

Everybody started talking at the same time as Speedy busied himself securing the boat. Finally, Mickey had to put up a hand for silence. "One at a time," he said.

Richie spoke first. "Mick, the police know we lied to them," he said. "They came by my house this morning and we're all in trouble. What are we going to do?"

"Mickey, the cops were at our house this morning," Diane said briskly. "They talked to mom. She told them she hadn't seen you. They didn't know I was there."

"Mickey, you can hide out here all day," Speedy said. "My parents ain't home. We can..."

"Hold it, everybody, will ya?" Mickey raised his hand again. He slowly walked out to the edge of the dock and stood there, looking out over the water. After a moment, he turned around and walked back to them. "I know what I gotta do," he said.

"What's that, Mick?" Speedy asked.

Mickey moved over next to Diane. "I ain't gonna let the cops arrest me for something I didn't do, so that means I gotta leave." He put his arm around his sister's shoulder. "Diane, would you do me a favor? I want you to go inside and call Eddie. Tell him to come over here as soon as he can."

"I don't want to talk to that creep, Mickey," Diane protested. "Me and Richie figured he must've told the cops everything."

"Well, if he did, we'll soon find out, won't we? Come on, Dee, I really need you to do this for me." Mickey looked at Speedy. "Okay if she uses the phone, Speedy?" he asked, almost as an afterthought.

"Sure, Mickey, no problem." Speedy gestured to Diane. "Come on, Diane, I'll show you where it is."

"Well, okay," Diane agreed reluctantly. "But I still don't understand why you want to involve Eddie. I don't trust him anymore." She started walking behind Speedy as he headed towards the house.

"You don't have to trust him. Just trust me instead." Mickey reached into his shirt pocket and took out his cigarettes. He tapped the end of one on his thumbnail and stuck it in his mouth, then offered the pack to Richie. "Cigarette, Rich?"

Richie shook his head. "No thanks."

Mickey lit the one in his mouth, took a deep drag and let the smoke out. He moved over to the side of the dock and leaned against the railing for a second, then turned and looked at Richie. "Rich," he began, "I'm sorry for the way things turned out. I didn't mean to get you in any trouble and as soon as I can, I'm gonna call the cops and explain to them that you were only trying to help me out." He took another drag and continued to stand there, looking out over the water.

Richie moved over and stood next to him. He didn't want Mickey to feel he was being backed into a corner and the thought of his friend leaving filled him with a terrible sadness. "There has to be a way out of this, Mick," he said. "Don't let them force you into doing something you don't want to do."

"I don't know, Rich," Mickey said with a sigh. "I don't think I have any choice."

"Why don't we just go to the police and talk to them? Explain everything. They'll believe us. They have to." Richie patted Mickey on the back in a gesture of friendship. "I know you didn't rob that house and I'm sorry I doubted you. I was just upset about Nancy, that's all. I never meant what I said."

Mickey looked at him and smiled. "I know you didn't, Rich, but thanks for telling me, anyway." He let the cigarette dangle from his mouth as his fingers beat out a drum rhythm on the top of the railing. "I'd go and talk to the police myself, but I know they won't believe me. Nobody believes anything I say, so what makes you think they would? Nah, I gotta do this my way."

"But, Mickey, running away isn't the answer. They'll find you sooner or later and then it'll be much worse. Let's just tell them the truth. That's the best way." Richie racked his brain to think of additional arguments he could present. In his heart, he felt Mickey's intended course of action just wasn't the right way to go.

Mickey flicked his cigarette into the water. "Rich, if I thought it would work, I'd go and talk to them, believe me. But it won't. You don't know the way things are out here. The cops are always looking for ways to hassle me. Ever since I got in trouble a couple of years ago, the cops have been treating me like a criminal. It just won't work."

"But..."

"Case closed."

Richie's jaw tightened and he started to grind his teeth. He was frustrated by Mickey's utter refusal to consider any other way. Realizing there were no further arguments, at least none that he could think of at the moment, he asked instead, "What happened that time, Mick?"

"You mean when I got expelled from school?"

"Yeah."

Mickey took a deep breath, then moved away from the railing and sat down on the edge of the dock. He drew his legs up against his chest and folded his hands on top of his knees. Richie moved over and sat down next to him.

Mickey was silent for a while, not saying anything, just gazing off into the distance. Finally, he spoke. "I stole money from the principal's office, Rich. Three hundred dollars. They caught me and I spent nine months up at Lincoln Hall. Reform School." He turned and looked at Richie. "I guess you want to know why I did it, huh?"

"Well, yeah, I guess so," Richie answered.

"I ain't a thief, Richie. Not really. I mean, sure, I stole stuff just like any other kid. Candy bars and junk from the five and dime but I never took any money before that."

"So, how come..."

"My old man needed it. He was in jail and had to have three hundred dollars to bail out."

Richie raised his eyebrows questioningly.

"It ain't like you think, Rich. My mother had him thrown in jail because he was behind in child support payments. They never got along too good and she did it just for spite. I begged her to drop the charges but she wouldn't listen. Told me she was gonna teach him a lesson." Mickey gave him a sardonic look.

"But how could he pay if he was in jail?" Richie asked.

"That was exactly my point. What good would it do to have him sitting in jail like that? He couldn't make payments from debtor's prison. She didn't care. She just wanted to punish him, that's why she did it." Mickey lit another cigarette.

"I kept after her, nagging her all the time, then one day she got drunk and beat the hell out of me. Kept screaming for me to mind my own business." Mickey massaged his arms as if remembering the beating. "I was only sixteen years old, Rich. What could I do? Nobody would help me. I even called some of my other relatives, but they weren't interested."

"Gee, I'm sorry, Mickey."

"That's okay. Anyway, after the beating, I got mad and ran away from home. Stayed gone for three days. Slept in the woods. The cops found me and brought me home. She gave me another beating, but I didn't care. I made up my mind I was gonna run away, soon as I could."

Mickey took a deep drag and exhaled. He held the cigarette in front of his face and blew on the tip, watching it as it glowed, then he took another drag.

"But first, I was gonna help the old man out. I wasn't gonna let him rot away in some jail cell, no sir." He flipped the cigarette into the water, then picked up several pebbles that were lying on the dock. He started tossing them into the water, one by one. "He didn't do nothing to deserve that, Rich. He was always good to me and Diane when he lived with us."

"So, what did you do?"

"First, I called the county jail in Riverhead and found out he needed three hundred bucks to get out. Then I made my plan. It was right before Easter vacation and they'd just had the Spring Bazaar at school. I knew they kept all the money in the principal's office over the weekend until the banks opened on Monday, so I knew I had to make my move before then."

Mickey found more pebbles and continued to throw them in the water. "I waited until Saturday night and then I broke into the office and grabbed the money. It was in a metal box in one of the desk drawers."

"How did you get in?" Richie asked, intrigued.

"Through a window. I wrapped a big rock in a towel and used it to break the window. Then I reached in, unlatched it and pushed it open. It was pretty easy, actually."

"Weren't you scared?"

"A little. I was more nervous than scared, I guess. Mainly, I was hoping the money would still be there and not someplace else."

"And it was?"

"Yeah. There was a lot more than three hundred in the box. Eight hundred and change, if I remember correctly. I only took the three, though. That's what I needed to bail my father out."

"And you were able to get him out of jail?" "Yeah. I hitched a ride to Riverhead the next day and bailed him out. I told him Aunt Rose - that's my mother's sister - gave me the money but not to say anything. Aunt Rose always liked my father, so he believed me."

"This is some story, Mickey," Richie said with amazement.

Mickey nodded. "Then I told him I wanted to come and live with him but he said it was impossible. He was living in a boarding house in Queens at the time and he didn't have any room for me. He told me to just stay put for a while, at least until I finished school, then maybe I could move in with him later. "I said I would."

"How did the police find out you stole the money?"

"I guess they put two and two together. They questioned a bunch of students and when they got to me, I was pretty nervous. It must have shown on my face or something. I never was much of a liar, Rich."

"Me neither," said Richie.

"They checked around and found out I put up the three hundred for bail and wanted to know where I got the money. I didn't really have an answer so I just admitted taking it. I was afraid they were gonna talk to my father but they didn't."

"You mean your father never knew you went to reform school?"

"Oh, he knew about it, but he thought it was for vandalism. He never knew I stole the money for his bail. I didn't want him to find out and he never did."

Twenty-Seven

"That's some story," Richie said. "I'm really sorry." He gave Mickey a sympathetic look. "I can understand why you did it, though."

"It was a stupid thing to do, Rich," admitted Mickey. "I never would have done anything like that but I just couldn't stand the thought of my father being in jail. It wasn't right and the whole thing got the better of me."

Richie watched as Mickey continued tossing pebbles into the water. He picked up a few of his own and did the same. "What was it like in reform school?" he asked in a soft voice.

"It was horrible." Mickey's face turned into a sneer. "Some of the kids in there were just like me, never really been in trouble before, but the rest of them were bad news." He glanced at Richie, but his eyes seemed to be looking somewhere else. "I got beat up a lot at first. There were fights almost every day over one thing or another."

"But didn't the people running the place protect you?" Richie asked. He was puzzled by this.

"Those creeps? Nah, they were worse than some of the clients. That's what they called us - clients. No, all they did was play us against each other." Mickey frowned. "I was lucky to get out of there in one piece," he said scornfully.

"Who were they?"

"The place was run by the Christian Brothers. Can you believe it? They were supposed to be some holy, religious order but all they were was a bunch of sadists and alcoholics." Mickey gave an involuntary shudder. "God, I hated those guys!"

"I'll bet," Richie said with sympathy.

"There was one guy up there I'll never forget. Brother Edward. He was really sick. Liked to use his pointer on us." Mickey stuck his hand out with his palm turned up. "He'd make you stick out your hand, like this, then he'd bring the pointer down hard across the tips of your fingers." He grimaced and wiggled his fingers.

"Man, that hurt like hell." Mickey brought his hand down and absentmindedly rubbed his fingers with his other hand. "Oh, yeah, if you moved your hand away or flinched, he'd add a couple more swipes. He really got a kick out of making us cry."

Richie made a face like he'd swallowed a piece of rotten fruit. "Gee, Mickey," he said, " I can't believe it!"

"I know, but it's true. We used to get it from both directions. The Brothers on one side and the clients on the other. I didn't think I was gonna make it out of there alive, or with my brain still intact," Mickey quipped.

"How did you ever get though something like that?" Richie asked, looking at his friend with awe.

"After I was there about three months, one of the older guys kind of took me under his wing. Taught me the ropes. I learned how to fight from hanging around with him." He turned to Richie. "You know what? His name was Richie, also. Richie Callow. From Hell's Kitchen."

"Where's that?"

"You never heard of it? It's in Manhattan. Over on the west side. From what I hear, it's a real tough neighborhood. That's why they call it that. Anyway, I'll never forget him. He probably saved my life. Once the other guys knew we were friends, they never bothered me again."

"What was he in for?" Richie asked.

"Callow? He stole a car and took it for a joy ride." Mickey chuckled. "Told me how he loved to drive."

"What happened to him?"

"They let him out when he was eighteen and I never heard from him again. Maybe he went back to Hell's Kitchen, I don't know." Mickey was thoughtful. "One of these days I plan on looking him up." He glanced at Richie. "He's the reason I ain't afraid of nobody, Rich. He could really fight, old Richie could. In fact, nobody ever beat him that I know of," he said admiringly.

"So what happened after that? How did you get out of there?" Richie was fascinated by Mickey's story and wanted to hear more. This was a part of Mickey he hadn't known about.

"Believe it or not, it was a Christmas present," Mickey said. I was supposed to be there until my eighteenth birthday, but right before Christmas they called me in to the Administrator's office and told me I was getting out." Mickey's face lit up and he broke into a grin.

"I couldn't believe it. The only condition they laid on me was, I had to promise to make restitution for the money I stole. Oh, yeah, and stay out of trouble after that. They told me I had to stay on probation until I paid back the money."

"And did you? Pay it back, I mean."

"Yeah. After they let me out, I got a job as a paper boy and paid back every cent. They let me off probation as soon as the money was paid." Mickey's voice took on a cheerful note. "Some Christmas present, huh, Rich? I was there for eight months, twenty-nine days and six hours, instead of the full two years I was supposed to serve. That was the best present I ever got in my whole life."

"I'll say."

Mickey lit another cigarette. "Two weeks ago, I took the train into Queens to visit my father. We had a great time. He took me to see the Mets play at Shea Stadium and afterwards we went to Coney Island and had hot dogs."

He glanced sideways at Richie. "Then...," Mickey laughed, "he took me for a ride on the merry-go-round! Can you believe it, Richie? I told him, Dad, I'm a little too old for this, don't you think?'" He laughed again. "He didn't care, he was having such a great time." Mickey's eyes were glowing and his face beamed.

"And you know what else, Rich?"

"No, what?"

"He's moving into his own apartment soon. He's doing real good and he said if I want, I can come and live with him."

"Really?"

"Yeah, cool huh? I mean, I'll feel bad about leaving Diane, but she's too young right now. My mother would never let her go. I'll visit her, though, and she can come to Queens and visit us." In spite of the trouble they were in, Mickey was the happiest Richie had seen him since they'd met.

"I'll be able to live with my old man again, Rich. We're gonna buy a clam boat and spend a lot of time together out on the bay. My father loves the water." Mickey folded his hands behind his head and leaned against the dock post. There was a dreamy look on his face.

"I'll finally be able to leave this hick town once and for all and live in the city. Hey, maybe we could even see each other there once in a while when summer's over, you think so?"

"Sure," Richie agreed. He was thoughtful. It was a nice idea but he wondered what Mickey was planning to do about the jam he was in. "But, Mickey..."

"I know, Rich, what about the cops, right?"

"Well, yeah."

"Look, I didn't rob that house and I'm not going to hang around here waiting for them to pick me up." Mickey unfolded his hands and pointed a finger at Richie. "If the cops want me, they're going to have to hunt me down and find me. I didn't do anything!"

"Yeah, but..."

"No buts. You want to know where I got that money for the fireworks? I'm sure you've been wondering about it." Mickey didn't wait for an answer. "From my father. He finally paid me back the three hundred I laid out for his bail. Told me to give it to Aunt Rose. Well, that money's mine, Richie. I already paid back the money I stole so it belongs to me."

"I guess so," Richie agreed. "But what're your plans, Mickey? How are you going to keep the police from finding you?"

"I'll have Eddy drive me to Queens. He'll do it, he owes me a favor. I'll hide out at the old man's. Once I'm gone, the cops will forget about me. I hope, anyway. Maybe they'll even find the real burglar."

"Do you think they will?"

"Maybe, maybe not." Mickey frowned. "All I know is, I'm not going to jail for something I didn't do. I'd rather be dead."

Richie didn't say anything. He knew there was no talking Mickey out of it. His mind was already made up. They sat there on the dock quietly, looking out at the water.

Maybe Mickey was right, Richie thought. Maybe the cops wouldn't look for him too hard and maybe they would find the real burglar. He silently wished him luck.

Mickey looked up. "Here comes Diane and Speedy."

"I just talked to Eddy, Mickey," Diane said as she and Speedy rejoined them on the dock. "He wasn't home the first time, so we waited ten minutes and called him again. He just got there."

"What did he say?" Mickey asked.

"He's coming over." Diane stood next to Richie and linked her arm through his. "He was out playing tennis but he said he'd be over as soon as he changes clothes."

"Good. The sooner the better." Mickey saw Diane's movement and smiled, but made no comment. Instead, he carefully looked at the three of them, then spoke. "You guys are my best friends," he began, "maybe when this blows over, we can all get together again." He stepped up to Richie and Diane and put a hand on each of their shoulders. "I'm just sorry I got you in trouble with the cops."

"I'm sure we'll come through it okay, Mickey," Richie offered. "Don't worry."

Mickey grinned. "What, me worry? Never!"

They left the dock and started walking out to the road to wait for Eddie. He showed up a few minutes later.

"Here comes Eddie now," Diane said.

Eddie pulled up and got out of the car. After listening to Mickey's request, he agreed to drive him in to the city. "We have to be careful, though, Mickey. Can't let the cops see us. I don't want to get in trouble, too."

Diane smirked behind his back as he walked over and opened the passenger side door for Mickey.

"I know," Mickey said. "We'll take the back roads."

Eddie turned around and leaned against the fender. "Before we do anything else, I want to apologize to all of you for my behavior the past few days," he said. "Especially to you, Richie."

Eddie took off his aviator's glasses and held them in his hand. He still had his black eye. "I never should have said anything to Sally," he continued. "I should have known she'd tell Pat." He offered his hand to Richie. "Will you forgive me, Rich?"

"Sure," Richie said, shaking Eddie's hand. "Water under the bridge."

Eddie walked around the car and opened the driver's side door, then climbed behind the wheel. "We'd better get going," he said. Mickey got in the passenger side.

"Why don't you two take a ride with us," Mickey said to Richie and Diane. "I might not see you for a long time."

Richie considered it. His parents were not due back until later that evening and today was most likely the last time he'd be allowed out of the house, once they found out about the police. What the heck!

He was already in trouble, anyway, so why not? What harm would there be in taking a ride to Queens? It was probably the last time he'd be seeing Mickey for a while and he wanted to spend a little more time with him. Besides, he'd be back long before his parents arrived home. He looked at Diane questioningly and she nodded.

"Let's do it, Richie," she said. "What have we got to lose?" They climbed into the back seat.

Speedy came over to the car and offered his hand to Mickey. "So long, you old trouble maker, you. I'm gonna miss ya."

Mickey took his hand. "Thanks for all you've done, Speedy. I'm gonna miss you, too. You're one of my best friends. I'll see you around."

They waved goodbye to Speedy as Eddie started the car and pulled away from the house. He made a u-turn and headed up the street towards Noyac Road. As he reached the corner and started to turn right, Richie looked back to see Speedy still standing there. He gave him a final wave until he disappeared from view.

Eddie headed west on Noyac Road. They had traveled only a mile or two when he glanced into the rearview mirror. "Oh, no!" he yelled, it's the police!"

Richie turned around and saw two Suffolk County Police cruisers behind them, closing in fast.

"Step on it, Eddie!" Mickey yelled. "You gotta lose them!"

"We can't do that, Mickey!" Eddie protested and started to pull the car over to the side of the road.

"Damn it, Eddie!" Mickey punched him hard in the arm. "Be a man for once in your life, will ya? Keep going!" Eddie gave Mickey a pained look.

"Come on, Eddie!" Diane yelled from the back seat. "Lose the bastards!"

"All right, you asked for it!" Eddie stepped on the accelerator and the car shot forward. He held the wheel tightly and the car picked up speed, tires squealing as he rounded a curve very fast. The distance between them and the pursuing vehicles increased.

"That's it, Eddie!" Mickey yelled. "Keep going! You're losing them!"

Richie had a feeling a deja-vu. Hadn't this already happened? With the top down and the wind whistling through his hair, he thought he was dreaming as he sat in the back of Eddie's speeding car. Diane was holding on to him for dear life. "Here we go again!" he yelled at the top of his lungs.

The police were closing the gap between them. Eddie pushed the gas pedal to the floor and gained slightly, but the police cars picked up speed and closed in again.

"It's no use, Mickey," Eddie yelled, "I can't shake them! They've got those big interceptor engines! We'll never lose them!" He eased off the pedal and the car immediately slowed.

"No! Damn it, Eddie, don't stop now!" Mickey's face was contorted with rage. He slammed his foot down on top of Eddie's and the car lurched forward. "Keep going! Keep going, I said!"

Eddie struggled to hold the wheel steady as the car entered a steep curve in the road. "Get your foot off!" he screamed, as the car crossed over the double lines. "I can't hold it!"

"Slow down, Eddie!" Diane yelled from the back seat. "Mickey, we've gotta stop! We're at Dead Man's Curve! Eddie, you're gonna wreck the car!"

Eddie cut the wheel sharply to the left, trying to straighten the car out but he over-corrected and they started to fishtail. He fought hard to maintain control, cutting the wheel back to the right.

The car swerved wildly from side to side and Eddie was unable to negotiate the last part of the steep curve. The car skidded off to the right and smacked into a large boulder sitting just off the road in the dirt. The collision with the boulder caused the vehicle to lift off the ground and the momentum carried it into a tree directly in its path. The car smashed into the tree with a sickening thud and the right passenger side was torn off.

Richie was thrown clear by the impact. He sailed through the air, then collided with another tree and was knocked unconscious.

Some time later as he began to come to, and somewhere at the far reaches of his senses, he was dimly aware of the continuous blaring of the car's horn. It was trying furiously to compete with the agonized howl of someone screaming. Would it ever stop?

Twenty-Eight

Richie woke up in the hospital with his right arm in a cast and his head wrapped in bandages. He had a splitting headache. He reached up with his left hand and felt the right side of his face. It was swollen.

He tried to look around the room. It was dark and he couldn't see much but it felt cold and gloomy. After a while, a nurse came into the room to check on him. Richie watched her out of the corner of his eye. She was middle-aged and had dark hair flecked with bits of gray. Her face was kind.

"How are you feeling, young man?" she inquired.

"My head hurts and my body aches all over," he replied weakly. "Where am I?"

"You're in Southampton Hospital. You've had a serious accident." She extended her hand to him. "Here, try to swallow this."

Richie took the pill from her and placed it in his mouth, then took a sip of water from the glass she offered. He groaned softly as he swallowed. Even his throat hurt. He wanted to ask the nurse about his friends but she left the room before he had the chance.

After a few minutes, the pill he'd taken started to make him feel drowsy and he fell asleep. He slept for hours. When he finally woke up, it was light. He looked around the room, taking it all in.

The room he was in was bright and cheerful, in stark contrast to the way it had looked and felt to him the night before. The walls were a pale blue and there was an overstuffed, high-backed chair in a matching blue pattern just off to the side of his bed.

On his left were double-sashed windows with the curtains tied back which allowed ample sunlight to enter the room.

He looked out the window but couldn't see anything except for blue sky, so he guessed he must be on an upper floor. He tried to remember what had happened, but couldn't. Everything was hazy.

All he remembered was being in Eddie's car with Eddie, Mickey and Diane. Had Speedy been there, too? He couldn't remember that part or where they had been going. Something to do with Mickey, he recollected. Eddie had been driving them somewhere, but where?

All of a sudden, part of his memory started to come back to him. Dramatic pictures began to flood his senses with vivid color and sound as they unfolded themselves before his eyes. It was almost like scenes from a frightening movie. They were in Eddie's car and the police were chasing them. Eddie and Mickey were arguing over whether or not to stop the car and Diane was screaming something about Dead Man's Curve. Beyond that, everything was a blank.

As he lay in the bed struggling to regain the rest of his memory, bits and pieces of what had actually happened began to come back to him. He vaguely remembered the car skidding around a sharp curve and then that he was flying and tumbling through the air. It seemed like a dream, but then if it was, what was he doing in the hospital?

And what about his friends? Were they all right? Beginning to feel restless and agitated, he tried to remember more. His face was contorted by frustration and he started thrashing from side to side in the bed, trying to kick his covers off so he could go outside and find them.

"Hello, Richard, how are you feeling this morning?"

Richie looked up into the bearded face of a young man in a white coat. Heavyset, he wore wire-rimmed glasses and had a stethoscope dangling from his neck. His hair was dark and cut very short, which made his ears appear larger than they really were. He was smiling.

"I'm Doctor Bauman, son." He adjusted his glasses and glanced at a clipboard he was carrying, then made a notation on it. "Can you tell me exactly what happened to you?" The doctor moved closer to the side of the bed and concern replaced the smile on his face. "I'm not sure," Richie replied softly. "I think I was in a car wreck."

"Yes, that's right," Doctor Bauman said. "It was quite a serious accident. What can you tell me about it?" He laid the clipboard on the small table next to Richie's bed and moved closer.

"I..., I don't remember much about it." Richie was trying hard to think. "I thought it was a dream."

"No, son, it was real. You sustained several injuries." The doctor looked him over. "Are you in any pain?" he asked gently.

"My head hurts, and my arm." Richie felt the side of his face. "This is sore, too."

Doctor Bauman examined Richie thoroughly, checking the cast on his arm, his head bandages and the right side of his face where it was bruised and swollen. He took a small instrument from his breast pocket and shined a light into each of Richie's eyes, then probed his chest and pelvic area. When he was finished with that, he placed the stethoscope on Richie's chest and listened to his breathing.

"Take a deep breath, Richard," he commanded.

Richie complied. "Am I going to be all right?" he asked.

"U'um h'mm." Doctor Bauman picked up his clipboard and made several notations. "I'll be honest with you, young man," he said, "I'm a little concerned about the injury to your head but the rest of you is in good shape. You've suffered a concussion and you have a compound fracture to your right arm, but it's not too serious. With proper care it should mend completely." He gave the cast on Richie's arm another quick examination, then shifted his attention back to his head.

He gently placed his hands on either side of Richie's head above the top of the bandages and gazed deeply into his eyes. "Because of this injury, though, you'll have to remain here in the hospital for at least two weeks, maybe even longer. I want to be sure that we can treat you properly."

"Oh," Richie said meekly.

The doctor continued. "I have already consulted with your parents and they are aware of the extent of your injuries. They are in complete agreement with me as to the direction your treatment should take."

He folded his arms in front of him. "You'll need to have absolute bed rest for the first few days. After that, and as your condition improves, we'll see about letting you move about a bit more."

"That's okay with me," Richie said. "I don't feel much like going anywhere right now, anyway."

Doctor Bauman gave a quick chuckle. "I'm glad to hear that. Some of the youngsters who come in here have to be tied down to the bed." He looked at his watch. "I've ordered you a sedative which will allow you to sleep for a few more hours. Your parents are expected to visit this afternoon."

A moment later, a different nurse from the night before entered the room carrying a small tray. This one was younger and prettier than the other one. She was slender with light brown hair cut to just above her collar and she had green eyes. On top of her head, she wore a white nurses cap.

"Good morning, Doctor Bauman," she greeted. "I've brought his meds." She took a paper cup from the tray and offered it to Richie. "Here," she said pleasantly, "take this."

Richie took the cup and looked inside. It contained a yellow pill. He put the cup to his lips and wriggled the pill into his mouth as the nurse handed him a glass of water.

"Drink this," she ordered.

"My friends. What about my friends?" Richie asked after swallowing the pill.

Doctor Bauman and the nurse glanced at each other but said nothing.

"Are they okay?" Richie tried to sit up in the bed but the doctor held him down by placing a hand gently on his chest. "I want you to relax now, son," he said. "Everything's going to be all right."

Richie settled back and watched as the doctor turned and spoke to the nurse. He used a lot of medical terms Richie didn't understand. The nurse left the room but came back a moment later and gave him another pill. After she left a second time, the doctor spoke to Richie.

"I've given you additional medication for the pain and also to relax you," he said. "Just try to stay calm and get some rest and I'll look in on you later."

Richie watched him leave the room. He tried to raise himself up on the bed again, but didn't have the strength. "My friends!" he called out weakly. "What about my friends?"

He began to feel drowsy as the pills took effect. "Mom, he called softly. "Mom, where are you? Can't anybody hear me?"

As he began to nod off, Richie imagined that he was leaving his body. He floated up from the bed and it felt as if he were flying through the air. He started to tumble upside down and as he twisted to keep himself upright, he looked down.

He was flying above Noyac Road and he could see Eddie's car spinning wildly out of control. It was heading straight for a large boulder and he could hear Diane screaming. Mickey was punching Eddie in the arm and yelling, "Go faster, Eddie! Go faster!"

Richie wanted to scream but nothing came out. He tried to warn Eddie by shouting, "Stop the car! Stop the car!" but the words just wouldn't come. He couldn't talk, but he could think. He'd think the words he needed. Eddie! Stop the car, you're going too fast!

He was flying faster through the air now and began to spin out of control. He tried to reach out to grab something, anything, but there was nothing to hold on to. He knew he was on a collision course with a tree because he could see himself heading straight for it. He would never be able to stop in time. He was going to hit the tree! I'm going to be killed, he thought. I'm going too fast! He tried to scream again but nothing came out. Oh, God, don't let me die!

His parents were in the room when he woke up. They looked worried. His mother was sitting in the chair next to him while his father quietly paced back and forth near the foot of the bed.

Mrs. Donnelly reached for Richie's hand when she saw that he was awake. "Oh, Richard," she said in a voice cracked with emotion, "whatever happened to you?"

"Hi, mom," Richie answered weakly. "We had an accident." She looked older than he remembered.

"Yes, dear, you certainly did."

Mr. Donnelly approached the bed and stood on the other side of it. His hair was slightly mussed and he looked very tired. "Richard, we were quite concerned about you and we're very upset. This is a grave situation you're involved in and we…"

Mrs. Donnelly interrupted her husband. "Fred, perhaps we'd better talk about this later, don't you think?"

Mr. Donnelly looked across the bed at his wife. "Yes, I suppose you're right," he agreed. "Another time would be better." He moved closer to Richie. "Richard, are you feeling all right, son?

He took a handkerchief from the pocket of his trousers and patted Richie's forehead with it. "We were very upset when we heard the news about the accident," he began, "however, the doctor has assured us you're going to be fine."

Richie managed a weak smile. "My head hurts and I broke my arm, dad." He glanced at his plaster cast.

"You also have a concussion and multiple contusions but Doctor Bauman says you will heal properly with good medical care," Mr. Donnelly said, matter-of-factly.

"My friends," Richie said, remembering that Mickey, Diane and Eddie had also been in the car. "What happened to them? Are they okay?"

Mr. Donnelly turned away without answering.

"Dad?" When his father didn't answer, Richie turned to his mother. She had tears in her eyes and was sobbing quietly. "Mom?" Richie was alarmed. "What's the matter? They're okay, aren't they?" He tried to sit up again. "What is it? Please! Tell me what's wrong!"

Mrs. Donnelly reached over to take his hand. "Richard…," she was grasping for words, trying hard, but not quite able to articulate what she wanted to say.

She looked to her husband for help, but Mr. Donnelly could only shrug his shoulders, his face betraying his own agony. He turned away again and quickly walked out of the room.

Mrs. Donnelly gripped Richie's hand and leaned closer to him. "Richard," his mother said softly, "your friend Mickey is dead!"

Twenty-Nine

"No!" Richie screamed. As the impact of his mother's words hit home, he began to have trouble breathing.

"It's true," Mrs. Donnelly said gently. She tightened her grip on his hand. "He was killed in the crash."

"No!" he screamed again. "Don't tell me that!" He yanked his hand away from her grasp and tried to sit up. His eyes were wide with fear as he looked wildly around the room, searching blindly for something he couldn't see.

Mrs. Donnelly reached for his hand again and managed a firmer grip. "He died instantly, Richard," she said. "He didn't suffer at all. Diane and Eddie were also hurt, but not too seriously. They're going to be all right."

Richie barely heard her. His legs started to thrash and he kicked wildly at the bed covers with savage bursts of movement. "No! Not Mickey! He's not dead! Why are you telling me this?" He managed to kick the covers off and tried to swing his legs over the side of the bed."

"Fred!" Mrs. Donnelly cried out. "Help me!" Mr. Donnelly, who was standing in the corridor just outside Richie's room, heard her call and ran into the room to assist. He leaned over the bed and helped his wife restrain their son. Together, they managed to get Richie settled back on the bed.

"I think you'd better try to find the nurse, Mary," he suggested to his wife. "Quickly. I'll stay here with Richard." Mrs. Donnelly hurriedly left the room.

"Richard, try to calm down, please!"

"Dad," Richie cried as tears flowed freely down his face. "Mickey's dead! It can't be! Please, tell me it's not true! Please, dad, tell me!" He let out a wail that could be heard outside the room, all the way to the other end of the corridor.

Mrs. Donnelly returned with the duty nurse. The nurse spoke softly to Richie and managed to calm him down slightly. "It's all right, Richard," she soothed. "It's all right."

Richie was still crying. "Mickey!" he sobbed. "Oh, please don't tell me he's dead!" His face was filled with anguish as he looked up at the three adults who were hovering over him. "I don't believe you!" he screamed. "He's not dead! Not Mickey! Mickey is alive!"

The nurse administered a sedative while continuing to speak to him in a soft voice. When Richie's agitation started to subside, the nurse instructed his parents, "Stay here with him while I locate his doctor. I'll be right back."

Mr. and Mrs. Donnelly sat with Richie and waited for the pill to take effect. A few minutes later, the nurse returned with Doctor Bauman, who examined him again and then motioned for his parents to follow him. Richie was just about to fall asleep while the nurse kept vigil and remained by his bed.

Outside the room, Doctor Bauman and the Donnellys gathered together in a close circle. "Do you think he'll be all right?" Mrs. Donnelly asked.

"Oh, absolutely," the doctor replied. "He's gone through a severe traumatic experience and you've just witnessed some of its effects. We'll have to keep a close watch on him, probably keep him sedated for the rest of today." Doctor Bauman gave them a reassuring smile. "I'm sure he'll be okay," he said. "Try not to worry."

"Thank goodness," Mrs. Donnelly said. "We were concerned about him. I mean, with his head injury and all..."

"I'm going to have Doctor Stevens take a look at Richard tomorrow," Doctor Bauman said. "He's our resident neurologist. It's only as a precaution, though, so there's no reason to be alarmed. He can fill you in on any further developments after the examination. Will you be here then?"

"We have a meeting over in Southampton with the police department at eleven, but we should be able to be here by early afternoon," Mr. Donnelly answered.

"Fine, then." Doctor Bauman looked at his watch. "Well, I've got a few things to do, but I will see you tomorrow."

"Thank you, doctor," Mrs. Donnelly said. "We appreciate all that you've done for our son."

"You're welcome, Mrs. Donnelly," the doctor replied. "Richard's been through quite an ordeal but he's young, he'll pull out of it, I'm sure. Take care."

"Goodbye doctor." The Donnellys watched him as he walked down the corridor, then returned to Richie's room.

The nurse looked up and smiled. "He's sleeping now, so I'll be on my way. The two of you can stay as long as you want. If you need anything, just ring." She showed them the call button by the side of the bed before she left the room.

Mr. and Mrs. Donnelly spent the rest of the afternoon in Richie's room, keeping watch by the side of his bed and talking quietly. Richie slept through it all.

During the following days in the hospital, Richie thought about Mickey constantly. At first, he refused to believe that his friend had been killed, but as the days went by and he started to come to grips with what had happened, he slowly began to accept Mickey's death as the truth. It was a grim reality and his own feelings of guilt were manifesting as an integral part of the tragic accident's aftermath.

His parents visited every day and tried to cheer him up. They brought him little gifts of food and some of his favorite books and other reading material. It helped. When they felt he was strong enough, they began to talk about some of the other things that needed to be discussed.

Richie knew that Diane and Eddie had been injured in the crash, though not too seriously. They'd been lucky, his parents had told him. They'd been sitting on the left side of the car and it hadn't been as severely damaged as the passenger side. Richie wanted to know more about them.

"Where's Diane?" he asked them. "Why hasn't she come to visit me? You said she wasn't badly hurt."

"No, she wasn't," his father answered. "Diane did receive some extensive cuts and bruises and she had her two front teeth knocked out, but otherwise wasn't hurt too seriously."

"Her teeth knocked out?" Richie tried to picture Diane with her front teeth missing. He shuddered at the thought.

"Yes, Richard," his father said. "She's all right, though," he added. "Already had them fixed by a dental surgeon. I believe Mr. Burkett, Eddie's father, took care of the arrangements."

Richie was glad to hear that. "What about Eddie? What happened to him? Is he okay?"

"Nothing more than a few bumps and bruises," his father said. "It seems he suffered the least. Of course, his automobile was a total wreck but I think that's the extent of his worries."

Mr. Donnelly took off his glasses and wiped them with his handkerchief. "Richard, now that you're feeling a little better, it might be time to discuss a few things." He put his glasses back on.

Richie knew what was coming and in a way, he was glad the moment had finally arrived. Maybe if he hadn't put things off, maybe if he had told the truth from the very beginning, the accident would never have happened. It was all his fault.

Maybe if he hadn't been so weak and hadn't allowed Mickey to talk him into telling that phony story to the police, Mickey would still be alive. He should have been stronger. He should have convinced Mickey to tell the truth. He should at least have done that.

"Your mother and I had a visit with Detectives Shaunessy and Robbins," Mr. Donnelly began. "They told us the entire story."

"I'm sorry, dad," Richie started to say, but couldn't finish the words. Tears formed in his eyes and he began to cry. "It's all my fault!" he sobbed. He began to shake and his body was wracked with involuntary spasms. "Mickey is dead because of me and now I'm going to prison!"

"No, Richard! No!" His father sat beside him on the bed and gently stroked his hair, smoothing it back away from his forehead.

"It's not your fault, son. You did not cause the accident. It was just a horrible twist of fate." Mr. Donnelly looked over his shoulder at his wife. "Mary?"

Mrs. Donnelly moved closer to the bed and switched places with her husband. "Everything's going to be all right, Richard," she said with a calming gentleness. "You're not going to prison." She placed the back of her hand against his neck, just as she had done many times to see if he was running a fever. His skin felt cool and after a few minutes, he stopped crying.

"We were very worried and, I admit, a little shocked when they told us what happened," his mother went on, "but the police said there are some new developments in the case and they aren't going to prosecute you or Diane for lying to them."

"They're not?"

"No. They said that because of what happened, they feel there is no reason to pursue the matter any further. They feel you and Diane have been punished enough."

His mother took his hand. "We can't quite understand how you let yourself get into this mess in the first place, why you didn't come to us but," she looked up at her husband, then back to Richie, "now is not the time to talk about it. Everything can wait until you're completely healed and out of the hospital. We just want you to get well, Richard."

Richie was grateful and breathed a sigh of relief. This latest bit of news wouldn't bring Mickey back but at least he and Diane wouldn't have to go to jail. It was just a tiny silver lining in an otherwise dark cloud.

He wondered what the detectives meant when they said there were new developments in the case. "What about Eddie?" he asked. "Is he in any trouble because of this?"

"No, son," his father answered. "Eddie did try to stop the car when he heard the police sirens so they decided not to press charges against him. I believe they did issue him a speeding ticket, though." A speeding ticket! Mickey was dead and all Eddie gets is a speeding ticket! Richie felt numb. It seemed ironic that after all that had happened, he and Diane were off the hook and the only legal ramification to come out of the entire episode was a speeding ticket for Eddie!

Mickey's dead, he thought. Not that he wanted to see anyone, including Eddie, in trouble, but it just didn't seem fair. Then again, life wasn't exactly fair.

"Life is hell and then we die," he remembered Diane saying. Maybe she was right. His life felt like hell right now and Mickey had certainly died. No, it just didn't seem fair. They had all been in it together but Mickey was the only one who had died.

He needed to see Diane, to talk to her. "Mom, could you call Diane and ask her to come and visit me?" he asked.

His mother pressed her lips together into a tight line before answering. "Diane moved away, Richard," she said as gently as she could. "She took Mickey's death really hard, from what we were told, and she went to live with her Aunt Rose in the city. Queens, I think."

"Oh." Richie turned away from her and stared at the wall. Diane, his only ally in all of this and now she wasn't even around anymore. He felt completely alone.

"I'm starting to feel a little tired," he told his parents. "Would you mind if I took a nap?" He wanted to be by himself for a while. He had a lot to think about. "Sure, son." His father motioned to his wife. Mr. and Mrs. Donnelly said their goodbyes and left the room, promising to see him later on that evening.

Richie laid his head back against the pillow and stared up at the ceiling. He could hear the hospital sounds as they drifted into his room from out in the hallway. They seemed loud to him at first, then gradually became dimmer, until finally, they were barely noticeable at all.

He thought back to the day when he'd first arrived in Sea Shell Harbor. It seemed like so long ago. He remembered how excited he'd been and how he'd looked forward to spending the entire summer here. It was supposed to be one of his best vacations ever.

Even his parents had said so. When they described the place to him just before they all left the city, they'd said, "There's plenty to do out there, Richard. Swimming, fishing, boating, water skiing, meeting new friends. You'll love it."

As he thought about it, most of what they'd said had been true. He'd done all that and more. And he'd met lots of new friends.

The image of Mickey popped into his mind's eye. He was standing at the front door of the cabin, holding a box of groceries. Smiling at Richie with that lopsided grin of his, he asked, "Is this the Donnelly place?"

As quickly as it came, the image left him. It was instantly replaced by Nancy's pretty face, dimples, freckles and all. She was looking up at him with her shimmering blue eyes and dazzling him with her perfect smile.

"Want to dance, Richie?" she asked. He glided over to her. They were on the dance floor of the Sugar Shack and when he reached for her, she pursed her lips and blew him a kiss. "I love you, Richie," she said. "I really do."

Before he could take her in his arms and profess his own undying love, the scene was suddenly washed away by a torrential downpour that flooded his vision and wiped away all the images. It was a river, a raging river. A river of tears. His own.

It formed a swift current that overtook him and swept him away. He fought it at first, then quickly submitted to it, letting it take him where it wanted. He couldn't fight it, nor was he going to try. It was in control now and he didn't care. Not anymore.

Thirty

Mickey was buried in Angel of Heaven, a small, private cemetery just outside Sag Harbor, after a funeral Mass at Saint Bridgets Church. The funeral had taken place three days after the accident but Doctor Bauman and Richie's parents had thought it best to avoid any mention of it because of his injuries.

Mr. and Mrs. Donnelly had attended, as had many of the townspeople who had known Mickey, including Speedy Downey, Frank Wittey and Danny Shaw. Mr. Treadway, who had never taken a day off since he'd opened his store, had closed up for the day and attended with his wife. Diane hadn't been there and neither had Eddie Burkett.

After he had been in the hospital for over two weeks, Richie was able to leave his bed and allowed to roam freely about the corridors. He kept himself busy, visiting with some of the younger children in the ward down the hall and spending the rest of his time reading and listening to the radio.

Thoughts of Mickey came and went, and with each passing day, the aching in his heart gradually diminished. He thought about Nancy and wondered whether or not she was still seeing her new friend, John. He guessed that she probably was, because she never came to the hospital to visit him.

He wished that he could see Diane. He had a lot of things he wanted to say to her. She was constantly on his mind and he vowed he would look her up in Queens as soon as he was able.

His parents visited every day, trying their best to cheer him up and giving him whatever news of the harbor they had. Some days were better than others and Richie was his old, happy self. Other days were pretty bad and he had all he could do to keep from crying for the slightest reason.

In addition to his medical treatment and physical therapy, the hospital provided the services of a psychologist who helped Richie to deal with his feelings. He looked forward to the sessions, feeling that they left him better able to deal with the aftermath of Mickey's death. After several visits, it was decided that his mental health was good and that no follow-up visits would be required.

A week later, on the day before he was to be released from the hospital, Richie was visited by the two detectives, Shaunessy and Robbins. Shaunessy seemed slightly ill-at-ease but Robbins was a completely different person than Richie remembered. He greeted him warmly and extended his hand in friendship.

"How are you, Richard?" Robbins asked.

"I'm doing real good," Richie said cheerfully. "The doctor says I can go home tomorrow."

Shaunessy moved forward and picked at an imaginary piece of lint on the sleeve of his jacket. "That's great, son." He shook Richie's hand gently as he eyed the cast on his arm. He looked around the room before speaking again. "I suppose your parents told you there won't be any charges filed against you or Diane?"

"Yes, sir, they did." Richie reached over and picked up a thin wooden rod from the table next to his bed. He inserted it under the cast and moved it back and forth several times. "Got an itch. Drives me crazy, sometimes. The doctor gave me this to scratch it with."

Shaunessy smiled. "How long will you have to keep the cast on, Richard?"

"Another three weeks, at least." Richie continued to scratch. "Summer'll be just about over by the time it comes off."

"That's too bad," Robbins said.

"It doesn't really matter." Richie placed the rod back on the table. "I can't do anything for the rest of the summer, anyway. My parents said I have to stay around the house until Labor Day. That's my punishment for what I did."

"Your parents are pretty strict, huh, Richie?" Robbins pointed to a pair of chairs near the window. "You mind if we sit down? We have a few things we'd like to discuss with you."

"Oh, sure," Richie said. "Excuse my manners. Please, sit down."

The detectives each took a chair, moved them closer to the bed and sat. Robbins continued speaking.

"We're sorry about your friend, Richard," he said. "We never wanted to see Mickey get hurt. It's a terrible tragedy that never should have happened."

"I know." Richie's eyes started to moisten at the mention of Mickey. "I still can't believe he's gone. In a way, he was like a big brother to me." He reached for a tissue and used it to wipe his eyes. "Sometimes I talk to him at night," he told the detectives. "I can feel his presence in the room."

"What do you talk about?" Shaunessy reached into his pocket and brought out a pack of chewing gum. He offered it to Richie. "Stick of gum?"

Richie shook his head. "No, thanks."

Shaunessy looked at his partner. "Bernie?"

"Nah."

"We talk about some of the good times we had," Richie continued. "Hanging around the Sugar Shack and Trout Pond. Jumping off trees, water skiing on Eddie's boat, things like that."

Richie looked out the window. A puffy white cloud floated in the sky, off in the distance. "It's all over now, though, Mickey's gone and he's not coming back." He wiped his eyes again.

Robbins looked at Shaunessy and shook his head. "I can't understand why you guys tried to make a run for it," he said. "Didn't you realize you couldn't get away from the police?"

"Bernie." Shaunessy gently nudged his partner.

Robbins caught himself. "Oh, sorry. Didn't mean to bring it up. I just..."

"It's okay," Richie said quickly. What's done is done. We can't change anything now." He looked past the two detectives to a picture hanging on the wall. It was a painting of a large sea shell.

Shaunessy followed his gaze. Underneath the picture was a small brass plaque with writing on it. Shaunessy silently read the words.

'The Chambered Nautilus: Symbol Of Continuity.'

"Build thee more stately mansions, O my soul

As the swift seasons roll! Leave thy low-vaulted past!

Let each new temple, nobler than the last,

Shut thee from Heaven with a dome more vast,

Till thou at length are free, Leaving thine outgrown shell by life's unresting sea." -- Dr. Oliver Wendell Holmes/1859

"I'm just happy for the time I got to spend with Mickey. He was a great guy!" Richie stopped talking and looked up at the two detectives. "He didn't rob that house," he said firmly. "His father gave him that money he used to buy the fireworks."

Shaunessy cleared his throat. "We know he didn't, Richard. That's what we wanted to talk to you about." He glanced at Robbins, then back to Richie. "We were wrong about Mickey."

Richie sat upright in the bed. "What?" His throat constricted and he was unable to speak.

"Do you know a guy by the name of Charlie McGee?" Robbins asked.

Richie swallowed twice. "I don't know him real well. I only met him once. He's a friend of Mickey's."

"He's no friend of Mickey's," Shaunessy said. "He's the one who burglarized that house in Southampton."

Richie took a deep breath. "Charlie did?"

"Yes, along with several others," Shaunessy added. "We caught him red-handed last week, trying to hit another house in the same neighborhood." He crossed his legs and folded his hands over his knees. "A real piece of work, that guy."

"He tried to deny it at first," Robbins said, "but after we questioned him a while, he finally broke down and admitted it." Robbins looked proud. "Confessed to all the burglaries over there, as a matter-of-fact."

Richie felt like someone had just kicked him in the chest. "Oh, my God!" he managed to gasp. He couldn't believe what he was hearing and had to take a drink of water before he could speak again.

"But how did Mickey's wallet get over there?"

"McGee stole it from him the day that Mickey was in Southampton running errands for his boss," Shaunessy answered.

"Picked his pocket," Robbins added.

Shaunessy went on, "He planted it outside another house he robbed a few days later. That's what made Mickey our prime suspect." Richie rubbed his face. "Just because you found his wallet?"

"That and the fact that he already had been busted for burglary," Robbins said. "He did time in reform school a couple of years ago."

"I know. He told me." Richie bit his lower lip, trying to keep his composure.

"Richard, when we questioned Mickey about it, he was very inconsistent, very nervous," Shaunessy said. "Kept changing his story. He just didn't sound credible and we felt sure he was lying."

Shaunessy fiddled with the buttons on his shirt. "First he said he was home sleeping and then he said he was with friends."

"We wanted to give him the benefit of the doubt," Robbins offered, "but when we tried to pin him down he changed his story again and said he was with you and Diane. Later on, when we talked to Frank Wittey and Eddie Burkett, we were convinced he was lying."

"Why? What did they say?" Richie asked.

Shaunessy consulted a small notebook that he pulled from his inside pocket. "Wittey told us he didn't remember seeing Mickey with you that night. Said you were by yourself."

"And Burkett told us Diane was with him that night," Robbins added.

"Mickey was afraid you wouldn't believe he was home sleeping that night," Richie explained. "That's why he made up that other story."

Robbins frowned. "And you went along with it, Richard, why?"

"Mickey asked me and Diane to back him up." He slowly shook

his head. "I know I shouldn't have lied to you. I did it for Mickey." He sniffed.

"We know," Shaunessy said soothingly. "You were just trying to help him out, that's all."

"I helped him out, all right! And now he's dead!" Tears welled up in Richie's eyes again.

"It's a terrible tragedy, son." Shaunessy reached over and patted Richie on the arm, then got up from his chair.

"It was a horrible mistake." Robbins stood and returned both chairs next to the window where they had been, then looked questioningly at his partner.

"We'd better be going," Shaunessy said. He looked down at Richie. "You know, Richard, you only did what you thought was right, and you were only trying to help out a friend. In a way, I admire that." He turned away from the bed.

"Take it easy, kid," Robbins said, and with that, both detectives left the room.

Richie stared at the doorway for several minutes after they had gone. Their words were playing over and over in his mind. A terrible tragedy. A horrible mistake. Mickey had to die because of a horrible mistake.

He lay back on the pillow and closed his eyes. He could see Mickey's face. Standing on Speedy's dock and smoking a cigarette, Richie could hear him say, "Don't worry, Rich. Every dog has its day. Things always have a way of working out, so don't worry about nothing."

That night, Richie cried himself to sleep.

Thirty-One

On the day Richie was released from the hospital, there was a letter waiting for him at the nurses station. It was from Diane and had a Flushing postmark. He held the envelope up to the light and examined the handwriting. It was neat and precise.

On the back side where the flap was sealed were the letters, S.W.A.K. Sealed With A Kiss. Off to the right of the nurses station was a little alcove. Richie sat in one of the chairs there and read the letter.

'Dear, Richie,

When I found out Mickey had been killed, I wanted to die myself. I just wanted to crawl under a rock and die because I didn't think there was any reason to go on living. I'm feeling better now.

I wanted to visit you in the hospital but I knew I couldn't bear to see you lying there all broken up. I couldn't deal with that. I didn't want you to see me, either, because my front teeth were knocked out and I was ashamed of the way I looked. I guess that was kind of silly of me, huh?

I look okay now, though. I had dental work done and they put caps on my teeth. You can't even tell the difference from my old ones. My face has healed up, too. They said I was lucky I didn't break my jaw in the crash and all, but all I got was a nasty bruise and some cuts and other things.

I wanted to write to you and tell you how I feel about you. I love you, Richie and I suppose I always will. I just know it wouldn't have worked out for us. I'm a girl who has been around the block a few times too many and you're too sweet a guy to be stuck with someone like me. I'm thankful for the time we did have together and even though you weren't my first love, you'll always be my best love.

I wouldn't have been able to stay in Sea Shell Harbor anymore anyway, there's just too many bad memories. So I decided after the accident that the best thing to do was leave. I'm living with my Aunt Rose in Flushing. That's in Queens County. She's a real nice lady and we get along great. I also see my father now and we're getting to know each other better than we ever did.

I don't know if you heard about what happened to my mother or not, but she had a nervous breakdown and they had to send her to Pilgrim State Hospital. I haven't visited her yet and don't know whether or not I will. I keep in touch with her doctors and I do write to her every week but so far I haven't received a reply from her. Her doctors say she's doing real well, so that's good, everything considered. Even though my mother and I never got along, I wish her good health.

There's not much more to say except that I love you and I hope you will not forget me. I don't think I'll be back out that way for a long time, except maybe to put some flowers on Mickey's grave. If you ever get a chance, maybe you could stop by the cemetery. I know Mickey would like that.

Well, that's about it. Take care of yourself, Richie. Someday we'll all be together again in heaven.

Love always, Diane.'

Richie read the letter several times before returning to his room and packing it away in his suitcase with his other things. It was nice of her to write to him, he thought.

He knew that their time together had been something special, something he would always cherish for the rest of his life, but he also knew in his heart that he didn't love Diane. For whatever reason, they'd needed each other. He'd needed her and she'd needed him. It didn't really matter why. Their time together had been but a fleeting moment in all eternity.

Although he was not allowed to leave the cabin and suffered from a severe case of boredom, surprisingly, the rest of the summer passed rather quickly. Richie took his punishment in stride. He sat in the yard and read. Books, newspapers, anything he could find.

He tried to keep his mind as occupied as possible, not only to pass the time, but to keep him from thinking about Mickey. The only bad days were when it was really hot and he longed for the beach and the way things had been.

When it rained, he stayed indoors and read or listened to the radio. Mainly, he did a lot of thinking. He realized that fate had played all of them a rough hand. Mickey, Diane, Eddie and himself, but somehow, he had lived through it. He had survived and for that he was grateful.

Life itself was the mystery and he wondered about the forces of fate and how they applied in different ways to different people. He, Diane and Eddie had survived the crash, but Mickey hadn't. What was behind these mysterious forces that could arbitrarily pluck one soul from life's sweetness and let others go on living?

He didn't understand it and perhaps he never would. He was lucky to be alive and he knew it. The hands of fate had reached down for him but chose someone else instead. That was the reality of life and he had to accept it. He had to because he knew he could never change it.

He remembered what Diane had said in her letter. Someday they'd all be together again in heaven. He hoped so. That would be wonderful. Whatever heaven was or could be, he knew it would be much better when all of them were there, together again.

A few days before Labor Day, his parents drove Richie back to the hospital to have his cast removed. The morning had started out to be gray and overcast but by eleven o'clock, the sun had managed to break through the clouds to bathe the village in its warmth and glimmering light.

The removal procedure was painless and after examining his arm thoroughly, Doctor Bauman pronounced it good as new. Richie bade goodbye to the nurses and some of the other medical staff while his parents took care of paperwork in the office.

On their way back to the cabin, Richie asked if they could stop by the cemetery to visit Mickey's grave. His parents agreed and they made a quick stop at a florist in Sag Harbor where they picked up a bouquet of flowers to place at the grave-site.

After receiving directions from the caretaker, they found the grave after a few minutes. It was at the far end of the cemetery, away from the main road. Mr. Donnelly parked the car and they walked down a grassy path between the rows of graves.

It was in a quiet and secluded area, separated from the others by a line of small willow and elm trees that looked like they had been planted only a few years before. The setting was peaceful and serene. Richie felt a chill down his spine as they approached Mickey's final resting place.

With his parents next to him, the three of them stood with heads bowed and said a silent prayer for Mickey. After a few minutes, they told Richie they would wait for him in the car so he could continue with his visit in private.

Seeing Mickey's name on the headstone started the tears flowing and Richie cried uncontrollably for ten minutes. As he wiped away the tears with his handkerchief he began to experience a soothing calmness that steadied his nerves and gave him a feeling of inner strength. Pleasant memories of Mickey came to him in waves, flooding his thoughts.

He sat down on the grass in front of the headstone and talked to his friend. He told Mickey how sorry he was for ever doubting him but how glad he was they had met. He promised that he would never forget him and would keep him forever in his thoughts. He told him about Diane's letter and how he wished the very best for her that life had to offer.

"I know you'll be keeping a good watch over her, Mick, so I guess she'll be okay," Richie said aloud. "I'm only sorry we didn't get to spend the rest of the summer together. We could've taken another plunge off Mighty Mo. I just...," the tears came to Richie's eyes and he faltered momentarily, "want you to know that the little bit of time I got to spend with you were some of the best times of my life."

Richie felt the tears threatening again, so he stood and blinked his eyes until the feeling passed. He looked down at Mickey's grave. As he was about to say a final goodbye, he had the distinct impression that he was hearing Mickey's voice. It was strong and it was speaking to him. It was telling him not to worry, that everything was going to be all right. He could hear Mickey clearly.

"I'm okay, Richie, really," Mickey said. "I'm happy here where I am. Don't forget about me but don't dwell on me, either. You have a good life ahead of you and it's time now to live it. We'll see each other again someday, Rich, I promise you that. You can count on it. Gotta go, now. Take care, buddy."

Richie gave Mickey's grave a long, last look. "So long, Mick," he said, then turned and walked away.

On Labor Day, Richie's parents informed him that his confinement was over and he was free to leave the cabin. He was elated. He decided to walk up to Noyac Road and then, as he passed Treadway's Market, found himself heading towards the Sugar Shack. It was late afternoon.

He reached Beach Road, turned left and walked down the hill past the Salty Pirate. Before long, he could see the magenta walls of the Sugar Shack, a half mile in the distance. On his left, the natural beauty of Noyac Bay was laid out before him in a panoramic view of vivid blue and aquamarine.

The air felt cooler to him and it seemed that the sultry heat of summer had begun to fade away, soon to be replaced by the cooler, crispier days of fall. Days when the leaves changed their color from green to glorious shades of red, yellow and orange and began to blanket the land around and beneath the trees.

As he approached the outside deck of the Sugar Shack, he noticed it was packed with teenagers. He walked up the stairs and sat at a table, looking cautiously around him for a familiar face. There didn't appear to be anyone he knew and he was starting to feel the same way he did his first day in Sea Shell Harbor.

After ordering a coke from the waitress, he sat there watching the crowd for several minutes. Finally, he got up and walked inside to the jukebox. He put a nickel in the slot and pushed B-3, 'Story

Untold', by The Nutmegs. He found an empty table and sat there, sipping his coke and listening to the song. The plaintive wailing of the lead vocalist was singing about a girl who had left him 'standing in the cold'.

As he listened to the words, similarities of the song's love story to his own sad romance with Nancy struck him as funny. Nancy had left him, too, only he'd been left standing in the heat, not the cold. That amusing thought brought a grin to his face. Just as the song ended, he finished the last of his drink, He placed the glass on the table and walked back outside and scanned the faces of the kids in the crowd again. Still no one he recognized. He began to wonder if indeed, there was anybody left in Sea Shell Harbor that he knew or had they all gone home or moved away?

Feeling slightly disappointed, he left the deck and started walking through the parking lot towards the beach. He decided he'd take one last look at the water before heading back home. Halfway through the lot, he heard someone call his name.

"Richie!"

He shaded his eyes from the last of the setting sun and looked around, trying to find the source of the voice.

"Richie, over here!" It was Nancy.

She was standing next to the fence which surrounded the parking lot, beckoning to him. He started walking over to her, feeling slightly self-conscious as he closed the distance between them.

She looked stunning. Her blond hair was lighter than he remembered and it had gotten much longer. It was almost as light as Diane's. She was wearing a lime-green blouse and a pair of cut-off jeans. Her legs were well tanned.

"Richie, how are you?" She gave him a shy smile and her closeness gave him the old familiar butterflies in his stomach.

He returned her smile and nervously ran his fingers through his hair. "I'm okay. Your hair is much lighter than I remembered," he said awkwardly, then felt foolish for having made such an inane remark.

"Yes, I guess it is," she agreed. "The sun bleached it. It's not usually this light."

"Oh." Richie put his hands in his pockets and shifted his weight back and forth. He felt a little uncomfortable and struggled to think of something to say. "So, how've you been?" he managed.

"Pretty good." She held on to the wooden post as she raised one foot to put her sandal on. "I was at the beach all afternoon but now it's time to go home."

As she raised her other leg her hand slipped from the fence and she lost her balance. She started to fall and Richie quickly reached out and held her arm to steady her.

"Thanks," she said as she recovered her balance. She gave him a half smile that was slightly self-conscious. "Guess I'm still a klutz."

"You're okay," he said, feeling more relaxed now.

She finished putting on her sandal while he stood ready to assist in case she slipped again. "We're leaving tomorrow," she said suddenly and then looked directly into his eyes. "I'm going to miss this place."

"We are, too." He studied her, trying hard not to be obvious about it. She was as pretty as he remembered. Even prettier. He thought about the nights they had spent together, holding each other and professing their undying love. He remembered her kisses and immediately felt an immense longing in his heart.

He wanted to say something to her, to tell her how much he missed her and how sorry he was for the way things had turned out. The words weren't there. He struggled to speak but only managed to take a deep breath and sigh.

"I'm sorry about what happened, Richie," Nancy said softly. "You know, about Mickey and all." She looked at him shyly. "I heard you were hurt pretty badly."

"Not too bad," he said. "Just a broken arm and a concussion. I'm okay, now."

"Just?" She sounded exasperated. "A concussion and a broken arm are more than just." She touched his right arm lightly. "This the one? It looks skinnier than the other one."

"Yeah. My right arm. They took the cast off the other day. I guess I'll have to start lifting weights or something to get it back in shape." Richie flexed his arm and made a muscle. "I look like the ninety-seven pound weakling you see in the Charles Atlas ads." He laughed.

Nancy laughed with him. "Oh, it's not that bad." She felt his muscle as he flexed it. "This part is fine. You just need a little help down there where the cast was. Shouldn't take too long."

"Shouldn't," he agreed.

"I haven't seen you around all summer," she said. "I thought maybe you left or something."

"No, my parents..., ah, no, I've been sticking close to home. I didn't feel much like coming out." Richie put his hands in his pockets again as he kicked at little mounds of sand with his sneaker. "What about you? What have you been doing?"

"Oh, the usual," she replied. "Swimming, water skiing, hanging out at the Sugar Shack."

"Oh." He took his hands from his pockets and leaned against the fence. "Seen any of the gang? Eddie? Pat and Sally?" he inquired.

"Not really." Nancy leaned on the fence next to him. "Eddie and Sally broke up. I heard he already left for college. Pat left at the end of July. She was pretty broken up when Mickey got killed. I haven't seen much of Sally. Heard she has a new boyfriend."

"Oh."

"I saw your friend, Speedy, a few times." Nancy gave a cute giggle. "He's so funny, always makes me laugh. He doesn't come around the Sugar Shack much anymore, though. She looked off into space for a moment. Abruptly, a cloud passed over her face and her mood turned somber. "He told me what happened."

"Good old Speedy," Richie said. "I really like him. He's a great guy. I should go and visit him before I leave." He molded the pile of sand into a tiny square with his foot. He

hoped she wasn't going to ask him anything about the accident. He'd probably start to cry in front of her and that would be embarrassing. "Tell him I said hello." She reached into her bag and brought out a lipstick. She dabbed at her lips with it and then put the case away. "Most of the old crowd left last month. There's a bunch of new kids here, now. Mostly, I've been spending a lot of time on my friend's boat."

"Who's boat, John's?"

"John? Oh, no." Nancy smiled self-consciously. "We broke up the night you saw me with him at the Sugar Shack. I didn't like the way he treated you and we ended up having a big fight about it." She frowned as she remembered it. "No, it's my girlfriend, Martha's boat. Her family has one. They go water skiing all the time and I go with them." Her blue eyes shined and a smile replaced the frown.

Richie felt slightly awkward. "Oh."

The sun was low on the horizon now and dusk was settling in around them. Nancy studied him for several moments. "Richie, I really wanted to come and see you in the hospital but I wasn't sure you wanted me to. Not after the way I treated you."

"You did?"

"Sure. I was concerned about you after I heard about that terrible accident and Mickey getting killed. I cried almost every night." She turned and looked at him. "I was even hoping you'd call me." She reached up and took a strand of her hair and began twirling it between her fingers. "Why didn't you?"

Richie's expression was blank as he thought about her question. He gazed off into the distance. "I don't know," he answered, then looked at her and smiled. "I thought you hated me."

"Oh, Richie. I could never hate you. I was jealous when I found out about you and Diane, that's all. I wanted to hurt you that night. Like you hurt me."

"I can understand that," Richie said. "I was acting like a real jerk. Especially that night."

"No, you weren't, Richie. I was. I never even gave you a chance to explain." She reached up and touched his cheek. "I only went out with John that night to make you jealous. It was Pat's idea. I never really liked him."

"You didn't?"

"No."

Richie was elated when he heard this. "Well, it worked," he said. "I sure was jealous."

"I guess that makes us even, then." Nancy held out her hand. "Friends?"

He took her extended hand. "Friends."

"You're not mad at me?"

"Water under the bridge."

"I'm glad." She glanced at her watch. "I'd better be going. Have lots of packing to do."

"Me, too."

"Richie?"

"Yeah?"

"Maybe we could see each other sometime, in the fall.

"Marine Park isn't too far from Flatbush, you know."

"Well, sure, If you want to."

"I would." Nancy reached into her bag again and brought out a slip of paper and a pencil. She scribbled something on it and handed it to Richie. "Here. My address and phone number. You'll call me?"

He took the paper and put it in his pocket. "I will."

"Oh, Richie." Nancy moved into his arms and kissed him.

He kissed her back, holding her tightly as memories of their earlier relationship came rushing back to him. He knew at this moment that Nancy meant more to him than he'd ever realized. I missed you, he thought.

Nancy broke off the kiss and looked up at him. "I love you, Richie, she said. There were tears in her eyes. "I always will."

"I love you, too, Nancy," he murmured. "With all my heart."

They kissed again for a long time, ecstatic about finding each other again. They ended the kiss and gazed into each others eyes.

"Want to walk me home?" she asked, finally.

"I'd be honored."

She linked her arm with his and they started walking out of the parking lot. At Beach Road they turned right and headed up the hill. When they had traveled about a quarter of a mile, Richie turned and looked back towards the Sugar Shack.

Someone was leaning against the wooden railing of the parking lot fence. From a distance, it looked like Mickey.

"Anything wrong, Richie?" Nancy asked, as he stopped.

"Oh, no. Just taking a last look at the old hangout." Richie squinted against the approaching darkness. The figure by the fence was waving to him now. It was Mickey and he was talking to him. Richie could hear his voice clearly.

"I see you're back with Nancy, Rich. Didn't I tell ya everything was gonna be all right, huh? Didn't I?" Mickey was smiling at him and his blue eyes had a mischievous sparkle to them. His image grew larger, before it moved up off the ground and into the air. It hovered there for a moment before starting to drift out over Noyac Bay.

"Remember what I told you, Rich," Mickey was saying. Don't worry about a thing. Everything's gonna be all right."

Richie watched as Mickey's image slowly faded from the sky. He took a deep breath and they continued walking. Nancy took his hand and held it tightly. There was a dreamy look on her face.

Richie looked down at the girl he was going to marry. The girl in my dreams, he thought, in reference to the song. She looked up at him and smiled. He smiled back at her and said aloud, "What, me worry, Mick? Never."